A DIAMOND FOR THE SHEIKH'S MISTRESS

BY
ABBY GREEN

MILLS & BOON

First Published in Great Britain 2017
By Mills & Boon, an imprint of HarperCollins*Publishers*
1 London Bridge Street, London, SE1 9GF

© 2017 Abby Green

ISBN: 978-0-263-92544-9

Our policy is to use papers that are natural, renewable and recyclable
products and made from wood grown in sustainable forests. The logging
and manufacturing processes conform to the legal environmental
regulations of the country of origin.

Printed and bound in Spain
by CPI, Barcelona

Irish author **Abby Green** threw in a very glamorous career in film and TV—which really consisted of a lot of standing in the rain outside actors' trailers—to pursue her love of romance. After she'd bombarded Mills & Boon with manuscripts they kindly accepted one, and an author was born. She lives in Dublin, Ireland, and loves any excuse for distraction. Visit abby-green.com or e-mail abbygreenauthor@gmail.com.

Books by Abby Green

Mills & Boon Modern Romance

Awakened by Her Desert Captor

Wedlocked!

Claimed for the De Carrillo Twins

Brides for Billionaires

Married for the Tycoon's Empire

One Night With Consequences

An Heir to Make a Marriage
An Heir Fit for a King

Billionaire Brothers

Fonseca's Fury
The Bride Fonseca Needs

Blood Brothers

When Falcone's World Stops Turning
When Christakos Meets His Match
When Da Silva Breaks the Rules

Visit the Author Profile page at
millsandboon.co.uk for more titles.

CHAPTER ONE

SHEIKH ZAFIR IBN HAFIZ AL-NOURY, King of Jandor, was oblivious to the exquisite mosaics on the path under his feet as he paced restlessly, and he was equally oblivious to the water burbling from the ornate central fountain. The tiny multicoloured birds darting between the lush exotic blooms also went unnoticed in this, just one of the many stunning courtyards of his royal palace in Jahor, the imposing capital city of his kingdom, which ran from snow-capped mountains in the east, across a vast desert to the sea in the west.

Zafir was oblivious to it all because all he could think about was *her*. It was getting worse. He'd had to call an important meeting to a premature end because he'd felt constricted and claustrophobic, aware of the heat in his blood and the ache in his core. An ache he'd largely managed to ignore for the last eighteen months.

Liar, whispered a voice, *those first three months were hell*.

Zafir scowled in remembrance. But then his father had died, and all his time and attention since then had been taken up with his accession to the throne and taking control of his country.

But now it was as if he finally had time to breathe again, and she was back. Infiltrating his thoughts and dreams. Haunting him.

Zafir loosened his robe at his neck with jerky movements. *Sexual frustration*, he told himself, momentarily coming to a halt on the path. It was just sexual frustration. After all, he hadn't taken a woman to bed since... *her*, and that incensed him even more now.

It wasn't due to lack of interest from women. It was due to Zafir's single-minded focus on his job and his commitment to his people. But he was aware of the growing pressure from his council and his people to find a suitable Queen and provide heirs, so they would have faith and feel secure in their King and future.

Zafir issued a loud curse, scattering the birds around him in a flurry. *Enough.* He whirled around and strode back out of the courtyard, determined to set in motion the search for an appropriate match and put *her* out of his head once and for all.

He stopped in his tracks, though, as he passed the overgrown entrance to the high-walled garden nearby. None of the gardeners had touched it in years, and Zafir hadn't had the heart to enforce its clean-up since taking power. He knew that his staff viewed it almost superstitiously; some believed it was haunted.

Maybe it was, he thought bleakly, his thoughts momentarily diverted.

He went and stood at the entrance and looked at the wildly overgrown space and realised with a jolt that today was the anniversary. The anniversary of his sister's death. Nineteen years ago. He'd been thirteen and she'd been just eleven. He stepped in, almost without realising what he was doing.

Unlike the rest of the pristinely manicured grounds, there was no water trickling into the circular pool that could barely be seen under greedy weeds. There were no lush flowers or exotic birds. It was dormant. Still. Dead.

He could still remember hearing the almost otherworldly scream of his brother Salim, Sara's twin. When Zafir had burst into the garden he'd found his brother cradling Sara's limp body, her head dangling over his arm at an unnatural angle. Her face had been whiter than white, her long black hair matted with the blood which had been dripping into the fountain's pool behind them, staining the water.

Salim had screamed at him to do something... *Save her...* But Zafir had known instinctively that she was gone. He'd tried to take Sara out of Salim's arms to carry her into the palace, to find help, see if there was any chance, but Salim, sensing Zafir's grim assessment, had only tightened his hold on his twin sister's body and shouted hoarsely, 'If you can't help, then don't touch her... Leave us alone!'

Sara had died from a massive head and neck injury after falling from the high wall around this garden where they'd used to play and climb, in spite of Zafir's protests. Salim hadn't spoken for weeks afterwards...

To Zafir's shame, the dominating thing he now recalled was the awfully familiar disconnect between him and his siblings. The sense of isolation that had pervaded his whole life. He'd always been envious of Salim and Sara's very special and close bond, which had been to the exclusion of everyone else. But right then he would have gladly given up his own life to see his sister's brought back...

'*Ahem*... Sire?'

Zafir tensed. Very few people managed to catch him unawares and he didn't appreciate this intrusion into such a private moment.

He didn't turn around as he responded curtly, 'Yes?'

There was some throat-clearing. 'The...ah... Heart of Jandor diamond, Sire. There are things we need to discuss about it, and the upcoming diplomatic tour.'

Zafir closed his eyes briefly, letting the painful past fade back to where it belonged, and when he was ready turned around to survey the young aide he'd taken on after his father's death almost fifteen months ago—much to his council's disapproval. They'd wanted him to keep his father's old guard and not rock the boat, but Zafir favoured a more modern outlook for his country's future and was slowly but surely implementing his ways.

He started walking back towards the palace, his aide hurrying alongside him, used to keeping up with his demanding King by now.

The Heart of Jandor diamond was a mythically rare gem. Thought for years to have been either stolen or lost, it had been found recently during archaeological excavations outside the palace walls. There had been much rejoicing and fervent whispering of it being a good omen. It was the largest known red diamond in the world, famed for its beauty. When it had first been discovered it had had a natural heart shape, and so had been cut and refined into its current incarnation, retaining its distinctive shape.

It had originally been unearthed in the eastern mountains of Jandor and given as a gift to woo Zafir's French great-grandmother. The fact that her marriage to his great-grandfather was the only one in his family history which had allegedly been a happy one merely confirmed for Zafir that love within marriage was as much of a rarity as the diamond itself—and about as improbable.

Irritated to find his mind deviating like this, Zafir said now, 'Well? What are your thoughts, Rahul?'

'We are starting the diplomatic tour in New York next week, as discussed.'

New York.

No one else would have noticed the slightest misstep in Zafir's authoritative stride. But *he* noticed. And he despised himself for it. Suddenly all thoughts of his sister and the lingering grief he felt were eclipsed by *her* again. The ease with which she could get to him after all this time only made him angrier.

What the hell was wrong with him today?

Manhattan was primarily where their relationship had played out over several months. And in spite of his best efforts his blood simmered, reminding him of just how far under her spell he'd fallen. Until it had been almost too late.

Zafir's strides got longer, as if he could outrun the past nipping at his heels, but even by the time he'd reached his palatial offices she was still there, those amber-hazel eyes looking up at him slumberously while a sinful smile made that famously sexy and lush mouth curve upwards. As if she'd known exactly what she was doing to him, drawing him deeper and deeper into—

'Sire?'

Zafir gritted his jaw against the onslaught of memories and turned around to focus on his aide. 'Yes, Rahul.'

The young man looked nervous. 'I…ah…have a suggestion to make regarding the jewel.'

'Go on,' Zafir bit out, curbing his impatience. His aide was not to know that he'd unwittingly precipitated the storm currently raging inside him.

'The diamond is being brought on your diplomatic tour as an exhibit and a stunning example of Jandor's many attractions in a bid to promote business and tourism.'

Zafir's impatience spiked in spite of his best efforts. 'I know very well why we're bringing it on the diplomatic tour. It was my idea.'

The man swallowed, visibly nervous. 'Yes, and we'd planned on displaying it in each city in a protected glass case.'

'Rahul…' Zafir said warningly, coming close to the end of his tether.

His aide spoke quickly now. 'The suggestion I want to make is this—rather than show it off in a sterile and protected environment, I thought it might prove to be far more dynamic if it were seen up close… We could let people see how accessible it is and yet still exclusive and mysterious.'

Now he had Zafir's attention. 'What are you talking about?'

'I'm talking about hiring someone—a model—someone who will actually wear the jewel and come with us on the tour. Someone who will walk with us among the guests at each function, so they can appreciate the jewel's full beauty, see how it lives and breathes—just like Jandor's beauty.'

Zafir looked at Rahul for a long moment. This was why he'd hired the younger man after all—to inject new blood into his father's archaic council.

The idea had merit, and Zafir assessed it in seconds. However he was about to dismiss it for various reasons—not least of which were to do with security—but just as he opened his mouth to speak an image exploded into his head, turning his words to dust.

He immediately turned away from the younger man, for fear that something would show on his face. All he could see was *her*, lying on a bed, with her long, sinuous limbs and her treacherously hypnotic beauty, naked but for the jewel that nestled between her high, full breasts. It would glow fiery red against that perfect pale skin.

As red as his blood—which wasn't simmering now. It had boiled over.

He'd allowed the floodgates to open, and right at that moment Zafir knew there was only one way to rid himself of this ache and move on. And he *had* to move on. His country depended on it.

Zafir's mind reeled as the idea took root and embedded itself deep inside him. Was he really considering revisiting the past and the one person he'd vowed never to think or speak of again?

A spurt of rebelliousness and something much more ambiguous ignited inside him.

Why not?

This could be the perfect opportunity to sate his desires before he committed to his full responsibilities and the people of Jandor owned him completely. And there was only one woman Zafir wanted.

She owed him, he told himself grimly. She'd lied to him. She'd betrayed him by not revealing her true self, her true nature. She'd walked out of his life eighteen months ago and he hadn't had enough of her. She'd left him aching and cursing her.

The fact that he'd once considered her suitable to be in his long-term future was a reminder that was unwelcome. This time when he took her he would know exactly who she was. And he would feel nothing but lust and desire. He would have her long legs wrapped around him again and he would sink deep enough inside her to burn away this irritating lingering lust.

He turned back to Rahul, who was looking nervous again.

'Sire, it was just a—'

Zafir cut him off. 'It was a brilliant suggestion and I know exactly who will be our model.'

Rahul frowned. 'Who, Sire?'

Zafir's pulse thundered in his veins. 'Kat Winters— the American supermodel. Find out where she is. Now.'

A week later, Queens, New York

Zafir observed her from the back of his car, with the window rolled down. He couldn't quite believe his eyes—that Kat Winters was working in a busy midrange restaurant in Queens. But, yes…one of the world's arguably most beautiful women was currently wearing skinny jeans and a white T-shirt with a black apron around her small waist. Her hair was piled up in a messy knot on her head and there was a pencil stuck through it, which she was now fumbling for as she took an order.

Everything in Zafir recoiled from this very banal scenario—except it wasn't disgust he was feeling, seeing her again. It was something much hotter and more urgent. Even dressed like this and without a scrap of make-up she was exquisite. A jewel such as she could not be hidden in a place like this. What the *hell* was she doing here? And what the hell was she doing going under another name—Kaycee Smith? And how dared she refuse to even consider the offer he'd sent to her via her agent?

Her agent had sent back a terse response:

> Kat Winters is no longer available for modelling assignments.
> Please do not pursue this request.

No one refused Zafir. Or warned him off. Least of all an ex-lover.

He issued a curt instruction to his driver now, and his window rolled up silently as he got out of the car and stretched to his full height of six foot four. He recalled Kat in vertiginous heels, the way it had put her mouth well within kissing distance. The way her added height had aligned their bodies so perfectly. He watched her walk away from the table and grimaced when he saw she was wearing sneakers.

Not for long, he vowed as he moved forward to the door of the restaurant. Soon she would be in heels again, and soon that lush mouth would be his again. All of her would be his again.

He had no idea what she was playing at, with this meek little game of being a waitress, but he was certain that once she heard what he had to say she'd be demonstrating her gratitude that he was prepared to give her another chance to be in his life and in his bed again, even just for a few brief weeks, in the most satisfactory way.

'Kat.'

It took a second for the significance of that word to sink in. No one here called her Kat. They called her Kaycee. And then there was the voice. Impossibly deep. And the way *Kat* had been pronounced, with the flat inflection that had always made it sound exotic. And authoritative—as if her name was a command to look at him, give him her attention.

It took another second for the realisation to hit her that there was only one person who could have spoken.

With the utmost reluctance, vying with disbelief, she looked up from the countertop.

Zafir.

For a moment she simply didn't believe it. He couldn't be here. Not against this very dull backdrop of a restaurant in Queens. He inhabited five-star zones. He breathed rarefied air. He moved in circles far removed from this place. This man was royalty.

He was a King now.

And yet her agent had told her only a couple of days ago that he'd asked for her, so she should have been prepared. But she'd blocked out any possibility of this happening. And now she was sorry, because she wasn't remotely prepared to see the man she'd loved with such intensity that it had sometimes scared her.

She blinked, but he didn't disappear. He seemed to grow in stature. Had he always been so tall? So broad? But she knew he had. He was imprinted on her brain and her memory like a brand. The hard-boned aristocratic features. The deep-set dark grey eyes that stood out against his dark olive skin. The thick dark hair swept back off his high forehead. That perfect hard-muscled body without an ounce of excess fat, its power evident even under a suit and overcoat.

He was clean-shaven now, instead of with the short beard he'd worn when she'd known him, and it should have made him look somehow *less*. But it didn't. It seemed to enhance his virility in a way that was almost overwhelming.

She hadn't even realised she'd spoken his name out loud until the sensual curve of those beautifully sculpted lips curved up slightly on one side and he said, 'You remember my name, then?'

The mocking tone which implied that it was laughable she could have possibly forgotten finally broke Kat out of her dangerous reverie and shock. He *was* here. In her space. The man she'd had dreams and nightmares about meeting again now that her life had changed beyond all recognition.

In her nightmares he looked at her with disgust and horror, and to her mortification she woke up crying more often than not. Her dreams were no less humiliating—they were X-rated, and she'd wake up sweating, believing for a second that she was still whole…still his.

But she was neither of those things. Not by a long shot.

Her pulse quickened treacherously, even though his presence heralded an emotional pain she'd hoped had been relegated to the past but which she was now discovering not to be the case.

She spoke sharply. 'What are you doing here, Zafir? Didn't you get my agent's message?'

He arched a brow and Kat flushed, suddenly aware of how she'd just addressed a man before whom most people would be genuflecting. A man who had two conspicuous bodyguards dressed in black just outside the main door.

She refused to be intimidated. It was almost too much to take in, thinking of the last time she'd seen him and how upset she'd been, and then what had happened…the most catastrophic event of her life.

'I got her message and chose to ignore it,' Zafir said easily, his tone belying the curious punch to his gut when he registered Kat's obvious reluctance to see him again.

Kat folded her arms, as if that could protect her from his all too devastating charisma. Typical arrogant Zafir. He hadn't changed.

Tersely she said, 'I'm working, so unless you've come here to eat this isn't appropriate.' *It'll never be appropriate.* But she stopped herself from saying that with some desperation.

Zafir's smile faded and those unusual dark grey eyes flashed. 'You refused to engage with my offer, which I do not accept.'

'No,' Kat said, feeling the bitterness that was a residue from their last tumultuous meeting, when she'd left him. 'I can well imagine that you don't accept it, Zafir, because you're used to everyone falling over themselves to please you. But I'm afraid I feel no such compulsion.'

His eyes narrowed on her and she immediately felt threatened. She'd always felt as if he could see right through her—through the desperate façade she'd put up to try and convince people she wasn't a girl who had grown up in a trailer with a drug-addicted, mentally unstable mother. A girl who hadn't even graduated from high school.

Yet Zafir hadn't—for all that she'd thought he might. Until he'd had the evidence shoved under his nose and he'd looked at her with cold, unforgiving eyes and had judged and condemned her out of his life.

'You've changed.'

His words slammed into her like a physical blow. He

was right. She *had* changed. Utterly. And this was her worst nightmare coming to life. Meeting Zafir again. And him finding out—

He wouldn't, she assured herself now, feeling panicky. He couldn't.

'Is this gentleman looking for a table for one, Kaycee?'

Kat looked blankly at her boss for a second, but she didn't mistake the gleam of very feminine appreciation in the older woman's eyes as she ogled Zafir unashamedly.

Galvanised into action, she took the menu out of her boss's hands and said firmly, 'No, he's not. He was just looking for directions and now he knows where to go.' She looked at Zafir, and if she could have vaporised him on the spot she would have. 'Don't you, sir?'

Her boss was pulled aside at that moment by another member of staff, and Zafir just looked at Kat for a long moment, before saying silkily, 'I'll be waiting for you, *Kat*. This isn't over.'

And then he turned and walked out.

Kat really didn't want to leave the restaurant when her shift was over, because Zafir's car was still outside. As was the very conspicuous black four-by-four undoubtedly carrying his security team.

She was more than a little shocked that he was still waiting for her. Two hours later. The Zafir she'd known a year and a half ago had never waited for anyone—he'd been famously restless and impatient. Fools had suffered in his presence. He'd cut down anyone wasting his time with a glacial look from those pewter-coloured eyes.

As Kat dragged on her coat and belted it she felt a sense of fatalism settle over her. If Zafir had ignored her agent and tracked her down this far, then he wouldn't give up easily. She should know more than anyone that when he wanted something he pursued it until he got it.

After all, he'd pursued *her* until he'd got her. Until he'd dismantled every defence she'd erected to keep people from getting too close. Until she'd been prepared to give up everything for him. Until she'd been prepared to try and mould herself into what he'd wanted her to be—even though she'd known that she couldn't possibly fulfil everything he expected of her.

Her hands tightened on her belt for a moment. He'd asked her to be his Queen. Even now she felt the same mix of terror and awe at the very thought. But it hadn't taken much to persuade him of her unsuitability in the end.

She steeled herself before walking out through the door, telling herself that she was infinitely stronger now. Able to resist Zafir. He had no idea of what she'd faced since she'd seen him last…

As soon as she walked outside though, the back door of Zafir's sleek car opened and he emerged, uncoiling to his full impressive height. Kat's bravado felt very shaky all of a sudden.

He stood back and indicated with a hand for her to get in. Incensed that he might think it could be this easy, she walked over to him, mindful of her limp, even though disguising it after a long evening on her feet put pressure on her leg.

'I'm not getting into a car with you, Zafir. You've had a wasted evening. Please leave.'

She turned to walk away and she heard him say,

'Either we talk here on the sidewalk, with lots of ears about us, or you let me take you home and we talk there.'

Kat gritted her jaw and looked longingly down the street that would take her to her apartment, just a couple of blocks away. But if she walked away she could well imagine Zafir's very noticeable car moving at a snail's pace beside her. And his security team. Drawing lots of attention. As he was doing now, just by standing there, drawing lingering glances. Whispers.

A group of giggling girls finally made Kat turn around. 'Fine,' she bit out. 'But once I've listened to what you have to say you'll leave.'

Zafir's eyes gleamed in a way that made all the hard and cold parts of Kat feel dangerously soft and warm.

'By all means. If you want me to leave then, I'll leave.'

His tone once again told Kat that that was about as likely as a snowstorm in the middle of the brutally hot Jandor desert, and that only made her even more determined to resist him, hating that his visit was bringing up memories long buried. Memories of his beautiful and exotic country and how out of her depth she'd felt—both there and in their relationship. Zafir had been like the sun—brilliant, all-consuming and mesmerising, but fatal if one got too close. And she had let herself get too close. Close enough to be burnt alive once she'd discovered that the love she'd felt had been unrequited.

She'd been prepared to marry him, buoyed up by his proposal, only to discover too late that for him it had never been a romantic proposal. It had been purely because he'd deemed her 'perfect.' Her humiliation was still vivid.

She stalked past him now and got into the car, burningly aware of his gaze on her and wondering what on earth he must make of her—a shadow of her former self. The fact that she didn't seem to be repelling him irritated her intensely.

Zafir shut the door once her legs were in the car and came round and got in the other side, immediately dwarfing the expansive confines of the luxurious car. For a moment Kat felt herself sinking back into the seat, relishing the decadent luxury, but as soon as she realised what she was doing she stiffened against it. This wasn't her life any more. Never would be again.

'Kat?'

She looked at Zafir, who had a familiar expression of impatience on his face. She realised she hadn't heard what he'd said.

'Directions? For my driver?'

She swallowed, suddenly bombarded with a memory of being in the back of a very similar car with Zafir, when he'd asked his driver to put up the privacy window and drive around until he gave further instructions. Then he'd pulled Kat over to straddle his lap, pulled up her dress and—

She slammed the lid shut on that memory and leaned forward to tell the driver where to go before she lost her composure completely.

She refused to look at Zafir again, and within a couple of minutes they were pulling up outside her very modest apartment block. Kat managed to scramble inelegantly out of the car before Zafir could help her. She didn't want him to touch her—not even fleetingly. The thin threads holding her composure together might snap completely.

Her apartment was just inside the main doors of the apartment block, on the ground floor, and Kat could feel Zafir behind her. Tall, commanding. Totally incongruous.

As if to underline it she heard him say a little incredulously, 'No concierge?'

Kat would have bitten back a smile if she'd felt like smiling. 'No.'

She opened her door and went into her studio apartment. What had become a place of refuge for the past year was now anything but as she put her keys down and turned around to face her biggest threat.

Zafir closed the door behind him and Kat folded her arms. 'Well, Zafir? What is it you have to say?'

He was looking around the small space with unmistakable curiosity, and finally that dark grey gaze came to land on her. To her horror, he started to shrug off his overcoat, revealing a bespoke suit that clung lovingly to his powerful body.

When he spoke he sounded grim. 'I have plenty to say, Kat, so why don't you make us both a coffee? Because I'm not going anywhere any time soon.'

Kat stared mutinously at Zafir for a moment, and for those few seconds he was transfixed by her stunningly unusual eyes—amber from a distance, but actually green and gold from up close, surrounded by long dark lashes. They were almond-shaped, and Zafir's blood rushed south as he recalled how she'd look at him after making love, the expression in her gaze one of wonderment that had never failed to catch him like a punch to his gut.

Lies.

It had all been lies. She might have been a virgin, but she'd been no innocent. It had been an elaborate act to hide her murky past. Suddenly he felt exposed. What was he doing here?

But just then something in Kat's stance seemed to droop and she said in a resigned voice, 'Fine, I'll make coffee.'

She disappeared into a tiny galley kitchen and Zafir had to admit that he knew very well why he was here—he still wanted her. Even more so after seeing her again. But questions buzzed in his brain. He put down his overcoat on the back of a worn armchair and took in the clean but colourless furnishings of the tiny space she now called home.

He'd never been in the apartment she'd shared with three other models when he'd known her before, but it had been a loft in SoHo—a long way from here.

She emerged a couple of minutes later with two steaming cups and handed one to Zafir. He noticed that she was careful not to come too close, and it made something within him snarl and snap.

She'd taken off her coat and now wore a long-sleeved jumper over the T-shirt. Even her plain clothes couldn't hide that perfect body, though. High firm breasts. A small waist, generous hips. And legs that went on for ever…

He could still feel them, wrapped around his back, her heels digging into his buttocks as she urged him deeper, harder—

Dammit. He struggled to rein in his libido.

'Take a seat,' she said, with almost palpable reluctance.

Zafir took the opportunity to disguise his uncontrollable response, not welcoming it one bit. He put it down to his recent sexual drought.

She sat on a threadbare couch on the other side of a coffee table. Zafir took a sip of coffee, noting with some level of satisfaction that she hadn't forgotten how he liked it. Strong and black. But then he frowned, noticing something. 'Your hair is different.'

She touched a hand to the unruly knot on her head self-consciously. 'This is my natural colour.'

Zafir felt something inside him go cold when he observed that her 'natural colour' was a slightly darker brown, with enticing glints of copper. Wasn't this just more evidence of her duplicitous nature? Her hair had used to be a tawny golden colour, adding to her all-American, girl-next-door appeal, but in reality she'd made a mockery of that image.

He put down his cup. 'So, Kat, what happened? Why did you disappear off the international modelling scene and who is Kaycee Smith?'

CHAPTER TWO

ALL KAT HEARD WAS, 'Why did you disappear off the international modelling scene?' For a moment she couldn't breathe. The thought of letting exactly what had happened tumble out of her mouth and watching Zafir's reaction terrified her.

She'd come a long way in eighteen months, but some things she wasn't sure she'd ever be ready for...namely revealing to him the full reality of why she was no longer a model, or who she was now. The graceful long-legged stride she'd become famous for on catwalks all over the world was a distant memory now, never to be resurrected.

She breathed in shakily. *Answer his questions and then he'll be gone.* She couldn't imagine him wanting to hang around in these insalubrious surroundings for too long.

'What happened?' she said, in a carefully neutral voice. 'You know what happened, Zafir—after all you're the one who broke it to me that I'd been dropped from nearly every contract and that the fashion houses couldn't distance themselves fast enough from the girl who had fallen from grace.'

Kat had been blissfully unaware of the storm headed her way. She'd been packing for her new life with her fiancé—filled with trepidation, yes, but also hope that she would make him proud of her... What a naive fool she'd been.

Zafir's face darkened. 'There were *naked* pictures of you when you were seventeen years old, Kat. They spoke pretty eloquently for themselves. Not to mention the not inconsequential fact of the huge personal debt you'd been hiding from me. And the real story of your upbringing—enabling a drug-addicted mother to find her next fix.'

Kat's hands tightened on her cup as she remembered the vicious headline Zafir had thrust under her nose. It had labelled her 'a white trash gold-digger.' A man like Zafir—privileged and richer than Croesus—could never have begun to understand the challenges she'd faced growing up.

Kat felt a surge of white-hot anger but also—far more betrayingly—she felt hurt all over again. The fact that he still had this ability to affect her almost killed her. Feeling too agitated to stay sitting, she put down her cup and stood up, moving to stand behind the couch, as if that could offer some scant protection.

Zafir was sitting forward, hands locked loosely between his legs. He looked perfectly at ease, but Kat wasn't fooled by his stance. He was never more dangerous than when he gave off an air of nonchalance.

'Look,' she said, as calmly as she could, 'if you've just come here to re-enact our last meeting, then I can't see how that will serve any purpose. I really don't need to be reminded of how once my so-called perfect image was tarnished you deemed me no longer acceptable in your life. We said all we had to say that night.'

Her hands instinctively dug into the top of the couch as she remembered that cataclysmic night—stumbling out of Zafir's apartment building into the dark streets, the pain of betrayal in her heart, her tear-blurred vision and then... Nothing but blackness and more pain, the like of which she hadn't known existed.

Zafir stood up too, dislodging the sickening memory, reminding her that this was the present and apparently not much had changed.

'Did we, really? As far as I recall you said far too little

and then left. You certainly didn't apologise for misleading me the whole time we were together.'

Struggling to control herself as she remembered the awful shock of that night, Kat said, 'You saw that article and you looked at those pictures and you judged and condemned me. You weren't prepared to listen to anything I had to say in my defence.'

Kat's conscience pricked when she recalled how she'd always put off telling Zafir the unvarnished truth of her background. And as for the debt... She'd never wanted to reveal that ugliness, or the awful powerlessness she'd felt. Not to someone like Zafir, who set such an exacting standard for moral strength and integrity.

'Dammit, Kat, you told me nothing about yourself—when were you going to reveal the truth? If ever?' He shook his head before she could respond, and repeated his accusation of that night. 'You were obviously hoping that I'd marry you before the sordid details came out and then you'd be secured for life even if we divorced.'

Kat felt breathless, and nausea rose inside her. 'It wasn't like that...'

Zafir looked impossibly stern. As unforgiving as he had been that night. He changed tack, asking her again, 'Who is Kaycee Smith?'

Kat swallowed painfully, not remotely prepared for her past transgressions to be visited upon her again like this. 'Kaycee Smith is the name on my birth certificate.'

A dark brow arched over one eye. 'A pertinent detail missed by the papers?'

She refused to let Zafir do this to her again. Humiliate her. Annihilate her.

Kat tipped up her chin. 'It was about the only thing they did miss.'

Thankfully, she thought now. Otherwise she would never have been able to fade away from view as she had.

'We have nothing to say to each other, Zafir. *Nothing*. Now, get out—before I call the police and tell them you're harassing me.'

Kat moved decisively from her spot behind the sofa towards the door, powered by anger and the tumult inside her, only to be stopped in her tracks before she reached it when Zafir asked sharply, 'Why are you limping?'

Immediately the adrenalin rush faded, to be replaced with a very unwelcome sense of exposure. There was nothing to hold on to nearby and it reminded her of how vulnerable she was now.

She turned around slowly and realised that she was far too close to Zafir. Every part of her body seemed to hum with electricity. It was as if her libido had merely been waiting for his presence again, and now it was no longer dormant but very much awake and sizzling back to life.

His scent wound around her like a siren call to lean closer...to breathe in his uniquely male smell. It had always fascinated her—the mixture of earthy musk and something indescribably exotic which instantly brought her back to her first and last visit to Jahor, with its awe-inspiring palace on a hill overlooking the teeming ancient city on the edge of the ocean.

She'd felt so awed and intimidated at the prospect of becoming a Queen of that land, and yet deep within her she'd thrilled to the challenge. But when Zafir had deemed her unsuitable to be his wife she'd realised what a fool she'd been to indulge in such a fantasy. She was no Queen, and she had no right to the ache of loss that still had the power to surprise her when she wasn't vigilant.

Her head snapped up. Zafir was still frowning. She moved back, aghast that her body could betray her like this. And then she remembered what he'd asked: *Why are you limping?*

Everything inside Kat recoiled from revealing herself to Zafir. The urge to self-protect was huge. He had no idea of the extent of the devastation in her life since she'd seen him—not all of which had to do with him. It also had to do with events totally beyond him.

But she knew that giving him nothing would only pique his interest even more, so reluctantly she said, 'I was involved in a road traffic accident a while ago. I injured my leg and I was out of circulation for some time.'

Try at least a year, Kat thought to herself, and held her breath, praying he wouldn't ask for more details.

Zafir looked at her assessingly. 'Is that why you haven't returned to modelling? And is that why you're living like this? Because you still haven't cleared your debts? You're obviously recovered now though, and I can't imagine the fashion world wouldn't have renewed your contracts eventually, once the story had died down.'

Kat hid her reflexive flinch at *'you're obviously recovered now.'* But she wasn't about to explain anything—not when Zafir was clearly no more ready to hear the truth now than he had been back then. And he was right—except when the fashion houses *had* come calling again she'd been in no position to consider going back…

Kat breathed out unsteadily. She avoided answering his questions directly and said, 'I do some hand modelling, but that's about it. And the waitressing.'

Zafir came closer, standing beside the chair. His gaze was far too keen on her and incisive. She could almost hear his brain working, trying to join the dots.

Kat just wanted him gone. He'd upended her world once before and she wouldn't survive him doing it again.

'Look,' she said now, trying to hide the desperation in her voice, 'did you really come here to rake over old ground, Zafir?'

She stopped and bit her lip as a dangerous thought

occurred to her—perhaps in spite of everything he *had* come to listen to her side of the story? Even belatedly?

For a moment Kat felt something very delicate flower deep inside her, but after a moment Zafir shook his head and said curtly, 'No. Of course not. That's in the past and I've no wish to revisit it any further.'

Kat's heart thumped. Hard. Of course he hadn't come here to hear her side of things. Apparently she was as pathetically susceptible to this man as she'd ever been, and in spite of everything she'd been through that was somehow more devastating than anything else. She felt a dart of panic at the knowledge that time had done little to diminish her feelings or her attraction to him. If anything, everything felt more acute than it had before.

She forced out words through a tight jaw. 'Then if you wouldn't mind leaving? We had a past and you pretty definitively ruled out any future, so what more could there possibly be to say?'

She regretted asking the question as soon as she saw the calculating gleam come into those slate-grey eyes.

'Our future is exactly what I'm here to talk about. A different future to the one previously envisaged, yes, but I don't see why we can't leave that in the past and move on.'

Kat's insides tightened as if warding off a blow. 'I'm not interested in discussing any kind of future or *moving on* with you, Zafir.'

Zafir's jaw clenched and he had to consciously relax it. He wasn't used to anyone talking to him like this—and he couldn't remember Kat ever being so combative. But he couldn't deny that somewhere deep inside him he thrilled to it. She *had* changed, and yet she was still intriguingly familiar. Achingly familiar. His whole body hummed with frustration to be so close and yet have her hold him at arm's length and look at him as if he was an unwelcome stranger.

In truth, he hadn't expected her to be so antagonistic towards him. He knew things had ended badly before, but she was the one who had kept the truth from him, clearly in a bid to avoid risking his commitment to marry her—which was exactly what had happened. Yet she was acting as if she was the injured party!

He cursed himself. He hadn't planned on rehashing the past, but obviously it had been inevitable. But, as he'd said, he was done talking about the past now—it was time for him to lay out his plans for Kat. For *them*.

In spite of everything, and even though he knew there were a thousand reasons for him to turn and walk away from Kat and forget he'd ever seen her again, he *couldn't*. Not now. But he assured himself that he could have what he wanted and get on with his life. And he fully intended to.

'I'm not leaving until I've said what I came to say, Kat.'

Dismayed, Kat watched as Zafir illustrated his point by sitting down again. He was an immovable force, and she recognised that steely determination all too well. The last thing she wanted was for him to see how raw she felt, so she schooled her features and sat down opposite him, as if this visit wasn't tearing her apart.

She looked pointedly at her watch and then back to him, 'It's getting late and I've got work early in the morning. I'd appreciate it if you could keep this short.'

Zafir inspected the bland expression on Kat's face. For a moment he'd caught a glimpse of something much more fiery, but it was gone now. She seemed to be determined to treat him as if he was someone she hadn't been intimately acquainted with. Soon, Zafir vowed, they would be intimately acquainted again, and she'd be moaning his name in ecstasy as her release threw them both over the edge and purged him of this ache.

He forced his mind out of his fantasies with effort and said, 'Did you even listen to the proposition I sent your agent?'

Kat shook her head, a long tendril of hair dropping from the knot on top of her head to curl around her neck. Zafir wanted to undo her hair and let it fall in a luxurious curtain down her naked back, the way it had before. He gritted his jaw at the image. This was ridiculous—he could barely conduct a coherent conversation without X-rated images flooding his mind.

Calling on every ounce of control he possessed, he said, 'What I'm proposing is a modelling assignment—'

He stopped and put up his hand as soon as he saw Kat's mouth open, presumably to protest. She closed it again, her lush lips compressing into a tight line. Zafir ignored the pulse throbbing in his groin.

He tried another tack. 'You might recall me telling you once about the famed missing jewel, the Heart of Jandor, the biggest red diamond in the world?'

Kat tensed opposite him, and then he saw a flush tinge her cheeks pink as if she too was remembering that moment—lying in her bed in Jahor, her limbs sprawled over his in sated abandon as he'd told her the story of the gem. He'd had to sneak into her rooms like a teenager, even though they'd been unofficially engaged at the time. His people would have been scandalised by such liaisons.

Kat had lifted her head from his chest and said huskily, 'That's so romantic... I hope they find it some day.'

Zafir could recall how a vague feeling of dread mixed with fear had washed over him on hearing the wistful tone in Kat's voice, and how he'd felt the urge to say something, *anything*, to take the dreamy look from her eyes, to tell her that such a thing as romance had no place in his life. Duty trumped emotion. Always. There would be no room for romance when he became King and she was Queen.

But then she'd reached up and kissed him…and he couldn't remember anything else.

'I remember something…vaguely,' she said tightly now, and Zafir desisted from arguing that she clearly remembered very well.

There was a curt edge to his voice after that memory. 'They found the diamond recently, during an archaeological dig. It was a cause of much celebration and my people have seen it as a good omen for the future.'

Kat's hands were clasped in her lap. 'I'm very happy for you…and them…but I fail to see what this has to do with me.'

Zafir said carefully, 'It has everything to do with you, Kat, because I've chosen you to be the model who will wear the diamond on our worldwide diplomatic tour to promote Jandor.'

The sheer arrogance of Zafir's pronouncement rendered Kat speechless for a moment. And then she spluttered, 'But that's ridiculous. I'm working here. I have a life here. I have no intention of going anywhere with you.'

Zafir stood up, and as if she hadn't spoken he said, 'It's a very select tour. The first function is the evening after tomorrow, at the Metropolitan Museum of Art. Then we and the diamond go to London, then Paris and then back to Jandor, where it will be put on permanent display.'

Kat stood up, quivering all over with volatile emotions. 'There is no *we* in this, Zafir.'

'If it had gone according to my plan, then, yes, I agree—I would have no need of you. But my chief aide came up with the idea of showing off the diamond in an infinitely more accessible way—instead of keeping it in a sterile environment, we will display it on a beautiful woman and have her meet and greet specially selected guests with us at each function, so that they can see how the gem really glows with a life force. It will bring the gem—and Jandor—alive.'

Kat folded her arms against the terrifying thought of people clamouring around her, too close, staring at her, pawing at her to get to the stone. One of the side effects of the accident she'd been involved in was that she felt claustrophobic in certain situations where she felt trapped.

She shook her head. 'No way, Zafir. I'm not interested. And surely if this is to promote your country, then you should be using a model from Jandor.'

Kat saw the steely glint in Zafir's eyes. It meant that he'd most likely anticipated every one of her arguments and was ready to counter them.

'We don't yet have a modelling agency in Jandor, but we *do* have aspiring fashion designers who are eager to showcase some of their designs during this tour. Also, I want someone who has the poise and grace of an experienced model—and they don't come more experienced than you.'

Feeling desperate, she said, 'There are a million models just as experienced as me—if not more.' A hint of bitterness crept into her voice. 'Models who don't come with negative baggage. If I appear in public with you as Kat Winters, the press will have a field day and all those stories will get raked up again.'

Kat sent up silent thanks now that their break-up had occurred before the official public announcement of their engagement had been made.

'Yes, they might,' he conceded, 'and I've considered that. But I have an excellent PR team, who will field any of the old stories and drown them out with this new one.

Resurrecting Kat Winters to wear the most famous re-discovered gem in the world will be an irresistible story.'

Kat went cold inside as the full extent of Zafir's cool calculation sank in. Her involvement would be purely to provide an angle. Something to fire up the headlines even at the expense of negativity. Everything Zafir was outlining was literally her worst nightmare. She felt pan-icky. She wasn't prepared to step back into the world of Kat Winters again—not for anyone.

She shook her head. 'The answer is no, Zafir. Now, please leave. I'm tired.'

But of course Zafir didn't turn around to leave, much as Kat wished he would. Even as she felt the betraying hum of awareness that flowed like illicit nectar through her blood.

'Obviously I wouldn't expect you to do this for free, Kat. I would be willing to pay handsomely for one of the world's most sought-after and elusive models. I'm well aware of the fees you once commanded, and as your credit history shows a lack of ability to hang on to your earnings, it looks like you're not really in a position to turn down such a lucrative contract.'

He illustrated his point with a sweeping glance around her studio apartment.

Kat's hands curled into fists. *Of all the patronising—* She stopped just as she was about to blurt something out. Something that would make those far too incisive eyes narrow on her and make him start asking questions again.

It was the last thing she wanted to bring up, but she had to. Maybe it was the thing that would finally push Zafir to leave. 'Have you considered the speculation that would inevitably be sparked about *us* again?'

He waited a beat and then said, 'Yes, I have, and I see no harm in it—not when it's likely to be confined to the duration of the tour and then it'll die away again.'

There was a rough quality to Zafir's voice that sent a rush of awareness through Kat's blood—as if her body was already reacting to some secret signal. For a moment she couldn't really comprehend the way he was suddenly so watchful, but then it sank in with horrifying clarity.

'You can't seriously mean for us to—' She stopped, afraid to speak the words out loud. Afraid to make herself look a fool again. Afraid she might be right.

Afraid she might be wrong.

'Can't seriously mean for us to what, Kat?'

Zafir moved closer and she was rooted to the spot. He stopped within reaching distance, the harsh lighting of her apartment doing nothing to leach away any of his sheer gorgeousness.

'I can't seriously mean for us to be together again?'

Kat looked at him, horrified and excited in equal measure. She half shook and nodded her head.

Zafir's face suddenly took on a harsh aspect. 'That's exactly what I mean. I want you back in my bed, Kat. We have unfinished business. When you walked out—'

'You mean when you cast me aside!' Anger flooded Kat's veins again, giving her the impetus to move back out of Zafir's dangerous proximity, crossing her arms defensively over her chest.

'We're not going to rake over that ground again,' Zafir said harshly. 'Suffice it to say that our engagement might have been over—there was no way I could have presented you as my future Queen after those headlines and pictures—but our relationship didn't have to be over.'

Shock mixed with affront, and hurt poured through Kat, making her tremble. She was back in time, standing before Zafir in far more luxurious surroundings saying incredulously, 'You don't love me.'

He'd slashed a hand through the air. 'This isn't about *love*, Kat. It's never been about love. It's about mutual respect and desire and the fact that I believed—mistakenly—that you were the perfect choice to be my wife and future Queen.'

'*Perfect...*' She'd half-whispered it to herself, never hating a word as much as she had then.

Her whole life she'd been told she had to be *perfect*. To win the next competition. To get the commercial over the other pretty girl. To get enough money to save her mother... Except she'd failed—miserably.

She'd looked at Zafir and said in a hollow voice, 'Well, I'm not perfect, Zafir. Far from it.'

And she'd walked out, leaving her engagement ring on the hall table. And now she was glad—because clearly he would have demoted her from the position of future wife, but kept her in his life as his mistress.

And she'd never been further from perfect than she was right now.

'Get out, Zafir, this conversation is over.'

But her words bounced off him as if an invisible shield protected him.

'Think about what you're turning down, Kat. A chance to restart your life and return to where you belong. Have you thought about what you'd be turning down?'

He mentioned a sum of money and it was literally life-changing. Kat felt her blood drain south.

He reached into an inside pocket and took out a card, holding it out to her. She unlocked her arms from her chest and took it reluctantly.

'That's my private number. I'll be staying at my penthouse apartment. I'll give you till tomorrow morning, Kat. If I don't hear from you I *will* find someone else and you will never hear from me again.'

She looked at him and marvelled that she'd once believed that he loved her because he'd asked her to marry him. Because she'd always had a romantic notion that that was what people did when they loved someone, in spite of being brought up as the only child of a single parent with no clue as to her father's whereabouts.

But Zafir's motives had been so much more strategic than that. She'd been scrutinised and deemed suitable. *Perfect.* And now he was asking her to step back into a world that had chewed her up and spat her out. Not only that, he was asking her to lay herself bare to him again, to let him carve out the last remaining part of her heart that still functioned and let him crush it until there was nothing left.

Kat was stronger now than she'd ever been, considering the trials she'd faced in the past eighteen months, but she was still only human and she wasn't strong enough for this. No matter how much money he was offering.

Without taking her eyes off Zafir's, as if some small, treacherous part of her wanted to commit them to her memory, she held up the card and ripped it in half, letting the pieces fall to the floor.

'Goodbye, Zafir.'

His eyes flashed and his jaw clenched. Kat could feel the waves of energy flowing like electricity between them, but after a tense moment he just stepped back and said, 'As you wish. Goodbye, Kat.'

But to Kat's dismay, when Zafir finally turned and walked out, picking up his overcoat as he did so, and when the door had shut behind him, the last thing she felt was triumph.

She found her feet moving towards the door instinctively, as if to rush after him and beg him not to go. She stopped in her tracks, shocked at the profound sense of loss that pervaded her whole body, and she wrapped her arms around herself as if that could hold back all the turmoil she was feeling.

Zafir had devastated her once before. She couldn't let it happen again.

So she stayed resolutely where she was, and after she'd heard the sound of his vehicles leaving from outside the apartment she breathed in shakily and sank down onto the couch behind her.

She looked around her, as if seeing the space for the first time again. She'd grown used to the bare furnishings and the sparse décor. It was all she'd been able to afford after the accident and her lengthy rehabilitation, even though the largest part of her debt had finally been gone.

And the reason it had been gone was because once those pictures of Kat had gone public, her blackmailer— the photographer who had taken them in the first place— had had no further means with which to blackmail her. After all, everything he'd always threatened her with had come true—her career had imploded in spectacular style.

Perversely, Kat had been grateful to whoever had found and leaked the pictures, because they had freed her from a malignant threat she'd had no idea how to deal with.

On numerous occasions she'd wanted to confide in Zafir, but then she'd feel too intimidated, or too scared of his reaction. How could a man like him, who had grown up in such a rarefied world, possibly understand why she would do such a thing? The thought of revealing all that ugly poison had pulled her back from the brink each time.

And in the end hadn't she been vindicated? She'd never forget the look of disgust and horror on his face as he'd confronted her with her past.

Kat stood up again, restless, as Zafir's visit sank in properly. She told herself that it was his arrogance that still left her breathless, but really it was the knowledge that he still wanted her, and the even more shattering knowledge that she still wanted him. The core of her body felt hot and achy, and her blood felt thick and heavy in her veins.

Damn him.

She paced back and forth, and as she did so her eye snagged on something in the corner of the room and she stopped. Zafir hadn't noticed them. Crutches and a folded-up wheelchair. She hadn't needed the wheelchair for some time now, but she would never *not* need one to hand. And she'd always need the crutches.

To Kat's shame, she knew that *this* was as much of a reason as any other as to why she'd all but pushed Zafir out through the door. Because she couldn't bear for him to know what had happened to her. Because she couldn't bear to think about the fact that, even if she *was* to ever be with Zafir again, he would not want to be with her.

Because she was irrevocably altered.

Kat picked up the crutches and went into her tiny bedroom. She took off her sneakers, undid her jeans and pulled them off, then stood in front of her mirror, inspecting herself critically.

At first glance Zafir might not notice anything different about Kat—after all she stood on two legs, and was the same height she'd always been, with the same straight back. But then she imagined his gaze travelling down and stopping on her left leg. Specifically on the prosthetic limb that now made up her lower left leg, with its mechanical ankle and fake foot.

Even now Kat couldn't recall anything about the accident itself on that fateful night. She only knew that one minute she'd been crossing the street and the next she'd been waking up, a day later, in a hospital, with a doctor informing her that they'd had to amputate below the knee to save her leg—which was kind of ironic, considering half of it was now gone.

She'd had flashbacks however, since then, of regaining consciousness and realising that her foot was trapped under the heaviest weight. People had crowded around her but she hadn't been able to move or speak. And then she'd slipped back into darkness.

That was why she got claustrophobic now.

Sometimes people gave her a second glance, but they soon dismissed her when they saw her slightly limping gait and figured this woman with darker hair and no make-up couldn't possibly be *the* Kat Winters.

A ball of emotion lodged itself in Kat's chest, and before she could stop them hot tears blurred her vision. But she dashed them away angrily as she sat down on her bed and set about removing her prosthetic limb with an efficiency born of habit.

It had been a long time since she'd indulged in self-pity. That had been in the dark early days, when she'd fallen down in many graceless heaps while trying to get to the bathroom during the night, when she'd hurled her crutches across the room in a rising tide of fury at the hand she'd been dealt. Or when she'd locked herself away for long days, sunk in such a black depression that she'd thought she might never emerge into daylight again.

It was her oldest friend, Julie, who was also her agent, who had finally saved her. And the local rehabilitation centre. It was there that she'd learnt how to deal with her new reality and had been able to start putting things into perspective after meeting a man who had lost both his legs in a war, and a woman who had lost an arm, and an endlessly cheerful little girl who'd lost her limbs after meningitis… They, and many more, had humbled her, and reminded her that she was one of the luckier ones.

And gradually she'd clawed her way out of the mire to a place of acceptance, where this was her new reality and she just had to get on with it. And she *had* been getting on with it, perfectly well, until a Zafir-shaped storm had blown everything up again.

Kat could be honest enough with herself to acknowledge that—as much as the accident and its consequences had made her feel as if her life had shrunk—she'd been living in a kind of limbo, taking one day at a time. The accident had been so catastrophic that she'd been able to block out that last night with Zafir for a long time, but recently it had been creeping back, as if now she was ready to deal with it…

Maybe he was right, whispered a coaxing voice. *Maybe you do have unfinished business. Perhaps if you took on the assignment you could lay more than one ghost to rest.*

The ghost of the relationship she'd *thought* she had with Zafir, but which had never really existed…only in her romantic fantasies.

The ghost of the Kat Winters she'd been before—in awe and intimidated by nearly everything and everyone around her in spite of her high-flying career, and by none more so than Sheikh Zafir Ibn Hafiz Al-Noury. The ghost of her mother's death and the constant feeling of failure Kat had grown up with when she hadn't been able to save a mother who hadn't wanted to be saved.

The thought lodged in Kat's head, and as much as she wanted to dismiss it out of hand she was afraid that she couldn't go back to fooling herself that Zafir was firmly in her past. She'd been too scared to really look at the repercussions of what had happened between them, but seeing him again this evening had roused more than one dormant part of her.

Not least of which was the reawakening of her sexual awareness. It was terrifying. The prospect of intimacy and what it would mean now was something she'd found easy to bury deep inside her since the accident. If she'd thought about it at all, she'd imagined that it would be with someone gentle, kind…patient.

Zafir was a force of nature—above such benign human virtues. He didn't have to deal with imperfection. He walked amongst the brightest, the best, the most beautiful. He was one of them.

Panic skittered up Kat's spine. There was no way she felt ready to trust Zafir on an intimate level again with her *new* self.

Resolutely shutting her mind to that scenario, she thought again of that fateful night and their fight.

Her conscience pricked when she remembered rushing out of his apartment—had she been too hasty? But once she'd known that he didn't love her, the last thing she'd wanted to do was try to defend herself to someone who had only ever seen her as some kind of a commodity.

That's how her mother had seen her—as a means to make money, capitalising on her daughter's beauty. Zafir had been no different—he'd all but admitted he'd only proposed because she'd fitted into his life on a superficial level and nothing more. It had driven home to Kat how much she hungered to be loved for her whole self.

But she had the sinking feeling that her secret wounds would remain raw until she confronted Zafir properly and forced him to listen to her side of the story behind those lurid headlines.

Not that she wanted anything more than that… The prospect of *more* made panic surge again even as her blood grew hot.

She would deny that her attraction to him was as strong as ever with every breath in her body—she had no intention of ever letting Zafir see her like this. She looked down at her residual limb and ran a hand over it almost protectively.

Yet even as she entertained the possibility of acquiescing to his demand—purely on a professional basis—she balked at the thought. The prospect of going back into that world and being scrutinised terrified her. And doing it all with Zafir by her side? Scrambling her brain to pieces? Making all the cold parts of her melt again after she'd spent so much time rebuilding her defences?

No way. She couldn't. She wasn't strong enough yet.

At that moment Kat caught sight of her reflection in the mirror as she sat on the bed. Her eyes were huge. She looked panicked and pale... Something inside her resisted that. She sat up straight and took in the full reality of who she was now. A damaged woman, yes, and less whole than she'd once been, but actually in many ways more whole than she'd ever been.

She'd always known on some level that she wasn't prepared to hide away as Kaycee Smith for ever, and Julie had been putting more and more pressure on her to come out of her protective cocoon, to let herself be seen again.

And now Zafir was asking her to take on a modelling assignment. That was all. *No, it's not*, whispered a snide voice, and Kat's heart thumped in response. Zafir had wanted perfection before, and he'd rejected her because she'd fallen from grace. She would never give him a chance to do that to her again.

She thought of the sum of money he'd mentioned and realised with a churning gut that it would allow her to pay Julie back. Her friend had helped support Kat through not only the first six months of her rehabilitation, but since then too, because Kat had only had the most basic of insurance. But also—and maybe more important—she realised that she would be able to help the rehabilitation centre that had been so instrumental in her recovery.

The St Patrick's Medical Centre for Traumatic Injuries was currently facing the prospect of closure due to lack of funds and resources. Kat would be in a position to give them enough money to avoid imminent closure until they could get back on their feet and raise more funds for their long-term future.

If she accepted Zafir's job offer.

Her heart sped up with a mixture of terror and illicit excitement—if she said yes, then she could use it as an exercise to prove to herself just how ill-suited she and Zafir had always been, in spite of the insane chemistry between them. Never more evident than now. She was no longer a wide-eyed virgin being initiated into a world that had moved at a terrifying pace—too fast for her to shout, *'Stop!'* and get off.

She was strong enough to take on Zafir and walk away with her head high.

Are you really, though?

Kat assured herself that, yes, she was.

This would be purely a professional transaction. Zafir would never touch her emotions again—or her body. He was the kind of man who relished the conquest, who relished making a woman acquiesce to him of her own volition, and she had no intention of acquiescing to an affair.

The walls Kat had had to build just to survive since the accident were impenetrable. He wouldn't break through. She could do this.

She picked up her mobile from the table near the bed before she lost her nerve, focusing on anything but the terror she felt at the thought of what she was about to do. And how it would affect her life.

This wasn't just about her. Not when she now knew she could put that money to good use. Vital use.

Zafir had made it clear that he would walk away, and if Kat knew anything about him it was that he meant what he said. He was a proud man. He wouldn't ask again and he certainly wouldn't beg.

As Kat dialled her friend's number and waited for her

to answer, she caught sight of her reflection in the mirror again. She scowled at her flushed face and the too-bright eyes that whispered that her decision had a lot less to do with altruism and more to do with something much darker and far more ambiguous deep inside her.

And then Julie answered and Kat had a split second to decide whether to take a step into a dangerous future or remain safe in the past.

CHAPTER THREE

ZAFIR STOOD AT the window of his penthouse study and looked out over Manhattan, sparkling under the autumn sun, with Central Park in the distance. He was trying not to acknowledge the sense of triumph and satisfaction rushing through his blood, but it was hard.

Along with it, though, had come something far more contradictory—a kind of disappointment—and Zafir realised that it was because when he'd walked away from Kat last night she'd seemed so resolute. And, as much as it had irritated him intensely, he'd admired it on some level. It was rare to find anyone going against him in anything—especially since he'd become King.

He recalled getting into his car last night and how stunned he'd been that she'd turned him down. And then how he'd had to physically restrain himself from instructing his driver to turn around so that he could go back to Kat's apartment and shatter that cooler than cool reception by reminding her in a very explicit way of just how good it had been between them. How good it could be again.

And yet before 8:00 a.m. this morning his personal phone had rung and it had been her agent, confirming that Kat had decided to take on the assignment after all.

At this very moment she was with her agent and his legal advisors, signing the contract, and then she was due to spend the rest of the day and tomorrow in preparation for the tour with a team of stylists. Rahul would go through the itinerary with her and make sure her passport and travel documents were in order for when they left the United States.

So her cold stonewalling and reluctance last night had been an act. Much like the act she'd fooled everyone with when he'd first met her, projecting a false persona of someone who was honest and hard-working, making the most of the opportunities presented to her.

She'd been honest, at least, about coming from a poor background—which in Zafir's eyes had only made her more commendable. She'd epitomised the American dream of grit and ambition and achieving success no matter what your circumstances were.

But in actual fact her story had been a lot darker and murkier. She'd had a huge personal debt she'd never revealed—in spite of commanding eye-wateringly high fees as one of the most in-demand models of her time. She'd had a drug-addicted mother, no father to speak of, and barely any education. Not to mention the coup de grâce—those provocative pictures taken when she was only seventeen years old, apparently in a bid to make money so her mother could score her next fix.

Even now when Zafir thought of those explicit pictures he felt his vision cloud over with a red mist and his hands curl to fists in his pockets. Kat had been so young, and yet she'd looked at the camera almost defiantly. The rage he'd felt towards the person behind the camera had scared him with its intensity. But what he'd felt towards Kat had been much more complicated—anger, disappointment. Protectiveness. *Betrayal.*

When he'd confronted her with the headlines due to hit the news stands within hours, he'd wanted to hear her say that she'd been an unwilling victim, so that he could apportion blame to someone else and not her... But she'd agreed with him that she was not perfect. That she was flawed. And then she'd walked out of his apartment and disappeared, leaving him with a futile anger that had corroded his insides as he'd gone over it in his head again and again, trying to make sense of how he could have been so naive…

It had made him doubt if she'd even been a virgin, or if that had been part of an elaborate ruse to attract his jaded interest. Certainly her innocence had shocked him at the time when she'd admitted it; he'd believed virgins in their twenties to be as mythical as unicorns, and it had dissolved some of Zafir's very cynical defences.

And yet in spite of that history he was bringing her back into his world. *Because he had to have her.* Zafir's jaw clenched. He did not like being at the mercy of desires he couldn't control. Maybe it had something to do with the fact that he'd been her first lover, making his connection to her feel somehow more primal…

But, he reasoned to himself, now he knew all Kat's secrets. Now he knew that she was suitable only to sate this fever burning in his body. He would never put her on a pedestal again, or imagine for a second that she could be the woman who would stand alongside him in front of his people.

Kat took in her reflection in the floor-length mirror. At that moment she was almost glad that Julie had had to leave her with the team of stylists and hair and make-up artists and go back to work. She needed to be alone right now.

She was dressed from head to toe in a black velvet sleeveless haute couture gown with a deep vee that ran almost down to her navel, exposing more skin than she had in years. Her hair was pulled back in a rough chignon. The heavy make-up felt strange on her face after not wearing any for so long. And she was wearing heels—albeit only two-inch heels.

Her critical gaze travelled down her body and she lifted up the bottom of the dress. Her breath caught. To the untrained eye her legs looked absolutely normal. As they'd always looked.

In the place of her habitual prosthetic limb was the cosmetic one that Julie had insisted on Kat being fitted for some months ago. It had been specially made for her in a factory in the UK, in a bid to show Kat that perhaps embarking on more than hand modelling was possible, but this was the first time she'd put it to use. And luckily the fit was still fine.

Kat looked down. It was remarkable. Her toenails were painted. She could even see veins. No one would notice a thing. A bubble of emotion rose up from her chest and she looked up again, letting the dress fall back, blinking her eyes rapidly to get rid of the sudden and mortifying onset of tears.

She was slightly ashamed of how overcome she felt to see herself like this, when she'd never expected to see herself like this again. When she'd thought she'd closed the door firmly on her old life. When she'd told herself that she'd never *really* felt a part of that world.

And yet here she was, feeling such a mix of emotions that it only proved to her that she was more tied to her old life than she'd realised.

A sharp rap sounded on the door to the bedroom in the lavish suite where she'd been changing into countless outfits and she called out hurriedly, 'Just a second.'

No doubt the stylists were eager to see the dress on her, as it was the one she'd wear on the first night of the tour, chosen for its clean lines so that the diamond would be shown to its best advantage.

She composed herself and held the dress to her chest where it was still a little loose. As she opened the door she said, 'The fit is fine. I just need to be zipped—'

The words died on her tongue and she had to look up and up again at the man filling the doorway. *Zafir.* She hadn't seen him when they'd arrived earlier to sign the contract, and she'd felt jittery with nerves, waiting for him to appear at any moment. When he hadn't, she'd almost fooled herself into thinking that this assignment was not at his behest.

But it was. And here he was, wearing a shirt and dark trousers, his top button open and sleeves rolled up. She guessed that he'd just come from his office. He always had been a workaholic.

He was as leanly muscled as she remembered, the power in his body evident in a provocatively subtle way that was mesmerising and made her think of how he'd looked in his traditional Jandori robes—like a fierce warrior.

His voice broke her out of her embarrassing trance. 'You'd like me to zip you up?'

Anyone but you.

Kat clutched the dress to her breasts even more tightly, suddenly feeling as shy as the virgin she'd once been, in front of him.

She tried to look past him. 'I can ask one of the stylists…' Then she realised how quiet it was. 'Where is everyone?'

'I sent them away for the evening.' Zafir looked at his watch. 'It's 4:30 p.m. They've been working all day and so have you.'

Kat looked at him a little stupidly. She hadn't even realised how late it had got.

He lifted his hands. 'The dress? I'd like to see how it looks with the diamond.'

Kat balked. 'You have it with you now?'

Zafir nodded.

With the utmost reluctance Kat moved closer and turned around, presenting her bare back to him. She'd never before realised how vulnerable it felt—exposing the most defenceless part of your body to someone you didn't trust.

Yet even as she told herself that she didn't trust him she had to suppress the betraying shiver of anticipation that ran through her body as she waited for Zafir to pull up the zip. It didn't help when countless memories bombarded her of similar moments, when he had pressed close behind her and moved his hands around and under her dress to cup her breasts, pressing a hot kiss to her neck.

She hadn't felt vulnerable or defenceless then. Far from it.

She'd trusted him.

Her nerves were jangling painfully when she finally felt his hands on the zip, just above her buttocks, and then its far too slow ascent up her back, pulling the dress tighter around her torso, so that her breasts were pushed together under the discreet boning, creating a voluptuous cleavage. Something that wouldn't have bothered her too much in the past, but which felt positively indecent now.

When the zip was up she quickly turned around and moved out of touching distance. Zafir's eyes were a dark grey. To her relief he moved back and stood aside so she could walk out of the bedroom and into the suite. The unsteadiness of her legs had nothing to do with her prosthetic limb.

Kat stopped in her tracks, though, when a young woman dressed in a sober black suit, with her dark hair pulled back, stepped out of the shadows to stand beside the table where a large black box sat.

She'd thought they were alone, but they weren't. Perversely, that didn't seem to be of any comfort.

Zafir walked over to the table with his innately masculine grace, saying as he did so, 'I'd like you to meet Noor Qureshi. She's going to be your personal bodyguard for the duration of the tour while you wear the diamond.'

Kat put out her hand, slightly in awe of the female bodyguard. 'It's nice to meet you.'

They shook hands, but Zafir was drawing Kat's attention to the box, where he had his hand on the open lid. Kat came forward as Zafir said something to Noor, and the woman nodded before slipping discreetly out of the main suite door, presumably to wait outside.

Kat barely noticed. She fancied she could almost see the red-hued glow before she saw the actual diamond, and when she stepped close enough to see the stone resting against the black silk she gasped.

It was literally breathtaking. A stone about the size of a golf ball, in a heart shape. It seemed to glow and emit some kind of luminosity. Kat could imagine how it must have appeared when it was first discovered, deep in the mines, even in its rough state.

Zafir lifted it out and Kat saw that the gem sat in a thick collar-style platinum setting, and that the platinum was inscribed with what looked like Arabic script. The diamond dropped from the collar, stark and hypnotic.

Zafir held the necklace up, clearly indicating that he wanted to put it on Kat, and once again she stood in front of him, and shivered slightly as his arms came around her and the red diamond necklace appeared in her eyeline. She could feel him behind her, the heat and strength of his body.

It was one of the things that had drawn her to him like a helpless moth to a bright burning flame. His very masculinity. And it had surprised her, because ever since she'd been tiny she'd been aware of men and their strength, and how they could use it against a woman, after witnessing her mother bringing home one abusive male after another.

But Zafir was the first physically powerful man who had connected with Kat on another level and she hadn't instinctively shied away from him. To the contrary. And now she was feeling that same pull—as if her body was a magnet, aligned only to his and no one else's.

She closed her eyes for a second, as if that would help fight his pull, and then she felt the weight of the stone land on her upper chest. It was warm, not cold, and she instinctively reached up to touch it, feeling the pointed end. The metal of the collar was cool where it touched her skin.

Zafir's fingers brushed the back of her neck as he closed the clasp and then they were gone, and the necklace felt heavy around Kat's neck. He came and stood in front of her, looking at the stone and then at her, critically.

'Move back,' he commanded.

Kat felt an urge to resist his autocratic demand, but she did as he asked, taking a step back.

This is just a job and he's your employer, she repeated to herself like a mantra.

Those impenetrable grey eyes raked her up and down. He walked around her, and even though she'd endured years of people inspecting her like a brood mare, she felt restless under Zafir's intense gaze. Self-conscious. The top of the liner which sat between her leg and the prosthesis suddenly felt itchy, and she had to stop herself from reaching down to touch it.

Zafir came and stood in front of her again, that gaze boring into her, making her skin heat up.

'Stunning,' he pronounced. 'You're per—'

'Don't say that word!' Kat interrupted in a rush, immediately regretting it when Zafir's eyes narrowed on her.

Of course Zafir ignored her. '*Perfect*? Well, you are.'

Kat felt very aware of her leg, and the discomfort of getting used to the new prosthesis. She felt like a fraud, and longed to pull the necklace off. The weight of it was oppressive now, and a panicky sensation was rising.

She couldn't do this.

She turned around and bent her head forward, saying tightly, 'Can you take it off, please?'

There was no movement for a second, but then Zafir's hands were at the back of her neck. She caught the diamond in her hands when the clasp was undone and turned around, holding it out to Zafir.

He was too close. Kat held up the necklace, silently begging Zafir to take it and put some space between them. Finally he did, and stepped aside to put it back safely in the box.

Kat immediately walked over to a window, needing the illusion of air at least. She put her hand to her throat and felt for a moment as if she wouldn't be surprised to see that the necklace had left some kind of a mark.

Like the mark Zafir left on you? Inside where no one can see?

The panic rose. Kat turned around and looked at Zafir, who was shutting the box again but watching her. So far they'd exchanged only a handful of words, but the silent communication between them was almost deafening. It was too much.

'I'm sorry,' she blurted out. 'I don't think I can do this after all.'

Zafir put his hands in his pockets, unperturbed by her outburst. 'You're a professional model. This is probably one of the easiest jobs you've ever been asked to do— walk amongst a crowd for a few hours over a handful of evenings.'

It was so much more than that.

Zafir's easy dismissal made Kat see red. 'I'm not a model any more, Zafir. I haven't done this in—' She stopped short of saying exactly how long and amended it to, 'Months.'

'I'm sure it's just like riding a bike,' he drawled infuriatingly.

Kat had to force oxygen to her brain by taking a big deep breath. Zafir had no idea what he was really asking of her, and she had no intention of revealing all to the man who had so casually stepped on her heart.

Thank God, she thought now, *I never actually told him I loved him.*

'Anyway,' he said, prowling closer to where she stood in fight-or-flight mode, 'it's too late. You've signed the contract and, as per your request, a sizeable sum of up-front money has been already wired to your nominated account. No doubt to fill the black hole your debt created. Unless, of course,' he added silkily, 'you want to give the money back?'

Kat sagged. For a moment she'd forgotten. The money wasn't to fill a debt hole—it was going straight to the rehabilitation clinic, whom she'd already informed about their unexpected windfall, much to their delight and relief. And to Julie, to reimburse her for what she'd paid for the cosmetic limb. Kat had insisted, in spite of Julie's protests, wanting to feel as if she was at least starting to make her own way again.

So, yes, it *was* too late.

Straightening her shoulders, she called upon the inner strength she'd never known she possessed until recently and said, 'No, I'm not giving the money back and, yes, I've agreed to the job so I'll keep my word. I'm going to change into my own clothes now, and then I'd like to go home.'

Zafir frowned. 'I've booked this suite for you for to-night and tomorrow night—until we leave for Europe.'

Kat shook her head firmly. 'No. I'm going back to my apartment tonight. There are still some things I need to pack, and I've got one last shift at the restaurant this evening.'

Zafir's eyes flashed. 'You are *not* working in that restaurant another minute. And my driver can wait for you and bring you back here when you're ready.'

This was what Zafir had done before, and she'd been too awed to say no.

'You're moving in with me, I want you in my bed when I wake up in the morning, Kat.'

A summons she'd been only too happy to comply with.

'Please do not tell me what I can and can't do, Zafir. I'm not officially working for you until tomorrow, when I will be here at the appropriate time to start preparing for the first function.'

She tore her gaze away from his and walked with as much grace as she could muster to the bedroom, shutting the door firmly behind her and resting against it for a moment.

Her heart was pounding. Underneath all Zafir's arrogance she could feel his compelling pull, asking her for so much more. It had been explicit in the way he'd looked at her wearing the diamond. As if he wanted to devour her. No wonder she'd panicked for a moment.

Was that why he'd dismissed all his staff? Had he really believed that that's all it would take? Seeing him, being enticed with the rarest jewel in the world, she'd fall back into his bed—except this time without any illusion that he wanted more than a finite affair.

This time there would be no marriage proposal to kick the earth from under her legs, making her feel for the first time in her life as if she truly was worth something to someone... She'd believed that Zafir had really wanted her and loved her for herself, and not just for the aesthetically pleasing sum of her parts.

Kat struggled with the zip on the dress, but she was damned if she was going to emit so much as a squeak to let Zafir know she might need help. Eventually she managed to get it down, after some serious body contortions, and stripped off to get back into her own clothes.

She caught a glimpse of herself in a mirror and stopped for a moment, reminded of the fact that at first glance no one would see anything amiss but that on closer inspection they'd see her leg, and frown, and think, *Wait a second...*

Kat went cold all over as she contemplated Zafir ever seeing her like this—naked and exposed, her wounds visible.

Suddenly conscious that he was mere feet away, and separated from her only by a door, Kat stopped dithering and got dressed in her own clothes again, before going into the bathroom to wash off the make-up.

When her face was clean she straightened up and looked at herself. This was her now. Unadorned. She was naturally pale, and her hair tumbled around her shoulders, messy after she'd brushed it so roughly and darker in hue than she'd had it before, with natural copper highlights. She could see the faint lines wrought on her face already—the marks of her experience. Marks of her new strength, which she'd never needed more than now.

Zafir only wanted her when she appeared as she just had—when she was Kat the Supermodel.

As long as she could keep him at arm's length and show him that she wasn't the same woman, he'd soon lose interest and move on to someone far easier and more docile. As she'd once been. And when Zafir did lose interest and move on she'd finally be able to let go of the ties that still bound her to him like a spider's resilient silken threads, because his behaviour would confirm for her that all he'd ever been interested in was the illusion of the perfect woman.

A small voice whispered to Kat that all she had to do was take off her jeans, walk out of the bedroom and show

Zafir exactly who she was. He'd never want anything to do with her when he saw that she wasn't everything she'd once been. He could handle the potentially negative PR fallout, but he surely wouldn't want to seduce an ex-lover who was now an amputee.

So why don't you just do it, then? crowed that inner voice. *Go on—walk out of here and show him who you are now.*

Kat's hands gripped the sink hard. Her gut churned. If she did, it would all be over. She'd have to give the money back. She'd have to go to the rehab centre and apologise for getting their hopes up.

She took a deep breath, forcing herself to be calm. She was overreacting. Panicking. She didn't owe Zafir anything. She didn't owe him any explanations. He would lose interest once he realised that Kat would resist him no matter what. A man like Zafir didn't want a strong, opinionated woman. He wanted someone who wouldn't challenge him.

She could do this. She *would* do this. And when she walked away from Zafir after this was over, it would be for good.

Zafir handed over the diamond in its box to Noor and her security team. When he'd closed the door behind them he paced up and down restlessly.

Kat was seriously perplexing him. The fact that she'd choose going back to her rundown neighbourhood over sleeping in luxury was simply inexplicable. Not to mention wanting to fulfil one last shift at that excuse for a restaurant.

Once he'd known that she'd acquiesced to the job, he'd assumed it meant that she was also agreeing to share his bed again. After all, he'd made it explicitly clear that he wanted her. And he knew she still wanted him—it throbbed in the air between them like live electricity.

He scowled at the closed bedroom door. So what was she up to? The sum of money she'd already received was enough for her to seriously upgrade her life. And yet just now, when he'd reminded her that it was too late for her to walk away, it had almost seemed as if she was reluctantly agreeing to commit to something burdensome—not embarking on a journey to one of the easiest paydays she'd ever had in her life.

He had to admit to a niggle of doubt that it was the money she was really interested in, even though he'd long ago come to the conclusion that Kat had refrained from telling him about her massive debt because she'd figured that once they were married he'd have no choice but to clear it for her.

He'd lavished her with gifts, yes, but she'd never seemed as enthralled by them as other women had. She'd get embarrassed, or try to convince him she didn't need whatever trinket he'd given her. When he'd given her underwear she'd blushed—and just thinking of that now made his body hard.

He went over to the window to look out broodingly. In the aftermath of their last bitter argument he'd summed their relationship up as nothing more than an elaborate act. Kat had been canny enough to try and secure a permanent position in his life before revealing the skeletons in her closet. In a way, with her coming from the background she had, he couldn't really blame her for developing such survival instincts...

He heard the bedroom door open and turned around to see her emerging, dressed down in a plaid shirt and faded jeans. Sneakers. Her hair was loose, the luxuriant waves tumbling around her shoulders, and his blood leapt. He realised that he preferred it like this—darker. It made her beauty somehow more dramatic, mature.

She was pulling a wheelie suitcase behind her and she caught his look and said defensively, 'I'm not staying. This is full of the accessories I told the stylists I'd bring from home.'

The uncomfortable assertion that she really wasn't playing hard to get made Zafir's skin prickle. He walked across the room and saw how she tensed visibly, her hand clutching the handle of the suitcase. It made something deep inside him roar like an animal. He knew this woman intimately. He'd been her first lover…the first man to bring her to orgasm…

A sense of extreme exposure that he wanted her so much—so much that he'd brought her back into his life and precipitated all these questions—propelled Zafir forward until he had both Kat's arms in his hands. He barely noticed the suitcase fall to the side because she was no longer holding it.

She was looking up at him, two spots of pink in her cheeks, her eyes huge and wary. Gold and green.

Something dark rose up inside him and he couldn't hold it back.

'How many have there been, Kat? How many men have you lain down for and fooled into believing that you're just a regular woman? Did they know who they were sleeping with? That the woman with her legs wrapped around their hips was really—'

'Stop it.'

Kat was as rigid as a board under his hands. 'How dare you? Who I have or haven't slept with is none of your business. I don't want the sordid details of your lovers, who I've no doubt you made sure met your exacting standards of moral integrity.'

Zafir's pulse thundered as Kat's sweetly evocative

scent tantalised him. The only woman he wanted was glaring at him and shooting gold sparks from her eyes.

He forced out through the hunger raging in his blood, 'Quite frankly, I'm a lot less fixated on moral integrity this time around.'

A shiver ran through Kat's body and Zafir felt it.

'There is no *this time*. This is just a job for me—that's all. I'm not interested in anything else.'

Everything in Zafir rejected that, and he lifted one hand to cup Kat's delicate jawline. Just the silken brush of her hair against the back of his hand had his body hardening all over again.

'Why are you denying this, Kat? Whatever is between us, it's mutual. And it's even stronger than before.'

She shook her head. 'It's not mutual.'

'Liar,' Zafir breathed, as every part of his body went on fire with an urgent and undeniable desire to prove Kat wrong. And along with that desire he felt something much more dangerous: *emotion*.

To block it out, deny it, Zafir cupped his hand behind Kat's neck and drew her to him until he could feel the length of her willowy body pressed against his.

Her hands came up between them to his chest. The wariness and anger was gone, to be replaced by something far more like panic. And why would she be panicky unless he was about to prove her very wrong?

'Zafir, what are you doing?'

His blood was pounding. 'I'm proving that once a liar, always a liar...'

And then he bent his head and covered Kat's mouth with his, and for the first time in eighteen months the roaring savage heat inside him was momentarily soothed.

Under the intense carnal satisfaction to be tasting her again was that emotion and a kind of relief. As if he'd found his way back to some place he'd been looking for.

It was so profound and overwhelming that for long seconds Zafir didn't even deepen the kiss—he just relished the sensation of Kat's soft, lush mouth under his.

And then she made a soft mewling sound and Zafir fell over the brink of his control and hauled Kat even closer, kissing her deep enough to see stars.

Time stood still. The earth might have stopped rotating. All Zafir was aware of was the feel of Kat's curves against his body, the stiffness of his arousal cushioned against her soft belly...and the desire to stop at nothing until he was deeply embedded between her legs and she was crying out his name as her climax sent them both into orbit.

It took a second for Zafir to realise that Kat had torn her mouth away and was pushing against his chest, breathing heavily enough for him to feel her breasts move against him. He almost growled. He felt feral.

She pushed hard and dislodged Zafir's arms, stumbling slightly as she stepped back. Her eyes were molten, her mouth was swollen and her cheeks were flushed, and the only thing keeping Zafir from reaching for her again was the knowledge that he'd already exposed himself.

'I do not want this, Zafir. I won't deny that the attraction between us is still there—'

Zafir snorted at the understatement and Kat's eyes turned steely.

'But I am not going there with you again. We had our moment and it's over. And unless you can promise to keep things between us on a professional footing I'll have no choice but to back out of our agreement and return the money you've already paid me. Don't think I won't, Zafir. The money is important to me, but not as important as not making the same mistake twice.'

No one spoke to Zafir like this. No one considered him a mistake.

But then an echo of his brother's voice whispered from the past, angry...

'Sara was a mistake, Zafir, our parents didn't even pretend to grieve when she died. Her life had no value because she couldn't rule when she came of age. They betrayed her more than you'll ever understand...'

Zafir pushed the past away, and with it the familiar ache of longing and disconnection. That ache shamed him, because he was above such weakness, or should be. He had to be. And he also ruthlessly shut out the niggling pain that his brother hadn't confided in him more.

Salim had shut Zafir out long ago, pursuing a life of debauched irresponsibility. Laughing in the face of his responsibilities. It was love that had done that to his brother—albeit sibling love. The twins had had their own little world, exclusive to everyone around them—even Zafir. And after Sara had died Salim had never been the same.

Seeing his brother's reaction to Sara's death, witnessing the pain of losing that intense bond, had bred within Zafir a lifelong desire to protect himself against such deep investment in another person. It appalled him that you could lose yourself like that.

Kat was looking at him now, and Zafir took a step back—as much from the intensity flowing between them as from his unwelcome reflections. He didn't appreciate Kat's ultimatum, but at the same time he didn't want to reveal the extent of his need. He'd already revealed too much. However, he could not let her rewrite their history.

He folded his arms. 'What happened between us was not a mistake, Kat. We were both adults, acting on mutual desire. The fact that it ended as it did was as much your responsibility as it was mine. You kept truths from me and I shouldn't have trusted you so easily.'

Kat seemed to go pale in the low lights of the room. 'Let's just leave it at that, then.'

Something in Zafir rebelled at that. 'By all means—if you think we can leave the past in the past. I, however, happen to believe that sooner or later you'll have to admit we have a present too.'

Kat bent down and picked up the handle of her suitcase. She looked at Zafir. 'The only present we have is a professional one, Zafir.'

For now, he told himself silently as he came forward and took Kat's suitcase out of her hand, leading her out of the suite and to his car downstairs.

She got into the car without looking at him once, keeping her face averted. Only that lingering sense of exposure stopped him from pulling her back out of the car to show her what a mockery this *professionalism* was.

He'd arrogantly assumed resuming a physical relationship with Kat would be easy. He couldn't have been more wrong. And yet he wasn't dissuaded. If anything, this pared down and feisty Kat was sparking his desire in a far deeper way than she ever had before.

As he watched his car slide away from the kerb and into the evening traffic he told himself that she wouldn't be able to hold out against this insane chemistry for long.

CHAPTER FOUR

'KAT, YOU LOOK...AMAZING.'

Kat heard the thickness in her friend's voice and tried not to let it affect her. She was having a hard enough time just breathing, and said shakily, 'Jules, I really don't know if I'm ready for this.'

Julie came and stood between Kat and the full-length mirror in the hotel suite bedroom, where Kat had returned some hours ago with her bags packed for the trip. They would leave tomorrow for London.

Kat was wearing the black velvet dress again. Her hair was in the chignon and her make-up had just been completed. Everyone had left, so now it was just the two of them.

Her petite blonde friend took Kat's hand in a firm grip and looked up at her steadily. 'I wouldn't push you if you weren't ready, Kat. But you are. You can't keep hiding from the world.'

Kat bit her lip to stop herself asking plaintively, *But this job? Now?* She looked at her reflection over her friend's head and saw the panicked look in her eyes, and forced herself to take in a breath.

Just then there was a knock on the door. Kat loved her friend for not jumping to answer it immediately, waiting to get a nod from Kat first. Gratitude made her chest swell because she knew that if she truly wanted to walk out of here right now her friend would support her. But she didn't want to let her down. And she didn't want to let the rehab centre down.

She could do this.

Before Julie had even opened the door Kat knew who it

was. Heat prickled over her skin. And, sure enough, when it swung back Zafir was there, filling the space effortlessly. He was dressed in a tuxedo and he was ridiculously gorgeous. And, even though Kat had seen him dressed like this before, it was still a shock to the system to behold such a formidable specimen of masculine perfection.

It was also the first time she'd seen him since yesterday, and the memory of that kiss made her pulse pound unevenly. Coming to terms with the resurrection of her sexual awareness was something she really hadn't expected to have to deal with for a long time. And yet it rushed through her now like an unstoppable wave.

Zafir was holding the necklace in his hand and he lifted it up. 'May I?'

Kat nodded dumbly and tensed against Zafir's effect on her as he walked in and came behind her, raising his hands up and over her head so that he could tie the clasp at the back of her neck.

The necklace felt warm and heavy against her skin and Kat touched it unconsciously. Julie's blue eyes had grown comically large and round as she took in the gem nestling against Kat's skin.

Kat looked at her reflection in the mirror and for a moment she was mesmerised too by the glowing red heart-shaped jewel. It did look somehow *alive*.

And then she raised her eyes and her gaze snagged on Zafir's. Those dark grey depths were focused solely on her. Not even looking at the gem. She swallowed. He was very close behind her, she could feel his heat, and only for the fact that Julie was still there, effectively acting as chaperone, stopped Kat from taking a step away.

He was the one finally to step back, and Kat breathed in shakily.

He went and stood beside Julie. 'You look stunning.' She was glad he hadn't said *perfect*.

He extended his arm towards the door. 'Shall we? My driver is waiting.'

As Kat stepped forward her friend touched her arm and mouthed *good luck*. And then it was just Kat and Zafir, stepping out of the suite to where the security team were waiting, looking serious and alert.

Noor got into the elevator with them, and Kat was relieved not to be alone in the small space with Zafir. When they got out on ground level they were ushered straight to Zafir's car, and Kat instinctively arranged the long dress over her left leg, conscious of her prosthetic limb. It had been a long time since she'd felt so undressed.

Thankfully Zafir had to take a call on his mobile as they cut through the early-evening Manhattan traffic, giving Kat time to gather herself before entering back into the fray in spectacular fashion.

By the time they pulled up in front of the iconic Metropolitan Museum Zafir was off his phone, and the palms of her hands were clammy with sweat. It got worse when she saw the hordes of paparazzi and reporters and other people already lining the red carpet in their finery.

Zafir touched her bare arm and she looked at him.

'Okay?'

Kat nodded jerkily. 'Fine.'

She'd never been less fine in her life.

'Just follow my lead.'

Zafir got out of the car then, and came around to Kat's side, opening the door and helping her out. Once again she was glad of the dress disguising her leg as she stood up and wobbled for a moment. Zafir's hand was on her arm again, holding her steady.

She stepped up onto the sidewalk and they moved forward. As people noticed who they were a hush seemed to fall over the crowd for a split-second, and then all hell broke loose as they walked onto the red carpet.

Zafir had tucked Kat's arm over his and she wasn't aware of how tightly she was holding on, she was being blinded by all the bright flashes going off in her face.

For a moment she was paralysed, and then Zafir's deep voice sounded in her ear, saying calmly, 'Start walking and smile—that's all you have to do.'

And suddenly she was moving, propelled forward by Zafir. They stopped periodically to let photographers take pictures, and Zafir stood back to let Kat be photographed on her own.

After a few long torturous minutes Kat found herself relaxing slightly, as if a long unused muscle was coming back to life. She knew how to do this—how to project a smiling façade. She'd done it for years. And slowly the ability returned.

And then someone shouted out, 'Where have you been, Kat? Are you and Zafir back together?' and all her fragile confidence shattered.

She stumbled, but Zafir was there in an instant, steadying her again. He replied to the questions smoothly and authoritatively.

'Persuading Kat Winters out of retirement was an unexpected coup and we're delighted she's working with us for this diplomatic trip. As for our relationship—that's none of anyone's business except our own.'

Eventually they reached the end of the red carpet. Kat was ready to crawl under a rock, but the evening hadn't even started yet. And she was angry.

She pulled away from Zafir and looked up at him, saying in a low voice, 'You could have shut down their questions about our relationship more comprehensively.'

Zafir just looked at her explicitly. 'I could have.'

But I didn't.

He didn't have to bother saying that part. Before she could react, though, he put her arm firmly in his again and propelled her forward to the main entrance of the function room. Her anger dissolved into panic at the sight of the packed room.

He stopped there for a second and looked at her again. 'Ready?'

No! she wanted to blurt out, but if she turned and ran she'd only have to face the red carpet again. There was literally nowhere to go except forward.

Not liking how symbolic this moment felt, Kat nodded jerkily and they stepped over the threshold of the room, its doors being held open by pristinely uniformed butlers.

Much like the hush outside when they'd arrived, as soon as they stepped in through the doorway everyone turned to look and there was an audible intake of breath. Kat realised that a spotlight rested on her—undoubtedly it was to showcase the diamond, not her, but she still felt utterly exposed.

Zafir took her arm from his and stepped to the side, leaving her feeling ridiculously bereft for a second. Then she heard his strong voice say, 'May I present to you Kat Winters and the Heart of Jandor?'

The enthusiastic clapping and gasps of wonder at the sight of Kat and the gem had faded away, to be replaced by the excited chatter of hundreds of VIP guests.

Zafir noted the presence of high-ranking politicians mixed with award-winning actors and actresses, world champion athletes, prize-winning authors and everyone who was anyone with satisfaction. And yet his feeling of satisfaction somehow fell short.

He found he was more interested in where Kat was and with whom. Currently she was standing a few feet away from him, surrounded by a small goggle-eyed crowd. Irritated by this dent in his sense of satisfaction, Zafir cursed himself.

This was exactly what he'd envisaged, wasn't it? To have one of the most beautiful women in the world standing amongst an awed crowd as she showcased his country's famed jewel?

But if anything she outshone the diamond. The inky black of the dress and its clean lines showcased the perfection of Kat's body. No other jewellery. Understated make-up. And not a bump or a mark or a blemish to mar that lustrous skin.

Zafir didn't recall her being so pale before, but presumably if she hadn't been travelling to exotic locations for fashion shoots, as she'd used to, then she'd lost her natural golden tan. And yet her skin seemed to glow even more. Like a pearl.

She was in profile to him now, and his gaze scanned down from the abundant dark hair artfully arranged in its chignon, to her high forehead, straight nose, lush mouth, delicate jaw and long, graceful neck.

The rare gem sat just below her collarbone, glowing as if lit from within by fire. Her shoulders were slim and straight. And then, as if compelled by the beat of his blood, his hungry gaze dropped to the voluptuous swells of her breasts.

Blood rushed to his groin and Zafir had to grit his jaw and use all of his control to stop making a complete fool of himself. He snapped his gaze back to her face, which he could see now was tense. Smiling, but tense.

He recalled how tightly she'd gripped his arm while on the red carpet, and how she'd wobbled precariously a couple of times as if her legs were unsteady. And the strangest thing... When he'd announced her arrival a short while before and watched her stand tall but alone, bathed in the spotlight, he'd felt a curious sense of pride, without even knowing why, exactly.

She turned her head then, as if sensing his intense regard, and looked at him, and before Zafir was even aware of what he was doing he ignored the veritable queue of people Rahul had lined up to speak to him and walked to Kat's side.

Hours later Kat ached all over, and she sank down into the hot bath as much as she could, wishing she could submerge herself completely and forget how exposed she'd felt as she'd been paraded through that enormous room like a thoroughbred horse at a bloodstock auction.

And yet, to her surprise, Zafir had stayed by her side more or less constantly—even though she'd seen the frustration on his aide Rahul's face as he'd tried to entreat Zafir to talk to this person or that person.

She didn't like to admit that his presence had steadied her as much as it had unnerved her, and made her feel more capable of bearing up to the scrutiny—which had been of *her* as much as the gem. And that had been Zafir's cynical plan all along, hadn't it? To get the most out of bringing the notorious Kat Winters out of the woodwork?

Yet, a small voice pointed out, he hadn't had to stay by her side like that. He could have quite easily ignored her all night...

But before she went down the dangerous path of believing that he'd stayed by her side out of concern or anything more, she reminded herself that Zafir's motivations had undoubtedly been to make sure that she didn't damage the Jandor 'brand' or upstage the diamond. And also because he was still messing with her head, not letting her forget the sensual threat he'd made.

At the end of the evening Zafir had been pulled aside to talk to an emissary from the American foreign office, and Rahul had come to let Kat know that she could hand back the gem if she so wished. Like a coward, she'd seized the opportunity, and he'd accompanied her to an anteroom where Noor had overseen the return of the gem to its box and it had been whisked safely away.

Then, when they'd re-emerged into the function room and Kat had seen that Zafir was still in conversation, she'd told Rahul that she was ready to leave.

Immediately he'd looked worried and said nervously, 'I should check with the King—'

Kat had cut in more firmly than she'd felt, 'I'm quite tired, and we have an early start to get to London in time for the function tomorrow evening, I'm sure you wouldn't want the King to be displeased because I don't appear rested.'

She'd almost felt sorry for how conflicted Rahul had looked, but eventually he'd agreed and had accompanied her down to the car and seen her off.

She'd just been breathing a sigh of relief when she'd received a text from Zafir while still in the car.

Next time, we leave together, Kat. Get some rest for tomorrow. Rahul will escort you to the royal plane in the morning and I'll meet you there.

Kat hadn't appreciated being made to feel like an admonished child, and yet now her mind drifted back to how Zafir had looked amongst the crowd earlier, how effortlessly he'd stood out with his height and dark good looks.

She couldn't stop a pulse fluttering between her legs as she recalled how she'd caught him looking at her with something raw in his eyes. Raw, and hungry. It had leapt across the space from him to her, and she'd felt it as strongly as if he'd physically reached out and touched her.

The pulse between Kat's legs intensified and she shifted in the bath, putting her hand down there, almost as if she could try to stop it. But once her fingers came into contact with her sensitised skin and she felt how slippery she was she sucked in a pained breath.

She'd been on a knife-edge of desire all evening, as much as she'd tried to ignore it. But she couldn't any more, and her fingers moved tentatively but far too easily against herself, helped by the water and her own slick arousal.

She'd never touched herself like this...not until Zafir had shown her how and had instructed her to do it for him. She thought of that now—how he'd sat naked in a chair and told her to get on the bed and spread her legs, to show herself to him, and then to touch herself. He'd held himself in his hand as she'd done his bidding, his fist moving up and down the stiff column of flesh in a slow, relentless rhythm.

It had been the singularly most indecent and erotic thing she'd ever experienced, and just as she'd exploded into pieces around her own fingers Zafir had surged up, taken her hand away, seated himself between her legs and thrust into her, deep and hard, and had kept her falling over the edge again and again until she'd screamed herself hoarse.

Kat could feel herself quickening now, tightening, as her movements became more feverish and desperate... and yet in the same moment she realised that Zafir wasn't watching her this time. She was alone in a bath...dreaming of the past and a scenario that would never be repeated.

Disgusted with herself, she took her hand away and opened her eyes, breathing harshly, ignoring the ache between her legs and the way her nipples were so tight they hurt. The truth was that she knew she would find no real satisfaction like this, and it killed her to admit it.

Kat pushed herself upright from the water and balanced on one leg. She sat on the edge of the bath, swinging herself over before drying herself roughly and reaching for the crutches she had nearby. Then she manoeuvred herself to standing, excess water dripping onto the towels she'd placed on the floor to stop herself from slipping and sliding when she got out.

Getting out of a bath was a process that was second nature now, but it had taken many months to perfect. It never ceased to amaze and humble her how much she'd taken for granted before.

She deliberately avoided her reflection in the countless bathroom mirrors, feeling like a coward. But right now she didn't need a reminder of exactly why Zafir would never look at her with that same hungry raw need again.

And the sooner she shut down these inappropriate fantasies, the better. Or she wouldn't survive another day, never mind another couple of weeks.

The following day Zafir was still stewing over the fact that Kat had left the function without him last night.

They'd departed from New York early in the morning, nearly six hours ago, so their landing in London was imminent.

Rahul had brought her to the plane and Kat had looked pale and tight-lipped, answering any questions Zafir had posed with monosyllabic answers. And then, when he'd suggested that she take advantage of the bedroom to rest, she'd disappeared for the rest of the flight.

Zafir sighed moodily and took in the sea of endless clouds outside his window. He really wasn't used to being thwarted like this. Especially not when the sexual tension between them was off the charts. He'd seen the way her gaze had roved over him hungrily when she'd first stepped into the plane, as if she wasn't even aware of her impulse. Which was the same as his. To devour her with his eyes at every opportunity.

He heard a noise from the back and that ever-present desire spiked as Kat's evocative scent reached him just before she did. She sat down in her seat again, asking huskily, 'We're nearly there?'

Zafir did his best to clamp down on the need to reach over and pluck her bodily from her seat and into his lap. 'Yes,' he gritted out. 'Within the next half hour. We've started our descent.'

Rahul's staff were at the front of the plane—out of sight and earshot—and his greedy gaze took in Kat's soft jeans and the loose, unstructured top that somehow still managed to mould itself to her curves. Her hair was down, and Zafir wanted to wrap it around his hand and force her to look at him.

'You won't turn to stone if you look at me, Kat.'

He couldn't disguise the irritation lacing his words. He saw how she tensed, but then eventually she turned her head and those glorious golden, amber and green eyes settled on him. Cool. Unreadable. *Why* was she so reluctant to take what he was offering? A no-strings-attached, very adult exorcism of this palpable connection between them.

He turned in his seat more fully, to face her. 'You must be hungry. You haven't eaten because you were sleeping.'

Before she could say anything he'd called for a steward, who materialised immediately. Zafir looked at Kat expressively. For a moment a mutinous expression crossed her face, but then she seemed to give in and said to the staff member, 'I'll just have something light…like an omelette, if you have it?'

Zafir added an order for coffee for both of them and the steward left.

Looking disgruntled, Kat said, 'You're still too bossy. And arrogant.'

Zafir shrugged, unperturbed. 'I'm a King now. I have a licence to be as bossy and arrogant as I want.'

Suddenly Kat looked stricken, and those eyes which had been so unreadable were now full of something far more readable. Sympathy.

'I never mentioned your father. I'm sorry for your loss. I know you weren't particularly close, but still it can't have been easy.'

Zafir's insides clenched. Plenty of people had offered empty platitudes when his father had died, but few had known just how barren their relationship had been. But he'd told Kat. And her simple sincerity now tugged on a deep part of him that *had* mourned his father—or at least mourned the fact that he'd never been a father in the real sense. The loving sense.

The steward arrived then, with Kat's food and the coffees, and Zafir said gruffly, 'Eat. We'll be landing soon and we have a busy schedule this evening.'

After a few moments Kat picked up her cutlery and ate with single-minded absorption.

When she'd finished, he mused out loud, 'You always did have a good appetite.'

Kat went still and pushed the plate away from her before taking up her cup of coffee. She glanced at Zafir without letting him see her eyes properly. Her mouth had gone tight and she said, 'When you grow up hungry it gives you an appreciation of food that others might not have.'

'Was it really that bad, Kat?'

She glared at him. 'You read that article along with everyone else in America, didn't you? The lurid details of my life in a trailer park?'

Zafir shook his head, his irritation mounting. 'I still don't know why you couldn't tell me the full details. There's no shame in growing up poor, *or* in a trailer park.'

'No,' she said, avoiding his eyes again. 'Only in the choices we make to survive.'

Kat felt bitterness corrode her insides even as she knew that this was her chance to spill it all out to Zafir. He was listening and receptive, and she'd always wanted to tell him, hadn't she? But suddenly the thought of laying it all out felt too huge. She still felt vulnerable after appearing in public again for the first time last night, and like a coward she clammed up, avoiding the opportunity.

Instead she looked at him and said, 'You called me a liar the other day, but I never lied to you. I just…didn't tell you everything.'

'A distinction that hardly exonerates you,' Zafir pointed out.

He felt frustration mount when she didn't respond, aware of a niggling sensation that she was still hiding things from him.

Just then the air steward arrived to clear Kat's plate and inform them that they'd be landing shortly, and to make sure they were ready. The tension dissipated and Kat broke their staring contest to turn her head and look out of her window.

The plane circled lower and lower over the private London airfield and Zafir addressed his question to the back of Kat's glossy head, unable to resist pushing her for a response. 'You never told me why you didn't go back into modelling full-time once you'd recovered.'

Zafir could feel her reluctance as she finally turned to look at him again, eyes guarded.

'It wasn't a career I'd ever really chosen for myself, and I discovered that if I had the choice I wouldn't necessarily step back into it.'

Which was more or less the truth, Kat reassured herself as Zafir's incisive gaze seemed to laser all the way into her soul. Even if she hadn't lost her leg she wouldn't have wanted to step back into that vacuous world. Being forced out of her old existence and into a new one had revealed a desire to find a more meaningful role in her life. What that might be, she wasn't even sure herself yet. She only knew that she wanted to help people as she had been helped...

The plane touched down with a brief jolt and Zafir finally looked away. Released from that compelling gaze, Kat took a breath. She'd tried to rest earlier, in the plane's luxurious bedroom, but sleep had proved elusive. She was too wound up after those illicit fantasies in her bath last night and the prospect of another public exhibition this evening.

Perhaps, she thought to herself a little hysterically, this was Zafir's retribution? Expose Kat to the ravenous judgmental hordes who would pick her over until there was nothing left?

Although, from what she'd seen of the headlines in the papers that Rahul had been poring over in the car earlier, there didn't seem to be much dredging up of the past—only feverish speculation as to why Kat had re-emerged and where she'd been and the nature of her relationship with Zafir. Kat wasn't sure whether to be relieved or even more anxious at the thought that someone from the rehabilitation clinic might recognise her and sell the story of what had really happened to her.

Before she could dwell on that too much Zafir was standing, holding her bag in one hand and his other hand out to her. She looked at it for a moment, and then realised how futile it would be to try and resist. She put her hand in Zafir's and let him pull her up. She stumbled slightly, falling against Zafir's chest. His eyes flared and his hand came up to steady her, curling around her arm tightly.

For a moment their bodies were welded together and the heat between them surged.

Roughly he said, 'Kat, why can't you just admit—'

'Sire, the cars are ready.'

Zafir clamped his mouth shut and didn't look around at Rahul, their interrupter.

Relief flooded Kat, because she realised that if Zafir had kissed her in that moment she'd have responded helplessly. She pulled free and walked to the entrance of the plane, taking care on the steps down, telling herself it was her prosthetic limb and not the throbbing arousal rushing through her body making her feel wobbly.

The event in London was even more impressive than the one in New York. Because of Zafir's royal status, senior members of the British royal family were present, imbuing the classic surroundings of one of London's oldest and most exclusive hotels with an elegance and gravitas Kat had never experienced before.

The ornate furnishings glittered under the flickering glow of hundreds of candles. A string quartet played on a dais at one end of the room. Pristine waiters moved silently and discreetly through the crowd, offering tantalising, exotic hors d'oeuvres prepared by Zafir's Jandori chef and glasses of priceless champagne.

Tonight Kat was dressed in a long strapless white dress. A sheath of simplicity which helped to show the red diamond to its best advantage. Zafir hadn't arrived at her suite to put the diamond around her neck earlier—it had been a stylist who had taken it from one of Noor's guards to place around her neck—and Kat denied furiously to herself that she'd missed his presence and his touch.

When Rahul had met her to walk her down to the function room, which was in the same hotel where they would stay the night, he'd explained that Zafir had had to take an important conference call and sent his apologies.

She'd denied the little dart of disappointment and

she'd ruthlessly quashed the relief she'd felt to see Zafir waiting outside the function room—pacing, actually— dressed once again in a classic tuxedo that did nothing to disguise his virile masculinity and everything to enhance it.

His gaze had swept her up and down. This evening her hair was tamed into a sleek bun, low at the back of her head, and she'd seen Zafir's gaze rest on it and how his eyes had flared with something unreadable. In that moment she'd gone breathless, imagining that she could almost feel his desire to undo it and let her hair fall down in its habitual unruly tumble of waves. He'd always loved it down...and the memory of that had made her weak.

But then he'd extended his arm, and she'd walked forward as the doors had opened and they'd stepped through.

And now Kat was standing beside Zafir on a small podium as he spoke to the hushed crowd and told them of the myriad opportunities available for business and recreation in his country. Kat found herself forgetting that she was under a spotlight while Zafir's deep and hypnotic voice painted a seductive picture of a land steeped in history and with boundless opportunities.

His love for his people and his country was evident in the passion in his voice, and she couldn't stop a dart of surprise and pride because she'd had no idea that Zafir was so determined to be a force for change in his country. The vision he outlined was modern and progressive, and was now being met with resounding applause.

She'd underestimated him, and that unsettled her as he stepped off the podium and held out a hand to help her down. She wasn't thinking, and she landed on her left leg a little awkwardly, wincing as the movement jarred her prosthesis. Any kind of steps, up or down, were more of a challenge than before.

Immediately he was sharp. 'Are you okay?'

'Fine—I just turned my ankle for a moment,' she embellished quickly.

Zafir frowned. 'Maybe we should have someone check it.'

Instant panic flooded her veins, turning her blood cold. 'No, I'm fine. Really.'

She spent the rest of the evening with a bright smile plastered on her face, even as her discomfort increased. She needed to take her prosthesis off to adjust it, but Zafir wouldn't leave her side and she was loath to attract his attention.

Finally, when she was wondering if the evening would ever end, the crowd thinned out and Zafir said, 'I'll take you to your suite and you can give the necklace back to the security guards for the night.'

Relief made her almost dizzy as he accompanied her out of the room and up in the elevator, with the ever-present Noor. Kat could be thankful for at least that much. As long as she wore the diamond, she wouldn't be alone with Zafir.

Once in Kat's suite, Noor stood at a respectful distance as Zafir took off the necklace and placed it into the box before handing it over.

Noor bowed her head. 'Good night, Sire... Miss Winters.'

She left the room and they were alone. Before Kat could say a word, though, Zafir put his hands on her shoulders and turned her around so she had her back to him. Then his hands were on her hair, plucking out the pins that had been holding the tight bun in place. As she felt it loosen and start to unravel, the discomfort of her limb was forgotten momentarily at the sheer bliss of *this*... Zafir's hands moving through her hair, massaging her skull.

His voice was low, husky. 'I've imagined doing this all evening.'

His body was close behind her and she could feel his heat and the whipcord strength of him. So close. So seductive. Treacherously, something gave way inside her, as if it was too strong for her to keep holding it back. Almost without realising what she was doing, she turned and looked up.

Zafir went still. Kat was looking up at him, eyes wide and molten, cheeks flushed. Every instinct within him called for him to claim her—finally. But something stopped him…a memory, brutally vivid and brutally exposing.

Kat sensed the chill even before she saw the heat in Zafir's eyes disappear. He dropped his hands and stepped back. She blinked, feeling vulnerable and hating herself for that small moment when he must have seen her desire laid bare.

When Zafir spoke he sounded harsh. 'Go to bed, Kat. I have some meetings here in the morning. Rahul will accompany you to the airport after lunch.'

And then he turned and walked out, the door closing behind him with an incongruously soft click.

Kat felt a little dazed, not sure what had just happened. She looked around and sank down onto the nearest chair. She could feel the discomfort in her leg again, and pulled up her dress in order to start taking off her prosthetic limb. But then she stopped, realising she needed to get her crutches first.

Feeling seriously on edge and irritable, she went into the bedroom, cursing Zafir for scrambling her brain so much that she forgot the fundamental basics.

But what irritated her the most, as she retrieved her crutches and started to undress so she could take off her prosthesis, was the fact that if he hadn't pulled back just now she'd most likely be on the nearest horizontal surface, giving up all her secrets to Zafir in the most humiliating way possible.

And that wasn't even the worst thing—because the worst thing was the insidious need to know, why had he stopped?

CHAPTER FIVE

LONDON UNDER MOONLIGHT twinkled benignly outside Zafir's suite window, with all of the famous landmarks lit up: the London Eye, the Shard, the dome and spires of St Paul's cathedral. But he couldn't care less about any of them. Or the fact that so far his diplomatic tour was a resounding success.

His head was filled with only one thing. Recrimination for letting a mere memory stop him from seeking the relief his body ached for. That was the past—this was the present. And yet the two were colliding far too vividly for his liking.

But when Kat had looked at him just now the sense of déjà vu had been strong enough to propel him out of her orbit. Déjà vu of the moment he'd proposed to her...

As much as Zafir would have liked to believe his proposal had been a well thought out and strategic move, it hadn't been. It had been spontaneous—not a behaviour that usually dictated his actions. They'd been travelling in his private jet, from London back to New York, and as he'd watched Kat across the aisle, staring dreamily out of the window, with his blood still humming after an overload of recent carnal satisfaction, she'd turned her head to look at him and he'd been overcome with a desperate and inexplicable need to ensure she never left his sight. And so he'd proposed, surprising her as much as himself.

He cursed himself now and turned from the view not liking the reminder that his proposal had been far less strategic than he liked to admit. He strode into the bedroom, shedding clothes as he went until he was naked.

When he reached the bathroom he stepped into the shower and turned it on. To cold.

He cursed volubly as the freezing water hit his skin, but it did little to douse the fever in his blood or the unwelcome memories in his head. He should have just followed his instincts and taken her. She wouldn't have stopped him this time—he felt it deep in his gut. And lower, where he still ached in spite of the cold water.

If anything, Kat had only proved that her defiance and reluctance were an act, and that she was biding her time before giving in. It was a little power play...she was messing with his head.

Next time he wouldn't let anything stop him, and when this tour was over and he'd slaked his lust he *would* walk away from Kat, and he would not feel the slightest ounce of regret because she'd be relegated to the past for good.

'Dinner, Kat. It's a social construct designed for people to sit down together and make conversation. Break bread together.'

Kat looked at Zafir suspiciously where he stood on the other side of her Parisian hotel suite's door. The Paris event wasn't due to take place until the following evening, and Kat had been savouring the thought of some breathing space while Zafir had meetings at the Jandor consulate nearby. She'd been looking forward to an early evening in bed, with a view of the Eiffel tower outside her window, watching old movies and eating ice-cream— her comfort staples. But now her peace was shattered.

'I know what dinner is.' She tried to keep her tone even. 'But what do you want to talk about? We have nothing to discuss.'

Zafir leaned a shoulder against the doorframe, supremely relaxed. Supremely dangerous. 'We're friends at least—aren't we, Kat?'

She scowled. 'You're my employer and I'm your employee.'

'We have history,' he countered.

'*Ancient* history,' she blasted back, panic rising as she realised that the past felt far too close for comfort. This Zafir was the one she remembered and feared. Relentless, seductive. Impossible to resist.

'We're ex-lovers,' he said silkily. 'I'd say we have plenty to talk about.'

And just like that a slideshow of explicit images bombarded Kat's memory banks, rendering her speechless.

As if sensing her momentary weakness, Zafir straightened from the door and said, 'I'll come back for you in an hour, Kat. Be ready.'

He was leaving before she could wrap her tongue around another word, but then he stopped abruptly and came back. 'Actually, I was going to go for a run, if you'd like to join me?'

A sharp pain lanced Kat right in the gut. She and Zafir used to jog together all the time. She'd taken great delight in keeping up with his punishing regular five-mile regime.

She felt hollow inside as she shook her head firmly. 'No, thank you.'

Zafir shrugged minutely and backed away again, oblivious to the turmoil caused by his easy invitation. 'As you wish—see you in an hour.'

She finally shut the door on his retreating back, and leant against it, an awful poignancy making her chest swell with emotion. Before it could turn into anything more she issued an unladylike curse and pushed herself away from the door.

The prospect of an evening with Zafir loomed large. The hollow feeling dissipated, to be replaced with a predictable array of physical reactions at the thought of sitting down with him one on one. Her skin grew hot, her pulse tripled and butterflies swarmed into her belly against her best efforts to quell his effect on her.

He was chipping away at the walls she'd erected around herself and he wasn't even aware of it. Yesterday evening she'd come so close to succumbing, and only because of *his* self-control she'd been saved from outright humiliation.

Damn him and his games. Damn him and his easy invitation to do something she'd never easily do again.

But he doesn't know about your leg, reminded a chiding voice.

And he never would, she vowed now. Because if he did it would mean he'd breached her last defences.

She walked over to the closet and opened the doors, purposely picking out the most casual clothes she possessed.

But when Zafir appeared at her door again, in exactly an hour's time, he looked smart and gorgeous in a dark suit, with his shirt open at the neck, and she felt like a rebellious teenager. His explicit look told her what he thought of the soft leather trousers, flat ankle boots and the loose, unstructured grey top. She'd left her hair down, wore minimal make-up, and reached for her light wraparound jacket and bag before coming into the hall and closing the door behind her.

Zafir appeared amused, which made her feel even more exposed and silly. 'Don't worry, Kat. I won't get the wrong idea, if that's what you're afraid of.'

He stood back to let her precede him into the elevator, and as it descended he leant against one mirrored wall with his hands in his pockets.

'You used to love wearing short skirts and high heels,' he observed. 'Is this some new feminist stance or is it just to ward me off?'

Kat's insides turned to ice. She *had* loved wearing the highest of heels and the shortest of dresses and skirts. And only ever for this man, because the carnal hunger and appreciation in his gaze had used to make her feel sexy and desired.

Relief warred confusingly with disappointment to hear that Zafir would obviously prefer to see her dressing as she'd used to.

Feeling exposed, she rounded on him, saying heatedly, 'No, it's not a feminist stance, actually. Women *should* be able to wear whatever they want—and not to entice a man. For themselves.'

He wasn't perturbed by her outburst. As the elevator doors opened he said easily, 'I was merely making an observation, not stating a preference, and I agree with you one hundred per cent. For what it's worth, Kat, you could wear a sack from head to toe and it wouldn't diminish how much I want you.'

Before she could respond to that, he took her arm in a loose but proprietorial hold to guide her across the exclusive Paris hotel lobby and out through the doors to his chauffeur-driven car.

She barely noticed the ubiquitous security vehicle waiting to tail their every move. Zafir had blindsided her a little. She'd always pegged him as being unremittingly traditional and conservative because he was so effortlessly alpha, but maybe that wasn't fair.

When they were settled in the back of his car she asked, 'Where are we going?'

He looked at her, his face cast into shadow, making it stern and even more compelling. 'It's a surprise.'

Kat's insides clenched. She had a feeling she knew exactly where, and if she was right she wanted to jump out of the car right now. Zafir had introduced her to a restaurant here on their first trip to Paris, shortly after they'd started seeing each other, and the experience was seared into her memory.

It was one of the city's oldest establishments, famous for its decadent furnishings and for its private dining rooms, which had been used in previous centuries for clandestine assignations of a very carnal nature. Zafir had, of course, booked one of those rooms, and Kat's memories of the evening had nothing to do with the food they'd eaten and everything to do with the wicked pleasures he'd subjected her to in the intimate and luxuriously furnished space...

She refused to let Zafir guess how agitated she was by these memories and looked out of the window, taking in the glittering lights and beautiful buildings. She'd always loved Paris as it had been the first place she'd visited outside of America in her early modelling days. Its beauty and history had astounded her, and nowhere else had ever had the same effect on her.

Her conscience twinged... Except for Jahor, the awe-inspiring capital city of Zafir's country, Jandor. It sprawled across a series of hills, overlooking the sparkling sea, and the skyline was made up of minarets and flat roofs, with children flying multicoloured kites as the sun went down. Overlooking it all was the golden-hued grand palace.

'We're here.'

Kat came out of the past and frantically checked where they were, a sigh of relief moving through her when she realised they weren't at the restaurant she'd been thinking of. Instead, as Zafir came around and helped her out of the car, she saw that they were in a small street on Île de la Cité—one of Paris's many small islands in the Seine.

Intrigued in spite of herself, she let Zafir lead her over to a small restaurant tucked between two tall buildings. From the outside it looked inviting, with golden light spilling out onto the street. And it was not like anywhere Zafir had ever brought her before.

In fact when he spoke he sounded almost…uncertain. 'This is one of Paris's best kept secrets.'

Kat looked at him and said drily, 'Were you expecting me to throw a tantrum because it's not a restaurant three hundred storeys up with a view of the Eiffel Tower?'

Zafir was unreadable, 'I'm not sure what to expect any more.'

Before she could respond, he was leading her into the restaurant. She was surprised to see that he got a warm welcome from the proprietor, who greeted Zafir like a long-lost son and her like an old friend.

Within seconds their coats had been taken and they were seated in a discreet corner, tucked away but able to see everything. The table was small, but exquisitely set with a white tablecloth and silver cutlery. Soft music played in the background and every other table was full, everyone engrossed in each other. It was achingly and effortlessly romantic.

Feeling vulnerable and defensive, Kat said, 'I wouldn't have thought this was your kind of place.'

Zafir shook out his napkin and laid it across his lap before reaching for a bread roll. 'I worked here in the kitchen as an apprentice chef while I was at the Sorbonne for a semester.'

Kat's jaw dropped. Zafir looked at her and smiled.

'Good to know I'm still capable of surprising you.'

Feeling even more vulnerable now, Kat said testily, 'You accused me of lying, but you weren't exactly forthcoming with information yourself.'

Zafir's smile faded and air between them crackled. 'It wasn't talking about myself I was most interested in where you were concerned.'

A waiter appeared then, and took their order, and he

was quickly followed by a sommelier who took their wine order. When the wine had been poured and they were alone again, Kat felt ridiculously self-conscious and aware of Zafir, his long legs bracketing hers beneath the table.

He sat back, the delicate stem of his wine glass between long fingers. 'Why did you do it, Kat?'

She looked at him, feeling panicked. 'What?'

His face was stark. 'The pictures. Why did you let a man see you like that when you were so young? Why weren't you in school?'

Kat's hand tightened on her glass. She hated that she still didn't feel ready to tell Zafir everything. She wondered if she ever would. '*Now* you want to know? It won't change anything.'

Their starter arrived—deliciously creamy mushroom soup with truffle oil. To Kat's relief, Zafir seemed happy to let the question go while they ate, and he told her some stories of working there under a famously mercurial chef.

She said, 'I had no idea you were interested in cooking. And why take a job when you didn't have to?'

'I may be privileged—'

Kat snorted indelicately at that understatement.

Zafir continued. 'But I soon got bored when I wasn't studying. I was walking past this place one day and saw a sign in the window advertising for kitchen help, so I applied. No one here knew who I was. To them I was just Zafir Noury, a foreign student. It was only when my bodyguards made themselves a little too noticeable that questions were asked. But they let me stay working here and protected my identity. When Marcel, the owner, got into financial difficulty some years ago I was able to help him out, so now I have a stake in the business too.'

Kat's jaw would have dropped again, but she kept her mouth firmly shut. This was a side to Zafir she'd never known existed. Happy to be anonymous. Not afraid of menial work. When she'd known him he'd been feted as the Crown Prince of Jandor, King in Waiting. Influential and imposing. Overwhelming.

To her surprise they fell into an easy conversation for the rest of the impeccably prepared meal. So when their plates had been cleared, and Kat was feeling semirelaxed in Zafir's company for the first time since she'd seen him again, and he repeated his question about those photos she felt almost betrayed. As if he'd been lulling her into a false sense of security on purpose.

Feeling prickly, because she knew she was being a coward, she said, 'What purpose will this serve, Zafir? You weren't interested in knowing before. Why now?'

He shrugged minutely. 'Let's just say that when you ran out of my apartment that night you left more questions than answers.'

Kat bit back the accusation that he'd not been remotely interested in hearing any explanations that night, because truly, how hard had she tried to get him to listen to her? Not hard at all. Not once she'd known how he really felt. Or *didn't* feel.

But she realised now that the time had come—ready or not—to tell him what she would have told him that night if she hadn't felt so betrayed by his admission that he didn't love her.

She took a breath and forced herself to look at him. 'By the time I was seventeen I was the main breadwinner. Thanks to the endless round of beauty pageants I'd been entered into ever since my mother realised my looks had currency, I was working almost full-time as a model and supporting us both. I badly needed money for her medical bills.'

Zafir frowned. 'Her drug use.'

Kat refused to let him intimidate her again. She said in a low, fierce voice, '*No*. I never funded her drug use. But no matter what I did, or how many rehab programmes I tried to get her onto, she always relapsed.' Kat could feel her cheeks grow hot with shame as she said, 'She used to steal from me to buy her drugs. No matter how careful I was, she always found the money.'

'But surely you had a bank account?'

'Yes,' Kat said tightly, 'but I was a minor, so she was the joint account holder. That was no safer place to hide my money than underneath my bed.'

Zafir's eyes flashed. 'You were a minor when that man took those photos.'

Kat felt bile rise when she thought of that awful day. A day when she'd crossed a line and knew she'd never feel clean again.

'My mother was in a bad way. She'd taken all my money and she'd almost overdosed to death. She was in hospital. My last resort was to try and get her into a private rehab facility…but it was expensive. This man—the photographer—he wasn't anyone I'd met before, but one of the girls I modelled with told me about him and about the money I could make…'

'If you took your clothes off.' Zafir's voice sounded cold and austere, and the look on his face was one of disgust.

Kat threw her napkin down and stood up, emotion making her voice shake. 'I am not here to be judged and condemned by you for a second time, Zafir. What I did, I did because I had no other choice. And it didn't do much good anyway, because the day before she was due to go to the facility my mother managed to do what she'd been trying to do for years—she successfully overdosed herself to death.'

Kat left the restaurant, weaving unsteadily through the tables, desperately trying to stem the onset of tears. Once out in the street, she hugged her arms around herself, suddenly cold. The bodyguards were alert, watching her from their car nearby. Noor didn't seem to be with them this evening, and Kat almost missed the other woman's presence.

She started to walk in the other direction, cursing her leg for a moment because she couldn't just run. The street was cobblestoned, and any uneven surface was treacherous for her now.

She heard steps close behind her and tensed, but then she felt something big and warm land on her shoulders and turned around to see a grim-looking Zafir holding her jacket and bag. He'd given her his coat.

She would have reached for her things, but she was afraid her hands would shake, so she clutched Zafir's coat around her, hating the fact that it felt so comforting and smelled so enticingly of him.

'I'm sorry,' he said abruptly.

Stunned by his apology, Kat responded unevenly, 'I… it's okay.'

Zafir ran a hand through his hair, his grim look being replaced by something close to anger. 'Dammit, Kat, if I'd known what had happened to you…why you were in that position…' He trailed off.

Old injury resurfaced and Kat said, 'You believed I didn't tell you because I was afraid you wouldn't marry me. That wasn't the reason at all, Zafir. I didn't tell you because I was ashamed of the choice I'd had to make. And because my world was so far removed from yours.'

'I might have at least been able to understand, though…'

Disgust crossed his face again, but this time Kat recognised it wasn't directed at her.

'That man took advantage of you when you were at your most vulnerable.'

She shook her head. 'He didn't take advantage of me,

Zafir. I made a choice to take up his job offer and earned a lot more money than I would have through a more traditional route. I have to take responsibility for that.'

Kat thought of telling Zafir everything—how the photographer had gone on to blackmail her once she'd become well-known—but something stopped her. It was an unwillingness to let him see just how far-reaching that bad choice had been, sending poisonous tendrils into her life for a long time afterwards. Better to let Zafir believe she'd just been bad with money than utterly naive. Because she'd been naive where he'd been concerned too. And the last thing she wanted was for him to know that.

Zafir's car pulled up alongside them with a low, sleek purr. They didn't go back into the restaurant and Kat felt bad now for rushing out, wondering what Zafir's friend and business partner must think.

As they drove silently back through the Paris streets Kat realised that the evening—apart from that abrupt ending—had been very pleasant. More than pleasant.

She said now, before she could censor herself, 'I liked that restaurant. Why did we never go there before?'

Zafir's face was cast into shadow and his voice sounded rueful. 'I liked to show you off...and, to be honest, I didn't think it was your scene.'

Kat fell silent, realising that she'd been so busy trying to live up to what she believed to be Zafir's high expectations of glamour and sophistication that she'd presented a largely false persona the whole time they'd been together.

Just before they reached the hotel, Zafir turned to her and asked, 'What was his name, Kat?'

Confused for a moment, she said, 'Who?'

'The man who took those pictures.'

Kat was shocked at the steel in Zafir's voice. She shook her head. 'It won't make any difference now—'

'Kat.' He cut her off. 'Either you tell me now or I'll find out my own way. All you'll be doing is saving my team some unnecessary work.'

She looked at him and knew it would be futile to deny Zafir when he was like this. 'What are you going to do?'

His mouth tightened. 'His name, Kat.'

Realising he'd only find out eventually anyway, she told him.

Satisfaction gleamed in Zafir's eyes as he got out of the car and came round to help her out. His hand was tight on hers, and he didn't let her go all the way up in the elevator and until he walked her to her door.

Her heart was thudding against her breastbone. She still had Zafir's coat around her shoulders and she shrugged it off now, handing it back. He took it, handing her her things.

Reluctant to look into those grey eyes, because it felt as if something fundamental had shifted between them and she wasn't sure where she stood any more, Kat turned to the door, inserting her key. It clicked and she pushed it open. She turned back at the last moment and forced herself to look at Zafir. His face was expressionless, but something burned deep in his eyes. Something that scared her as much as it excited her.

Her hand tightened on the door handle. 'Good night, Zafir.'

For a heart-stopping moment she thought he was about to step forward and kiss her, and she knew that if he did that she wouldn't be able to resist. She felt as if an outer layer of protective skin had been removed.

But Zafir just took a step back and said, 'Good night, Kat. Get some rest.'

Kat watched him leave, and a minute later she was still rooted to the spot and trembling all over. That explicit look had been hot enough to make her feel scorched all over. And hot enough to confuse the hell out of her. Because he'd walked away again.

She was also still reeling from his sincere apology. And his anger on her behalf at the photographer. He still didn't know the half of it. About the blackmail...

An insidious though sneaked into her head... Maybe she'd finally done it. Maybe the truth of her past had been enough to drive him away.

Realising she was still standing outside her room, Kat quickly went inside and rested her back against the door, doing her best to ignore her thumping pulse and the betraying feeling of disappointment.

But it was clear now: her past was a passion-killer. Zafir might still be attracted to her, but he didn't really want the whole unvarnished truth of her past getting in the way. She told herself that she should be happy. Relieved. This is what she wanted, wasn't it? To prove to herself that Zafir only wanted the superficial and nothing deeper.

But she wasn't happy—or relieved. She was in more turmoil than ever.

A short while later, in his own suite, Zafir paced up and down, his head reeling with what Kat had told him.

He knew he wouldn't be able to rest until he'd started a search for the man who had taken such advantage of her. Despite her insistence that she had been just as responsible.

Zafir had had no idea how erroneous those salacious newspaper reports had been, or how cruel. And when he thought of a much younger Kat, in dire straits, needing help, he felt a helpless raw fury rise up within him.

She hadn't kept all this from him for fear he'd break the engagement and because she'd sought financial security—it had been because she hadn't trusted him enough to accept her past. And she'd been right.

Recrimination blasted him. He'd judged and condemned her before she'd had a chance to say anything.

There was so much more to her than he'd ever given her credit for, and this insight was proving yet again that something he'd thought would be easy—seducing Kat into his bed again—was anything but. And yet he'd never wanted her more.

When Zafir met Kat at the door of her room, early the following evening, he stopped in his tracks. For a heart-stopping, pulse-pounding moment he thought she was naked. But then he realised that she was wearing a flesh-coloured dress that moulded to her every curve, dip and hollow. It had a high neck and long sleeves, so she was effectively covered up, and yet he'd never seen anything more provocative.

Her hair was up again, and she already wore the diamond. It sat, glittering, over the dress against her breast-bone. Only the presence of the stylist and Noor and her guards stopped Zafir from overreacting and sending Kat back into her suite to change into a sack that would cover her from head to toe.

He was the one, after all, who had specified a wardrobe of clothes designed to show off the diamond to best advantage, and this dress did it perfectly. The problem was that it set Kat off to best advantage too, and the truth was that once again she effortlessly outshone the rare stone.

His eyes met hers and something clenched tight inside him when he saw a hint of vulnerability before she quickly masked it.

Willing the heat in his body down to a dull roar, he held out his arm to her and said, 'Shall we?'

* * *

The function was taking place in a ballroom at the very top of the hotel in which they were staying. It was sumptuous and decadent—and a blur to Kat. As was the view of Paris visible through open French doors on this unseasonably warm autumn evening. Apparently the rolling bank of clouds on the horizon heralded a storm, and Kat didn't appreciate the irony that the weather was mirroring her feelings so accurately.

She'd barely slept a wink last night, tossing and turning, wondering if she *had* driven Zafir away. As dawn had risen she'd felt gritty-eyed and hollow. Fully expecting that the next time she saw Zafir he would be looking at her with pity, or a kind of cool reserve.

But he hadn't. He'd looked at her with explicit heat in his eyes. And now she hated him for doing this to her, making her feel so confused and on edge.

Compounding her inner storm was the fact that Zafir had barely left her side. He was touching her constantly, either taking her arm or her hand, or placing his hand low on her back, just above her buttocks. She was hot all over and between her legs there was a merciless throb. Her breasts felt full and heavy, her nipples pressing against the material of the dress, but thankfully not glaringly obvious under the heavy material of the gown.

He'd turned away from her for a brief moment, and she was relishing the chance to get her breath and try to bring her heart rate under control again. But just as she was relaxing slightly a vaguely familiar voice called out.

'Kat! It's really you!'

Kat turned and a jolt of pure shock ran through her to see one of the only models she'd been relatively close with.

Her old friend stepped forward and enveloped Kat

in a huge hug. When she pulled back Kat saw the body-guards hovering protectively and said faintly, 'It's fine… I know her…'

She looked back at her friend and to her horror felt emotion threaten as remorse gripped her. Remorse for cutting her friend off after the accident. Cassidy had tried to contact her on numerous occasions, but Kat hadn't been capable of talking to anyone.

'I'm so sorry, Cass… I should have been in touch…'

Her friend took her hand and shook her head, 'No, Kat, you don't have to say anything. It's enough to see you now…' The stunningly beautiful Irish model, with her dark red hair, pale skin and blue eyes, smiled crookedly, 'But, *God*, I've missed you on the circuit.'

Kat smiled back, squeezing her friend's hand, appreciating this acceptance of her behaviour. She knew it was down to Zafir that her emotions were closer to the surface than usual, but that didn't help much.

Far too belatedly she spotted a tall, imposing man at her friend's side. He was dark and stern-looking, with compelling dark brown eyes. He also looked vaguely familiar… It was only when Zafir stepped up to Kat's side again that she saw it—a distinct resemblance.

She also noted how this man slid his arm possessively around her friend's waist. Clearly they were lovers. He was looking at Kat's necklace and said in a deep and slightly accented voice, 'So this is the famous Heart of Jandor?'

Kat resisted the urge to touch the stone. 'Yes, it is.'

Then Zafir surprised her by saying, 'Welcome, Riad. Kat, this is my very distant cousin, Riad Arnaud, a descendant of my French great-grandmother who was gifted this very diamond. And this is Kat Winters, who I'm sure needs no introduction.'

Riad inclined his head towards Kat, and then he drawled, 'Some might say I have a claim on this diamond.'

Zafir responded, sounding unperturbed. 'It belongs to Jandor—as you very well know. Left to us by your ancestor.'

Zafir's cousin looked as if he was considering this, but then he smiled and his face was transformed from stern to gorgeous. The tension dissipated as he clapped Zafir on his shoulder and said, 'You do know how I like to wind you up about the diamond, and it never fails.'

Zafir let out a short laugh. 'It's good to see you, Riad. It's been far too long.'

Kat turned to Zafir then, and said, 'This is Cassidy O'Connor—an old friend of mine. We modelled together.'

Cassidy stepped out of Riad's embrace to shake Zafir's hand. Kat noted with interest how Riad's face tightened as he watched the two greet each other. There was something very proprietorial in his dark gaze and he quickly drew Cassidy back to his side. For a moment Kat felt a twinge of envy.

Riad was saying something about arranging a meeting and stepping back, but Kat's friend stepped forward to hug her again. She whispered into Kat's ear, 'Is everything okay? You look great, but...different.'

Kat pulled back and smiled weakly. 'I have a lot to tell you, Cass. I'll call you when I get home?'

Cass took her hand and squeezed it. 'Promise me you will. I don't want to lose touch again.'

Kat nodded and said, 'Promise.' Then she added impulsively, 'And you, Cass, are you okay? Are you both...?' She trailed off ineffectually.

To her surprise her friend paled slightly, but then she smiled brightly and said, 'I'm fine. And we...well, I'm not quite sure what we are, to be honest.'

And then her friend was gone, sucked back into the crowd with her brooding and enigmatic lover by her side, leaving Kat pondering that perhaps all was not as straightforward as it had seemed between them.

A while later, after a seemingly endless round of being introduced to people and being stared at, Kat's nerves were on end and she felt close to breaking point—physically and emotionally.

As if sensing her vulnerability, Zafir took advantage of a moment when they were alone and bent down to say, sotto voce, 'It's going to happen, Kat. Tonight.'

Those words…said with such implacable arrogance after his mixed messages pushed Kat over the edge of her control. She hissed up at him. 'No, it's not, Zafir. It's really not.'

She walked away as steadily as she could and felt his gaze boring into her from behind. She went through the open French doors and breathed in deep, hoping the cool air would calm her down.

Dark storm clouds were gathering on the horizon and she heard a distant crack of thunder. She was aware of someone hovering nearby—a bodyguard. And now she felt foolish for stalking off.

She wished in that moment that Zafir had never reappeared in her life. And then the thought of that made her suck in a pained breath and put a hand to her belly as if someone had just punched her.

Taking another deep breath, and assuring herself that she still had everything under control, Kat turned around and walked back into the room—only to see Zafir smiling indulgently down into the upturned face of a famous French actress, a renowned beauty, who had her scarlet-tipped nails firmly on Zafir's arm as she told him something undoubtedly scintillating and hilarious.

As if feeling the weight of her gaze, Zafir turned his head for a second and looked straight at her, with no expression on his face, and then he deliberately turned his back on her and his attention to the other woman.

The speed with which Kat became engulfed in a red mist of jealousy shocked her. As did the speed with which she could already imagine that Zafir had decided she was too much trouble to pursue, and was now turning to an easier and far more accommodating prospect.

Kat had made Zafir wait before finally agreeing to date him that first time. He'd been too overwhelming... intimidating. But a woman like that wouldn't make him wait. He'd give and she'd take and then move on...not like Kat, who'd never really moved on.

She turned away from the sight just as Rahul passed close by. Kat caught his arm impulsively. 'I've got a headache—do you think it'd be okay if I left now?' She crossed her fingers at the white lie.

Rahul immediately looked concerned and anxious. 'Let me just check...'

He was gone before she could stop him, and suddenly Kat couldn't bear to watch Zafir's face change expression as he was told that she wanted to leave early. She threaded her way through the crowd to where another of Noor's men was waiting and told him she was ready to give the necklace back. He looked unsure, but took her aside to a secure area and waited as she removed it and handed it over.

He and his colleague had it boxed up and whisked away within seconds. Discreet and efficient.

When Kat stepped back into the room she let out a sigh of relief that she couldn't see Zafir or Rahul. She pressed the button for the elevator, wanting to get out of Zafir's orbit before she made a complete fool of herself.

It finally arrived with a soft *ping* and the doors opened. She'd stepped in, and had just pressed the button to go down when a hand inserted itself into the closing doors, forcing them open again.

Zafir.

CHAPTER SIX

ZAFIR WAS ANGRY. 'Leaving so soon?'

Kat forced herself to sound cool. 'I have a headache.' She wasn't even lying now. She could feel a throbbing at her temples.

He frowned and stepped into the elevator with her as the doors closed. Instantly the space was dwarfed by his tall and broad masculine form. 'I'll see you down to your room.'

Panic surged. 'You don't have to—you shouldn't leave the function.'

Zafir shrugged even as his eyes stayed on her, alert. 'They'll hardly notice now, the champagne and cocktails have been flowing for a couple of hours. The object of the evening has been achieved. Jandor will be indelibly imprinted on their minds, thanks to you and the diamond.'

Zafir pressed the button and the elevator started moving with a little jolt. It was enough to make Kat sway and go off balance, falling backwards. As quick as lightning Zafir reached for her, taking her arms and hauling her against him.

They both sucked in a breath at the contact, and with a muttered curse Zafir reached out and slammed a hand on the stop button. Kat's hands were pressed against his chest as the elevator came to a juddering halt.

'What are you doing?'

'Do you really have a headache, Kat?'

She looked up at him helplessly. She knew if she tried to move he'd only pull her even closer, and as it was she could feel every hard plane of his chest, and down lower the unmistakable thrust of something much more potent. His arousal. For her? Or for that woman?

Heat and self-disgust flooded her body. She pushed herself away, stepping back until she hit the wall and could go no further.

Zafir took a step closer. 'You don't have a headache, do you?'

Kat bit her lip, but the sharp pain made no difference. Images of him laughing down at that woman, made her say rashly, 'What do you even care, Zafir? I'm just a living, breathing mannequin. Your guests will be missing your presence.'

Zafir's eyes flashed and then narrowed on her, and he came even closer. So close that she could see the beginnings of stubble along his hard jaw. The darker flecks of grey in those mesmerising eyes.

Softly he asked, 'You wouldn't be jealous, would you, Kat? Jealous that I was giving attention to a woman who made it obvious that she'd welcome me to her bed if I just said the word?'

Aghast that she'd exposed herself so easily and quickly, Kat blurted out, 'Don't be ridiculous. I don't care who you sleep with.'

Zafir stepped even closer. Close enough to touch. 'Liar,' he breathed. 'I think you do care.'

The expression on his face was fierce now. He put his hands on the wall, either side of her head, enclosing her with his whole body.

Kat was barely breathing. The tension was thick enough to cut with a knife. Her hands were balled into fists at her sides in an effort to stop herself from grabbing him—or smacking him.

'The truth is that you've reduced me to crude methods not even used by hapless teenage boys.'

Kat shook her head, finding it hard to focus. 'What are you talking about?'

Zafir's jaw clenched. 'I'm talking about making you jealous, Kat. I wanted to make you jealous. I wanted to provoke you into showing me something...anything...so that I don't feel as if I'm the only one going crazy here.'

Kat swallowed, all her turmoil dissolving and being replaced by a dangerous tenderness. She whispered unevenly, 'You're not going crazy...'

'The problem is,' he said, as if she hadn't spoken, his voice rough, 'that I *do* care who I sleep with, and unfortunately there's only one woman I want to sleep with. She's haunted me for months and I can't get her out of my head...not till I've tasted every inch of her again.'

Kat felt a dangerous languor steal over her. She was oblivious to the fact that they were in a stalled elevator. 'Who...?' she managed to croak out. 'Who is this woman?'

Zafir lowered his hands from beside her head and expertly wrapped one arm around her waist, pulling her into him. His other hand found and started plucking the pins from her hair as he said throatily, 'You know it's you, Kat...it's always been you.'

It's always been you...

Kat could feel tendrils of her hair falling down around her shoulders. She didn't have the strength to resist Zafir any more. She wanted him with an ache that was painful. And when his mouth touched hers she couldn't stop a helpless whimper of need escaping. Her hands were already unfurling and climbing up to wrap around his neck.

The kiss quickly became carnal and explicit. This was no gentle exploration. This was months of hunger and frustration. Months of X-rated dreams. Zafir demanded Kat's response and she gave it, arching her whole body into his as if they could just fuse there and then.

She was dizzy, ravenous for the taste of Zafir's mouth, sucking his tongue deep, nipping with her teeth. He was hot and hard against her belly, and she longed to wrap her hand around him and squeeze his flesh, remembering the way his breath would hiss between his teeth.

His hands roved over her back, slipping over her dress, feeling her curves. She felt constricted, her breasts pushing against the heavy fabric, nipples tingling with need.

Zafir's hands went lower, covering her buttocks, squeezing with his big hands, pulling her dress up. It was the sensation of air on her bare leg that finally managed to cut through the heated haze in Kat's brain, and with a stark feeling of sheer panic and dread she realised that Zafir was about to expose her in more ways than one.

She broke away from his kiss and opened her eyes. It took a second for her to focus, and her breathing was as jagged as her heart rate. The fact that Zafir looked similarly dishevelled was no consolation.

She'd almost forgotten...

She stepped to the side, her dress falling down around her legs. Covering her again. Her mouth felt swollen. Other parts of her felt sensitive. Slick. *God.* He'd been moments away from lifting her up so she could wrap her legs around his waist.

'What is it, Kat?'

She couldn't look at him. Her hair was half up, half down, and she raised trembling hands, trying to repair the damage. 'Please...just take me back to my room.'

For a long moment there was only the sound of harsh breathing in the small space, and then Zafir turned away and pressed a button. The elevator started moving again, and this time Kat put a hand on the wall to steady herself. She saw her clutch bag on the floor, where she must have dropped it, and bent down to pick it up with nerveless fingers.

Zafir's back was impossibly broad and remote in front of her. She longed to say something. Anything. But her tongue was frozen.

When the elevator doors opened Zafir stepped out. Kat followed him down the corridor to her room. She opened her clutch to get her key, but her hand was shaking too much to put it in the door. Any hope of disguising his effect on her was well and truly gone.

Her key was plucked out of her hand by a much bigger one and Zafir opened the door efficiently, waiting for her to go in. Kat wanted to sag down into a chair and take the weight off her quivering legs, but Zafir followed her in, closing the door behind him.

She faced him, heart thumping. 'Zafir, I didn't mean for you to—'

'Continue what we just started?' he inserted harshly.

He folded his arms. He'd never looked more formidable or gorgeous.

'Well, tough,' he said. 'Because I have every intention of finishing what we started.'

Kat shook her head and forced herself to speak as calmly as possible. 'I'm sorry, Zafir, if I gave you the impression…'

But the words dried up in her throat under his quelling look. She knew Zafir was more sophisticated than that. Just because they'd kissed, he wouldn't expect more now. But it wasn't about that. She'd felt the conflagration between them. It was unique. Unprecedented. Undeniable.

He unlocked his arms and shed his jacket, tossing it on a nearby chair. Then he reached for his bow tie and undid it with jerky moves, yanking open his top button.

He looked around. 'Do you have anything to drink in here?'

Kat lifted her hand and pointed to the drinks tray on a table near the window. Zafir strode over, more animal than man. He poured himself a shot of something and drank it back in one.

Then he looked at her. 'Do you want anything?'

Kat was shocked. It was as if a layer of civility had been stripped away. She'd never seen him like this. Not even that night when her world had crumbled to pieces around her.

She shook her head, even though her mouth was dry. 'No, I'm fine.'

Zafir slugged back another shot and turned around to face her. 'You're not, though, are you?'

Kat could feel herself pale.

How did he know?

'What do you mean?'

'What I mean is that for some reason you're determined to deny us this closure.'

Relief warred with anger.

He didn't know.

'You're so certain that resuming our physical relationship will end with everything neatly tied up in a bow?'

Hurt lanced her that Zafir could believe it would be so simple. But it would be…for him. Because he had no feelings involved. Only lust. She wished it could be so easy for her.

His mouth was a tight line. 'It's inevitable, Kat. We can't be within two feet of each other without going up in flames. Can you handle another week of this? Because I know I can't.'

One week. Surely she could survive one more week and then walk away, heart and soul still intact?

She lifted her chin. 'I can, Zafir. I'm sorry for what just happened…' A sudden flash of their two bodies welded together and how good it had felt to have him kiss her made her falter, but then she regained her composure and said, 'But it was a mistake.'

'A word I've heard more times than I care for lately,' Zafir said.

He started to pace then, and that only drew Kat's hungry eyes to his lean form.

He stopped suddenly to look at her. 'What is it, Kat? Is this punishment for what happened before? This is your retribution? Because I didn't give you a chance to explain your past? Because I judged you too harshly?'

Kat's eyes widened. It was so much more than that. That had been just the tip of the iceberg.

He hadn't loved her.

She backed away. '*No*, Zafir. I'm not that petty.'

She whirled away from him, afraid he'd see something of the emotion she was feeling on her face.

A bleak, futile anger rose up and she turned around again. 'It's not all about you, you know. There are things…things you don't understand.'

He frowned, and then his gaze moved over Kat's shoulder to something behind her and he frowned even harder.

She only had the barest moment of premonition before he said, 'Why are there crutches in your room?'

Kat wanted to close her eyes. She wanted to be on her own so she could curl up in a ball and pretend she'd never seen Zafir again. Pretend that her body wasn't pulsating with awareness just to be near him.

This was the moment of truth. It had been spectacularly naive or stupid of her to believe that she could keep her secret from Zafir. It was amazing that he hadn't found out already. And she'd never been less ready to tell him. Especially not after that moment in the elevator, reminding her of just how explosive it had always been between them. And how it could never be again. Not after this.

'Kat?' There was something stark in his voice. 'Who do the crutches belong to?'

She looked at him and swallowed painfully. 'Me. Because I need them.'

Zafir shook his head. Not understanding. And why would he?

'Tell me why you need them when you're standing in front of me right now.' He sounded harsh now.

It was time to stop hiding. Kat reached down and caught her dress in one hand. She pulled it up, revealing her prosthetic limb and the joint where it met her leg.

Even so, it took a few seconds for Zafir to understand what he was looking at—and when it finally registered he went pale. Eventually his gaze lifted back to her face. The room was so silent it felt like time had stopped.

'What are you showing me?' Zafir's voice was hoarse.

The dress fell from nerveless fingers to cover her leg again. She started to tremble and felt cold. She was going into shock. 'The accident…the one I mentioned. It was worse than I let you believe. They had to amputate… My foot…was crushed.'

She must have swayed or something, because suddenly Zafir was there, hands on her shoulders, pushing her down into a chair. He disappeared for a moment and then reappeared with a glass in his hand.

He held it up to her mouth. 'Drink some of this.'

Kat's eyes were on his as she lifted shaking hands to the glass and tipped back her head. The liquid burned down her throat and she coughed. Zafir took the glass away as fire bloomed in her chest, having an almost immediate effect on the numb coldness that had gripped her.

He put down the glass. His hands were on the chair's armrests either side of her. He looked as if he'd just been punched in the gut.

'Why didn't you tell me?'

Because I was using it as a crude defence to resist you.

Kat opened her mouth and shut it again uselessly, before saying finally, 'At first I didn't see that it was any of your business. And then…when you offered all that money to do the job… I couldn't afford to say no and I was afraid if you knew you'd think I couldn't do it.'

Zafir's grey gaze bored all the way through her. 'I don't think that's it at all—or not all of it.'

Feeling threatened, and horribly exposed, Kat pushed herself up out of the chair, forcing Zafir to stand. She stalked away from him, acutely aware of her limp now.

She whirled back, the truth spilling out. 'I'm different now, Zafir. You want the Kat I was before, and she doesn't exist any more. I didn't want to see you look at me the way others do—with horror and pity.'

She'd dreaded this moment ever materialising, and she feared that she'd avoided it for so long for the most basic reasons of vanity more than anything more noble. And that killed her when she knew she was so much stronger than that. But standing here now, in front of the only man who'd ever made her feel truly alive, she couldn't bear it. Tears weren't far away, and that would be the worst humiliation.

'You know where the door is, Zafir. Please, just go.'

But he didn't go. He came closer, and Kat held herself rigid for fear she'd shatter into a million pieces before she was alone again, when she could lick her wounds without that devastating gaze on her.

When Zafir spoke, he sounded harsh. 'You really think I hadn't realised that you'd changed in some very fundamental way? Have you not noticed that if anything it's only made me want you more?'

Kat blinked. She'd expected to be looking at a retreating back and a closing door. Not listening to Zafir sounding almost…hurt.

'You really think I'm that shallow?' he asked.

She might have before, when he'd more or less admitted he'd only proposed because she embodied some physical ideal, but now everything she'd thought she'd known about this man was jumbled up and contradictory.

She couldn't speak. The fact that he was still here was too much. The tears she was desperately holding back filled her eyes. She heard a curse, and then Zafir's white shirt became a blur in her vision as she was enveloped in strong arms and held tight against his body.

It was heaven and hell as a storm took hold of Kat that she had no control over and no choice but to give in to it. She wept for everything: her heartbreak, the loss of her leg, for her deceased and damaged mother and for the fact that she'd longed for Zafir's arms around her so many times…even though she'd denied it to herself.

For a long time she stood in the harbour of Zafir's arms as his hands moved soothingly over her back. *Compassion.* Another facet to this man she hadn't seen before, adding to the complexity she felt around him now.

When her sobs had finally died away she pulled back and looked with horror at Zafir's wet shirt. She could see the darkness of his skin underneath, and despite her paroxysm of emotion she felt awareness sizzle deep inside. Mortified—because any desire Zafir had ever felt for her must have been incinerated by now—she pulled herself free of his arms completely, wiping the backs of her hands across her hot, wet cheeks.

He was the last person in whose arms she'd expected to find solace. Her eyes felt swollen. She must have rivers of mascara down her cheeks. This truly was her lowest moment. And that was saying a lot, considering what she'd been through.

'I'm sorry,' she said thickly, avoiding his eyes, 'I don't know what came over me.'

He took her by the hand and led her over to a chair, pushing her down gently. He reappeared with a tissue, and another shot of alcohol in a glass. He crouched down before her and made her take a sip of the drink, until gradually she felt seminormal again.

He dipped another tissue in a glass of water and gently rubbed at her cheeks.

She was mortified at the emotional storm she'd just unleashed all over him—and at the way he was tending to her so easily.

When he'd put the tissue down she forced herself to look up from his damp shirt to his face, which was tense and unreadable. 'Your shirt is ruined.'

His mouth tightened. 'I couldn't care less about my shirt. In fact—' He broke off and stood up, starting to undo his buttons.

Kat's mouth opened as his impressive chest was revealed, bit by bit. 'What are you doing?' she squeaked, holding the glass to her like some sort of shield.

Zafir's shirt was open now, and he made short work of the cufflinks, throwing them on a nearby table before he let the shirt drop to the ground and then he knelt down in front of her again.

His naked and very masculine chest filled her vision. It was deliciously broad, with dark hair dusting defined muscles. And dark, flat nipples that she remembered were sensitive to the touch, earning her a hiss through his teeth whenever she'd lavished attention on them...

She felt bewildered and exposed. 'Zafir—'

'I want to see it, Kat. Show me your leg.'

Her insides clenched hard in rejection of that. But he looked determined. 'Why would you want to see it?'

Zafir couldn't exactly articulate why he needed to see Kat's leg, but it came from a visceral place deep within him that was boiling over with a mixture of volatile emotions. Reverberating shock, futile anger, and a kind of grief he'd only ever felt before for his sister.

'I want to see what happened to you.'

He could see the myriad expressions crossing her face, dominated by clear reluctance, and it made him want to go out and smash whoever had done this to her into tiny pieces. But then something else crossed her face that he couldn't decipher—something like resignation—and she put her hands on her dress, pulling it up over her knees.

The sparkling folds of the dress were gathered on her smooth thighs and he could see now where thick material like a sock came halfway up the thigh of her left leg. It was flesh-coloured. So it wouldn't be too noticeable? That sent another spurt of raw emotion through Zafir.

He moved back to give Kat room, watching as she pressed a button at the bottom of the prosthetic limb and then she pushed at it firmly, so that the whole apparatus slid down and off.

He absorbed fresh shock seeing her amputated leg, which now ended just a few inches below her knee. The thick, sock-like liner stretched from above her knee, to the bottom of her limb, where it was rounded and had a pin, which obviously slotted into the prosthetic leg to help keep it in place.

Her hands moved to the liner covering her leg and he could see that they were trembling. He moved forward and covered her hands, forcing her to meet his gaze by sheer will.

When she eventually looked at him he said, 'Let me?'

She bit her lip, and it looked so painful that Zafir wanted to reach out and rescue it, but then she said hoarsely, 'You don't have to do this.'

He reminded her, with an arrogance that felt hollow now, 'I don't have to do anything.' There was a heavy weight in his chest, an ache he'd never felt before.

Eventually she lifted her hands from under his and Zafir looked down and took a breath before carefully rolling the liner down Kat's thigh, over her knee and off, taking in the enormity of the moment as her naked leg was revealed.

He put both hands on her leg, cupping it, feeling the skin where it was so brutally cut short. The scar was a jagged but neat line, and he ached even harder to imagine the pain she must have gone through. The weeks and months of rehabilitation. The fact that he hadn't noticed anything before now was testament to her sheer will.

The earth could have stopped revolving outside, he was so focused on Kat and this moment. He looked at her. 'Tell me what happened?'

Her hands were tightly clasped in her lap, knuckles white. Her face was pale, eyes huge. 'It was dark. I was crossing a road... There was a truck and a motorcycle. They told me afterwards that the truck's brakes failed and it went out of control, hitting the motorcycle. I ended up in the middle. My foot...was crushed.'

Zafir thought of her broken, lying still on the road, and felt a dizzying surge of panic. It took him a moment to compose himself, but then he said, 'I'm so sorry, Kat... that this happened to you.'

She half shrugged, as if it was no big deal, but he could see the vulnerability in her eyes.

'The man on the motorcycle died, Zafir. He was only twenty-two. When you consider that... I was lucky.'

For a second Zafir's mind blanked as he thought of how easily it might have been Kat who had lost her life.

Bitterly he said, 'It sounds like the truck driver was the lucky one.'

Kat shook her head. 'He has to live with the guilt he feels every day. He came to visit me and I've never seen anyone so haunted.'

Zafir was humbled by her compassion. He realised now where her new steely strength came from, and he felt something like awe. He also felt a very sharp pang at the assertion that he should have been there for her.

But he hadn't—because he'd judged her on the basis of lurid headlines without really giving her a chance to explain her side. For the first time, Zafir felt a rush of remorse and regret. Everything had changed and yet, conversely, nothing had changed.

Kat felt so delicate and vulnerable under his hands, and yet strong. It made his blood pulse faster through his veins. Acting on pure instinct and need, Zafir spread his hands out, encompassing Kat's leg completely. He bent forward and pressed a kiss to her knee, then lower, to the top of her shin, his hands moving down and cupping her residual limb.

He heard her sucked-in breath and a strangled-sounding, 'What are you doing?'

He lifted his head and looked at her with explicit intention. He moved both hands up her leg at the same time, until they encircled her bare thigh. Blood thundered in his veins.

'What do you think I'm doing, Kat? I'm finishing what we started.'

CHAPTER SEVEN

KAT COULDN'T BREATHE. Again. It was a miracle that any oxygen was reaching her brain. Somehow, from somewhere, she managed to suck in a breath. And another one. Her heart rate wouldn't slow, though. She felt flayed alive. Raw. But deep within her core burnt a fire that not even her turmoil could quench.

She'd expected Zafir to be long gone by now. But he wasn't. He was kneeling at her feet, looking up at her with that molten silver gaze. It was uncompromisingly direct, leaving her nowhere to hide.

And yet her mind reeled. He'd just looked at her... touched her leg. Inspected it. Cupped it reverently. Kissed it.

Emotion threatened again. The only people who'd touched her there since the accident had been medical professionals, or herself when she'd had the nerve to, and it had taken a long time to do it without crying.

Yet Zafir had just done it, and he hadn't looked remotely horrified or disgusted. He'd looked sad. Angry. Fierce. And there'd been something unmistakably possessive in his touch too—as if he was claiming some kind of ownership of her damaged limb. Which was obviously just a figment of her overwrought brain.

She shook her head, forcing herself to articulate her scattered thoughts. 'You don't mean that...'

Something struck her then, and she went cold all over. Zafir was a proud man. A very alpha man. A man full of integrity.

She recoiled back in the seat. 'You don't have to prove

anything, Zafir. If you stand up and walk away it won't make you less of a man.'

His hands tightened on her thigh and his eyes widened. A look of affront came over his hard-boned face. 'First you think I'm too shallow to handle this news and now you're accusing me of being too proud to walk away from something I don't want to do?'

Kat swallowed. She'd never seen Zafir look more stern.

His voice resonated deep within her. 'I would have thought that the least you know about me by now, Kat, is that I don't ever do anything I don't want to. I want something and I go after it. Do I need to remind you of how I went after you?'

She shook her head quickly. She did not need a reminder of that all-consuming seduction right now—her brain was addled enough as it was.

'I am here,' he said, 'because I want you, Kat. I tracked you down because I couldn't get you out of my head. Because I believe we have unfinished business. Because I believe that I won't be able to get on with my life until I've tasted you again…until I'm buried so deep inside you that I might finally be able to think clearly again. What happened to you changes nothing about how much I want you.'

All Kat heard was 'until I'm buried so deep inside you' and her whole lower body clenched, as if it was already anticipating taking his body into hers. As if some muscle memory was already reacting just to his words.

She clamped her thighs together, trapping Zafir's hand. His eyes flashed. He knew. He could sense her helpless response. But insecurity warred with desire. Did he really still want her?

With gentle but remorseless force, Zafir pushed her knees until they were spread apart and he was between them. Her dress was ruched up around her thighs, and if he looked he would see her very plain white panties.

As if reading her mind, his hands moved upwards, and Kat's breathing grew ragged and fast. Within seconds he would know just how badly she ached for him. She'd be utterly exposed.

She reached down and covered his hands, stopping their progress, and shifted, sitting up straighter in the chair, trying to put some space between them. She seized on something, *anything*, that might restore sanity, even though the blood rushing through her body wasn't asking for sanity at all. The opposite…

'I haven't been with anyone since—' She stopped. She'd been about to say *since you*, but she didn't want Zafir to know that. It would mean too much. She hoped he'd assume she'd meant to say *since the accident*.

Zafir shook his head. 'None of that matters. What matters is here and now.'

He rested his arms on the armrests of her chair and just looked at her. Her thighs were bracketing his chest…she could feel the tiny abrasions of his chest hair against the delicate skin of her inner thighs. Between her legs she was so damp and hot it was embarrassing.

'You're so beautiful,' he said simply.

Kat wanted to duck her head, avoid that blistering gaze, but she couldn't. She couldn't speak.

Zafir bent forward and touched his mouth to hers.

Kat closed her eyes and a helpless sound of need flowed from her mouth to his as the kiss hardened and deepened. It was too late for sanity. She couldn't resist this. *This* was what she wanted and needed to make all of the questions and doubts and insecurities fade away. When Zafir touched her she couldn't think of anything else. And she didn't want to.

On every level he'd defeated her. Kat's whole body

arched towards his, her arms finding and twining their way around his neck as his kiss got deeper and darker, and so explicit that it sent electric shocks all the way through her core, against which Zafir's taut belly provided a delicious friction.

His hands were on her thighs, lifting them up to hook around his hips. Kat didn't have time to think about how she looked, or how the lack of her limb felt. Zafir was too all-consuming.

One hand was on her back now, finding the top of the zip at her neck. He tugged it down and she felt air touch her bare skin as the dress slackened around her breasts. Zafir took his mouth off hers to pull back. They were both breathing harshly.

Without taking his eyes off hers, he pulled her dress forward and down, easing it off her shoulders and down her arms until she was naked from the waist up. The design of the dress had precluded the need for a bra.

Then he looked down at her.

She saw the way his eyes grew even darker, and colour slashed across his cheeks as he took in her bare breasts.

He said something guttural in Arabic. And then he brought his hands to her flesh, cupping her and squeezing. Her nipples were hard, stinging points, and when Zafir passed a thumb over each of them she almost cried out, they were so sensitive.

He looked at her and said raggedly, 'I've dreamt of this. Of you…'

He put one hand on her back, encouraging her to arch towards his mouth. He cupped her breast with his other hand, and then surrounded first one nipple and then the other in hot sucking heat. Kat's hands were buried in his hair, clinging on for dear life as he stoked her arousal to painful levels.

It was as if a wire was directly connecting Zafir's

mouth on her breasts to her core. The deliciously wicked combination of his rough tongue and teeth on her sensitive flesh pushed her right over an edge she didn't see coming, and she found herself shuddering in his arms as an orgasm gripped her and threw her high, before letting her float back down to earth.

She stiffened and pulled back in mortification, her cheeks burning. Her body had just betrayed her spectacularly. She shook her head. 'I'm sorry... I—'

He stopped her with a finger to her mouth. He looked wild. 'Don't you dare apologise. If I don't get inside you soon, Kat, I'm in danger of disgracing myself in a way that only used to happen when I was a boy and unable to control my body.'

Her eyes widened as comprehension sank in. 'You mean you—'

'Yes,' he said succinctly. And then, 'Where's the bedroom?'

All semblance of civility was gone now. And it was the sexiest thing Kat had ever seen.

'Behind you.'

With effortless strength, Zafir stood and scooped Kat up against his chest. Her arms went around his neck as he kicked open the bedroom door and brought her into the dimly lit room.

The gathering storm clouds outside went unnoticed as Zafir lowered Kat to the bed. So did the jagged fork of lightning and the first drops of heavy rain.

A part of Kat couldn't believe this was happening, and she needed a moment to assimilate everything and analyse the consequences. And yet, in spite of this knowledge, she couldn't bring herself to utter a word as she lay back and watched Zafir strip off the rest of his clothes with all the natural-born confidence of a spectacularly beautiful, sexually virile man.

Kat's eyes widened as she took in a sight she'd thought she'd never see again. A very aroused Zafir. Her greedy gaze avidly took in his whole body, noting that his muscles seemed even harder than before. His body bigger. And yet he was leaner. As if he'd shed some softer layer. Maybe becoming a King had done that to him.

'You, Kat,' he said gutturally. 'I want to see you too.'

He started to tug at her dress, pulling it down over her hips and off completely. Now she only wore her plain white panties, and she felt embarrassed. She'd always made an effort before, aware that Zafir had once liked wispy concoctions of lingerie—usually sent to her by him. But as he came down beside her on the bed now, his eyes gleamed with a hunger that turned any doubts to dust.

His hand smoothed over her chest and belly, which contracted with need. When his hand reached her underwear and his fingers slid underneath to explore she put a hand down instinctively. He looked at her. Once again she bit her lip. Unsure. As if she hadn't ever lain with this man before. As if he hadn't just seen her fall apart after barely touching her.

'I haven't… I don't look after myself down there like I used to.' Her cheeks burned.

Zafir's nostrils flared. 'Kat…when are you going to get it? *Nothing* about you could turn me off.'

His words unleashed a fresh flood of heat, and she realised now how careful she'd always been to live up to some ideal that she'd thought he wanted. His hand explored further, over the curls she'd always been told she had to remove for the sake of lingerie modelling contracts.

When his fingers touched her very core she arched her back off the bed. Within seconds her panties were gone and her legs were splayed. Zafir clamped big hands on her thighs, holding her captive as he bent his head and proceeded to explore her drenched sex with a thoroughness that rendered her insensible.

Her first orgasm had taken her by surprise. This one built and built until she almost screamed with the need to release the tension—and then Zafir circled her clitoris with his tongue, sucking it roughly, and she exploded into a million pieces.

When he loomed up over her he looked like a god. A dark, sexy, dangerous god. His muscles gleamed with sweat and she could smell his arousal—and hers. And even though her body wanted to float on a sea of bliss after that orgasm, when she heard the snap of latex and looked down to see Zafir's hands on his straining erection, need gripped her like a vice again. He made her insatiable. Greedy. She felt as if she'd been starved of some vital thing and was only now realising how empty she'd been.

He came down over her and aligned their bodies. She could see nothing else but him, feel nothing else but him. He surrounded her utterly.

After a breath he thrust into her body, deep and hard and unequivocal. As if stamping his brand on her. Kat breathed in the sheer expanse of him, awed at the way he filled her so completely. It was all at once familiar and altogether new. It was exquisite.

For a heart-pounding moment Zafir stayed embedded in her like that, as if he too was savouring the moment. And then something inside Kat broke apart. She reached for him, wrapping her arms around his neck, arching upwards. And as he started to move in long slow strokes in and out of her body's tight clasp, she gave herself over to the sensations racing through her body, rendering her mute.

His movements quickened and became less controlled,

he reached for her left thigh and brought it up, holding it firmly, deepening his penetration. Kat was only aware of the pinnacle of pleasure beckoning. It came at them like a steam train, blasting them apart and then welding them back together as Zafir's big body slumped over hers. They were so joined at every possible point, Kat wasn't sure she'd ever been a separate entity.

She fell into an exhausted slumber under Zafir's weight, unaware of him moving off her and standing up from the bed, looking at her as though he'd never seen her before.

Zafir was still reeling a few hours later as he looked out at the dawn breaking over the Paris skyline. The storm had passed—a storm he'd only been peripherally aware of. He felt as if a bigger storm had just happened in this hotel room.

In him.

He could see the shape of Kat on the bed in the reflection of the window, her elegant curves, her breasts...

He turned around and looked at her properly, his gaze inevitably tracking to her left leg, where it ended so cruelly short. He could see the faint imprint of his hand on the pale skin of her thigh, where he'd obviously gripped her in the throes of the most urgent lust that had ever gripped him.

As if hearing his thoughts, she moved minutely on the bed, and Zafir's chest tightened when he saw how her left leg instinctively wanted to stretch out. He wondered if she experienced the 'phantom limb' that people spoke of, when they could feel the pain of their amputated limb even though it wasn't there any more.

Seeing her like this... It made him feel so many different emotions he wasn't sure where one started and the other ended. But mostly he felt angry that she hadn't trusted him enough to tell him. And, worse, that she'd clearly expected him to turn tail and run.

But then, he had to concede heavily, why would she have thought otherwise? After all, he'd pursued her relentlessly after seeing her model lingerie on a catwalk. Why wouldn't she believe that he was shallow enough to value physical perfection over anything else?

He shook his head. Sex with Kat had always been amazing. So amazing that it had prompted him to track her down again. But this…what they'd just shared…had reached a whole new level. He didn't remember it ever being so carnal or so visceral. He'd literally had to have her…or die. Sinking into her that first time had impacted on him on a level where sex never usually did.

He went cold as the significance of that sank in. It had felt like coming home. But not in the way that returning to Jandor always felt like coming home… This had been far more profound and disturbing. It had felt like coming back to a place he'd longed for without even realising it.

Zafir's immediate reaction was to negate this revelation as a lust-induced delusion, but the truth was harder to deny.

Things with Kat had morphed out of all recognition. And it had nothing to do with the fact that she'd been hiding the truth that she was an amputee. It had everything to do with the fact that after having sex with this woman closure had never seemed more distant.

He dragged his gaze back up her body to her face. She was awake now, and looking at him with wide golden eyes. And just like that desire returned—urgent and swift.

Her gaze tracked down his body, obviously taking in his helpless physical reaction. Her cheeks coloured as she said in a sleepily husky voice, 'You showered…'

For a second Zafir warred with his emotions and tendrils of panic growing inside him. This was so far beyond what he'd expected to experience with Kat again that he wanted to tell her that last night had been enough. He wanted to walk out through the door and never look back. Because suddenly things weren't as simple as he'd thought they would be.

But that urge to leave curdled in his belly.

He didn't want to leave. He wanted her.

Compelled by a force stronger than he could deny, he twitched his towel off his hips and stalked back to the bed. He lay down alongside Kat and touched her thigh, seeing how something in her eyes veiled itself.

'I marked you...'

She looked down and saw his handprint. Her hair hid her face as she said in a slightly breathless voice, 'It's okay...it doesn't hurt.'

Zafir scooped her hair over her shoulder and tipped her chin up so she had to look at him. She was wary, but he could see the heat in her eyes. He kept his eyes on hers as he moved so that he was between her thighs... his erection notched against the place where she was hot and wet. Ready for him.

It was too much. Zafir didn't have a hope as he gave in to the raging desire inside him, blocked out all the warning voices and slid home. Again. And again. Until he was reduced to rubble and the voices were mercifully quiet.

Kat woke up surrounded by steel and heat. She couldn't breathe. Panic gripped her and she instinctively thrashed out, flailing uncontrollably.

She vaguely heard a sound, but it took long seconds for her to realise that Zafir had all but pinned her to the bed and was now looming over her saying, 'Kat, relax— it's me... You're okay.'

She went still, even though panic still raced through

her blood. Eventually it dissipated and she asked shakily, 'What happened?'

'You were lashing out…screaming. "Get it off me! Get it off…"'

The first tendrils of understanding sank in, quickly followed by embarrassment. She breathed deep. Zafir's very naked body was over hers, but even that couldn't distract her from the fact that she'd just had the same nightmare she'd had for months after the accident.

She pulled back from Zafir's embrace and he let her go reluctantly, as if he knew she needed space but didn't want to allow it.

She struggled to find a way to explain herself. 'I'm sorry… If I feel claustrophobic it brings back the accident…when I was trapped under the truck.'

Zafir reared back. 'I make you feel claustrophobic?'

Kat was shocked at the hurt she heard in Zafir's voice. '*No*…no. I'm just not used to waking up in bed with someone.'

Kat realised that part of it was disbelief that Zafir was still here—that she'd woken in his arms. The claustrophobia lingered, but it had nothing to do now with traumatic memories and everything to do with feelings rising inside her that she didn't want to analyse, like a coward.

She sat up and avoided his eye. 'I think I'll take a bath. Could you pass me my robe, please?'

Zafir said nothing for a long moment, and then he got out of the bed, unashamedly naked, and handed her a silken robe. Kat watched him walk into the bathroom and registered the sound of water running. She quickly pulled on the robe, covering her own nakedness, and scooted to the edge of the bed.

Zafir reappeared in the doorway, still naked. Ridiculously, Kat felt like blushing and she blurted out, 'Could you hand me my crutches?'

Zafir strode over, saying, 'You don't need your crutches.'

He was about to bend down and pick her up into his arms but Kat put out her hands, heart thumping treacherously at the innately masculine reaction.

'No, Zafir, I can do it myself.'

He drew back and looked down at her, a muscle pulsing in his jaw. 'Very well.'

He went and retrieved her crutches from the other room and Kat pulled herself upright on them, making her way into the bathroom, burning with self-consciousness. The only people who had seen her like this were medical professionals and Julie. Not a lover. Not Zafir.

She didn't want to turn around to see what might be on his face and she shut the bathroom door behind her, feeling alternately stronger than she'd ever felt but also weak. As if she'd scored some useless point.

She turned off the taps of the bath and disrobed, carefully stowing the crutches and lowering herself into the steaming, fragrant water.

The water lapped around her and a sense of déjà vu struck her as she recalled the last time she'd had a bath and where her mind had gone. She couldn't stop the images of the night they'd just shared from circling in her head like a lurid movie.

When he'd come back to the bed as dawn had broken they'd made love again. He'd pulled her over his body so that she was straddling him, and just before he'd thrust up into her body he'd asked, 'Is this okay? Are you comfortable?'

She'd nodded, aghast at how overcome she'd felt in that moment. She'd never seen this far more tender and gentle side to Zafir before. Even though there was nothing tender or gentle about their lovemaking.

She'd been so…uninhibited. Sex with Zafir had never felt like this. Before, she'd always felt somehow…aware of herself. Aware of all the women he'd been with before her and of her inexperience. It was as if a wall of glass had separated them, and no matter how skilful Zafir had been Kat had never lost herself completely, always holding some part of herself back.

But last night had been different. She'd lost herself completely. There'd been nothing between them but heat and lust and desperate need. It was as if she'd undergone some seismic shift.

There was a knock on the door, making her jerk upright. 'Kat, are you all right?'

Her voice sounded strangled as she called out, 'Fine. I'm fine.'

Zafir scowled on the other side of the door. Everything in him burned to go to her. He could imagine Kat's naked body all too well—slick and wet, droplets of water beading on her nipples...

He paced back and forth, aware of his body responding to his imagination. Cursing softly, he pulled a towel around his waist, as if that could douse his desire.

She'd looked so proud just now, walking into the bathroom on her crutches, back straight and tall. The stark reality of what she'd gone through had impacted on him all over again. It had almost but not quite eclipsed what he'd felt when she'd told him she felt claustrophobic. *Hurt.* An emotion he'd only ever felt around his siblings when they'd used to shut him out.

Hurt was not an emotion he welcomed. He'd always liked and respected Kat, but he'd never claimed to love her. He wanted no part of that—not after seeing his brother so destroyed by it.

Once again Zafir felt the urge to just walk away. Consign this to the status of a one-night stand. A slaking of lust. But even as he thought that he knew it was a lie. His body burned for her. One night would never be enough.

Just then there was the sound of splashing and a muffled curse. Zafir didn't even think. He walked straight into the bathroom.

Kat was sitting up in the bath and she looked at him. All he saw was gleaming pale skin and those glorious breasts rising from the water.

'I heard…something…' he said, feeling ridiculous.

'I just dropped the soap.'

Kat's cheeks were pink. Her hair was piled high, but long tendrils clung to her skin. Giving up the fight, Zafir muttered a curse and dropped the towel from around his hips, seeing Kat's eyes widen as she took in his helplessly rampant response.

Zafir was climbing into the bath before Kat could react. She squeaked as he settled himself behind her, making water slosh over the edge of the bath. 'What are you doing?'

His arms were around her, pulling her back against his broad chest, and the past and present meshed painfully for a moment, reminding of her of many such shared moments before.

'Zafir…' she protested weakly.

'Yes?' Zafir started to lather his hands with soap and then spread them over her body.

'You don't have to do this…' Kat tensed her body, trying to hold back the emotion she was feeling.

Zafir's hands stilled. He angled himself around to see her face. 'What is it?'

Kat shrugged, as if this wasn't a big deal. 'I just… This kind of thing has been so far from my mind… I certainly never expected that when the time came it would be you…'

Her heart beat fast. This was the closest she could come to trying to articulate the tangled feelings in her breast.

'And are you glad it's me?'

Kat knew now that she was in serious trouble, because experiencing this reawakening with him was more profound than she liked to admit. Not that she could tell him that. Not when to him this was just an affair to gain *closure*.

She shrugged again and said—as nonchalantly as she could when he was at her back, surrounding her in heat and desire, 'You're a good lover, Zafir…'

A good lover.

Zafir curbed his tongue. How did she manage to make that sound almost insulting? As for the thought that she would have let some other man see her for the first time as she was now… Zafir didn't even want to contemplate that scenario.

He concentrated instead on washing Kat's body with an explorative zeal that would soon make her admit that— *what?* What did he want her to admit? Zafir suddenly wasn't sure…

But then he felt Kat start to soften against him, her back arching against his chest, her body moving restlessly under the water, and as he found the slick centre of her body and made her moan he told himself he didn't care. *This* was all he cared about. Here and now.

It was enough. It would be enough.

CHAPTER EIGHT

SOME HOURS LATER Kat was dressed and ready to go, but she was delaying her exit from the bedroom to join Zafir in the suite, where he'd gone to make some calls, because the full significance of the previous night and everything that had happened was sinking in fully—and very belatedly. As if she'd been blocking it out until now.

Just thinking of Zafir's easy acceptance of her secret and how tender he'd been was overwhelming. At every step when she'd expected him to look at her in horror, turn and walk away…reject her…he'd done the opposite.

A flashback came of sweaty limbs entwined, his hand hard on her thigh, clamping her in place so he could thrust even deeper…

Kat felt a fine sweat break out over her body.

To say she was raw and exposed was an understatement. She hadn't felt like this since the aftermath of the accident. It was as if he'd torn her apart and put her back together, and now she wasn't sure who she was any more.

The thought of that grey gaze narrowing on her made her pace back and forth now, gnawing at a nail. A bad habit she'd cut out years before.

Zafir had effectively demolished every wall she'd erected around herself last night, and now there was nothing left to hide behind. The knowledge that she'd been using her leg as a defence mechanism to keep him at a distance was not welcome. And the thought of another night like last night was terrifying.

She was very much afraid he'd effortlessly expose things that she wasn't even ready to admit to herself yet. Like how far he'd burrowed under her skin again. Like how much she yearned for him to look at her as he had before, when she'd done no wrong in his eyes.

He'd used to look at her and say, 'I can't believe someone like you exists in this world…'

A curt rap on the door stopped Kat in her tracks.

'Kat? Are you ready? My car is waiting to take us to the airport.'

To take them to Jandor. Back to the place where Kat had realised just how ill-suited she was to become a permanent part of Zafir's life. And yet she'd tried to convince herself it would be all right.

Her recent thoughts and revelations still reverberating in her head sickeningly, she walked to the door and opened it. Zafir filled her vision. He'd changed into a charcoal suit and looked regal and impressive.

Before she could stop herself, she blurted out, 'There's something I need to say before we leave.'

Unfazed, even though Kat could imagine the veritable army of people waiting for them to leave, he just said, 'Okay.'

She was glad of her slim-fitting trousers and silk shirt. She wanted to send out a no-nonsense vibe.

She walked into the suite and turned around to face Zafir, steeling herself. 'What happened last night won't be happening again.'

Even as she said it she could feel her heart give a betraying lurch. And between her legs pulsed as if in protest.

Zafir leant his shoulder against the doorframe and folded his arms. He raised a brow. 'And why would that be?'

Kat wanted to pace, but forced herself to stand still and sound cool and blasé. 'Because last night was enough for me. And, in any case, Jandor is hardly an appropriate location for the King to be conducting an illicit affair with someone who is eminently unsuitable.'

Zafir straightened up from the wall, his gaze narrowing on her just as she'd feared. 'You never did like Jandor.'

Kat thought she detected a note of bitterness in his voice, and she responded defensively. 'That's *not* true. From the moment I first saw it from the plane I thought it was magical...'

Zafir looked sceptical.

'It's true,' Kat said, less vehemently now, afraid of revealing too much. 'I loved Jahor too. It was just... The palace was so huge and intimidating.'

She shivered now, remembering the massive empty corridors. The hushed reverence. Her fear of doing something wrong. The feeling of hundreds of eyes on her that she couldn't see.

'And you were so busy. I hardly saw you.' Kat hated the accusing note in her voice.

To her surprise, Zafir unfolded his arms and ran a hand through his hair.

He sighed. 'Maybe you're right. My father monopolised my attention.' Those grey eyes pinned her to the spot. 'I shouldn't have left you alone so much.'

Kat broke eye contact, not wanting him to see how much that impacted on her. 'It wouldn't have changed anything in the end,' she said. She had to keep reminding herself of that fact. If not him.

'I'm sorry I hurt you, Kat. I never meant to do that.'

Kat went very still. *This* was why they couldn't sleep together again. Zafir was getting far too close to the beating heart of her, and she didn't want him to suspect that that was why she couldn't repeat last night.

She looked at him and said, very deliberately, 'I was infatuated with you, Zafir. Not in love. It was for the best. I wasn't ready to step into such a hugely responsible role. I would have disappointed you. And, even though I know you would have been happy with a marriage based on respect and chemistry, it wouldn't have been enough for me in the end.'

She knew that much now—indelibly. She needed to be loved in a way that had eluded her all her life. For herself. Not just because she represented some ideal and as such could be used as a commodity, as her mother had used her so shamelessly. And as she had used herself when she'd had to.

An impulse rose from deep inside her at that moment, a desire to unsettle Zafir as much as he unsettled her. 'What about you, Zafir?' she asked before she could stop herself. 'Would a marriage in little more than name really have been enough for you? Are you so cold?'

Zafir was silent for a long moment, and then he said, almost harshly, 'Yes, I am that cold. I was brought up to rule a country, not to fall in love. My parents' marriage was borne out of a need to unite two warring countries. There was no love lost between them, and yet together they brought peace to a region. Surely that's more important than the selfish desires of one person to indulge in the myth of a fairy tale?'

Kat tried to hide her shock. 'I know things are different for you…that you're not the same as the average person…' *Not remotely*, said a little voice. 'But I don't think it's too much to ask, Zafir…even for you.'

He started to pace, and as much as Kat had wished to unsettle him, now she regretted it. He stopped and looked at her accusingly. 'Love tore my brother apart. Destroyed him.'

Kat put a hand on the back of a chair near to her, as if that might steady her. 'What do you mean?'

Zafir had never really talked about his younger brother before, but she knew he existed. He had a reputation as a debauched playboy, and from the photos she'd seen of him in passing, in the gossip pages, he was as tall, dark and handsome as his brother, with a roguish edge that had earned him a place as one of the world's most elusive bachelors.

Zafir said, 'I had a younger sister—Sara. She was Salim's twin. They were playing one day in a walled garden. They were messing about as usual...' Zafir lifted a hand and let it drop. 'I heard Salim scream and I ran to them. She was dead when I got there...a massive head injury... She'd fallen from the high wall...'

Kat wanted to go and touch Zafir as anguish filled her chest, but it was as if he was still surrounded by that wall. 'Oh, Zafir... I'm so sorry. How old was she?'

He looked bleak. 'Just eleven.'

He went over to a window and looked out, his back to Kat. She sat down in the chair.

'They were so close, the two of them. From the moment they were born they had their own little world. Even spoke a language no one else could decipher. When she died...and when Salim realised how little our parents had valued Sara because she'd been a girl and not a boy... something broke inside him.'

After a long moment Zafir turned around. He was expressionless.

'I saw what loving someone and losing them did to Salim. It changed him for ever. I have no intention of ever investing so much in one person that they have the power to destroy you.'

A million things crowded onto Kat's tongue. She wanted to say to Zafir that Salim and Sara had obviously had a very strong twin bond, and of course Salim had taken her death hard, but that was no reason to believe Zafir would experience the same thing. But Kat's tongue wouldn't work. She guessed that whatever she said would be met with deep cynicism.

She stood up and tried to ignore the tightness in her chest. 'I'm sorry you had to experience losing your sister like that, Zafir. I think I would have liked to know her...'

'Yes...' he said almost wistfully. 'I often wonder how she would be now. I think she would be formidable.'

No more formidable than her older brother, thought Kat.

There was a sharp rap on the door at that moment, and Kat flinched.

Rahul's anxious voice floated through the door. 'Sire, the cars are waiting.'

Zafir's gaze narrowed on Kat again as he called out, 'Just a minute.'

She felt a frisson of danger as he walked over to where she stood with all the inherent grace and menace of a predatory animal. Their recent conversation was forgotten as that grey gaze skewered her to the spot.

'You meant what you said? You're certain this affair ends here?'

For a heart-jolting moment Kat thought that Zafir might just leave her here in Paris and go on without her. Maybe she'd pushed him too far, asking those questions...

She forced herself to nod.

Zafir snaked a hand around the back of her neck, under her hair. She went on fire.

He shook his head. 'It's not over, Kat—not yet. You can delude yourself that it is, but when you're ready to be honest and admit that it's not I'll be waiting.'

The worst thing, as he stepped back and she struggled to find some pithy response, was the relief rushing through her that he wasn't leaving her behind.

Not yet.

* * *

The setting sun bathed Jahor in warm golden light. Kat couldn't believe how overwhelmed she was to be back here again, but she told herself it had nothing to do with learning about Zafir's sister and brother or her renewed intimacy with Zafir.

She'd once had a very real fantasy of becoming Queen of this land, humbled and awed by Zafir's belief in her, but that fantasy had been cruelly shattered. She felt it keenly now, though—the sense of loss—even though she knew that it was better this way.

She wouldn't have known the first thing about being Queen. She would have let Zafir down. And she went cold now, thinking of how much worse it would have been if her past had come out after she had become Queen.

Zafir was sitting beside her in the back of a chauffeur-driven car, speaking on his phone in a low, deep voice as they wound their way through the ancient streets and up to the palace on the hill, overlooking the ancient city.

She was glad his attention wasn't focused on her for this moment. During the flight from Paris she'd found his gaze resting on her every time she'd looked at him, and by the time they'd disembarked her senses had been jangling with awareness.

She just had to resist him. That was all.

She could see people through the tinted windows of the car, bowing reverently as they passed by. And then a gaggle of gap-toothed boys chased the car, waving manically even though she knew they couldn't see her or Zafir. She felt an impulse to open her window and reach out to touch their hands, and it shocked her.

It was another reminder of how she'd never have had the decorum to be Queen. So why didn't that thought comfort her? Why did it leave her feeling hollow?

They were sweeping through the palace gates now, and

into the majestic forecourt. Nerves fluttered in Kat's belly as Zafir ended his phone call and said enigmatically, 'You might find some things a little changed since last time.'

When she got out of the car she could see several aides waiting, and Rahul, looking as efficient as ever. Staff greeted them, dressed in long, light-coloured tunics and close-fitting trousers. They were smiling as they took her luggage and Zafir's.

The last time she'd been there the staff had been dressed in black, and they'd had a dour air. There'd also been an oppressive atmosphere, but now there was an air of infectious joyousness.

A smiling young woman came forward to greet Kat, saying in perfect English, 'I'm Jasmine. I'll be your maid while you're here, Miss Winters. If you'd like to follow me?'

Kat looked over to where Zafir was still watching her, and he said, 'Go—settle in and rest. I'll come and find you.'

Then he was striding away, his aides and Rahul hurrying in his wake. And, in spite of Kat's intentions to put some distance between herself and Zafir, all she felt right then was bereft. But, she told herself sternly, that this was a good thing if it reminded her of how out of place she'd felt here before. It would help her to resist Zafir.

She was led over to a nearby golf buggy and the younger woman indicated for Kat to get in. Kat did so, and soaked up the glorious lingering heat and the beautifully cultivated gardens as Jasmine carefully drove them round to where Kat's suite was located, at the other side of the palace.

On her first visit, Kat remembered walking miles and miles through vast corridors behind a silent woman as she'd been led to her quarters, feeling as though she was being punished for something she hadn't done.

Her rooms were different this time—which she was grateful for. She had enough memories bombarding her brain without adding more to the mix. Memories of long hot nights when Zafir had crept into her bed and woken her up with his mouth on her…

'You'll see here, Miss Winters, that your wardrobe is fully stocked with clothes from our finest designers.'

Kat's cheeks burned as she diverted her mind away from X-rated memories, and her mouth fell open as she took in the acres of sumptuous fabrics hanging in the massive wardrobe. She put out a hand, touching an emerald-green gown reverently, and breathed, 'This is too much.'

But Jasmine was already opening drawers nearby, showing her a vast collection of brand-new lingerie and more casual wear. Everything and anything Kat could possibly need.

Except Zafir's trust and love.

She cursed herself for even thinking it. She might have had his trust, before she'd broken it, but she'd never had his love.

She thought of what he'd said before they'd left Paris, and wondered with a pang if any woman would be able to entice him out from behind the rigid wall he maintained around his heart.

Jasmine left Kat alone after she'd given her an exhaustive tour of the vast suite and shown her where a tray had been laid out with mouth-watering refreshments and a jug of iced water infused with lemons and limes.

After eating a little, Kat explored the bathroom, and was alternately shocked and moved to find that someone—*Zafir*—had obviously given instructions to have the shower made more accessible for her, with a chair and rails.

After a refreshing shower, she put her prosthesis back

on and slipped into a long kaftan she'd found among the clothes hanging in the wardrobe. It was dark gold, and it glided over her body like a cool breeze. She lifted her hair up and off her neck, twisting it into a knot on her head, and went outside the French doors to explore the grounds.

The sun was setting in a blazing ball of orange on the horizon and Kat watched it for a long moment, a sense of peace she hadn't experienced in a long time stealing over her. She took a deep breath, revelling in the heat and the rich, exotic scents around her.

This place resonated deep within her in a way that she couldn't explain. A familiar refrain popped into her head: she came from a trailer park in one of the poorest parts of Midwest America and she hadn't even completed her high school education. She had no right to feel an affinity with this place.

Kat pushed the assertion down. She could recognise how intimidated she'd been before, but of course she had a right to be here—no matter what her background was. If anything, the last eighteen months had shown her where her true strengths lay, and she wasn't as wide-eyed and naive as she'd once been.

She walked along a path shaded by the overhanging branches of a tree that bore small black fruits like berries. It truly was paradise. She spotted a walled garden ahead, but came to a stop at the entrance when she saw that it was untended and overgrown—in stark contrast to the lush perfection surrounding it.

Something about it called to her, and she stepped inside. She could just make out an empty dry fountain, and beautiful mosaics that were cracked and broken.

She felt as if she was intruding on a private space, and was just turning to go when she heard a noise. She whirled around to see Zafir standing in the entrance to the garden, breathtaking in traditional flowing cream robes.

As soon as she saw the look on his face something clicked in her mind, and she said slowly, 'This is where she died, isn't it? Sara...?'

He nodded once, curtly, and stepped inside the garden.

Kat said, 'I didn't mean to intrude. I was just passing...'

Zafir came and stood near the overgrown fountain. 'It's fine. How were you to know?'

He didn't look at Kat, and impetuously she asked, 'Tell me about Sara. What was she like?'

She held her breath for a moment, not sure if Zafir would indulge her, but then she saw the corner of his mouth twitch.

'She was beautiful and stubborn and mischievous.'

'Did she have your eyes?'

Zafir shook his head. 'No, she had blue eyes—like Salim. Long dark hair. They were inseparable like I told you, from the moment they were born. Like a little unit.'

'What about you?'

Zafir shrugged minutely. 'They didn't need me. They had each other.'

Kat didn't know what to say to that. She was blindsided by an image of a young Zafir, always on the outside of his siblings' intense bond, and how lonely that must have been.

'I can't believe your parents weren't affected when Sara died. They couldn't have been so cruel.'

Zafir turned around then, and the cold look on his face made Kat suck in a breath.

'Yes, they could and they were. Don't you remember meeting them?'

Of course she did. She'd met them on her first visit and endured an excruciating lunch during which they'd spoken their own language and made no attempt to speak with her, directing all their conversation to Zafir. They'd clearly deemed the prospect of her becoming a daughter-in-law a total travesty.

Zafir shook his head. 'I can't believe you still retain such optimism about people when your own mother exploited you so shamelessly.'

Kat's face grew hot. She felt like that naive virgin all over again. Mocked by Zafir's deep well of cynicism.

She lifted up her chin. 'I'd prefer to be optimistic about people rather than believe there's no hope for love or redemption. You're not your brother, Zafir. Or your parents.'

Suddenly acutely aware of the small space, and its air of general decay, Kat felt claustrophobic.

She started to walk out, but Zafir caught her by the arm. 'Where are you going?'

She looked at him, and hated the ease with which he could strike at her very heart. 'Back to my room.'

'I've arranged dinner for us in my private suite.'

Zafir's hand was warm on her arm, and it made her think of how it would feel on other parts of her body. It would be so easy just to say *yes*—to go with Zafir to his suite and let the inevitable happen. Her blood grew hot just from thinking about it. But she couldn't. Not if she wanted to walk away relatively intact when all this was over.

She pulled her arm free. 'No, Zafir. I'm tired and I'd like to go to bed—*alone*. I'm here to complete the job of promoting the diamond and Jandor and that's all I'm interested in.'

Zafir's eyes took on a gleam she didn't want to interpret. But he just said, 'Very well, Kat. I'll see you after lunch tomorrow, then.'

She had turned to walk away again before she stopped and asked suspiciously, 'The function is in two days. What's happening tomorrow?'

Zafir folded his arms and looked powerful and dangerous. 'A little sightseeing tour of my country. I'm making up for the fact that you saw very little of Jandor last time.'

Panic skittered along Kat's skin. 'You really don't have to do that. You're busy. I can sightsee on my own.'

He walked forward and caught her arm again, escorting her out of the garden in a smooth motion. 'Your concern for my schedule is commendable—but, yes, Kat, I am doing this. Jasmine will help you pack for the trip.'

Kat pulled herself free. *'Pack?'*

'I'm taking you into the desert for the night—a unique experience, and one I'd hate for you to miss out on before you leave.'

Before you leave.

Kat stifled the dart of pain. She recognised his look of steely determination. 'Fine, Zafir,' she bit out eventually. 'But don't think that this changes anything—all you'll be doing is wasting your own precious time.'

Zafir watched Kat walk back to her suite of rooms, her slight limp the only hint that there was anything different about her.

When he'd seen her standing in Sara's garden—as he called it—he'd expected to feel a sense of intrusion. But he'd felt the opposite. He'd felt as if a weight was being lifted off his shoulders. He'd found himself avoiding her eye, embarrassingly afraid of the compassion he suspected he'd see in those amber depths and what it might unleash inside him.

And then, when he'd told her about Salim and Sara and their bond, she'd asked, 'What about you?'

Her innocent question had impacted on him like a blow to the gut. No one had ever said that to him before—*What about you?*—because no one had ever really cared.

Zafir's hands curled into fists now, as if that could

halt the rise of something dark and tangled that he didn't want to decipher.

He turned around and strode back to his rooms, irritation and sexual frustration making his movements jerky. Damn her for throwing up more questions than answers. Damn her for not making this as easy as he'd expected it to be. And damn her for looking so right here...as if she belonged.

She couldn't belong here. Zafir had closed the door on that possibility comprehensively and for ever. He had a future to build, and Kat was not a part of that future. Very soon she would be in his past and Zafir would have no regrets.

But in the meantime he would use every skill he possessed to make her acquiesce one last time, and then—*then*—he would be able to let her go, and when he moved on and chose his Queen it would be someone who didn't look at him and make him feel as though she could see all the way to the depths of his soul...

Late the following afternoon Kat was in a helicopter, looking down in awe as they flew over the vast Jandor desert. The spiderlike shape of the helicopter's shadow undulated over high sand dunes as the sun set in the distance. It was magical.

Much as she had intended blocking out Zafir's far too magnetic presence, it was almost impossible. The space in the back of the helicopter was small, and his thigh was pressed firmly along hers. And she didn't like the look in his eye—far too intense and determined. As if he knew something she didn't.

She hated that he'd checked if she'd be okay in the confined space before they'd left, mindful of her claustrophobia. At every point where she was doing her best to rebuild her walls of self-defence, he was just kicking them down again.

After about thirty minutes they landed in a small airfield and Kat saw a fleet of four-by-fours waiting. One for them, and the rest for the security team and entourage. Zafir led Kat to the first four-by-four, and when she was in he got into the driver's seat. They drove out of the airfield and into the desert, surrounded on all sides by nothing but sand and massive dunes.

Kat was surprised to feel a sense of liberation—as if there was nothing but this in the world. She looked at Zafir's proud profile and the inevitable stubble shadowing his jaw. She wanted to reach out and touch it but she kept her hands to herself.

'How do you know where to go?'

Zafir looked up to where the sun was lowering in the sky. 'The position of the sun tells me where to go...and this...' He tapped at a navigation dial on the dashboard. He glanced at her. 'I know this place like the back of my hand. I used to come here a lot as a teenager.'

Kat turned to face him more, curious. 'What did you do out here?'

Zafir looked away and shrugged. 'Dune racing with my bodyguards. Meeting the nomads and hearing their stories. Learning how to fight and shoot. Training my peregrine falcon.'

Kat didn't say it, but she thought it: he'd obviously done all that alone. Her heart ached in spite of her best efforts.

Gradually she could make out a shape in the distance. She squinted, wondering if she was hallucinating, but it got bigger and bigger until she could see that it was green and lush. Trees... A circle of tall palm trees... An oasis!

She'd been to oases before, for fashion shoots, but they had invariably been close to cities. Not like this, in the middle of an ocean of sand, with nothing as far as the eye could see except sky.

When they stopped she got out of the four-by-four, shading her eyes against the setting sun that was burnishing everything red and gold. She stepped forward to join Zafir, who was rounding the bonnet, and stumbled in the sand, her leg momentarily stuck in the soft surface. Before she could take another step Zafir had caught her and swung her up into his arms.

Kat hated how breathless it made her when Zafir lifted her into his arms, and she huffed against his shoulder. 'I hate this aspect of my disability—that I can't just walk where I used to and that I'm so portable.'

Zafir snorted inelegantly. '*Disability?* I've never met anyone more able in my life!'

Kat's chest swelled, and she hated him at that moment for making it so hard to resist him or to stay cool towards him. She felt hot all over now, and it had nothing to do with the temperature of the desert and everything to do with that inner fire Zafir stoked so effortlessly.

The oasis was indeed ringed with palm trees, and when they stepped through the perimeter Kat gasped. Zafir let her stand, as the terrain here was more solid, and she looked around, drinking in the sight of the lush green idyll.

The oasis was carved out of a natural gorge that held a pool of crystal-clear water. There was a small waterfall down at the one end, sending up a spray of white foam. It was breathtaking.

There was one tent set apart from all the others, with a tented domed roof and lanterns outside, already lit. Zafir led her to this tent, and Kat's heart was thumping unevenly.

He had brought her here to seduce her.

How could she resist him in this place of pure fantasy?

Maybe you don't have to, whispered a wicked voice that she tried to quash.

When they got inside the tent a few more of Kat's defences crumbled. The interior was lit only by candles, and it was a sumptuous decadent fantasy, straight out of an Arabian fairy tale. An X-rated fairy tale. Because what dominated the lush scene was an enormous bed, on top of which lay jewel-coloured cushions and satin bedding. Or maybe the bed was all she saw because she couldn't stop thinking about sex with Zafir again.

One last time.

She somehow managed to tear her gaze from the bed and looked at Zafir. He stood near the entrance, watching her with that intent gaze.

Even though she suspected she already knew the answer she asked, 'Where are you sleeping?'

Zafir even allowed his mouth to tip up minutely, as if she merely amused him. 'In here—with you.'

He moved into the tent. Kat panicked even as her insides quivered with anticipation. If he touched her—which she yearned for as much as she feared—he'd surely guess how far she'd fallen for him all over again.

She put up a hand, seizing on *anything* to try and remind Zafir that she wasn't worth pursuing. She blurted out the first thing she could think of. 'You've accused me of having no ability to manage money and you're right!'

Zafir shook his head. 'Kat, we're not here to discuss your credit rating.'

She ploughed on, determined to try and make him turn away in disgust. 'The money you've given me upfront for this job? It's gone. Already.'

She waited with bated breath, but Zafir just kept coming closer and said easily, 'It's none of my business what you do with your money, Kat. But as a matter of interest what did you spend it on?'

Kat was deflated. She wished she could brandish some gaudy bauble under Zafir's nose, but of course she couldn't—and she also couldn't lie.

She avoided his eye. 'I gave it to the rehabilitation centre where I went after my accident because they're in trouble. And some to Julie, because she supported me.'

Zafir's feet came into her line of vision. He put a finger under her chin, tipping her face up. There was an enigmatic look on his face.

'I know, Kat.'

Her eyes widened with shock. 'How did you know?'

'Because whenever such a large sum of money is wired to another account the bank checks to make sure it's a genuine transaction. My accountants had to verify it. If you'd told me your intentions I could have given it directly to them…'

Kat couldn't escape his gaze and she shifted uncomfortably. 'I hadn't told you yet…about my leg.'

She pulled her chin free and stepped back a few paces, sensing the walls of the tent closing in around her—but not in a scary way. It was in a way that made her blood leap with illicit excitement. Still she resisted, though.

She wrapped her arms around herself. 'That's why I agreed to the job, Zafir, because I realised I could use the money for good. I wasn't looking for an affair—or an easy payday.'

His mouth tipped up wryly. 'I think you've made that clear.'

He came towards her again, as if determined not to give her any space, and for a moment Kat might have believed that they'd slipped through time to another age, where he was a medieval warrior king and there was nothing beyond this place but untamed lands and fierce desires.

He put his hands on her arms.

Far too weakly, Kat said, 'Zafir, *no.*'

His eyes were silver in the flickering candlelight. 'Kat, *yes.* All that matters is this moment. Here and now.'

His words impacted on her like little bombs, blasting the last of her shaky defences.

He pulled her so close that she could feel his chest moving against hers, and the blunt thrust of his burgeoning arousal. Then he cupped her face with his hands, tipping it up to his, and as his mouth covered hers Kat stayed tense, even though she knew it was futile. She wanted this as much as he did.

She was fooling herself if she thought that denying herself this would make things easier in the end... Or at least that's how she justified it to herself as she found herself softening, tipping over the edge of resistance, responding to Zafir's expert touch and kisses, letting his strength hold her up because hers was gone...

CHAPTER NINE

HOURS LATER, WHEN the oasis was bathed in silvery moonlight, and after they had gorged themselves on a succulent feast and then made love again, Kat was curled into Zafir's side, one arm across his chest, her hand idly tracing patterns on his skin. He felt sated, languid, and at peace.

Peace?

When that registered, a prickle of panic skated over his skin. He wasn't looking for peace. He had peace—*didn't he?* He was just looking for an end to this insatiable hunger he felt.

So why did you bring her here to this place? asked a snide voice.

To seduce her ruthlessly and get her to admit she still wanted him. That was why. And Zafir had felt ruthless as he'd noted Kat's attempts to ward him off. The fact that she'd done it by trying to remind him of the accusations he'd thrown at her before had impacted on him in a place he didn't like to acknowledge.

He'd wanted to stop her saying those things, stop reminding him of how wrong he'd been about her...

Kat moved beside him then, coming up on one elbow. He looked at her and his chest tightened. She was sexily dishevelled and still flushed. His hunger was like a sharp spike, clawing at his insides all over again.

She looked at him, and he saw how her eyes had turned more green than amber and she seemed concerned. A sense of desperation joined his panic. Everything in him resisted letting her see the pit of emotions he couldn't analyse in his gut. And so, in a crude reflex to avoid hearing what she was thinking, he moved, gently disentangling himself from her to sit up and reach for a robe.

'Where are you going?'

Her voice was husky, and even that had an effect on him. Zafir gritted his jaw.

He handed her another, smaller robe and watched as she sat up and pulled it on. 'I want to show you something.'

She came to the edge of the bed and started to reach for her prosthesis, but Zafir lifted her into his arms, saying gruffly, 'You don't need it.'

'Zafir, I *do* need it,' she said, her breath warming his neck. 'I don't want to get too used to this—it'll make me lazy.'

There was something in her voice—an edge that made Zafir's jaw clench even tighter. Especially when he thought of any other faceless man lifting her into his arms. But he was already walking out through the tent opening and across the oasis.

Kat curled into him and hissed, 'Someone will see us.'

'No, they won't. We're totally private.'

He walked until they reached the edge of the large pool, its surface rippling and glistening under the moonlight. The waterfall fell nearby—a muted roar. Zafir put Kat down on her good leg and held her steady as he let his robe drop. Then he pulled hers off so they were both naked.

He lifted her again, and stepped into the pool. Kat clung on and squeaked as Zafir lowered them both into warm, silky water. He held her until they were deep enough to float, feeling her nipples pebble into hard points against his chest, which almost undid him.

And then he asked, 'Okay?'

She nodded.

Zafir let her go and Kat swam a couple of metres

through the satin water before flipping onto her back, her wet breasts gleaming enticingly above the waterline in the silver light.

Zafir's body was so hard it ached, and he swam towards her like a magnet drawn to true north. He couldn't help smiling when he saw the grin on her face, and the way her hair was spread out around her like skeins of silk.

'You like this?'

She flipped over again, treading water. 'Swimming was my favourite part of rehab… For a moment I could almost forget what had happened, pretend I was whole again…'

Moved by something that scared him with its intensity, Zafir caught her under the arms and pulled her into him, so their bodies were touching. 'You *are* whole, Kat.'

Her eyes were huge and unreadable in the darkness, but even though Zafir couldn't analyse what was in their depths it didn't make him feel any less exposed. He knew now that he'd crossed an emotional line that he'd never wanted to cross with anyone, and he was afraid there was no way back.

'I feel whole when I'm with you.'

Kat immediately bit her lip, as if regretting what she'd just said.

The water lapped around them and Zafir gave in to the carnal dictates of his body with an eagerness that spoke of his desire not to think about emotions. He pulled her close, catching her thighs and wrapping them around his hips.

She reached down a hand and curled it around his erection, making him suck in a breath and see stars. *Witch.*

'Make love to me, Zafir…' she breathed.

He needed no further urging. He walked in the water until Kat could rest her back against the soft grassy bank. She arched towards him, offering herself. It was all Zafir

could do not to tremble in the face of such sheer feminine power as he smoothed a hand down over her breasts
and belly.

Catching her around her waist, he drew her closer so
that his erection nudged against where she was slick and
hot. He stroked himself against her body, teasing them
both unmercifully until she was begging… Only then did
he plant his legs wide and hold her steady as he thrust up
into her body, making everything explode around them
and finally, mercifully, dulling the tangled voices in his
head and soothing the ache in his chest.

At least for now.

Early the following morning Kat tried not to be so aware
of Zafir watching her from a slight distance as one of the
senior nomads instructed her patiently on how to let the
peregrine falcon fly from where it was perched on her
arm, protected by a heavy glove.

Her eyes were as wide as saucers as she listened, and
she tentatively stroked the belly of the majestic bird. She
was terrified of this beautiful creature, with its huge tal-
ons, sharp beak and beady eyes, but trying not to show it.

She lifted her arm to let the bird go free, as she'd
been instructed, and it flew up into the air before landing on a nearby stand. The old man with the turban on
his head, the wrinkled face and kind eyes, put some food
on Kat's glove and the bird swooped back to land on her
hand again.

She felt a ridiculous sense of triumph, even though
she knew the bird had been trained for years to do exactly this. She couldn't stop smiling, and looked at Zafir.

The smile slid from her face when she saw his expression. He looked as if someone had punched him in the
gut. He was pale, and staring at her so intently that she

instinctively moved towards him, forgetting about the bird until it moved.

She stopped. The nomad took the bird off her glove then, enticing it to hop back onto his own arm, and when Kat looked at Zafir again it was as if she'd imagined it— now he looked completely fine... Well, except for the intense way he was looking at her.

Memories of their X-rated swim in the pool rushed back, and she was glad of the long traditional kaftan she wore that would hopefully hide the effect Zafir had on her body from these strangers who had appeared to pay homage to their King.

He came towards her, his expression inscrutable. 'It's time to leave. We have a busy day ahead of the function this evening.'

Kat forgot about his enigmatic look as she realised that this was the last function and then she'd be free to go. She nodded quickly and avoided Zafir's eye as took off the glove, handing it back to the nomad with a smile that disguised her sorrow that she'd never see this place again.

Sitting in the back of Zafir's car on their way to the palace, an hour later, Kat was trying not to feel needy. She had to keep reminding herself that their night at the oasis hadn't really meant anything other than a lavish attempt on Zafir's part to prove that he could still seduce her.

And he had.

It was all a game to him. A battle of wills. She had told him she wouldn't sleep with him again, and naturally he had done his utmost to prove her wrong.

Self-disgust curled through her that she'd been so easy. And yet could she regret the intensity of their lovemaking in that idyllic fantastical place, where it had felt as if they were the only two people on the planet? Or the magic of that pool at midnight?

No. Already she wanted to hug those memories to her, like a miser protecting her gold. And Zafir hadn't made any great attempt to engage her in conversation since they'd left, so it couldn't be any clearer really...

She was so distracted with her thoughts that it took a second before she heard Zafir calling her name. She turned her head and looked at him, steeling herself. He was holding out his palm tablet and he looked grim.

'There's something you should see.'

It took her a second to absorb the headline.

The Real Reason Kat Winters Disappeared!

She scanned the piece with a growing sense of panic mixed with terror. Apparently 'a source' close to Kat had told the papers all about her accident, and the subsequent amputation and rehabilitation, with some added salacious details about how she'd wanted to hide away from the world because she was so ashamed of what had happened to her.

Anger flooded her veins...

She looked at Zafir, handing back the tablet as if it was poison. 'I was never ashamed—why would someone say that? I was hurt and in pain, struggling to come to terms with a new reality—'

Kat stopped abruptly, realising how close to full-on panic she was. She'd always dreaded this scenario—the story being leaked—and she realised now that she'd always hoped—naively, obviously—that she would be able to control the story before it came out.

The last thing she had ever wanted was for other people who were in a similar situation to feel she was ashamed to be one of them. She *was* one of them. They had helped her to get through it.

Zafir looked angry. 'Do you know who might have leaked it? Your agent?'

Kat drew back. 'No, Julie is my best friend—she wouldn't do something like this.'

Zafir made some remark under his breath about people and money, and Kat said, 'Give me your phone and I'll call her now.'

He handed over his phone and she made the call. Relief flooded her when Julie sounded as upset as she was, and she hated Zafir for infecting her with his cynicism for a moment, making her doubt her friend's loyalty.

When she'd handed back the phone she said, 'Julie thinks it was someone at the hospital I was taken to directly after the accident. That they saw the new pictures of me and put two and two together.' She grimaced. 'When you lose a leg you tend to be a memorable patient—even if I was using another name and was hardly recognisable at the time.'

Zafir still looked livid. Immediately she thought of something, and her belly sank. 'I'm sorry.'

He frowned. 'What do you have to be sorry about?'

Kat swallowed. 'No doubt the last thing you want is for this news to come out now—before the final event and the last showing of the diamond. It's bound to draw negative press.'

There was a sharp rap on Zafir's window, but he ignored it. They'd arrived back at the palace.

He turned to face Kat. 'There will be no negativity. The diamond will become even more famous when your story of courage is revealed. But I won't force you to go out there this evening if you feel it's asking too much of you. You're the one who will be put under more scrutiny than ever now.'

Kat felt alternately comforted by Zafir's words and bereft. He sounded as if he didn't care what she did either way.

She shrugged minutely. 'It's not as if I've got anything

more to hide than this. It was going to come out sooner or later. If you're not afraid of it impacting the campaign negatively, then of course I'll go out there this evening.'

Even as she said that though, she felt flutters of trepidation—but she also had to acknowledge a fledgling sense of liberation, as if a weight was being lifted off her shoulders.

Zafir looked at her enigmatically before saying, 'Very well—as you wish.'

As if he'd sent a psychic message to someone, his door was opened by a waiting attendant and he got out. The driver opened her door, and when she emerged into the sunlight Rahul was walking over to her, looking pale.

'Miss Winters, I am so sorry. I had no idea about… If I'd known…'

He looked so miserable in his inarticulacy that Kat touched his arm. 'Rahul, you don't need to apologise. You did nothing wrong. And no one knew.'

Rahul walked back to Zafir, who broke away from his attendants to come over to where she was standing. The expression on his face reminded her of the enigmatic way he'd looked at her in the desert before they'd left. It was profoundly irritating that she couldn't read it.

Zafir gestured with a hand. 'Jasmine is waiting to go through your wardrobe and she'll help you choose an outfit for this evening.'

Kat looked to where he was indicating, to see Jasmine and the golf buggy nearby.

Zafir stepped back. 'I'll come to your rooms for you at six.'

Kat wanted to cling to his robes and demand of him, *Where are we now? What did last night mean?*

She watched him walk away and chastised herself. Last night had just been a last slaking of lust. No doubt now that the end was in sight Zafir was already casting his mind ahead to the future and lining up suitable candidates to be his Queen.

Kat shoved down the rise of a very uncharacteristic bitterness and forced a smile as she greeted a serious-looking Jasmine, who was unusually quiet on their way back to the suite. Kat surmised that the news had obviously spread like wildfire.

When they got to her rooms Jasmine looked at Kat with big eyes and asked hesitantly, 'Is it really true, Miss Winters?'

Kat took a deep breath and nodded. Then she sat down and pulled up her kaftan, showing the young girl her leg.

Jasmine sank down at Kat's feet. When she looked up at Kat her eyes were brimming over with tears, and for the first time since her accident Kat felt a sense of liberation bubble up inside her as she reached out and wiped Jasmine's tears.

'It's not that bad, really,' she said with a wry smile. 'Here, let me show you...'

That evening, Kat paced back and forth unevenly across her suite. In spite of her bravado earlier, her nerves were intensifying with every moment at the thought that when she was presented tonight everyone would *know*.

Jasmine melted away discreetly when Zafir appeared at the entrance to her main reception room. Kat stopped pacing and looked at him, her nerves dissolving for a moment as she took him in, resplendent in cream and gold robes, every inch the powerful and impressive King of his country.

His grey eyes raked her up and down. 'You look beautiful.'

Kat felt ridiculously shy and half shrugged. 'Jasmine liked this dress the best.'

It was a long traditional Jandori kaftan, with deceptively simple flowing lines and a V-neck that showed off the diamond she was already wearing. Noor had delivered it shortly before. Over the kaftan she wore a long sleeveless robe inlaid with gold embroidery.

She noticed then that she and Zafir were almost matching, as her kaftan was a similar colour to his. For a second her rogue imagination wondered if this was close to what the bride of Zafir would wear on her wedding day.

It took her a second to realise that Zafir had spoken and she hadn't even heard him. Mortified, she said, 'I'm sorry, what did you say?'

She noticed then that he appeared less than his usual composed self.

He ran a hand through his hair and looked at her. 'There's something I need to tell you. I was going to wait until later, but...'

Kat went cold inside. 'What is it?'

He was grim. 'It's something I discovered this afternoon—a couple of things, actually.'

Kat wasn't sure why, but she felt she needed to sit down on a nearby chair. 'What things?'

Zafir started to pace back and forth, exactly where Kat had just been. He stopped and said abruptly, 'My father was the one who leaked those pictures and the story of your background to the press.'

Kat went very still. Zafir's father's cold features came back into her mind's eye. She stood up again. 'I know he didn't approve of me... But how...? Where did he find the pictures?'

Zafir was pacing again, energy crackling around him like a forcefield. 'He hired investigators to look into your past. They found the photographer and paid him a lot of money to hand over some of the photos.' He stopped again and looked stricken. 'I'm sorry, Kat. I had no idea... If I'd known...'

Kat walked blindly over to another chair, and clutched the back of it. Faintly, she said, 'You couldn't have known.'

She looked at Zafir and tried to push down the feeling of betrayal, even though it hadn't had anything to do with him. She'd known his parents hadn't liked her, but to go that far was hurtful in the extreme.

'It's not relevant now, anyway. What's done is done... your father is dead.'

'There's something else too.'

Kat's hand tightened on the chair. She regretted standing up. 'What?'

'I tracked down the photographer—or rather my team did. That's how I found out about my father's involvement.'

He paced again and then stopped. He'd never reminded Kat more of a caged animal than right now.

His face was all stark lines and hard jaw. 'You should have told me everything, Kat. You should have told me that the photographer was blackmailing you.'

She blanched. 'He told you...?'

Zafir nodded. 'I wanted to make sure that he had no more images of you, and I made sure that the ones that did get leaked to the press were destroyed. They'll never surface again. He was still very bitter about having had his payday taken away from him when the pictures were leaked and published. You could have told me, Kat,' Zafir said now, with an almost bewildered tone in his voice. 'Was I such an ogre?'

Her weak heart clenched. 'No, of course not. I didn't tell you because I was ashamed. You weren't an ogre, but you were a Crown Prince, Zafir. You didn't suffer fools lightly. And I felt like a fool for allowing myself to get into that situation. So many times I wanted to tell you what had happened, but at the last second I couldn't… I never wanted you to find out. Not even now.'

Zafir's jaw clenched. 'No, you would have preferred to go into marriage bringing your baggage with you— bleeding us *both* dry.'

Kat's blood drained south. This was proof, if she'd ever needed it, that nothing had changed between them. She was still in disgrace.

Kat lifted her chin and said, as coolly as she could, belying her profound hurt, 'That would never have been my intention, Zafir.'

Zafir cursed and ran a hand through his hair again. 'I'm sorry… You didn't deserve that…'

Kat refused to let his apology impact on her and forced herself to say, 'Even if you'd known the truth it wouldn't have changed anything. I still would have been deemed unsuitable. I broke your trust, Zafir. I know that.'

His mouth tightened into a grim line. The pain cut deeper when he didn't contradict her. As she watched she could see him retreat somewhere, become stiff, expressionless.

'You don't need to go out there this evening if you don't want to, Kat. I know it must terrify you, in spite of what you said earlier. I hired you and put you in front of the world's media again, and it was through your involvement with me that you had to endure your career and reputation being ruined in the first place. It's my fault you're under this renewed scrutiny.'

He sounded like a stranger. A civil stranger. Not the man who had taken her into a magical pool last night and made love to her as if his life depended on it. But then she hardly needed reminding of where this had been headed all along.

Kat stepped out from behind the chair. She said, 'No.

I committed to doing a job and I'm not going to renege on that.'

Just then there was a knock on the door, and Rahul's voice saying, 'Sire, they're ready for you and Miss Winters.'

Zafir looked at Kat. His insides felt as if they were being corroded by acid. He felt tainted by his father's machinations.

He was still reeling from the revelations of the previous few hours, but now he felt something similar to the way he'd felt much earlier that day, when he'd watched Kat with that bird of prey on her arm, clearly scared but determined not to show it. *Proud.* She'd looked regal, and it had impacted on him like a punch to his gut.

She stepped forward now, and she was a vision in gold with the red diamond glowing at her throat.

He said, 'Are you sure, Kat? You really don't have to do it if you don't want to. I've asked enough of you.'

An inner voice mocked him. *You asked for nothing less than her unconditional surrender and you got it.*

'I'm sure.'

And then she walked to the door, straight-backed and proud. Zafir battled an almost feral urge to grab her and shut the door—as if he knew that as soon as she walked through it she would be lost to him in a way he'd never really appreciated before.

But he couldn't stop her.

He followed her out to the corridor, where Noor and Rahul were waiting. Kat was staring straight ahead and he took her arm, leading her towards the ceremonial room. She didn't resist his touch but he could feel her tension.

Just before the doors to the ceremonial room opened Zafir gripped her arm hard and willed her to look at him.

After a few seconds she did—with clear reluctance. He couldn't read anything in those golden eyes. Could see nothing but a distance he'd never seen before.

His bleakness intensified. For the first time in his life he was floundering. The big doors were slowly opening, and with a heavy weight in his chest he said, 'I'm sorry, Kat.'

'I'm sorry, Kat.'

Zafir's words reverberated in Kat's head as she wound her way through the crowd, with Noor hovering protectively at her side. She'd smiled so much she thought she'd never be able to crack a smile again, even while her heart was shattering.

When Zafir had looked at her outside the door and said those words Kat had known then that it was over. It couldn't have been clearer.

Their past had been resurrected in spectacular fashion and now Zafir knew Kat's story—warts and all. Clearly he was taking responsibility for his father's actions and felt guilty, but Kat couldn't let him own all that guilt.

She should have told him everything. She should've have trusted that he wouldn't reject her... And even if he had—well, then she might possibly have saved herself the negative press fallout because he might have pursued the photographer earlier to protect his reputation as much as hers.

But she'd been living in a dream...fantasising that Zafir loved her and that she would make a great Queen... until it had all shattered. The truth was that their bond hadn't been strong enough to hold them together.

Then...or now.

For a moment the crowd seemed to thin around her and she sucked in a breath, relaxing her facial muscles for the first time in hours. Zafir was on the opposite side of the room, and Kat saw that for once there were no body-guards close by. She had the crazy sensation that she wanted to run from the room, taking the diamond with her—as if it was all she had left to bind her to Zafir, and once it was taken off at the end of the evening she'd disappear completely and he wouldn't even notice she'd gone.

Kat looked over to where Zafir was and at that moment, as if feeling the weight of her gaze on him, he turned his head and his gaze zeroed in on her immediately. Not wanting him to read her far too expressive face, Kat turned and took advantage of the lull to escape to a quieter part of the room.

She saw open French doors nearby, and was almost there when she bumped into someone. She started to apologise, but the words died on her tongue as she recognised who it was. Zafir's mother. And suddenly everything she was feeling coalesced into a very familiar sense of inadequacy. The sense of déjà vu was overwhelming.

Zafir's mother was a tall and regal woman, with cold dark eyes and a strong-boned handsome face. Her head was veiled and she wore an elaborate royal blue kaftan. Kat felt ridiculously ill-prepared, and found herself doing what she'd done the first time—bending in an awkward curtsey, with the vague idea that all royalty had to be curtsied to. Not that she'd ever done that to Zafir, of course.

When she stood again the older woman was managing to look down her nose at Kat, even though she was about the same height.

In perfect English she said, 'I hadn't expected to see you here again.'

Kat tried to ignore the dart of hurt at the thought of what this woman's husband, and possibly she too, had done. Kat didn't need to be reminded that she was not of this world and never would be. 'Your son was kind enough to offer me a job opportunity...'

To be in his bed.

Kat didn't say it.

But as if reading her mind, the older woman made a rude sound. 'If you want to call it that.' And then she said, 'Is it true what they're saying? You lost your leg?'

'Yes.' Kat stood tall. 'My left leg—below the knee.'

Someone who looked like a personal maid came forward then, and whispered something in Zafir's mother's ear.

When the maid melted away again she gave Kat a glacial once over and said, 'If you'll excuse me, please?' And then she swept off with a veritable retinue of people in her wake.

Kat was left reeling a little at the woman's ill manners. And then, remembering that she'd wanted to escape Zafir, she quickly walked outside to a blissfully deserted terrace. She went over to the wall overlooking Jahor and sucked in some air. Thousands of lights lit up the city, making it look even more exotic than usual.

For a moment she stood tthere, soaking in the view, because as of tomorrow morning when her flight took off she wouldn't ever see it again.

Her peace was shattered, though, when a group of laughing, chattering people came out to the terrace. Kat tensed and turned around warily, ready to project her model persona again.

When the group of about five men and six women saw who it was they stopped, before smiling and moving forward towards Kat, evidently excited that they had a private audience with her.

Kat smiled, but the wall was at her back and the people were pressing closer. They weren't speaking English and they were all talking at once, crowding around her to see the diamond.

Kat tried to look around them, to see if she could see

Noor or another bodyguard, but there was no sign of anyone from the security team and she cursed herself for fleeing.

Someone reached out to touch the diamond and Kat started to panic, her breath growing choppy. They were closing in on her and she had nowhere to go. She couldn't see past them, and one of the women had very strong perfume, which made it even harder to breathe.

Someone caught at Kat's arm then, in a surprisingly firm grip which only intensified her panic and growing sense of claustrophobia. She pulled her arm free and stepped to the side in a bid to escape—and found she was stepping into nothing as she discovered too late that there must have been a step she hadn't noticed.

She couldn't stop herself falling helplessly, and all she heard at the last minute was a familiar voice saying, 'Kat!'

She had flashes of being held in Zafir's arms as he strode through the crowd, saying angrily, 'Where the hell were you, Noor? Those people were all over her...'

Kat tried desperately to speak, to say something, but her tongue wouldn't work and then everything faded out.

CHAPTER TEN

A COUPLE OF HOURS later Zafir was still experiencing waves of relief reverberating through his system. Kat had apparently not suffered any major injury apart from a bump to her head when she'd tumbled down those steps that of course she wouldn't have seen with that thick crowd of people pressing around her.

His hands instinctively clenched tighter when he recalled seeing her lying there, so pale and unmoving, the crowd just gaping at her ineffectually.

She'd come round soon after arriving at the hospital, and her first concern had been to tell him that it hadn't been the security team's fault—she'd slipped away from them. Her instinct to protect their incompetence had only increased his ire at them. And made him realise how much he'd underestimated Kat's innate loyalty.

Zafir was standing on the other side of a door with a window in it, looking at Kat, who was sitting on a bed dressed in a hospital gown. She'd had an MRI scan and they were just waiting to hear the results. Even in an unflattering hospital gown she took his breath away.

She wasn't wearing her prosthesis and there was a wheelchair nearby. But she wasn't alone—there was a little girl sitting beside her aged about nine or ten. The little girl was also a below-the-knee amputee.

He couldn't hear what they were saying, but the little girl was looking at Kat with wide eyes. And then suddenly a hesitant smile bloomed across her pretty face. She'd had tear-stained cheeks when a doctor had brought her to see Kat a short while before.

The little girl's doctor came alongside Zafir now, and

said in a low, awestruck voice, 'Thank you for agreeing to let Amira visit with Miss Winters.'

Zafir desisted from saying that as soon as he'd told Kat about the young girl she'd insisted on him letting her come to visit.

The doctor continued, 'Amira lost her leg due to meningitis. She hasn't spoken a word in months to anyone—not even her family. But now look at her...' The doctor shook his head. 'Miss Winters is a remarkable woman.'

Zafir curbed his irritation that the doctor felt the need to point out to him what he already knew. He was on edge and unsettled.

The doctor pushed open the door and went in to get Amira. She hopped off the bed and got into her wheelchair and waved goodbye to Kat.

Zafir got down on his haunches as she was being wheeled out of the room and her eyes grew as round as they'd been when she'd seen and recognised him the first time.

He held out his hand and she put her much smaller one into his. Something completely alien inside him shifted and expanded.

'Hello, Amira. I believe you've been a very brave young lady?'

She nodded soberly, her huge brown eyes wide with an awe that Zafir was sure wasn't solely for him. Then she said something to him in their own language with an endearing lisp and that alien sensation inside him expanded even more, stopping his breath for a second.

He had to stand to let the doctor wheel her out, and he heard Kat ask, 'What is it? You look as if you've seen a ghost. What did she say to you?'

He turned to Kat, and for the first time in his life he knew that he was being a coward when he said, 'Nothing important.' He went over to her. 'How are you feeling?'

Kat grimaced and put her hand up to where she'd hit her head. 'I think I'll have a headache for about a week, but other than that I'm fine.' She looked at him. 'I didn't mean to disrupt the evening so dramatically.'

Zafir shook his head, feeling anger rise again. 'Those people were practically pushing you through the wall.'

Kat tried not to let herself read anything into Zafir's concern—the way he'd stayed by her side from the moment he'd brought her to the hospital. She tried again, saying, 'You really don't have to stay…'

He shook his head and folded his arms. 'I'm not moving.'

Just then the kind doctor arrived, smiling. He closed the door behind him and came over, saying, 'Good news—nothing untoward appeared on the scan. I'm afraid you'll just have a nasty bump for a couple of weeks, but it should go down in time.'

Zafir looked at the doctor. 'You're sure she's okay?'

'Yes. I can let her go home as long as someone keeps an eye on her overnight for signs of concussion.'

Zafir said immediately, 'I'll make sure she's watched tonight.'

Jasmine arrived then, with some clothes for Kat, and helped her to put on her prosthetic limb and get dressed once the men had stepped outside.

The diamond had been dispatched shortly after Kat had arrived at the hospital—taken by a very meek-looking security guard.

Kat was wheeled out of the hospital in a wheelchair, as per regulations, but once outside she stood up, unsteady for a moment.

Zafir took her arm, leading her over to where his car was waiting.

When they were moving through the narrow streets

towards the palace Kat said as lightly as she could, 'I should still be able to make my flight tomorrow morning.'

Zafir looked at her, and the expression on his face brooked no argument. 'I've postponed it, Kat. You need a day to recover. At least.'

Kat's heart thumped at the thought of another day and night here, knowing that Zafir was just biding his time till she was gone. 'But I'm fine.'

He shook his head, and something sparked in his eyes. 'Is one more day really too much, Kat? You want to leave that badly?'

She was shocked. 'No... I love it here.'

But I also love you, and one more minute than necessary is torture.

But of course she didn't say that.

She swallowed her emotion and said, 'It's fine. I'll stay.'

She turned her head to look out of the window. After their explosive conversation before the event, and Zafir's 'I'm sorry,' Kat knew there was nothing more for them to say to each other. The past had been laid to rest. Now she would just have to suck up the fact that Zafir was acting out of a sense of responsibility. And possibly still that misplaced guilt. No doubt he wanted her continued presence here as little as she did.

When they arrived back at the palace Jasmine was waiting for them, and also Rahul, both looking worried. Zafir gave instructions to Jasmine in his own language and she whisked Kat back to her suite, shooting her concerned glances.

When Kat had had a bath and was re-emerging from the bathroom, feeling a little more human again without half a ton of make-up on her face, Jasmine was still there and looking determined.

Before Kat could say anything the younger woman

said, 'I'm not leaving. The King has told me someone needs to watch over you tonight in case of concussion.'

Kat knew that arguing would be futile. 'Very well…'

She got into bed as Jasmine curled up on a large love seat nearby, her pretty face illuminated by the screen of her palm tablet. Kat felt a surge of gratitude at the thought of how much the girl had already come to mean to her.

Before she tried to go to sleep she said, 'Thank you, Jasmine.'

The girl looked up and smiled. 'You're welcome, Miss Winters. Now, get some rest.'

Kat thought she'd toss and turn for a while, but she actually slipped into sleep almost immediately.

When she woke some time later the room was in darkness and her throat was dry. She struggled to sit up in the bed, and immediately saw movement in the corner—something big and dark. A scream stuck in Kat's throat for a second, before she realised with a hammering heart that it was Zafir looming over her in the moonlight.

'What is it?' he asked. 'Are you all right? Is your head hurting?'

'No, I'm just thirsty. Where's Jasmine?'

Zafir sat down on the edge of the bed and turned on a low light. Kat saw that stubble darkened his jaw and that his hair was mussed up as if he'd been running a hand through it.

He reached for some water and handed Kat the glass. She took a few gulps, hating how aware she was of Zafir's big body. Was it only a couple of days ago he'd been making love to her with such zealous passion? Now he couldn't be more distant.

He took the glass and put it back. His body was rigid with tension and something inside Kat broke. Clearly he couldn't stand to be near her any more.

She sank back under the covers. 'You don't need to watch me, Zafir. I'm fine.'

He reached over and turned off the light and said, 'I'm not going anywhere, Kat.'

And then he stood up and retreated back into the shadows.

When Kat woke up the next morning Jasmine was the first person she saw, and she wondered for a moment if she'd imagined Zafir being there during the night. She was too scared to ask.

Kat ate breakfast, and then took a shower and dressed. Jasmine helped her to put on her prosthetic leg—the girl was totally unfazed now by the whole thing.

She'd deliberately chosen from her own clothes, knowing that she'd be leaving all the other gorgeous garments behind. They belonged to a Kat who had lived a stolen dream for a short time.

After packing most of her things she looked up flights from Jahor to America, and saw that there was one late that night. On impulse she booked a seat, even though her flight home was meant to have been on Zafir's private plane.

She stood up then, determined to go and find Zafir and tell him she was leaving and not to let him persuade her otherwise.

Kat made her way slowly to where Zafir's office was located, absorbing the understated finery of the palace for the last time—its ancient murals and hidden inner courtyards covered in mosaics, and the peacocks strutting around loose and free, as if they owned the place.

When she got to the office she was surprised not to see Rahul outside, in his usual spot, but his cell phone sat on the table so presumably he wasn't far away. Then

Kat heard raised voices, and one familiar one sent icicles down her spine.

Zafir's mother.

Instinctively Kat wanted to turn away from that strident voice, but something kept her rooted to the spot, near the half-open door to Zafir's office.

'What are you going to do about Salim? Your brother is out of control, and meanwhile the country he is meant to be ruling—*my* homeland—is falling into chaos.'

Kat recognised the tension in Zafir's voice as he replied.

'I am not my brother's keeper, Mother, and maybe you should have thought of this a long time ago, when you proved how little we all really meant to you when Sara died. But if it's any consolation I'm hiring someone who is an expert in diplomatic relations to help oversee Salim's accession to the throne in Tabat.'

His mother sniffed and said ungraciously, 'That's something, at least.'

Kat's heart clenched for Zafir and his siblings, and then his mother changed tack.

'And what is *she* still doing here? Wasn't she meant to be gone this morning?'

Kat's heart stopped.

There seemed to be a year of silence before Zafir said coldly, 'I presume you're referring to Kat Winters?'

His mother made a rude sound. 'If you're thinking of making her your Queen again, then you've learnt nothing about being a King, Zafir. She is the most singularly unsuitable woman to be Queen of this country. There's her scandalous past to think of—not to mention the fact that she made a complete fool of herself last night and ruined the event!'

Kat somehow managed to take in some oxygen at that point. She whirled around and walked away as fast as she could—before she could hear Zafir assure his mother that of course he wouldn't be making Kat his Queen. She tried not to feel hurt at what Zafir's mother had said, but it was hard when it echoed her own deepest insecurities.

She didn't see Rahul until it was too late and they collided. Kat said sorry and kept going, terrified that he'd see how upset she was.

When she got back to her rooms she was glad to find them empty, and was relieved she'd gone ahead and booked that plane ticket. She continued packing, telling herself she'd go to the airport early. She would wait there.

'What are you doing?'

She whirled around at the deep and familiar voice, holding some trousers up to her chest. Zafir was inside her room, the door closed behind him. He was clean-shaven now, making Kat suspect again that she'd dreamt his presence during the night. He was the *King*! And she was now his inconvenient ex-mistress. Of course he hadn't been there.

She turned around again and forced her voice to sound cool. Unconcerned. 'I'm packing. I've booked a commercial flight home tonight, Zafir, there's no need for me to prolong my stay.'

He came over and took her arm, turning her to face him. 'You said you'd stay another day.'

She pulled free and let the trousers fall to the floor, stepping back. 'I'm fine. I don't need to stay—and you have stuff to do.' She cringed inwardly at *stuff*.

'I want to talk to you.'

Something illicit fluttered in Kat's belly. 'What is there to talk about? I think we've said everything that needs to be said.'

'Rahul told me he bumped into you outside my office just now… You obviously came to talk to me. Why did you leave?'

Kat glanced away. 'You were busy.'

'I suspected as much,' he breathed. 'How much did you hear of my conversation with my mother, Kat?'

She looked back at Zafir and pain scored her insides. She backed away further. He was too close. 'I heard enough,' she said painfully. 'I didn't stick around to hear you agree with her assessment that I'm entirely unsuitable.'

A flush stained Zafir's cheeks. 'Dammit, Kat, you are *not* unsuitable.' Then he stopped. 'You didn't hear what I said to her?'

You are not unsuitable.

She cursed her silly heart for leaping at that. Kat wanted to look anywhere but at him, but she couldn't look away. He was like the sun—blinding and devastating.

She lifted her chin. 'No. I told you. I'd heard enough.'

'So you didn't hear me tell her that I've no intention of letting you go anywhere?'

She just looked at Zafir, her brain moving sluggishly. A tangled mass of sensations roiled in her gut, but worst of all was a kernel of something that felt awfully like hope.

Kat refused to give in to it. 'Why would you want to keep me here? Our liaison is over.'

Zafir stepped closer to her, his eyes intense. 'Is it?'

Kat felt flustered. 'Well, of course it is. It was never going to last beyond this job, and you couldn't have made it more clear after our conversation yesterday that whatever was there is gone...' Kat was breathing jaggedly and tried to compose herself.

Zafir grimaced. 'When I found out about my father... Kat, it was a huge shock. It made me realise how badly I'd judged you...how badly I'd disrupted your life. But it hasn't changed how much I want you. Do you know how hard it was for me not to touch you last night?'

His words were like a punch in the gut. She breathed, 'So you *were* there...'

He frowned. 'Of course I was—who else would it have been?'

Kat shook her head and muttered, 'I thought it was a dream.'

She took another step back, putting her arms around herself. 'So...you're saying you still...' She trailed off.

Zafir nodded and his mouth compressed. 'I don't think I'll ever *not* want you, Kat.'

Something painful gripped her insides. 'So what are you suggesting, Zafir? Are you going to lock me in your harem and make a carnal visit when you feel the urge, while you marry your suitable bride and have a legion of heirs?'

'What are you talking about? There's no such thing as a harem here and there hasn't been for years.'

Mortified, because she was giving herself away spectacularly, she looked away, wishing she had something to hold on to. 'Forget it.'

Zafir came close and put a hand to her chin, forcing her to look at him. He had a fierce light in his eye. 'Do you really think that I would want to set you up as my mistress?'

She swallowed. 'I don't know what to think any more.'

Zafir shook his head. 'I don't want a mistress, Kat. I want a wife—a Queen.'

The pain was excruciating. She pulled away from Zafir and somehow managed to say, 'And that's what you deserve. I'm sure you'll choose the perfect Queen.'

Zafir folded his arms. His eyes were like laser beams now. 'I've already chosen her.'

Kat looked at him and felt a surge of jealousy at the thought of this mystery woman. 'Then how can you not let me go? I can't be here now—it's unconscionable.'

Zafir shook his head. 'It's very conscionable, actually, because I want you to be my Queen, Kat. And *that's* what I told my mother—before I told her to get out of my sight and that I wanted her gone from Jandor within a week. She's no longer welcome.'

Kat shook her head. Something was happening inside her…something was cracking open… But she couldn't let it. There was too much at stake, too much not yet said. Too much had happened in the past. There had been too much hurt.

'You wanted to make me your Queen before, so what's changed, Zafir? Is it the fact that the truth of my history is a little more palatable? Or is it because you feel guilty that your father interfered? It doesn't change the fact that I did keep things from you. I'm just as guilty for what happened.'

Zafir looked pale now. 'No, it's not because your history is more palatable, or because of the guilt I feel—which I don't think I'll ever *un*feel.' He said heavily, 'The truth is that I didn't fight hard enough for you before.'

'Because you didn't really want to marry me.'

Kat was trying desperately to get Zafir to admit that he didn't really mean what he said. Because if she believed him and he didn't…she'd never recover.

He looked at her for a long time. And even trapped under that intense gaze Kat couldn't help but be acutely aware of his powerfully lean body in dark trousers and a white shirt.

After a long moment he said, 'I can't deny that.'

She sucked in a painful breath. She hadn't actually expected to hear him agree with her, and it should have been a relief but it wasn't.

'But not because of why you're thinking, Kat.'

Kat's circling thoughts came to a halt.

'I was very careful to keep my feelings for you superficial, Kat. I had you on a pedestal as this perfect paragon of beauty and morality—a small-town girl who had worked hard to get where she was. A woman who was unbelievably innocent. I put you in a box and I didn't look any deeper. I know it sounds crazy, and contradictory, but by proposing to you and convincing myself it was for those shallow reasons, I was able to keep you with me while not admitting the depth of my emotions—the real reason I wanted to marry you. Because I loved you. You see, I told myself I'd never allow love to impact my life. I was so sure that I wouldn't ever succumb to such an emotion that I arrogantly denied to myself that I felt anything deeper than liking and respect for you.'

Kat wasn't sure she could speak now, even if she wanted to.

Zafir grimaced. 'When those headlines surfaced and I confronted you... I didn't really give you a chance to explain your side because on some cowardly level it was easier for me to break the engagement and tell you I didn't love you than to admit how I really felt. How could I? When I wouldn't even admit it to myself?'

Zafir stepped closer to Kat.

'I love you, Kat. I know that now, and I always did... I was just too scared to admit it before. Seeing how Salim was so destroyed after Sara's death, feeling that loss myself—it terrified me. I never wanted to love someone so much that it would send my life into a tailspin if something happened to them. And our parents hardly provided us with any kind of healthy example...'

He shook his head, his face paling.

'But when I saw you on the ground last night, lying so still, I realised then that it would be far worse if I'd never told you how I felt than if I'd tried to protect myself from the pain. Even if you don't love me.'

Kat couldn't breathe. She felt as if she was hanging

over a huge abyss by a thread. But as she looked at Zafir, into those slate-grey eyes, the light in them died and he took a step back.

Before she could reach out or say anything he said, 'There's something I've suspected for a while, but I've been too afraid to ask…'

'What?' she managed to croak out.

'The accident…it happened that night, didn't it? The night we fought.'

Kat felt the blood drain from her face, and Zafir's own face paled even more. She'd never seen him look so stricken.

'Kat…what did I do to you?'

He backed away even further, as if he couldn't bear to be near her. Everything in her rebelled at that. He'd told her he loved her. She had to believe. To trust.

She closed the distance between them and took his hands in hers. They felt cold. 'No,' she said, and then more firmly, when she saw his eyes so bleak, '*No*, Zafir. You do not get to do this. What happened that night was no one's fault. It could have just as easily been you. You don't get to take responsibility for an accident.'

She clung onto his hands, willing him to come back to her.

'I was an emotional coward too… As soon as I heard you say you didn't love me I ran—because I wasn't brave enough to fight for myself or for you.'

He shook his head, his face etched with pain. 'I have no right to ask you to stay now. I've brought nothing but destruction into your life.'

He wouldn't look at her, so Kat let one hand go and reached up to touch Zafir's face, smoothing the lines, the tension in his jaw. She turned his face until their eyes met and she said, 'Well, tough, because I'm not going anywhere—unless you didn't mean any of what you said?'

Fire flashed in his eyes and Kat breathed a sigh of relief.

'Of course I meant what I said.'

She took a deep breath. 'I love you too, Zafir. What I felt for you before was immature... I couldn't handle it. It was too much. I don't think either of us were ready to deal with the enormity of how we felt. It killed me to think you'd only valued me for my physical attributes. I felt worthless. I felt like no one had ever really loved me for me—not even my mother.'

Zafir reached out and cupped Kat's jaw. His eyes were suspiciously bright.

'I love all of you, Kat—every bit. I love the little girl who was pushed out in front of cameras and lights at far too young an age. I love the young teenager who struggled to protect her mother and who did something radical to keep her mother alive because she had no other choice. I love the young woman who didn't let her experiences make her bitter, but who clung on to something good in spite of being blackmailed by an arch manipulator... And I love the woman who overcame a massive life event to become even stronger and more proud. You have a huge life ahead of you, and you're going to be an inspiration to so many people.'

Zafir got down on one knee in front of Kat and she stopped breathing. He pulled a black box out of his pocket and looked ridiculously nervous. He opened it to reveal a square-shaped Art Deco ring, with a red stone surrounded by white diamonds.

'Is that...?' She couldn't even finish the question.

Zafir nodded, his eyes on her as he took the ring out of the box. 'It's part of the Heart of Jandor red diamond. My great-grandfather had it made for my great-grandmother out of an offcut of the original stone. It wasn't her engagement ring, but she wore it every day. I wanted to give you a different ring, Kat. To symbolise a fresh start… That is…if you'll have me?'

Kat's chest had swelled so much that her eyes stung. She felt as if she might float away, but Zafir was anchoring her to the ground, waiting for her answer.

At the last moment old insecurities surfaced. 'What if your mother is right, Zafir? I'm not cut out to be Queen… I'll let you down…'

Zafir stood up, looking fierce. 'You will make a great Queen, Kat. You're compassionate and passionate. You're intelligent and endlessly kind—and stronger than anyone else I know. Jasmine adores you and Rahul would die for you. When I saw you holding that falcon you humbled me with your innate grace. It was then that I knew I couldn't let you go. And then I found out about my father and I knew I had no right to ask anything more of you. Do you want to know what Amira said to me at the hospital?'

Kat nodded, feeling overwhelmed at everything he was saying, each word soothing the wounds of her soul.

'She said to me, "Your Queen is beautiful," and she was right. You are beautiful—inside and out. My mother was born and bred to be Queen and she spread nothing but pain and misery… You are more of a Queen than she could ever be.'

Kat eventually held out her hand and said in a choked voice, 'Then, yes, I'll be your Queen. I love you, Zafir.'

He grew blurry in her vision as he put the ring on her finger, and then she was being lifted into his arms and taken over to the bed.

He laid her down and said fervently, 'I need you, Kat, so much…'

She put her arms around him and arched into his body. 'I'll never walk away from you again,' she said emotionally. 'You're my King and my home, Zafir.'

Six months later

Kat stood behind the curtain with Amira's hand tightly clasped in hers. They looked at each other and Kat winked. Amira smiled widely. In the last few months the little girl had been transformed into her normal gregarious self again, with a new prosthetic leg.

A woman stepped forward and whispered, 'Your Majesty, whenever you're ready...'

Kat wasn't sure she'd ever get used to being called *Your Majesty*, but slowly, with each day, it was sinking in that she was a Queen.

She looked at Amira to make sure she was ready, and then took a breath, pushing the curtain aside and stepping forward.

Lights illuminated their path down the long catwalk. They were both dressed in the latest designs from Jandor's best designers for Jahor's inaugural fashion week, with all proceeds from the show going to the global amputee fund that Kat and Zafir had set up in recent months. The fund gave money to all aspects of limb loss, including research into prosthetic limbs.

Kat had been persuaded out of retirement by Julie, but was only agreeing to modelling work that didn't conflict with her role as Queen of Jandor, and work that didn't disguise her limb—and, again, all proceeds were going to charity. She was determined to make her face and her body work for the best causes this time, and she'd never felt more fulfilled or happier.

But then, her work wasn't the most important thing in her life. Not by a long shot.

As they reached the end of the catwalk and Amira twirled around just as Kat had instructed her earlier, Kat caught Zafir's eye where he was sitting in the front row. His grey gaze blazed into hers, and then it dropped explicitly to where the swell of her six-months-pregnant belly was visible under the kaftan she wore.

The baby kicked, and Kat couldn't stop a huge grin breaking across her face as her eyes met Zafir's again. And then she turned and walked serenely back down the catwalk with the little girl.

The following morning the headline on the front page of the *Jahor Times* simply said The Look of Love. And below it was a picture of Kat and Zafir gazing at each other, with her hand protectively cradling the swell of her belly.

Zafir threw down the newspaper and turned to face Kat, where she lay in bed. He splayed a big hand possessively over her naked pregnant belly and Kat rolled her eyes when the baby kicked.

She grumbled good-naturedly, 'It's already two against one…'

Zafir pulled Kat close and smoothed his hand down her body until he found her left thigh. He lifted it up so that the centre of his body came into contact with the centre of hers. She gasped when she felt him, hard and ready.

'No, my love…' he said huskily. 'It'll never be two against one. It's going to be three against the world…' He bent his head and kissed her before lifting his mouth for a second to say, 'And then four…' Another kiss. 'And then five…'

Kat huffed out a chuckle that turned into a moan of pleasure as Zafir angled his body against hers in a very intimate way. She gripped his shoulders and bit her lip, and whispered as he filled her with a smooth thrust, 'I love you, Zafir…'

He kissed her again. 'And I love you…for ever.'

* * * * *

DEDICATION

I'd like to dedicate this story and give huge thanks to Peggy Chenoweth, who runs the website AmputeeMommy.com. I thank her for her kind patience and her answers to my questions. Her website and blog are an invaluable resource for anyone seeking information and/or support around being an amputee. Any inaccuracies relating to Kat's limb loss in this story are purely my own.

If you enjoyed
A DIAMOND FOR THE SHEIKH'S MISTRESS
why not explore these other
Abby Green stories?

AN HEIR TO MAKE A MARRIAGE
MARRIED FOR THE TYCOON'S EMPIRE
CLAIMED FOR THE DE CARRILLO TWINS

Available now!

Nola felt her stomach flip over, and images from that night they'd spent together exploded inside her head like popping corn. Suddenly her whole body was quivering, and it was all she could do not to lean over and kiss Ramsay, to give in to that impulse to taste and touch that beautiful mouth once again…

Gripping the underside of the hard plastic chair, she steadied herself. And, taking a quick breath, forced herself to meet his eyes head-on. 'You said you wanted to finish this, Ram, but we can't,' she said hoarsely. 'Because it never started. It was just a one-night stand, remember?'

'Oh, I remember every single moment of that night. As I'm sure you do, Nola.'

His eyes gleamed, and instantly her pulse began to accelerate.

'Only this isn't about just one night any more. Our one-night stand has got long-term consequences.' He gestured towards her stomach.

'But not for you.' She looked up at him stubbornly, her blue eyes wide with frustration. 'Whatever connection we had, it ended a long time ago.'

'Given that you're pregnant with my child, that would seem to be a little premature and counter-intuitive,' he said softly.

Secret Heirs of Billionaires

There are some things money can't buy...

Living life at lightning pace, these magnates are no strangers to stakes at their highest. It seems they've got it all... That is until they find out that there's an unplanned item to add to their list of accomplishments!

Achieved:

1. Successful business empire

2. Beautiful women in their bed

3. *An heir to bear their name?*

Though every billionaire needs to leave his legacy in safe hands, discovering a secret heir shakes up his carefully orchestrated plan in more ways than one!

Uncover their secrets in:

Unwrapping the Castelli Secret by Caitlin Crews

Brunetti's Secret Son by Maya Blake

The Secret to Marrying Marchesi by Amanda Cinelli

Demetriou Demands His Child by Kate Hewitt

The Desert King's Secret Heir by Annie West

The Sheikh's Secret Son by Maggie Cox

The Innocent's Shameful Secret by Sara Craven

The Greek's Pleasurable Revenge by Andie Brock

The Secret Kept from the Greek by Susan Stephens

Carrying the Spaniard's Child by Jennie Lucas

Look out for more stories in the
Secret Heirs of Billionaires series coming soon!

KIDNAPPED
FOR THE
TYCOON'S BABY

BY
LOUISE FULLER

First Published in Great Britain 2017
By Mills & Boon, an imprint of HarperCollins*Publishers*
1 London Bridge Street, London, SE1 9GF

© 2017 Louise Fuller

ISBN: 978-0-263-92544-9

Printed and bound in Spain
by CPI, Barcelona

Louise Fuller was a tomboy who hated pink and always wanted to be the Prince—not the Princess! Now she enjoys creating heroines who aren't pretty push-overs but strong, believable women. Before writing for Mills & Boon she studied literature and philosophy at university, and then worked as a reporter on her local newspaper. She lives in Tunbridge Wells with her impossibly handsome husband, Patrick, and their six children.

Books by Louise Fuller

Mills & Boon Modern Romance

Blackmailed Down the Aisle
Claiming His Wedding Night
A Deal Sealed by Passion
Vows Made in Secret

Visit the Author Profile page
at millsandboon.co.uk for more titles.

For Adrian. My brother, and one of the good guys.

CHAPTER ONE

'I'M SORRY ABOUT THIS, Ms Mason. But don't worry. I'll get you there on time, just like always.'

Feeling the car slow, Nola Mason looked up from her laptop and frowned, her denim-blue eyes almost black within the dark interior of the sleek executive saloon.

Glancing out of the window, she watched a flatbed truck loaded with cones lumber slowly through the traffic lights. There had been some kind of parade in Sydney over the weekend, and the police and street cleaners were still dealing with the aftermath.

Thankfully, though, at five o'clock on Monday morning the traffic was limited to just a few buses and a handful of cars and, closing her laptop, she leaned towards her driver.

'I know you will, John. And please don't worry. I'm just relieved to have you.'

Relieved, and grateful, for not only was John punctual and polite, he also had near photographic recall of Sydney's daunting grid of streets.

As the car began to move again she shifted in her seat. Even after two months of working for the global tech giant RWI it still felt strange—fraudulent, even—having a chauffeur-driven limo at her disposal. She was a cyber architect, not a celebrity! But Ramsay Walker, the company's demanding and maddeningly autocratic CEO, had insisted on it.

Her mouth twisted. It had been the first time she'd objected to something, only to have Ramsay overrule her, but it hadn't been the last. His dictatorial behaviour and her stubborn determination to make a stand had ensured that they clashed fiercely at every subsequent meeting.

But now it was nearly over. Tomorrow was her last day in Sydney and, although, she and her partner Anna were still under contract to troubleshoot any problems in the RWI cyber security framework, they would do so from their office in Edinburgh.

She breathed out softly. And what a relief to finally be free of that intense grey gaze! Only, why then did what she was feeling seem more like regret than relief?

Glancing up at the imposing RWI building, she felt her heart begin beating hard and high in her chest. But right now was *not* the time to indulge in amateur psychology. She was here to work—and, if she was lucky, at this time of the morning she could expect a good two to three hours of uninterrupted access to the security system.

But as she walked past the empty bays in the visitor parking area some of her optimism wilted as she spotted a familiar black Bentley idling in front of the main entrance.

Damn it! She was in no mood for small talk—particularly with the owner of that car—and, ducking her chin, she began to walk faster. But she was not fast enough. Almost as she drew level with the car, the door opened and a man slid out. A woman's voice followed him into the early-morning light, together with the faintest hint of his cologne.

'But, baby, why can't it wait?' she wheedled. 'Come on—we can go back to mine. I'll make it worth your while...'

Unable to stop herself, Nola stole a glance at the man. Predictably, her breath stumbled in her throat and, gritting her teeth, she began to walk faster. She couldn't see his face, but she didn't need to. She would recognise that profile, that languid yet predatory manner anywhere. It was her boss—Ramsay Walker. In that car, at this time of the morning, it was always her boss.

Only the women were different each time.

Ignoring the sudden slick of heat on her skin, she stalked into the foyer. She felt clumsy and stupid, a mix of fear and restlessness and longing churning inside of her. But longing for what?

Working fourteen-hour days, and most weekends, she had no time for romance. And besides, she knew nobody in Sydney except the people in this building, and there was no way she would *ever* have a relationship with a colleague again. Not after what had happened with Connor.

Remembering all the snide glances, and the way people would stop talking when she walked by, she winced inwardly. It had been bad enough that everyone had believed the gossip. What had been so hurtful—so hurtful that she'd still never told anyone, not even her best friend and business partner, Anna—was that it had been Connor who'd betrayed her. Betrayed her and then abandoned her—just like her father had.

It had been humiliating, debilitating, but finally she had understood that love and trust were not necessarily symbiotic or two-way. She'd learnt her lesson, and she certainly wasn't about to forget it for an office fling.

She glanced back to where the woman was still pleading with Ramsay. Gazing at the broad shoulders beneath the crumpled shirt and the tousled surfer hair, Nola felt her heart thudding so loudly she thought one of the huge windows might shatter.

Workplace flings were trouble. But with a man like him it would be trouble squared. Cubed, even.

And anyway her life was too complicated right now for romance. This was the biggest job Cyber Angels had ever taken on, and with Anna away on her honeymoon she was having to manage alone, and do so with a brain and a body that were still struggling to get over three long-haul flights in as many weeks.

Trying to ignore the swell of panic rising inside her, she smiled mechanically at the security guard as he checked her security card. Reaching inside her bag, she pulled out her lift pass—and felt her stomach plummet as it slipped from her fingers and landed on the floor beside a pair of handmade Italian leather loafers.

'Allow me.'

The deep, masculine voice made her scalp freeze. Half turning, she forced a smile onto her face as she took the card from the man's outstretched hand.

'Thank you.'

'My pleasure.'

Turning, she walked quickly towards the lift, her skin tightening with irritation and a sort of feverish apprehension, as Ramsay Walker strolled alongside her, his long strides making it easy for him to keep pace.

As the lift doors opened it was on the tip of her tongue to tell him that she would use the stairs. But, given that her office was on the twenty-first floor, she knew it would simply make her look churlish or—worse—as though she cared about sharing the lift with him.

'Early start!'

Her skin twitched in an involuntary response to his languid East Coast accent, and she allowed herself a brief glance at his face. Instantly she regretted it. His dark grey eyes were watching her casually…a lazy smile tugged at his beautiful mouth. A mouth that had been kissing her all over every night since she'd first met him—but only in her dreams.

Trying to subdue the heat of her thoughts, praying that her face showed nothing of their content, she shrugged stiffly. 'I'm a morning person.'

'Is that right?' he drawled. 'I like the night-time myself.'

Night-time. The words whispered inside her head and she felt her body react to the darkness and danger it implied, her pulse slowing, goosebumps prickling over her skin. Only how was it possible to create such havoc with just a handful of syllables? she thought frantically.

'Really?' Trying her hardest to ignore the strange tension throbbing between them, she forced her expression into what she hoped looked like boredom and, glancing away, stared straight ahead. 'And yet here you are.'

She felt his gaze on the side of her face.

'Well, I got waylaid at a party...'

Remembering the redhead in the car, she felt a sharp nip of jealousy as stifling a yawn, he stretched his arms back behind his shoulders, the gesture somehow implying more clearly than words exactly what form that waylaying had taken.

'It seemed simpler to come straight to work. I take it you weren't out partying?'

His voice was soft, and yet it seemed to hook beneath her skin so that suddenly she had no option but to look up at him.

'Not my scene. I need my sleep,' she said crisply.

She knew she sounded prudish. But better that than to give this man even a hint of encouragement. Not that he needed any—he clearly believed himself to be irresistible. And, judging by his hit rate with women, he was right.

He laughed softly. 'You need to relax. Clio has a party most weekends. You should come along next time.'

'Surely that would be up to Clio?' she said primly, and he smiled—a curling, mocking smile that made the hairs on the back of her neck stand up.

His eyes glittered. 'If I'm happy, she's happy.'

She gritted her teeth. Judging by the photos of supermodels with tear-stained faces, papped leaving his apartment, that clearly wasn't true. Not that it was any of her business, she thought quickly as the lift stopped.

There was a short hiss as the doors opened, and then, turning to face him, Nola lifted her chin. 'Thank you, but no. I never socialise with people at work. In my opinion, the disadvantages outweigh the benefits.'

His eyes inspected her lazily. 'Then maybe you should let me change your opinion. I can be very persuasive.'

Her stomach dipped, and something treacherously soft and warm slipped over her skin as his grey gaze rested on her face. When he looked at her like that it was hard not to feel persuaded.

She drew a breath. Hard, but not impossible.

'I don't doubt that. Unfortunately, though, I always put workplace considerations above everything else.'

And before he had a chance to respond she slipped through the doors, just before they slid shut.

Her heart was racing. Her legs felt weak. Any woman would have been tempted by such an invitation. But she had been telling the truth.

Since her disastrous relationship with Connor, she had made a decision and stuck to it. Her work life and her personal life were two separate, concurrent strands, and she never mixed the two. She would certainly never date anyone from work. Or go to a party with them.

Particularly if the invitation came from her boss.

Remembering the way his eyes had drifted appraisingly over her face, she shivered.

And most especially not if that boss was Ramsay Walker.

In business, he was heralded as a genius, and he was undeniably handsome and sexy. But Ramsay Walker was the definition of trouble.

Okay, she knew with absolute certainty that sex with him would be mind-blowing. How could it not be? The man was a force of nature made flesh and blood—the human personification of a hurricane or a tsunami. But that was why he was so dangerous. He might be powerful, intense, unstoppable, but he also left chaos and destruction behind him.

Even if she didn't believe all the stories in the media about his womanising, she had witnessed it with her own eyes. Ramsay clearly valued novelty and variety above all else. And, if that wasn't enough of a warning to stay well away, he'd also publicly and repeatedly stated his desire never to marry or have children.

Not that she was planning on doing either any time soon. She and her mother had done fine on their own, but getting involved on any level with a man who seemed so determinedly opposed to such basic human connections just wasn't an option. It had taken too long to restore her pride and build up a good reputation, to throw either away for a heartbreaking smile.

Three hours later, though, she was struggling to defend both.

In the RWI boardroom silence had fallen as the man at the head of the table leaned back in his chair, his casual stance at odds with the dark intensity of his gaze. A gaze that was currently locked on Nola's face.

'So let me get this right,' he observed softly. 'What you're trying to say is that I'm being naive. Or complacent.'

A pulse of anger leapfrogged over his skin.

Did she *really* think she was going to get away with insulting him in his own boardroom? Ram thought, watching Nola blink, seeing anger, confusion and frustration colliding in those blue, blue eyes.

Eyes that made a man want to quench his thirst—and not for water. The same blue eyes that should have warned him to ignore her CV and glowing references and stick with men in grey suits who talked about algorithms and crypto-ransomware. But Nola Mason was not the kind of woman it was easy to ignore.

Refusing his invitation to meet at the office, she had insisted instead that they meet in some grimy café in downtown Sydney.

There, surrounded by surly teenagers in hoodies and bearded geeks, she had shown him just how easy it was to breach RWI's security. It had been an impressive display—unorthodox, but credible and provocative.

Only not as provocative as the sight of her long slim legs and rounded bottom in tight black jeans, or the strip of smooth bare stomach beneath her T-shirt that he'd glimpsed when she reached over to the next table for a napkin.

It wasn't love at first sight.

For starters, he didn't believe in love.

Only, watching her talk, he had been knocked sideways by lust, by curiosity, by the challenge in those blue eyes. By whatever it was that triggered sexual attraction between two people. It had been beyond his conscious control, and he'd had to struggle not to pull her across the table by the long dark hair spilling onto the shoulders of her battered leather jacket.

But it was the dark blue velvet ribbon tied around her throat that had goaded his senses to the point where he had thought he was going to black out.

Those eyes, that choker, had made up his mind. In other words, he'd let his libido hire her.

It was the first time he'd ever allowed lust to dictate a business decision. And it would be the last, he thought grimly, glancing once again at the tersely written email she had sent him that morning. He gritted his teeth. If Ms Nola Mason was expecting him to pay more, she could damn well sing for it.

Nola swallowed, shifting in her seat. Her heart was pounding, and she was struggling to stay calm beneath the battleship-grey of Ram's scrutiny. Most CEOs were exacting and autocratic, but cyber security was typically an area in which the boss was almost always willing to hand over leadership to an expert.

Only Ram was not a typical boss.

Right from that first interview it had been clear that not only was his reputation as the *enfant terrible* of the tech industry fully justified, but that, unusually, he could also demonstrate considerably more than a working knowledge of the latest big data technologies.

Truthfully, however, Ram's intelligence wasn't the only reason she found it so hard to confront him. His beauty, his innate self-confidence, and that still focus—the sense that he was watching her and only her—made her heart flip-flop against her ribs.

Her blue eyes flickered across the boardroom table to where he sat, lounging opposite her. It might be shallow, but who wouldn't be affected by such blatant perfection? And it didn't help that he appealed on so many different levels.

With grey eyes that seemed to lighten and darken in harmony with his moods, messy black hair, a straight nose, and a jaw permanently darkened with stubble, he might just as easily be a poet or a revolutionary as a CEO. And the hard definition of muscle beneath his gleaming white shirt only seemed to emphasise that contradiction even more.

Dragging her gaze back up to his face, Nola felt her nerves ball painfully. The tension in his jaw told her that she was balancing on eggshells. *Concentrate*, she told herself—surely she hadn't meant to imply that he was naive or complacent?

'No, that's not what I'm saying,' she said quickly, ignoring the faint sigh of relief that echoed round the table as she did so. She drew in a deep breath. 'What you're actually being is arrogant, and unreasonable.'

Somebody—she wasn't sure who—gave a small whimper.

For a fraction of a second Ram thought he might have misheard her. Nobody called him arrogant or unreasonable. But, glancing across at Nola, he knew immediately that he'd heard her correctly.

Her cheeks were flushed, but she was eyeing him steadily, and he felt a flicker of anger and something like admiration. She was brave—he'd give her that. And determined. He knew his reputation, and it had been well and truly earned. His negotiating skills were legendary, and his single-minded ruthlessness had turned a loan from his grandfather into a global brand.

A pulse began to beat in his groin. Normally she would be emptying her desk by now. Only the humming in his blood seemed to block out all rational thought so that he felt dazed, disorientated by her accusation. But why? What was it about this woman that made it so difficult for him to stay focused?

He didn't know. But whatever it was it had been instant and undeniable. When he'd walked into that coffee shop she had stood up, shaken his hand, and his body had reacted automatically—not just a spark but a fire starting in his blood and burning through his veins.

It had been devastating, unprecedented. At the time he'd assumed it was because she was so unlike any of the other women of his acquaintance. Women who would sacrifice anything and *anyone* to fit in, to make their lives smooth. Women who chose conformity and comfort over risk.

Nola took risks. That was obvious from the way she had dressed and behaved at her interview. He liked it that she broke the rules. Every single time he came into contact with her he liked it more—liked *her* more.

And she liked him too.

Only every single time she came into contact with him she gave him the brush-off. Or at least she tried too. But her eyes gave her away.

As though sensing his thoughts, Nola glanced up and looked away, her hand rising protectively to touch her throat. Instantly the pulse in his groin began to beat harder and faster.

He had never had to chase a woman before—let alone coax her into his bed. It was both maddening and unbelievably erotic.

At the thought of Nola in his bed, wearing nothing but that velvet choker, he felt a stab of sexual frustration so painful that he had to grip the arms of his chair to stop himself from groaning out loud.

'That's a pretty damning assessment, Ms Mason,' he said softly. 'Obviously if I thought you were being serious we'd be having a very different conversation. So I'm going to assume you're trying to shock me into changing my mind.'

Nola took a breath. Her insides felt tight and a prickling heat was spreading up her spine. Could everyone else in the room feel the tension between her and Ram? Or was it all in her head?

Stupid question. She knew it was real—and not just real. It was dangerous. Whatever this thing was between them, it was clearly hazardous—not only to her reason but to her instinct for self-preservation. Why else was she picking a fight with the boss in public?

Abruptly he leaned forward, and as their eyes met she shivered. His gaze was so intent that suddenly it felt as though they were alone, facing each other like two Western gunslingers in a saloon bar.

'Nice try! But I'm not that sensitive.'

Without warning the intensity faded from his handsome features and, glancing swiftly round the room, she knew her anger must look out of place—petulant, even. No doubt that had been his intention all along: to make her look emotional and unprofessional.

Gritting her teeth, she leaned back in her chair, trying to match his nonchalance.

Watching her fingers curl into a fist around her pen, Ram smiled slowly. 'I don't know whether to be disappointed or impressed by you, Ms Mason. It usually takes people a lot less than two months to realise I'm arrogant and unreasonable. However, they don't tend to say it to my face. Either way, though, I'm not inclined to change my mind. Or permit you to change yours. You see, I only have one thousand four hundred and forty minutes in any day, and I don't like to waste them on ill-thought-out negotiations like this one.'

Watching the flush of colour spread over her pale skin, he felt a stab of satisfaction. She had got under his skin; now he had not got under hers, And he was going to make sure it stung.

'I gave you a budget—a very generous budget—and I see no reason to increase it on the basis of some whim.'

Nola glared at him. 'This is not a whim, Mr Walker. It is a response to your email informing me that the software launch date has been brought forward by six weeks.'

Had he stuck to the original deadline, the new system would have been up and running for several months prior to the launch, giving her ample time to iron out any glitches. Now, though, the team she'd hired and trained for RWI would have to work longer hours to run all the necessary checks, and overtime meant more money.

Ram leaned forward. 'I run a business—a very successful one—that is currently paying your salary, and part of that success comes from knowing my market inside out. And this software needs to be on sale as soon as possible. And by "as soon as possible" I mean *now*.'

She blinked trying to break the spell of his eyes on hers and the small taunting smile on his lips.

Taking a breath, she steadied herself. 'I understand that. But *now* changes things. *Now* is expensive. But not nearly as expensive as it will be when your system gets hacked.'

'That sounds awfully like a threat, Ms Mason.'

She took another quick breath, her hand lifting instinctively to her throat. Feeling the blood pulsing beneath her fingertips, she straightened her spine.

'That's because it is. But better that it comes from me than them. Hackers break the rules, which means *I* have to break the rules. The difference is that I'm not about to steal or destroy or publicise your data. Nor am I going to extort money from you.'

'Not true.' The corner of his mouth lifted, as though she had made a joke, but there was no laughter in his eyes. 'Okay, you don't sneak in through the back door. You just give me one of those butter-wouldn't-melt-in-your-mouth smiles and put an invoice on my desk!'

'I can protect your company, Mr Walker. But I can't do that if my hands are tied behind my back.'

He tilted his head, his expression shifting, his dark gaze locking onto her face. 'Of course not. But, personally, I never let anyone tie me up unless we've decided on a safe word beforehand. Maybe you should do the same.'

There was some nervous laughter around the table. But before she could respond, he twisted in his seat and gestured vaguely towards the door.

'I need to have a private conversation with Ms Mason.'

Stomach churning, Nola watched as the men and women filed silently out of the room. Finally the door closed with a quiet click and she felt a ripple of apprehension slither over her skin as she waited for him to speak.

But he didn't say anything. Instead he simply stared out of the window at the blue sky, his face calm and untroubled.

Her heartbeat accelerated. *Damn him!* She knew he was making her wait, proving his power. If only she could tell him where to put his job. But this contract was not only paying her and Anna's wages, RWI was a global brand—a household name—and getting a good reference would propel their company, Cyber Angels, into the big time.

So, willing herself to stay cool-headed, she sat as the silence spread to the four corners of the room. Finally he pushed back his seat and stood up. Her pulse twitched in her throat as she watched him walk slowly around the table and come to a halt in front of her.

'You're costing me a great deal of money already. And now you're about to cost me a whole lot more.' He stared at her coolly. 'Are you sure there's nothing else you'd like, Nola? This table, perhaps? My car? Maybe the shirt off my back?'

He was looking for her to react. Which meant she should stay silent and seated. But it was the first time he had said her name, and hearing it spoken in that soft, sexy drawl caught her off guard.

She jerked to her feet, her body acting independently, tasting the sharp tang of adrenaline in her mouth.

Instantly she knew she'd made a mistake. She was close enough to reach out and touch that beautifully shaped mouth. In other words, too close. *Walk away*, she shouted silently. *Better still, run!* But for some reason her legs wouldn't do what her brain was suggesting.

Instead, she glowered at him, her blue eyes darkening with anger. 'Yes, that's right, Mr Walker. That's exactly what I want. The shirt off your back.'

But it wasn't. What she really wanted was to turn the tables. Goad him into losing control. Make him feel this same conflicted, confusing mass of fear and frustration and desire.

His fingers were hovering over the top button of his shirt, his eyes holding hers. 'You're sure about that?' he said softly.

The menacing undertone beneath the softness cut through her emotion and brought her to her senses.

At the other end of a table, surrounded by people, Ram Walker was disturbing, distracting. But up close and un-chaperoned he was formidable.

And she was out of her depth.

Breathing in sharply, she shook her head, her pulse quickening with helpless anger as he gave her a small satisfied smile.

'And I thought you liked breaking the rules.'

His eyes gleamed and she knew he was goading her again, but she didn't care. Right now all she wanted was to be somewhere far away from this man who seemed to have the power to turn her inside out and off balance.

'Is there anything else you'd like to discuss?' he asked with an exaggerated politeness that seemed designed to test her self-control.

He waited until she shook her head, and then, turning, he walked towards the door.

'I'll speak to the accountants today.'

It was with relief bordering on delirium that she watched him leave the room.

Back in her office, she sat down behind her desk and let out a jagged breath.

Her hands were trembling and she felt hot and dizzy.

Leaning back in her chair, she picked up her notebook and a pencil. She knew it was anachronistic for a techie like herself to use pen and paper, but her mother had always used a notebook. Besides, it helped her clear her mind and unwind—and right now, with Ram Walker's goading words running on a loop round her head, she needed all the help she could get.

But she had barely flipped open her notebook when her phone buzzed. She hesitated before picking it up. If it was Ram, she was going to let it ring out. Her nerves were still jangling from their last encounter, and she couldn't face another head-to-head right now. But glancing at the screen, she felt a warm rush of happiness.

It was Anna.

A chat with her best friend would be the perfect antidote to that showdown with Ram.

'Hey, I wasn't expecting to hear from you. Why are you calling me? This is your honeymoon. Shouldn't you be gazing into Robbie's eyes, or writhing about with him on some idyllic beach?'

Hearing Anna's snort of laughter, she realised just how much she was missing her easy-going friend and business partner.

'I promise you, sex on the beach is overrated! Sand gets everywhere. And I mean *everywhere*.'

'Okay, too much information, Mrs Harris.' She began to doodle at the edges of the paper.

'Oh, Noles, you have no idea how weird it is to be Mrs Somebody, let alone Mrs Harris.'

'No idea at all! And planning to stay that way,' she said lightly.

Marriage had never been high on her to-do list. She was happy for Anna, of course. But her parents' divorce had left her wary of making vows and promises. And her disastrous relationship with Connor had only reinforced her instinctive distrust of the sort of trust and intimacy that marriage required.

Anna giggled. 'Every time anyone calls me that I keep thinking my mother-in-law's here. It's terrifying!'

She and Nola both burst out laughing.

'So why are you ringing me?' Nola said finally, when she could speak again.

'Well, we were at the pool, and Robbie got talking to this guy, and guess what? He's a neurosurgeon too. So you can imagine what happened next.'

Nola nodded. Anna's husband had recently been appointed as a consultant at one of Edinburgh's top teaching hospitals. He was as passionate about his work as he was about his new wife.

'Anyway, I left them yapping on about central core function and some new scanner, and that made me think of you, slogging away in Sydney all on your own. So I thought I'd give you a call and see how everything's going…'

Tucking the phone against her shoulder, Nola rolled her eyes. 'Everything's fine. There was a bit of a problem this morning, but nothing I couldn't handle.'

She paused, felt a betraying flush of colour spreading over her cheeks, and was grateful that Anna was on the end of a phone and not in the same room.

There was a short silence. Then, 'So, you and Ramsay Walker are getting on okay?'

Nola frowned.

'Yes…' She hesitated. 'Well, no. Not really. It's complicated. But it's okay,' she said quickly, as Anna made a noise somewhere between a wail and groan.

'I knew I should have postponed the honeymoon! Please tell me you haven't done anything stupid.'

Nola swallowed. She had—but thankfully only in the safe zone of her imagination.

'We had a few words about the budget, but I handled it and it's fine. I promise.'

'That's good.' She heard Anna breathe out. 'Look, Noles, I know you think he's arrogant and demanding—'

'It's not a matter of opinion, Anna. It's a fact. He *is* arrogant and demanding.'

And spoiled. How could he not be? He was the only son and heir to a fortune; his every whim had probably been indulged from birth. He might like to boast that he said no to almost everything, but she was willing to bet an entire year's salary that nobody had ever said no to him.

'I know,' her friend said soothingly. 'But for the next twenty-four hours he's still the boss. And if we get a good reference from him we'll basically be able to print money. We might even be able to pay off our loan.' She giggled. 'Besides, you have to admit that there are *some* perks working for him.'

'Anna Harris, you're a married woman. You shouldn't be having thoughts like that.'

'Why not? I love my Robbie, but Ram Walker is *gorgeous*.'

Laughing reluctantly, Nola shook her head. 'He is so not your type, Anna.'

'If you believe that you must have been looking too long into that big old Australian sun! He's *every* woman's type. As long as they're breathing.'

Opening her mouth, wanting to disagree, to deny what she knew to be true, Nola glanced down at her notepad, at the sketch she had made of Ram.

Who was she trying to kid?

'Fine. He's gorgeous. Happy now?'

But as she swung round in her seat her words froze on her lips, and Anna's response was lost beneath the sudden deafening beat of her heart.

Lounging in the open doorway, his muscular body draped against the frame, Ram Walker was watching her with a mocking gaze that told her he had clearly heard her last remark.

There was no choice but to front it out. Acknowledging his presence with a small, tight smile, she closed her notebook carefully and, as casually as she could manage, said, 'Okay, that all sounds fine. Send the data over as soon as possible and I'll take a look at it.'

Ignoring Anna's confused reply, she hung up.

Her heart was ricocheting against her ribs.

'Mr Walker. How can I help you?'

He stared at her calmly, his grey eyes holding her captive.

'Let's not worry about that now,' he said easily. 'Why don't we talk about how I can help *you*?'

She stared at him in silence. Where was this conversation going?

'I don't understand—*you* want to help *me*?'

'Of course. You're only with us one more day, and I want to make that time as productive as possible. Which is why I want you to have dinner with me this evening.'

'You mean tonight?'

Her voice sounded too high, and she felt her cheeks grow hot as he raised an eyebrow.

'Well, it can't be any other night,' he said slowly. 'You're flying home tomorrow, aren't you?'

Nola licked her lips nervously, a dizzying heat sliding over her skin. Dinner with her billionaire boss might sound like a dream date, but frankly it was a risk she wasn't prepared to take.

'That would be lovely. Obviously,' she lied. 'But I've got a couple of meetings, and the one with the tactical team at five will probably overrun.'

He locked eyes with her.

'Oh, don't worry. I cancelled it.'

She gazed at him in disbelief, and then a ripple of anger flickered over her skin.

'You cancelled it?'

He nodded. 'It seemed easier. So is seven-thirty okay?'

'Okay?' she spluttered. 'No, it's *not* okay. You can't just march in and cancel my meetings for a dinner date.'

He raised an eyebrow and took a step backwards. 'Date? Is that why you're so flustered? I'm sorry to disappoint you, Ms Mason, but I'm afraid we won't be alone.'

His words made her heart hammer against her chest, and a hot flush of embarrassment swept across her face. She was suddenly so angry she wanted to scream.

'I don't want to be alone with you,' she snapped, her hands curling into fists. 'Why would I want that?'

He smiled at her mockingly. 'I suppose for the same reason as any other woman in your position. Sadly, though, I've invited some people I think you should meet. They'll be good for your business.'

She stared at him mutely, unable to think of anything to say that wouldn't result in her being fired on the spot.

His gaze shifted from her face to her fists, grey eyes gleaming like polished pewter.

'Nothing else to say? You disappoint me, Ms Mason! I was hoping for at least one devastating comeback. Okay, I'll pick you up from your hotel later. Be ready. And don't worry about thanking me now. You can do that later too.'

'But I've got to pack!' she called after him, the bottle-neck of words in her throat finally bursting.

But it was too late. He'd gone.

Staring after him, Nola felt a trickle of fury run down her spine. *Any other woman in your position.* How dared he lump her in with all his other wannabe conquests? He was impossible, overbearing and conceited.

But as a hot, swift shiver ran through her body she

swore under her breath, for if that was true then why did he still affect her in this way?

Well, it was going to stop now.

Standing up, she stormed across her office and slammed the door.

Breathing out hard, she stared at her shaking hands. It felt good to give way to frustration and anger. But closing a door was easy. She had a horrible feeling that keeping Ram Walker out of her head, even when she was back in Scotland, was going to be a whole lot harder.

CHAPTER TWO

FROM HIS OFFICE on the twenty-second floor, Ram stared steadily out of the window at the Pacific Ocean. The calm expression on his face in no way reflected the turmoil inside his head.

Something was wrong. He looked down at the file he was supposed to be reading and frowned. For starters, he was sleeping badly, and he had a near permanent headache. But worst of all he was suffering from a frustrating and completely uncharacteristic inability to focus on what was important to him. His business.

Or it had been important to him right up until the moment he'd walked into that backstreet café and met Nola Mason.

A prickling tension slid down his spine and his chest squeezed tighter.

Down in the bay, a yacht cut smoothly through the waves. But for once his eyes didn't follow its progress. Instead it was the clear, sparkling blue of the water that drew his gaze.

His jaw tightened, pulling the skin across the high curves of his cheekbones.

Two months ago his life had been perfect. But one particular woman, whose eyes were the exact shade as the ocean, had turned that life upside down.

Nola.

He ran the syllables slowly over his tongue. Before he'd met her the name had simply been an acronym for New

Orleans—or the Big Easy, as it was also known. His eyes narrowed. But any connection between Nola Mason and the city straddling the Mississippi ended there. Nola might be many things—sexy, smart and seriously good at her job. But she wasn't easy. In fact she was unique among women in that she seemed utterly impervious to his charms.

Thinking back to their conversation in the boardroom, remembering the way she had stood up to him in front of the directors, he felt the same mix of frustration, admiration and desire that seemed to define every single contact he had with her.

It was a mix of feelings that was entirely new to him.

Normally women tripped over themselves to please him. They certainly never kept him at arm's length, or spouted 'workplace considerations' as a reason for turning him down.

Turning him down! Even just thinking the words inside his head made him see every shade of red. Nobody had ever turned him down—in the boardroom *or* the bedroom.

He glanced down at the unread report, but there was no place to hide from the truth: despite the fact that his instincts were screaming at him to keep his distance, he couldn't stop thinking about Nola and her refusal to sleep with him. Her stupid, logical, perfectly justified refusal to break the rules. *Her* rules.

He closed the file with a snap. His rules too.

And that was what was really driving him crazy. The fact that up until a couple of months ago he would have agreed with her. Workplace relationships were a poisoned chalice. They caused tension and upset. And not once had he ever been tempted to break those rules and sleep with an employee.

Only Nola Mason was not just a temptation.

She was a virus in his blood.

No. His mouth twisted. She was more like malware in

his system, stealthily undermining his strength, his stability, his sanity.

But there was a cure.

His groin hardened.

He knew what it was, and so did she.

He'd seen it in the antagonism flickering in those blue eyes, heard it in the huskiness of her voice. And her resistance, her refusal to acknowledge it was merely fuelling his desire. His anticipation of the moment when finally she surrendered to him.

He tossed the file onto his desk, feeling a pulsing, breathless excitement scrabbling up inside him.

Of course, being Nola, she would offer a truce, not a surrender. Those eyes, that mouth, might suggest an uninhibited sensuality, but he sensed that the determined slant of her chin was not just a pose adopted for business but a reflection of how she behaved out of work and in bed.

Picturing Nola, her blue eyes narrowing into fierce slits as she straddled his naked body, he felt his spine melt into his chair. But truces could only happen if both parties came to the table—which was why he'd invited her to dinner. Not an intimate, candlelit tryst. He knew Nola, and she would have instantly rejected anything so blatant. But now she knew it was to be a business dinner at a crowded restaurant, she would relax—hell, they might even end up sharing a dessert.

His mouth curved up into a satisfied smile. Or, better still, they could save dessert until they got back to his penthouse.

So this was what it felt like to be famous, Nola thought as she walked self-consciously between the tables in the exclusive restaurant Ram had chosen. It was certainly an experience, although she wasn't sure it was one she'd ever want to repeat.

The Wool Shed was the hottest dining ticket in town, but even though it was midweek, and the award-winning restaurant was packed, to her astonishment Ram hadn't bothered to book. For any normal person that would have meant looking for somewhere else to eat. Clearly those rules didn't apply to Ram Walker, for now, within seconds of his arrival, the maître d' was leading them to a table with a view across the bay to the Opera House.

'I think I may have told our guests that dinner was at eight, so it's going to be just the two of us for a bit. Sorry about that.'

Nola stared at him warily. He didn't sound sorry; he sounded completely unrepentant. Meeting his gaze, she saw that he didn't look sorry either. In fact, he seemed to be enjoying the uneasiness that was clearly written all over her face.

Sliding into the seat he'd pulled out, Nola breathed out carefully. 'That's fine. It'll give you a chance to brief me on our mystery guests.'

She felt him smile behind her. 'Of course—and don't worry, your chaperones will arrive very soon. I promise.'

Gritting her teeth, she watched him drop gracefully into the chair beside her. At work it had been easy to tell herself that the tension between them was just some kind of personality clash or a battle of wills. Now, though, she could see that ever since she'd met Ram that first time, the battle had been raging inside her.

A battle between her brain and her body...between common sense and her basest carnal urges. And, much as she would have liked to deny it, or pretend it wasn't true, the sexual pull between them was as real and tangible as the bottles of still and sparkling water on the table. So much so that only by pressing her fingers into the armrests of her chair could she stop herself from reaching out to touch the smooth curve of his jaw.

Her hand twitched. It was like trying to ignore a mosquito bite. The urge to scratch was overwhelming.

But surely walking into this restaurant with him was just what she'd needed to remind her why it was best not to give in to that urge—for Ram wasn't just her boss. He was way out of her league.

In a room filled with beautiful people, he was the unashamed focus of every eye. As he'd strolled casually to their table conversations had dwindled and even the waiters had seemed to freeze; it had been as though everyone in the restaurant had taken a sort of communal breath.

And it was easy to see why.

Glancing up, she felt a jolt of hunger spike inside her.

There was something about him that commanded attention. Of course he looked amazing—each feature, from his long dark eyelashes to the tiny scar on his cheekbone, looked as though it had been lovingly executed by an artist. But it wasn't just his dark, sculpted looks that tugged at the senses. He had a quality of certainty that was unique, compelling, irresistible.

He was the ultimate cool boy at school, she decided. And now he was sitting next to her, his arm resting casually over the back of her chair, the scent of his cologne making a dizzy heat spread over her skin.

Unable to stop herself, she glanced sideways and felt her breath catch in her throat.

He was just too ridiculously beautiful.

As though sensing her focus, he turned, and the air was punched out of her lungs as his dark grey gaze scanned her face.

'What's the matter?'

'Nothing,' she lied. 'Are you going to tell me who we're meeting?' She tried to arrange her expression into that same mix of casual and professional that he projected so effortlessly. 'Are they local?'

'They're a little bigger than just Australia. It's Craig Aldin and Will Fraser. They own—'

'A&F Freight,' she finished his sentence. 'That's the—'

'The biggest logistics company in the southern hemisphere.'

His eyes glittered as he in turn finished *her* sentence, a hint of a smile tugging at his mouth. 'Maybe we should try ordering dinner this way. It would be like a new game: gastronomic consequences.'

She tried not to respond to that smile, but it was like trying to resist gravity.

'It could be fun,' she said cautiously. 'Although we might end up with some challenging flavour combinations.'

His eyes didn't leave her face. 'Well, I've never been that vanilla in my tastes,' he said softly.

Her heart banged against her ribs like a bird hitting a window. There it was again—that spark of danger and desire, her flint striking his steel.

But as he picked up the water bottle and filled her glass she bit her lip, felt a knot forming in her stomach. Flirting with Ram in this crowded restaurant might feel safe. Playing with fire, however, was never a good idea—and especially not with a man who was as experienced and careless with women as he was.

She needed to remember that the next time he made her breath jerk in her throat, but right now she needed to dampen that flame and steer the conversation back to work.

'Is A&F looking to upgrade its system?' she asked quickly, ignoring the mocking gleam in his eyes.

Ram stared at her for a moment and then shrugged.

It was the same every time. Back and forth. Gaining her trust, then losing it again. Like trying to stroke a feral cat. Just as he thought he was close enough to touch, she'd retreat. It was driving him mad.

He shifted in his seat, wishing he could shift the ache inside his body. If he couldn't persuade her to relax soon he was going to do himself some permanent damage.

His eyes drifted lazily over her body. In that cream blouse, dark skirt and stockings, and with those blue eyes watching him warily across the table, she looked more like a sleek Siamese than the feisty street cat she'd been channelling in their meeting that morning.

'Yes—and soon. That's why I want you to meet with them today.'

As he put the bottle back on the table his hand brushed against hers, and suddenly she was struggling to remember what he'd just said, let alone figure out how to reply.

'Thank you,' she said finally.

His expression was neutral. 'Of course it might mean coming back to Australia.'

Frowning, she looked into his face. 'That won't be a problem.'

'Really? It's just that you live on the other side of the world. I thought you might have somebody missing you. Someone significant.'

Nola blinked. How had they ended up talking about this? About her private life.

Ram Walker was too damn sharp for his own good. He made connections that were barely visible while she was still struggling to join the dots.

His gaze was so intense that suddenly she wanted to lift her hand and shield her face. But instead she thought about her flat, with its high ceilings and shabby old sofas. It was her home, and she loved it, but it wasn't a *somebody*. Truthfully, there hadn't been anyone in her life since Connor.

Her throat tightened. Connor—with his sweet face and his floppy hair. And his desire to be liked. A desire that had meant betraying her trust in the most humiliating way possible. He hadn't quite matched up to her father's level of unreliability, but then, he'd only been in her life a matter of months.

Of course since their break-up she hadn't taken a vow of celibacy. She'd gone out with a couple of men on more than a couple of dates and they'd been pleasant enough. But none had been memorable, and right now the only significant living thing in her flat was a cactus called Colin.

She shook her head. 'No,' she said at last. 'Anna's the home bird. I've no desire to tie myself down any time soon. I like my independence too much.'

Ram nodded. Letting his gaze wander over her face, he took in the flushed cheeks and the dilated pupils and felt a tug down low in his stomach. A pulse of heat flickered beneath his skin.

Independence. The word tasted sweet and dark and glossy in his mouth—like a cherry bursting against his tongue. At that moment, had he believed in soulmates, he would have thought he'd found his. For here was a woman who was not afraid to be herself. To stand alone in the world.

His heart was pounding. He wanted her more than he'd ever wanted anyone—anything. If only he could reach over and pull her against him, strip her naked and take her right here, right now—

But instead a waiter brought over some bread and, grateful for the nudge back to reality, Ram leaned back in his chair, trying to school his thoughts, his breathing, his body, into some sort of order.

'She's impressive, your partner,' he said, when finally the waiter left them alone.

He watched her face soften, the blue eyes widen with affection, and suddenly he wondered how it would feel to be the object of that incredible gaze. For someone to care that much about him.

The idea made him feel strangely vulnerable and, picking up his glass, he downed his water so that it hit his stomach with a thump.

She nodded eagerly. 'She was always top of the class.'

He nodded. 'I can believe that. But I wasn't talking about her tech skills. It's her attitude that's her real strength. She's pragmatic; she understands the value of compromise. Whereas you...'

He paused, and Nola felt her skin tighten. That was Anna in a nutshell. But how could Ram know that? They'd only met once, when they'd signed the contracts.

And then her muscles tensed, her body squirming with nerves at what he might be about to reveal about her.

'You, on the other hand, are a rebel.'

Reaching out, he ran his hand lightly over her sleeve and she felt a thrill like the jolt of electricity. This wasn't like any conversation she'd ever had. It was more like a dance—a dazzling dance with quick, complicated steps that only they understood.

She swallowed. 'What kind of rebel works *for* the system?'

Beneath the lights, his eyes gleamed like brushed steel. 'You might look corporate on the outside, but if I scratched the surface I'd find a hacker beneath. Unlike your partner—unlike most people, really—you like to cross boundaries, take risks. You're not motivated by money; you like the challenge.'

The hum of chatter and laughter faded around them and a pulse began to beat loudly inside her head. Reaching forward to pick up her glass, she cleared her throat with difficulty.

'You're making me sound a lot edgier than I am,' she said quickly. 'I'm actually just a "white hat".'

'Of course you are!'

Ram shifted in his seat, his thigh brushing against her leg so that her hand twitched around the stem of the glass. It was a gambler's tell—a tiny, visible sign of the tension throbbing between them.

'It's not like I'd ever catch you hanging out in some grimy internet café with a bunch of wannabe anarchists.'

He lounged back in his seat, one eyebrow lifted, challenging her to contradict him.

Remembering their first meeting, Nola felt her heart beat faster, her stomach giving way to that familiar mix of apprehension and fascination, the sense that there was something pulling them inexorably closer.

But even as she felt her skin grow warm his teasing words stirred something inside her. Suddenly the desire to tease him back was overwhelming—to put the heat on *him*, to watch those grey eyes turn molten.

'Actually, wannabe anarchists are usually pretty harmless—like sheep. It's the wolf in sheep's clothing you need to worry about.'

She kept her expression innocent, but heat cascaded down through her belly as his gaze locked onto hers with the intensity of a tractor beam. A small, urgent voice in the back of her head was warning her to back down, to stop playing Russian roulette with the man who'd loaded the gun she was holding to her head.

But then suddenly he smiled, and just like that nothing seemed to matter except being the focus of his undivided attention. It was easy to forget he was self-serving and arrogant…easy to believe that breaking the rules—*her* rules—wouldn't matter just this once.

Her heart began to beat faster.

Except she knew from experience that it *would* matter. And that smile wasn't a challenge. It was a warning—a red light flashing. *Danger! Keep away!*

Breathing in, she gave him a quick, neutral smile of her own. 'Now, this menu!' Holding her smile in place, she forced a casual note into her voice. 'My French is pretty non-existent, so I might need a little help ordering.'

'Don't worry. I speak it fluently.'

'You do?' She gazed at him, torn between disbelief and wonder.

He shrugged. 'My mother always wanted to live in Paris, but it didn't work out. So she sent me to school there.'

Nola frowned. 'Paris! You mean Paris in France?'

'I don't think they speak French in Paris, Texas.'

His face was expressionless. but there was a tension in his shoulders that hadn't been there before.

Her eyes met his, then bounced away. 'That's such a long way from here,' she said slowly.

'I suppose it is.'

Her pulse twitched.

It would have been easy to take his reply at face value, as just another of those glib, offhand remarks people made to keep a conversation running smoothly.

But something had shifted in his voice—or rather left it. The teasing warmth had gone, had been replaced by something cool and dismissive that pricked her skin like the sting of a wasp.

It was her cue to back off—and maybe she would have done so an hour earlier. But this was the first piece of personal information he had ever shared with her.

She cleared her throat. 'So how old were you?'

Along the back of her seat, she could feel the muscles in his arm tensing.

'Seven.' He gazed at her steadily. 'It was a good school. I had a great education there.'

She knew her face had stiffened into some kind of answering smile—she just hoped it looked more convincing than it felt. Nodding, she said quickly, 'I'm sure. And learning another language is such an opportunity.'

'It has its uses.' He spoke tonelessly. 'But I wasn't talking about speaking French. Being away taught me to rely on myself. To trust my own judgement. Great life lessons—and brilliant for business.'

Did he ever think of anything else? Nola wondered. Surely he must have been homesick or lonely? But the expression on his face made it clear that it was definitely time to change the subject.

Glancing down at her menu again, she said quickly, 'So, what do you recommend?'

'That depends on what you like to eat.'

Looking up, she saw with relief that the tightness in his face had eased.

'The fish is great here, and they do fantastic steaks.' He frowned. 'I forgot to ask. You do eat meat?'

She nodded.

'And no allergies?'

His words were innocent enough, but there was a lazy undercurrent in his voice that made the palms of her hands grow damp, and her heart gave a thump as his eyes settled on her face.

'Apart from to me, I mean…'

Her insides tightened, and a prickling heat spread over her cheeks and throat as she gave him a small, tight, polite smile.

'I'm not allergic to you, Mr Walker.' She bit her lip, her eyes meeting his. 'For a start, allergies tend to be involuntary.'

'Oh, I see. So you're *choosing* to ignore this thing between us?'

She swallowed, unable to look away from his dark, mocking gaze.

'If by "ignore" you mean not behave in an unprofessional and inappropriate manner, then, yes, I am,' she said crisply.

He studied her face in silence, and as she gazed into his flawless features a tingling heat seeped through her limbs, cocooning her body so she felt drowsy and blurred around the edges.

'So you do admit that there is something between us?'

His words sent a pulse up her spine, bringing her to her senses instantly, and she felt a rush of adrenaline. Damn him! She was in security. It was her job to keep out unwanted intruders, to keep important data secret. So why was it that she fell into each and every one of his traps with such humiliating ease?

She wasn't even sure how he did it. No one else had ever managed to get under her skin so easily. But he seemed not only able to read her mind, but to turn her inside out so that she had nowhere to hide. It made her feel raw, flayed, vulnerable.

Remembering the last time she had felt so vulnerable, she shivered. Connor's betrayal still had the power to hurt. But, even though she knew now that it was her ego not her heart that he'd damaged, no good was going to come of confessing any of that to Ram—a man who had zero interest in emotions, his own and other people's.

And that was why this conversation was going to stop.

Lifting her chin, she met his gaze with what she hoped was an expression of cool composure.

'I don't think a business meeting is really the right time to have this particular conversation,' she said coolly. 'But, as you have a girlfriend, I'm not sure when or where *would* be right.'

'Girlfriend?' He seemed genuinely surprised. 'If you mean Clio, then, yes, she's female. But "girlfriend"? That would be stretching it. And don't look so outraged. She knows exactly what's on offer, and she's grateful to take it.'

She stared at him in disbelief. 'Grateful! For what? For being fortunate enough to have sex with the great Ramsay Walker?'

'In a nutshell.'

He seemed amused rather than annoyed.

'You surprise me, Ms Mason. Given the nature of your job, I thought you of all people would know that it pays to look beneath the surface.' His eyes gleamed. 'You really shouldn't believe everything you read on the internet.'

A quivering irritation flickered through her brain, like static on the radio.

'Is that right? So, for example, all those times you're meant to have said you don't want to get married or have children—that was all lies? You were misquoted?'

Ram stared past her, felt the breath whipping out of him. Used to women who sought to soothe and seduce, he felt her directness like a rogue wave, punching him off his feet. Who did she think she was, to question him like this? To put him, his life, under a spotlight?

But beneath his exasperation he could feel his body responding to the heat sparking in her eyes.

Ignoring his uneven heartbeat, he met her furious blue gaze. 'I'm not in the business of explaining myself, Ms Mason. But this one time I'll answer your question. I wasn't misquoted. Everything I said was and is true. I have no desire whatsoever to marry or have children.'

That was an understatement. Marriage had never been a priority for him. Parenthood even less so. And for good reason. Both might appear to offer security and satisfaction, but it had been a long time since he'd believed in the myths they promised.

Out in the bay, the Opera House was lit up, its sails gleaming ghost-white. But it was the darkness that drew his gaze. For a moment he let it blot out the twisting mass of feelings that were rising up inside him, unbidden and unwelcome.

Commitment came at a cost, and he knew that the debt would never be paid. A wife and a child were a burden— a responsibility he simply didn't want. Had never once wanted.

And he didn't intend to start now.

Leaning back in his chair, he shrugged. 'Marriage and parenthood are just a Mobius strip of emotional scenes that quite frankly I can do without. I'm sorry if that offends your romantic sensibilities, Ms Mason, but that's how I choose to live my life.'

There was a moment of absolute silence.

Nola drew a breath. By 'romantic', he clearly meant deluded, soppy and hopelessly outdated. It was also obvious that he thought her resistance to him was driven not by logic but by a desire for something more meaningful than passion.

She felt a pulse of anger beneath her skin. Maybe it was time to disabuse him of that belief.

Eyes narrowing, she stared at him coldly. 'Sorry to disillusion you, Mr Walker, but I don't have any "romantic sensibilities". I don't crave a white wedding. Nor am I hunting for a husband to make my life complete. So if I actually had an opinion on how you live your life it would be that I have no problem with it at all.'

His watched—no—*inspected* her in silence, so that the air seemed to swell painfully in her lungs.

'But you do have a problem...' He paused, and the intent expression on his face made her insides tighten and her throat grow dry and scratchy. 'You think I say something different in private to the women you refer to as my "girlfriends".'

He shook his head slowly. 'Then it's my turn to disillusion you. I don't make false promises. Why would I?

It's not as if I need to. I always get exactly what I want in the end.'

She shook her head. 'You're so arrogant.'

'I'm being honest. Isn't that what you wanted from me?'

'I don't want anything from you,' she said hoarsely, trying to ignore the heat scalding her skin, 'except a salary and a reference. I certainly have no interest in being some accessory to your louche lifestyle.'

Watching his mouth curl into a slow, sexy smile, she felt her stomach drop as though the legs of her chair had snapped.

'So why are you blushing?' he asked softly. 'Surely not because of my "louche lifestyle". I thought you were more open-minded than that.'

She glowered at him.

'I'm as open-minded as the next woman. But not if it means being a part of your harem. That's never been one of my fantasies.'

'Sadly, I'm going to have to put your fantasies on hold,' he said softly, raising his hand in a gesture of greeting to the two tall blond men who were weaving their way towards them. 'Our guests are here. But maybe we could discuss them after dinner?'

'I think that's the first time I've seen you relax since you arrived.'

Glancing up at Ram, Nola frowned.

Dinner was over, and his limo had dropped them back at the RWI building. Now they were standing in the lift.

Like many of his remarks, it could be read in so many ways. But she was too tired to do anything but take it at face value.

'It was fun,' she said simply. 'I enjoyed the food and the company.'

He did a mock stagger. 'I'm flattered.'

Glancing up, she saw that he was smiling, and she felt a panicky rush of nerves. In daylight, Ram Walker was flawless but unattainable. Now it was night-time, and beneath the low lighting, with his top button undone and a shadow of stubble grazing his face, he looked like the perfect after-dark female fantasy.

But the point about fantasies was that they were never supposed to become reality, she told herself quickly.

Shaking her head, she gave him a small, careful smile. 'I suppose it hasn't occurred to you that I might be talking about Craig and Will?'

His eyes gleamed. 'Nope.'

She swallowed. 'They're nice people.'

'And I'm not?'

Her throat felt as though it was closing up. And, was it her imagination, or was the lift getting smaller and hotter?

'You can be,' she said cautiously. She felt her pulse twitch beneath his gaze. 'But I don't know you very well. We don't know each other very well.'

Suddenly she was struggling to breathe, and her heart was beating very fast.

He smiled. 'Oh, I think we know each other very well, Nola!'

Her stomach dropped as though the lift cable had suddenly snapped, and somewhere at the edge of her vision stars were flickering—only that couldn't be right for they weren't outside.

'And I think you're a lot like me,' he said softly. 'You're focused, and determined, and you like breaking the rules. Even when you're scared of the consequences.'

There was a tiny shift in the air…softer than a sigh.

She watched, dry-mouthed, her stomach twisting into knots as he reached out and ran his finger along her cheekbone. She could feel her heartbeat echoing inside her head like footsteps fleeing. As she should be.

Except that she couldn't move—could hardly breathe.
He moved closer, sliding his hand through her hair.

'When I met you in that café you took my breath away.
You still do.'

There was silence as she struggled to speak, struggled
against the ridiculous pleasure his words provoked. Pleasure she knew she shouldn't acknowledge, let alone feel.
Not for her boss anyway.

But maybe she was making too big a deal about that. He
might be a CEO, but he was just a man, and as a woman
she was his equal. Besides, as of tomorrow he wouldn't
even be her boss.

The thought jumped inside her head like popping candy,
and then somehow her hand was on his arm, the magnetic
pull between them impossible to resist.

'Ram...' She whispered his name and he stared down at
her mutely. His eyes were dark and fierce, and she could
see that he was struggling for control.

She felt a shiver of panic tumble down her spine.

But why?

What did she care if he was struggling? So was she.
Like her, he was fighting himself—fighting this desire.

Desire.

The word jangled inside her head like a warning bell,
for was desire a big enough reason to play truth or dare
with this man? After all, she knew the risks, knew the
consequences.

Her head was spinning. Memories of that first kiss with
Connor were slip-sliding into an image of his face, resentful and distant, on that last day.

But there was no reason it would be the same with Ram.

Nola knew she had been reckless with Connor—clue-
less, really. She'd jumped off the highest board and hoped
for what? Love? A soulmate? A future? But *this* was never

going to be anything but lust. There was no expectation. No need to make promises.

And, most importantly, there would be no consequences. After tomorrow they would never see one another again. It would be a perfect moment of pure passion. So why shouldn't she give in to it?

But even as the question formed in her mind she knew two things. One, it was purely rhetorical. And two, it was too late.

The warmth of his body had melted away the last of her resistance; the battle was already lost.

And, as though he could read her mind, Ram leaned forward and kissed her.

Groaning softly, he reached out blindly for the wall of the lift, trying to steady himself. He'd expected to feel something—hell, how could he not after the tension that had been building between them for weeks?—but the touch of her lips on his was like being knocked sideways by a rogue wave.

His head was spinning. Somewhere, the world was still turning, but it didn't matter. All that mattered was here and now and Nola. Her body was melting into him, moving as he moved, her breath and his breath were one and the same. He felt her lips part and, deepening the kiss, he pulled her closer.

As the doors opened he pulled her against him and out of the lift. Hands sliding over each other, they staggered backwards, drunkenly banging into walls, barely noticing the impact. Somehow they reached his office, and as he pushed open the door they stumbled into the room as one.

Nola reached out for him, her fingers clutching the front of his shirt. He could feel her heart pounding, hear her breath coming in gasps. She pulled him closer and, groaning softly, he wrapped his fingers around hers and dragged her arms behind her back, holding her captive.

Ram shuddered. His heart was pounding so hard he thought it might burst and, reaching down, he jerked her closer, crushing her body against his. But it wasn't enough. He wanted more. Breathing out shakily, he nudged her backwards, guiding her towards the sofa.

As they slid onto the cushions he dragged his mouth from hers and she gazed up at him, her eyes huge and dazed.

His breath caught in his throat. He wanted her so badly, but he needed to know that she wanted what *he* wanted—what he could give.

'I don't do for ever. Or happy-ever-after. This is about now. About you and me. If you're hoping for something more than that—'

In answer, she looped her arm about his neck, gripping him tightly. 'Stop talking and kiss me,' she whispered, her fingers tugging at his arms, his shirt, his belt.

He knew that relief must be showing on his face, but for once he didn't care that he'd shown his true feelings. She had said what he wanted to hear and, lowering his mouth, he kissed her fiercely. As her lips parted he caught hold of the front of her blouse and tugged it loose.

Instantly he felt his groin harden. For a moment his eyes fed hungrily on the soft, pale curve of her stomach, and the small rounded breasts in the black lace bra.

She was beautiful—every bit as beautiful as he'd imagined.

And he couldn't wait a moment longer.

Leaning forward, he fumbled with the fastening of her bra and it was gone. Then he lowered his mouth to her bare breast, feeling the nipple harden beneath his tongue.

Nola whimpered. His tongue was pulling her upwards. She felt as if she was floating; her blood was lighter than air.

Helplessly, she let her head fall back, arching her spine so that her hips were pressing against his thighs. Her head was spinning, her body so hot and tight with need that she hardly knew who she was. All she knew was that she wanted him—wanted to feel him on her and in her.

She couldn't fight it anymore—couldn't fight herself.

Desperately she squirmed beneath him, freeing him with her fingers. She heard him groan, then a choking sound deep in his throat as she slid her hand around his erection.

For a moment he steadied himself above her, the muscles of his arms straining to hold his weight, his beautiful clean profile tensing with the effort.

Breathing out unsteadily, he gazed down at her. 'What about—?' he began. 'Are you protected?'

Nola gazed at him feverishly. She didn't want to talk. Didn't want anything to come between them—and, besides, there was no need.

'It's fine,' she whispered.

His eyes flared, his expression shifting, his face growing tauter as slowly he pushed the hem of her skirt up around her hips. She shivered, the sudden rush of air cooling her overheated skin, and then she breathed in sharply as he pressed the palm of his hand against the liquid ache between her thighs.

Helplessly, eagerly, she pressed back, and then suddenly he pulled her mouth up to meet his and pushed into her.

His fingers were bumping over her ribcage, his touch making her heartbeat stagger. She reached up, sliding her hand through his hair, scraping his scalp. The ache inside her was beating harder and faster and louder, the urge to pull him closer and deeper overwhelming her so that suddenly she was moving desperately, reaching for him, pressing against him.

She felt a sting of ecstasy—a white heat spreading out like a supernova—and then she arched against him, her breath shuddering in her throat. As her muscles spasmed around him he groaned her name and tensed, filling her completely.

CHAPTER THREE

Nola woke with a start.

For a moment she lay in the darkness, her brain still only on pilot light, wondering what had woken her. Almost immediately the warmth of her bed began tugging her back towards sleep and, stifling a yawn, she wriggled drowsily against the source of the heat.

And froze.

Not just her body, but her blood, her heartbeat. Even the breath in her throat hardened like ice, so that suddenly she was rigid—like a tightrope walker who'd just looked down beyond the rope.

Head spinning, she slid her hand tentatively over her thigh and touched the solid, sleeping form of Ram. As her fingers brushed against him she felt him stir and shift closer, his arm curving over her waist, and instantly she was completely, fiercely awake.

Around her the air stilled and the darkness closed in on her. Someone—Ram?—had turned off the lights in the office. Or maybe they just switched off automatically. But her eyes were adjusting now, and she could just make out the solid bulk of his desk. And strewn across the floor, distorted into strange, unfamiliar shapes, were their discarded clothes.

Picturing how they had torn them off in their hurry to feel each other's naked skin, she felt her cheeks grow hot and she blew out a breath.

Finally they'd done it. They'd had sex.

Her skin tightened in the darkness, her heartbeat fluttering, as a smile pulled at her mouth.

Sex! That made it sound so ordinary, or mechanical. But it had been anything but that.

Beside her, Ram shifted in his sleep, and the damp warmth of his body sent a tremor of hot, panicky excitement over her skin.

Remembering his fierce, hard mouth on hers, his hands roaming at will over her aching, desperate body, she pressed her hand against her lips, her stomach flip-flopping as she felt the slight puffiness where he'd kissed her again and again.

She'd expected the sex to be incredible. But now, with his hard, muscular arm curled possessively around her waist, and her body still throbbing from the frenzied release of their lovemaking, she knew that what she and Ram had shared had been more than incredible.

It had been—she searched for a word—it had been *transformative*. Beautiful and wild and breathless, flaring up like a forest fire, so hot and fast that it had consumed everything in its path straight to the sea.

And then afterwards calm, a peace such as she had never known. Just the two of them glowing in each other's arms, spent, sated, their bodies seeping into one another.

It had felt so right. *He'd* felt so right.

She shivered again. Ram had been the lover she'd imagined but never expected to meet in real life. Intuitive, generous, his touch had been a masterclass in power and precision.

He had demanded more from her than she had been willing to give, but she had yielded, for it had been impossible to resist the strength of her desire. The intensity of his.

Over and over he had pulled her against him, touching her, finding the place where liquid heat gathered, using his lips, his hands, his body to stir and torment her until the blood had beaten inside her so hard and so fast she'd thought she would pass out. She had been frantic and feverish—hadn't known who or where she was. Her entire being—every thought, every beat of her heart—had been concentrated on him, on his mouth, his body, his fingertips…

A memory of exactly what he'd done with those fingers dropped into her head and she squirmed, pressing her thighs together.

She couldn't understand why she was feeling this way. Why she had responded so strongly to a man she barely knew and didn't even really like.

She'd loved Connor—or at least she'd thought she had—yet sex with him had only ever been satisfying. Whereas with Ram it had been sublime.

It made no sense.

But then, nothing she'd thought, said or done in the last twenty-four hours had even come close to making sense. Not least sleeping with the man who, for the next twelve hours or so, was still her boss.

Her breath felt thick and scratchy in her throat.

Oh, she knew why she'd done it.

Ram Walker was not your average man. Even just being in his orbit made her feel as if someone had handed her the keys to a top-spec sports car and told her to put her foot down. He was exhilarating, irresistible.

But she knew from sleeping with Connor that giving in to temptation had consequences. Messy, unexpected and painful consequences. And so she'd waited until now, until the day before her contract ended, to give in, believing that she was being smart.

Believing it would just be one perfect night of pure pleasure.

Her skin grew hot, then cold.

She'd thought it would be so easy. Not just the sex, but

the aftermath. Maybe there might be a few awkward moments. But surely nothing too dramatic or life-changing. After all, she barely knew Ram.

It had never once crossed her mind that she would feel this way—so moved, so alive.

She'd thought once would be enough. That her body would be satisfied and she could forget him and move on.

She almost laughed out loud.

Forget him!

As if she could ever forget him.

Right now, there was only him.

It was as though he'd wiped her mind—erased every memory and experience she'd ever had. And it wasn't only the past he'd obliterated. Her future would never be the same now either. How could it be after last night? She might not have a crystal ball, but she didn't need one to know that sex was never going to be as good with any other man.

But what if today was the last time she ever saw Ram?

Was she really that naive? So stupid as to imagine they were done? That she could put last night in a box, wrap it up neatly with a bow and that would be it.

Her pulse began to race.

Since breaking up with Connor she'd been so careful. She'd had a couple of short relationships, but at the first hint of anything serious she had broken them off. It had seemed safer, given her bad luck when it came to men. Or was it bad judgement?

Her father, Richard, had been charming—financially generous. But even before her parents' divorce he had been unreliable—often disappearing without explanation, and always utterly incapable of remembering anything to do with his wife and daughter, from birthdays to parents' evenings.

Then she'd met Connor—sweet, funny Connor—who

had cared about everything from saving the planet to the trainers he wore. Miraculously, he had cared about her too, so she'd thought it would be different with him.

And it had been—for a time.

Until he'd betrayed her trust…shared the most private details of their life together over a pint in the pub. And then not even stepped up to defend her reputation.

She almost laughed, but felt more as if she was about to cry.

Her reputation.

It made her sound like some foolish eighteenth-century heroine who'd let the wrong man pick up her fan. But that was what she'd felt like. Foolish and powerless. And the fact that her supposed boyfriend had sacrificed her to impress his mates still had the power to make her curl up inside with misery.

Breathing out silently, she closed her eyes.

She'd vowed never again to trust her judgement. And with Ram she hadn't needed to. Her opinion of him was irrelevant; the facts spoke for themselves.

Even before they'd met in that café in Sydney she'd known his reputation as a ruthless womaniser. Yet she'd still gone ahead and slept with him.

And why?

Because she'd become complacent.

She'd assumed, like last time, that the worst-case scenario would be the two of them having to work in the same building. Now, though, she could see that geography didn't matter, and that the worst-case scenario was happening inside her head. And it was all to do with *him*, and how he'd made her feel.

But she couldn't think about this anymore. Not with his body so warm and solid beside her.

Her breathing faltered.

It was time to leave.

Moving carefully, so as not to wake him, she slid out from beneath his arm and began groping in the darkness for her discarded bra and shoes. Her bag was harder to find, but finally she located it by one of the armchairs.

Clutching her blouse in one hand, she tiptoed to the door and gently pushed down the handle. There was a tiny but unmistakable click and she held her breath. But there was no sound from within the darkened office and slowly, carefully, she pulled open the door and slid through it into the empty corridor.

As she waited for the lift her heartbeat sounded like raindrops on a tin roof. Every second felt like a day, and she couldn't shift the feeling that at any moment she would hear Ram's voice or his footsteps in the darkness.

Pressing her forehead against the wall, she breathed out slowly. She should be feeling relief, and in some ways she was, for now she wouldn't have to go through that horrific about-last-night conversation, or the alternative—the awkward let's-pretend-it-never-happened version.

But she couldn't help feeling that somehow she was making a mistake. That what had happened between them had been so rare, so right, that she shouldn't just walk away from it.

She turned and gazed hesitantly down the darkened corridor.

Was she doing the right thing?

Or was she about to do something she'd regret?

But what would happen if she stayed?

Her heart was racing like a steeplechaser. What should she do?

She needed help. Fifty/fifty? Ask the audience?

She felt a rush of relief.

Phone a friend.

Stepping into the lift, she pulled out her mobile. It was four in the morning here, which made it two in the afternoon in Barbados. She would let it ring three times and then hang up.

Anna picked up on the second ring.

'Hi, you. This is a surprise…'

She paused, and for a moment Nola could almost picture her friend's face, the slight furrow between her eyes as she mentally calculated the time difference between the Caribbean and Australia.

'Have you been pulling an all-nighter or did you just randomly get up to watch the sunrise?'

Anna's voice was as calm as ever, but there was a brightness to it that Nola recognised as concern. And, despite everything, that made her feel calmer.

She swallowed. 'Neither. Look, I'm not hurt or anything, but…' She breathed out slowly. 'I've just done something really stupid. At least I think it was really stupid.'

There was the shortest of silences, and then Anna said firmly, 'In that case I'll get Robbie to make me a Rum Punch and you can tell me all about it.'

It was not the daylight creeping into his office that woke Ram. Nor was it the faint but aggravating hum of some kind of machinery. It was Nola.

Or rather the fact—the quite incredible fact—that at some unspecified point in the night she had gone.

Left.

Done a runner.

Hightailed it.

He felt a sudden sharp, inexplicable spasm of…of what? Irritation? Outrage? Disappointment?

No. A twitch ran down his spine and, breathing out, he sat up slowly and ran his hand over the stubble already shadowing his jaw. It was shock. That was all.

Sitting up, he stared in disbelief around the empty office. This had *never* happened. Ever. And, despite the evidence proving that it had, he still couldn't quite believe his eyes.

His heart started to beat faster. But, really, should he be that surprised? Every single time he thought he'd got Nola Mason all figured out she threw him a curveball that not only knocked him off his feet but left him wondering who she really was.

Who *he* really was.

He scowled. In this instance that should have been an easy question to answer.

He was the one who dressed and left.

He was always the one who chose the venue, and he never slept over.

Spending the night with a woman hinted too strongly at a kind of commitment he'd spent a lifetime choosing to avoid.

His face hardened. That didn't mean, though, that women upped and left him.

But, squinting into the pale grey light that was seeping into the room, he was forced to accept that on this occasion, with this woman, it did mean exactly that.

Which should be a good thing. Most women were tedious about their need to be held, or to talk, or to plan the next date, even when he couldn't have made it any clearer that none of the above was on offer.

Only for some reason Nola's departure felt premature. Incomprehensible.

Maybe he was just overthinking it.

But why did her leaving seem to matter so much?

Probably because, although superficially she might have seemed different, he'd assumed in the end that she would behave like every other woman he knew. Only nothing about last night had turned out as he'd imagined it would.

He'd thought he was seducing her, but he'd never lost control like that.

He certainly hadn't planned to have sex with her *here*,

on the sofa in his office. But could he really be blamed for what had happened?

The tension between had been building from the moment they'd first met. In the restaurant it had been so intense, so powerful, he was surprised the other diners hadn't been sucked in by its gravitational pull.

She'd been as shaken by it as him—he was sure of it—and in the lift she had responded to his kiss so fiercely, and with such lack of inhibition, that he'd never got as far as inviting her back to his apartment.

Remembering that beat before they'd kissed, he felt his heart trip, heat and hunger tangling inside him. Watching that to-hell-with-you expression on her face grow fiercer, then soften as she melted into him, he'd wanted her so badly that he would have taken there and then in the lift if the doors hadn't opened.

Glancing round his office, his eyes homed in on his discarded shirt and he felt suddenly breathless, winded by the memory of how he'd sped her through the building with no real awareness of what he was doing, no conscious thought at all, just a need to have her in the most primitive way possible.

Reaching down, he picked his shirt up from the floor and slid his arms carelessly into the sleeves.

He hadn't hurt her. He would never do that. But he hadn't recognised himself. Hadn't recognised that fire, that urgency, that need—

The word snagged inside his head. No, not *need*.

It had been a long time since he had let himself *need* anyone. Not since he'd been a child, fighting misery and loneliness in a school on the other side of the world from his mother. Needing people, being needed, was something he'd avoided all his adult life, and whatever he might have felt for Nola he knew it couldn't have been that.

No, what he'd felt for Nola had been lust. And, like

hunger and thirst, once it had been satisfied it would be forgotten. *She* would be forgotten.

And that was what mattered. After months of feeling distracted and on edge, he could finally get back to focusing on his work.

After all, that was the real reason he'd wanted to sleep with her. To soothe the burn of frustration that had not only tested his self-control but made it impossible for him to focus on the biggest product launch of his career.

Now, though, just as he had with every other female he'd bedded, he could draw a line under her and get on with the rest of his life.

Straightening his cuffs, he stood up and walked briskly towards the door.

Ten hours later he was wrapping up the last meeting of the day.

'Right, if there's nothing else then I think we'll finish up here.'

It was five o'clock.

Ram glanced casually around the boardroom, saw his heads of department were already collecting their laptops and paperwork. His loathing of meetings was legendary among his staff, as was his near fanatical insistence that they start *and* end on time.

Pulling his laptop in front of him, he flipped it open as they began to leave the room.

The day had passed with grinding slowness.

Nothing had seemed to hold his attention, or maybe he simply hadn't been able to concentrate. But, either way, his thoughts had kept drifting off from whatever spreadsheet or proposal he was supposed to be discussing, and his head had filled with memories of the night before.

More specifically, memories of Nola—her body straddling his, her face softening as his own body grew harder than it had ever been...

He gritted his teeth. For some reason she had got under his skin in a way no woman ever had before. He'd even fallen asleep holding her in his arms. But for once intimacy had felt natural, right.

Staring down blankly at his computer screen, he felt his chest tighten. So what if it had felt right? He'd held her *in his sleep*. He hadn't even been conscious. And of course he would like to have sex with Nola again. He was a normal heterosexual man, and she was a beautiful, sexy woman.

Abruptly his muscles tensed, his eyes narrowing infinitesimally as through the open door he caught a glimpse of gleaming dark hair.

Nola! His stomach tightened involuntarily and he felt a rush of anticipation.

All day he'd been expecting to bump into her, had half imagined that she might seek him out. But now he realised that wouldn't be her way. She'd want it to play out naturally—like the tide coming in and going out again.

He breathed out sharply, his pulse zigzagging through his veins like a thread pulled through fabric, and before he even knew what he was doing he had crossed the room and yanked open the door.

But the corridor was empty.

Anger stuttered across his skin.

What the—? Why hadn't she come in to talk to him? She *must* have seen him.

Breathing out slowly, he stalked swiftly through the corridor to his office.

Jenny, his secretary, glanced up from her computer, her eyes widening at the expression on his face.

'Get Nola Mason on the phone. Tell her I want her in my office in the next five minutes.'

Slamming his office door, he strode across the room and stared furiously out of the window.

Was this some kind of a game?

Hopefully not—for *her* sake.

There was a knock at the door, and he felt a rush of satisfaction at having dragged Nola away from whatever it was she'd been doing.

'Come in,' he said curtly.

'Mr Walker—'

He turned, his face hardening as he saw Jenny, hovering in the doorway.

She smiled nervously. 'I'm sorry, Mr Walker. I was just going to tell you, but you went into your office before—'

He frowned impatiently. 'Tell me what?'

'Ms Mason can't come right now.'

'Can't or won't?' he snapped.

Jenny blinked. 'Oh, I'm sure she would if she were here, Mr Walker. But she's not here. She left about an hour ago. For the airport.'

Ram stared at her in silence, his eyes narrowing.

The airport?

'I—I thought you knew,' she stammered.

'I did.' He gave her a quick, curt smile. 'It must have slipped my mind. Thank you, Jenny.'

As the door closed his phone buzzed in his jacket and he reached for it, glancing distractedly down at the screen. And then his heart began to beat rhythmically in his chest.

It was an email.

From *Nola_Mason@CyberAngels.org*.

The corner of his mouth twisted, and then the words on the screen seemed to slip sideways as he slowly read, then reread, the email.

Dear Mr Walker

I am writing to confirm that in accordance with our agreement, today will be the last day of my employment at RWI. My colleague, Anna Harris—nee Mackenzie—and I will, of course, be in close contact with the on-site team, and remain available for any questions you may have.

I look forward to the successful completion of the project, and I wish to take this opportunity to thank you for all your personal input.
Nola Mason

Ram stared blankly at the email.

Was this some kind of a joke?

Slowly, his heart banging against his ribs like bailiffs demanding overdue rent, he reread it.

No, it wasn't a joke. It was a brush-off.

He read it again, his anger mounting with every word. Oh, it was all very polite, but there could be no mistaking the thank-you-but-I'm-done undertone. Why else would she have included that choice little remark at the bottom?

I wish to take this opportunity to thank you for all your personal input.

His fingers tightened around the phone.

Personal input!

He could barely see the screen through the veil of anger in front of his eyes, and it didn't help that he knew he was behaving irrationally—hypocritically, even. For in the past he'd ended liaisons with far less charm and courtesy.

But this was the woman he was paying to protect his business from unwanted intruders. Why, then, had he let her get past the carefully constructed emotional defences he'd built between himself and the world?

CHAPTER FOUR

Three months later

GLANCING UP AT the chalkboard above her head, Nola sighed. It was half past ten and the coffee shop was filling up, and as usual there was just too much choice. Today though, she had a rare morning off, and she wasn't about to waste the whole of it choosing a hot drink! Not even in Seattle, the coffee-drinking capital of the world.

Stepping forward, she smiled apologetically at the barista behind the counter. 'Just a green tea. Drink in. Oh, and one of those Danish, please. The cinnamon sort. Thanks.'

The sun was shining, but it was still not quite warm enough to sit outside, so she made her way to a table with a view of Elliott Bay.

Shrugging off her jacket, she leaned back in her seat, enjoying the sensation of sunlight on her face. Most of her time at work was spent alone in an office, hunched over a screen, so whenever she had any free time she liked to spend it outside. And her favourite place was right here, on the waterfront.

It was a little bit touristy. But then she *was* a tourist. And, besides, even if it did cater mainly to visitors, the restaurants still served amazingly fresh seafood and the coffee shops were a great place to relax and people-watch.

It was two weeks since she'd arrived in Seattle. And three months since she'd left Sydney. Three months of picking over the bones of her impulsive behaviour. Of wondering why she had ever thought that the consequences of sleeping with her boss would be less messy than sleeping with any other colleague?

Her pulse hopscotched forward. It was a little late to start worrying about consequences now. Particularly when one of them was a baby.

Breathing out slowly, she glanced down at her stomach and ran her hand lightly over the small rounded bump.

She had never imagined having a child. Her parents' unhappy marriage and eventual divorce had not exactly encouraged her to think of matrimony as the fairy-tale option that many of her friends, including Anna, believed it to be.

Being a mother, like being married, had always been something she thought happened to other people. Had she thought about it at all, she would probably have wanted the father of her baby to be a gentle, easy-going, thoughtful man.

She took another sip of tea.

So not Ram Walker, then.

And yet here she was, carrying his baby.

Across the café a young couple sat drinking *lattes*, gazing dotingly at a baby in a buggy. They looked like a photoshoot for the perfect modern family, and suddenly the cup in her hand felt heavy. Almost as heavy as her heart. For it was a life her child would never enjoy.

Not least because she hadn't told Ram about the baby.

And nor would she.

Had he shown any sign, any hint that he wanted to be a father, she would have told him the moment she'd found out. But some men just weren't cut out for relationships and commitment, and Ram was one of them.

He'd said so to her face, so it had been easy at first to feel that her silence was justified—especially when she was still struggling not just with the shock of finding out she was pregnant but with nausea and an exhaustion that made getting dressed feel like a tough mission.

Only now, when finally she was in a fit enough state to think, she was almost as overwhelmed with guilt as she had been with nausea.

Evening after evening had been spent silently arguing with herself over whether or not she should tell him about the baby. But with each passing day she'd convinced herself that there really was no point in letting him know.

He'd clearly stated that he didn't want to be a father, and she knew from the way he lived his life that he wasn't capable of being one.

She didn't mean biologically. He clearly could father a child—and had. But what kind of a father would he be? His relationships with women lasted days, not years—not much use for raising a child to adulthood. Their brief affair had given her first-hand experience of his limited attention span. That night in his office she had felt as though he was floating through her veins. But afterwards he'd barely acknowledged the email she'd sent him. Just sent a single sentence thanking her for her services.

Her face felt hot. Was that the real reason why she hadn't told him about the baby? Her pride? Her ego? A yearning to keep her memories of that night intact and not made ugly by the truth? The truth that he'd never wanted anything more than a one-night stand. Never wanted her *or* this baby.

She felt the hot sting of tears behind her eyes as silently she questioned her motives again. But, no, it wasn't pride or sentimentality that was stopping her from saying anything.

It was him. It was Ram.

She didn't need to confront him to know that he wouldn't want to know about the baby, or be a father, or be in their lives. Whatever connection there had been between them had ended when she'd crept out of his office in the early hours of that morning. Nothing would change that, so why put herself through the misery of having him spell it out in black and white?

She shifted in her seat. So now she was three months pregnant, unmarried, living out of a suitcase—and happy.

It was true that she sometimes got a little freaked out at the thought of being solely responsible for the baby growing inside her. But she knew she could bring a child up on her own—better than if Ram was involved.

Her mum had done it and, besides, Anna and Robbie would be there for her—when she finally got round to telling them.

She felt a twinge of guilt.

Unlike with Ram, she didn't have any doubts about telling her friends about the baby. Quite the opposite. She wanted them to know. But by the time she'd done a test she'd been in Seattle, struggling with morning sickness. Besides, she wanted to tell her friend face-to-face, not over the—

Her phone rang and, glancing down at the screen, she frowned. It was Anna. Quickly, she answered it.

'That is so weird. I was literally just thinking about you.'

Anna snorted. 'Really? What happened? Did you eat some shortbread and finally remember your old pal in Scotland?'

'I spoke to you three days ago,' Nola protested.

'And you said you'd call back. But what happens? Nothing. No text. No email…'

'I've been busy.'

'Doing what?' Anna paused. 'No, let me guess. Drinking coffee?'

Nola smiled. Since her arrival in Seattle, it was a private joke between them that Nola was drinking coffee every time her friend called.

Tucking the phone under her chin, she smiled. 'Actually, it's green tea, and it's delicious. And the Danish isn't bad either!'

'You're eating a Danish? That's fantastic.'

The relief in Anna's voice caught Nola off guard. They might barely have seen one another over the last few months but she knew her friend had been worried about her, and if she wasn't going to tell her about the baby, the least she could do was put Anna's mind at rest.

'Yeah, you heard it here first. The appetite's back. Pizzerias across the entire state of Washington are rejoicing! In fact I might even get a national holiday named after me.'

Anna laughed. 'I always said you had Italian roots.'

'Was it my blue eyes or my pale skin that gave it away?' Nola said teasingly. 'Okay, that's enough of your amateur psychology, Dr Harris. Tell me why you've rung.'

There was a slight pause.

'You mean I need something more than just being bossy?'

Nola frowned. There was something odd about her friend's voice. She sounded nervous, hesitant. 'I don't know—do you?'

There was a short silence, then Anna sighed. 'Yes. I still can't believe it happened, but...you know how clumsy I am? Well, I was out walking yesterday with Robbie, and I tripped. Guess what? I broke my foot.'

Relief, smooth and warm, surged over Nola's skin.

'Oh, thank goodness.' She frowned. 'I don't mean thank goodness you broke your foot—I just thought it was going to be something worse.' She breathed out. 'Are you okay? Does it hurt? Have you got one of those crazy boot things?'

'I'm fine. It doesn't hurt anymore and, yeah, I've got a boot. But, Noles...'

Anna paused and Nola felt the air grow still around her.

'But, Noles, what?' she said slowly.

'I can't fly for another week. It's something to do with broken bones making you more at risk of blood clots, so—'

Nola felt her ribcage contract. Glancing down, she noticed that her hands were shaking. But she'd read the email. She knew what was coming.

'So you want me to go to Sydney?'

Nola swallowed. Even just saying the words out loud made panic grip her around the throat.

'I really didn't want to ask you, and ordinarily I'd just postpone it. But the launch is so close.' There was another infinitesimal pause. 'And we *are* under contract.'

Anna sounded so wretched that Nola was instantly furious with herself.

Of course she would go to Sydney. Her friend had been a shoulder to cry on after she'd slept with Ram and generally fallen apart. She damn well wasn't going to make her sweat and feel guilty for asking one tiny favour.

'I know, and I understand—it's fine,' she heard herself say.

'Are you sure? I thought there might be a problem—'

There definitely *would* be a problem, Nola thought dully. About six feet of problem, with tousled dark hair and cheekbones that could sharpen steel. But it would be *her* problem, not Anna's.

'There won't be!' Nola shook her head, trying to shake off the leaden feeling in her chest. 'And it's me who should be sorry. Moping around and making a huge fuss about some one-night stand.'

'You didn't make a fuss,' Anna said indignantly, sounding more like herself. 'You made a mistake. And if he wasn't paying us such a huge sum of money, I'd tell him where he could stick his global launch.'

Nola laughed. 'Let's wait until the money clears and then we can tell him together. Look, please don't worry,

Anna. It'll be fine. It's not as if he's going to be making an effort to see me.'

'Oh, you don't need to worry about that,' Anna said quickly. 'I checked before I called you. He's in New York on some business trip. He won't be back for at least five days, so you definitely won't have to see him. Not that you'd have much to say to him even if he was there.'

Hanging up, Nola curled her arms around her waist protectively.

Except that she did.

She had a lot to say.

Only she had no intention of saying any of it to Ram— ever.

Glancing out of the window of his limo, Ram stared moodily up at the RWI building with none of the usual excitement and pride he felt at seeing the headquarters of his company. His trip to New York had been productive and busy—there had been the usual hectic round of meetings—but for the first time ever he had wanted to come home early.

As the car slowed he frowned. He still didn't understand why he'd decided to shorten his trip. But then, right now he didn't understand a lot of what was happening in his life, for it seemed to be changing in ways he couldn't control or predict.

Nodding at the receptionists on the front desk, he strode through the foyer and took the lift up to the twenty-second floor. Closing the door to his office, he stared disconsolately out of the window.

The launch date was rapidly approaching, but he was struggling to find any enthusiasm and energy for what amounted to the biggest day of his business career.

Nor was he even faintly excited about any of the beautiful, sexy women who were pursuing him with the determination and dedication of hungry cheetahs hunting an impala.

Why did he feel like this? And why was he feeling like it *now*?

He gritted his teeth. He knew the answer to both those questions. In fact it was the same answer. For, despite his having tried to erase her from his mind, *Nola* was the answer, the punchline, the coda to every single question and thought he'd had since she'd left Australia.

It might have been okay if it was just every now and then, but the reality was that Nola was never far from his thoughts. Even though she'd been gone for months now, every time he saw a mass of long dark hair he was still sure it was her. And each time that it wasn't he felt the same excitement, and disappointment, then fury.

There was a knock at the door, and when he was sure his face would give away nothing of what he was feeling, he said curtly. 'Come in.'

It was Jenny.

'I emailed you the data you asked for.' She handed him a folder. 'But I know you like a hard copy as well.'

He nodded. 'Anything crop up while I was away?'

'Nothing major. There were a couple of problems with some of the pre-order sites, and the live stream was only working intermittently on Tuesday. But Ms Mason sorted them out so—'

Ram stiffened. 'Ms Mason? Why didn't you tell me she called?'

Jenny's eyes widened. 'Because she didn't call. She's here.'

He stared past her, his chest tightening with shock.

'Since when?'

'Since Monday.' She smiled. 'But she's leaving tonight. Oh, and she's pr—'

He cut her off. 'And nobody thought to tell me?' he demanded.

'I thought you knew. I— Is there a problem?' Jenny stammered. 'I thought she was still under contract.'

Blood was pounding in his ears.

Glancing at his secretary's scared expression, he shook his head and softened his voice. 'There isn't, and she is.'

He could hardly believe it. Nola was in the building and yet she hadn't bothered to come and find him.

As though reading his thoughts, Jenny gave him a small, anxious smile. 'She probably thinks you're still in New York. I'm sure she'd like to see you,' she said breathlessly.

Remembering the email Nola had sent him, he felt his pulse twitch. That seemed unlikely, but it wasn't her choice.

He smiled blandly. 'I'm sure she does. Maybe you could get her on the phone, Jenny, and tell her I'd like to see her in my office. When it's convenient, of course. It's just that we have some unfinished business.'

But it wasn't going to stay unfinished for long.

Watching the door close, he leaned back in his chair, his face expressionless.

Finally she was done!

Resting her forehead against the palms of her hands, Nola stifled a yawn. It might only be four o'clock in the afternoon, but it felt as if she'd worked an all-nighter. If only she could go back to bed. Really, though, what would be the point? The fact she was sleeping badly was nothing to do with jet lag.

It was nerves.

She scowled. Not that she had any real reason to be nervous. Anna had been right—Ram was in New York on business. But that hadn't stopped the prickling sensation in the back of her neck as she'd walked into the RWI foyer, for even if the man himself wasn't in the building his presence was everywhere, making it impossible to shake off the feeling that there was still some link between them—an invisible bond that just wouldn't break.

Lowering her hands, she laid her fingers protectively over her stomach.

Not so invisible now.

For the last few weeks she'd been wearing her usual clothes, but today, for the first time, she'd struggled to get into her jeans. Fortunately she'd packed a pair of stretchy trousers that, although close-fitting, were more forgiving. She glanced down at her bump and smiled. It wasn't large, but she definitely looked pregnant now, and several people—mostly women—had noticed and congratulated her.

It was lovely, seeing their faces light up and finally being able to share this new phase of her life. But she would still be glad when it was all over and she could walk out through the huge RWI doors for the last time. And not just because of Ram's ghostly presence in the building. It felt wrong that people she barely knew—people who worked for Ram—knew that she was pregnant when he didn't.

And somehow, being here in his building, telling herself that he wouldn't want to know about the baby or be a father, didn't seem to be working anymore. He *was* the father. And being here had made that fact unavoidable.

Thankfully her train of thought was interrupted as her phone rang. Glancing at the screen, she frowned, her stomach clenching involuntarily.

It was Ram's secretary, Jenny.

'Hi, Jenny. Is everything okay?

'Yes, everything's fine, Ms Mason. I was just ringing to ask if you'd mind popping up to the office? Mr Walker would like to see you.'

Mr Walker.

She opened her mouth to say some words, but no sound came from her lips.

'I thought he was away,' she managed finally. 'On business.'

'He was.' To her shell-shocked ears Jenny's voice sounded painfully bright and happy. 'But he flew back in this afternoon. And he particularly asked to see you. Apparently you have unfinished business?'

Nola nodded, too stunned by Jenny's words even to register the fact that the other woman couldn't see her.

'Okay, well, he said to come up whenever it's convenient, so I'll see you in a bit.'

'Okay, see you then,' Nola lied.

As she hung up her heart began leaping like a salmon going upstream. For a moment she couldn't move, then slowly she closed her laptop and picked up her jacket.

Where could she go? Not her hotel. He might track her down. Nor the airport—at least not yet. No, probably it would be safest just to hide in some random café until it was time to check in.

On legs that felt like blancmange, she walked across the office and out into the corridor.

'Mr Walker? I'm just making some coffee. Can I get you anything?'

Ram looked up at Jenny.

'No, thank you, Jenny. I'm good.'

He glanced down at his phone and frowned. It was half past four. A flicker of apprehension ran down his spine.

'By the way, did you call Ms Mason?' he asked casually.

She nodded. 'Yes, and she said she'd be up in a bit.'

He nodded. 'Good. Excellent.'

He felt stupidly elated at her words, and suddenly so restless that he couldn't stay sitting at his desk a moment longer.

'Actually, I might just go and stretch my legs, Jenny. If Ms Mason turns up, ask her to wait in my office, please.'

The idea of Nola having to wait for him was strangely satisfying and, grabbing his jacket, he walked out through the door and began wandering down the corridor. Most of his staff were at their desks, but as he turned the corner into the large open-plan reception area he saw a group of people waiting for the lift.

Walking towards them, he felt a thrill of anticipation at the thought of finally seeing her again—and then abruptly he stopped dead, his eyes freezing with shock and disbelief. For there, standing slightly apart from the rest, her jacket folded over her arm, was Nola.

He watched, transfixed, as she stepped into the lift. Her long dark hair was coiled at the nape of her neck, and a tiny part of his brain registered that he'd never seen her wear it like that before.

But the bigger part was concentrating not on her hair but on the small, rounded, unmistakable bump of her stomach.

He heard his own sharp intake of breath as though from a long way away.

She was pregnant.

Pregnant.

A vice seemed to be closing around his throat. He felt like a drowning man watching his life play out in front of his eyes. A life that had just been derailed, knocked off course by a single night of passion.

And then, just as his legs overrode his brain, the lift doors closed and she was gone.

He stood gazing across the office, his head spinning, his breath scrabbling inside his chest like an animal trying to get out.

She was pregnant—several months pregnant at least—and frantically he rewound back through the calendar. But even before he reached the date when they'd slept together he knew that the baby could be his.

The blood seemed to drain from his body.

So why hadn't she said anything to him?

She'd been in the office for days. Yes, he'd been in New York when she arrived, but Jenny had spoken to her earlier. Nola knew he was in the building. Knew that he wanted to see her—

Remembering his remark about unfinished business, he almost laughed out loud.

Unfinished business.

You could say that again.

So why hadn't she said anything to him?

The question looped inside his head, each time growing louder and louder, like a car alarm. The obvious and most logical answer was that he was not the father.

Instantly he felt his chest tighten. The thought of Nola giving herself to another man made him want to smash his fists into the wall.

Surely she wouldn't—she couldn't have.

A memory rose up inside him, stark and unfiltered, of Nola, her body melting into his. She had been like fire under his skin. For that one night she had been his.

But was that baby his too?

A muscle flickered along the line of his jaw and he felt his anger curdle, swirling and separating into fury and frustration. Turning, he strode back into his office.

There was no way he could second-guess this. He had to know for certain.

'Tell Mike to bring the car round to the front of the building—*now*,' he barked at Jenny. 'I need to get to the airport.'

Ten minutes later he was slouched in the back of his limo. His head was beginning to clear finally, and now his anger was as cold and hostile as the arctic tundra.

How could she do this?

Treating him as if he didn't matter, as if he'd only had some walk-on part in her life. If he was the father, he should be centre stage.

His hands clenched in his lap. He hated the feeling of being sidelined, of being secondary to the key players in the drama, for it reminded him of his childhood, and the years he'd spent trying to fit into his parents' complex relationship.

But he wasn't a child anymore. He was man who might be about to have a child of his own.

His breath stilled in his throat.

Only *how* could he be the father? She had told him she was safe. But there was always an element of risk—particularly for a man like him, a man who would be expected to provide generous financial support for his child. Which was why he always used precautions of his own.

Except that night with Nola.

He'd wanted her so badly that he couldn't bring himself to do anything that might have risked them pausing, maybe changing their minds—like putting on a condom.

Feeling the car slow, he glanced up, his pulse starting to accelerate.

Was the baby his? He would soon find out.

Before the limo had even come to a stop, he was opening the door and stepping onto the pavement.

Dragging her suitcase through the airport, Nola frowned. She had waited as long as possible before arriving at the airport, and now she was worried she would be too late to check in her luggage.

But any worry she might be feeling now was nothing to the stress of staying at the office. Knowing he was in the building had been unsettling enough, but the fact that Ram had asked to see her—

She didn't need to worry about that now and, curving her hand protectively over her stomach, she breathed out slowly, trying to calm herself as she stopped in front of the departures board.

She was just trying to locate her flight when there was some kind of commotion behind her and, turning, she saw that there was a crowd of people pointing and milling around.

'They're shooting a commercial,' the woman standing next to her said knowledgeably. 'It was in the paper. It's for beer. Apparently it's got that rugby player in it, and a crocodile.'

'A real one?'

The woman laughed. 'Yes, but it's not here. I just meant in the advert. I don't think they'd be allowed to bring a real croc to an airport. That'd be way too dangerous.'

Nodding politely, Nola smiled—and then she caught her breath for, striding towards her, his lean, muscular body parting the crowds like a mythical wind, and looking more dangerous than any wild animal, was Ram Walker.

CHAPTER FIVE

As she watched his broad shoulders cutting through the clumps of passengers like a scythe through wheat Nola couldn't move. Or speak, or even think. Shock seemed to have robbed her of the ability to do anything but gape.

And as he made his way across the departures lounge towards her she couldn't decide if it was shock or desire that was making her heart feel as if it was about to burst.

Mind numb, she stood frozen, like a movie on pause. It was just over three months since she'd last seen him. Three months of trying and failing to forget the man who had changed her life completely.

She'd assumed she just needed more time, that eventually his memory would fade. Only now he was here, and she knew she'd been kidding herself. She would never forget Ram—and not just because she was pregnant with his baby.

Her body began to shake, and instinctively she folded her arms over her stomach.

A baby he didn't even know existed.

A baby she had deliberately chosen to conceal from him.

And just like that she knew his being here wasn't some cosmic coincidence: he was coming to find her.

Before that thought had even finished forming in her head he was there, standing in front of her, and suddenly she wished she was sitting down, for the blazing anger in his grey gaze almost knocked her off her feet.

'Going somewhere?' he asked softly.

She had forgotten his voice. Not the sound of it, but the power it had to throw her into a state of confusion, to turn her emotions into a swirling mass of chaos that made even breathing a challenge.

Looking up at him, hoping that her voice was steadier than her heartbeat, she said hoarsely, 'Mr Walker. I wasn't expecting to see you.'

He didn't reply. For a moment his narrowed gaze stayed fixed on her face, and then her skin seemed to blister and burn as slowly his eyes slid down over her throat and breast, stopping pointedly on the curve of her stomach.

'Yes, it's been a day of surprises all round.'

His heart crashing against his ribs, Ram stared at Nola in silence. He had spent the last two hours waiting at the check-in desk for her, his nerves buzzing beneath his skin at the sight of every long-haired brunette. At first when she hadn't turned up he'd been terrified that she'd caught another flight. But finally it had dawned on him that she was probably just hoping to avoid him, and therefore was going to arrive at the last minute.

Now that she was here, he was struggling to come to terms with what he could see—for seeing her in the office had been such a shock that he'd almost started to think that maybe what he'd seen might not even have been real. After all, it had only been a glimpse…

Maybe it had been another woman with dark hair, and after months of thinking and dreaming about her he'd just imagined it was Nola.

Now, though, there could be no doubt, no confusion.

It was Nola, and she was pregnant.

But that didn't mean he was the father.

He felt himself jerk forward—doubt and then certainty vibrating through his bones.

If that baby was another man's child, he knew she would

have met his gaze proudly. Instead she looked hunted, cornered, like a small animal facing a predator it couldn't outrun.

In other words, guilty as hell.

With an effort he shifted his gaze from her stomach to her face. Her lips were pale, and her blue eyes were huge and uncomprehending. She looked, if possible, more stunned than he felt. But right now feelings were secondary to the truth.

'So this is why you've been giving me the runaround?' he asked slowly. 'I suppose I should offer my congratulations.' He paused, letting the silence stretch between them. *'To both of us.'*

Watching her eyes widen with guilt, he felt new shoots of anger pushing up inside him, so that suddenly his pulse was too fast and irregular.

'I wonder—when, exactly, were you going to tell me you were pregnant?'

Looking up into his face, Nola felt her breath jerk in her throat. He was angrier than she'd ever seen him. Angrier than she'd ever seen anyone. And he had every right to be.

Had she been standing there, confronted by both this truth and the months of deception that had preceded it, she would have felt as furious and thwarted as he did. But somehow knowing that made her feel more defensive, for that was only half the story. The half that *didn't* include her reasons for acting as she had.

Lifting her chin, she met his gaze. 'Why would I tell you I'm pregnant? As of twenty minutes ago, I don't actually work for you anymore.'

Her hands curled up into fists in front of her as he took a step towards her.

'Don't play games with me, Nola.'

His eyes burned into hers, and the raw hostility in his

voice suffocated her so that suddenly she could hardly breathe.

'And don't pretend this has got anything to with your employment rights. You're having a baby, and we both know it could be mine. So you should have told me.'

Around her, the air sharpened. She could feel people turning to stare at them curiously.

Forcing herself to hold his gaze, she glared at him. 'This has got nothing to do with you.'

A nerve pulsed along his jawline.

'And you want me to take your word for that, do you?' He gazed at her in naked disbelief. 'On the basis of what? Your outstanding display of honesty up until now?'

She blinked. 'You don't know for certain if you're the father,' she said quickly, failing to control the rush of colour to her face.

His eyes locked onto hers, and instantly she felt the tension in her spine tighten like a guy rope.

'No. But *you* do.'

She flinched, wrong-footed.

How was this happening?

Not him finding her. It would have been a matter of moments for his secretary to check her flight time. But why was he here? Over the last three months she'd spent hours imagining this moment, playing out every possible type of scenario. In not one of them had he pursued her to the airport and angrily demanded the truth.

Her heart began to pound fiercely.

It would be tempting to think that he cared about the baby.

Tempting, but foolish.

Ram's appearance at the airport, his frustration and anger, had nothing to do with any sudden rush of paternal feelings on his part. Understandably, he hadn't liked finding out second-hand that she was pregnant. But that didn't mean he could just turn up and start throwing his weight around.

'I don't see why you're making this into such a big deal,' she snapped. 'We both know that you have absolutely no interest in being a father anyway.'

Ram studied her face, his pulse beating slow and hard.

It was true that up until this moment, he'd believed that fatherhood was not for him. But he'd been talking about a concept, a theoretical child, and Nola knew that as well as he did.

His chest tightened with anger.

'That doesn't mean I don't want to know *when* I am going to be one. In fact, I think I have a right to know. However, if you're saying that you really don't know who the father is, then I suggest we find out for certain.' His eyes held hers. 'I believe it's a fairly simple test. Of course it would mean you'd have to miss your flight...'

Imprisoned by his dark grey gaze, Nola gritted her teeth.

He was calling her bluff, and she hated him for it.

But what she hated more was the fact that in spite of her anger and resentment she could feel her body unfurling inside, as though it was waking from a long hibernation. And even though he was causing mayhem in her life, her longing for him still sucked the breath from her lungs.

Glancing at his profile, she felt a pulse of heat that had nothing to do with anger skim over her skin. But right now the stupid, senseless way she reacted to Ram didn't matter. All she cared about was catching that plane—and that was clearly not going to happen unless Ram found out, one way or another, if this baby was his.

So why not just tell him the truth?

Squaring her shoulders, she met his gaze. 'Fine,' she said slowly. 'You're the father.'

She didn't really know how she'd expected him to react,

but he didn't say or do anything. He just continued to stare at her impassively, his grey eyes dark and unblinking.

'I know you don't want to be involved, and that's fine. I'm not expecting you to be,' she said quickly. 'That's one of the reasons I didn't tell you.'

'So you had more than one reason, then?' he said quietly.

She frowned, unsure of how she should respond. But she didn't get a chance to reply, for as though he had suddenly become conscious of the sidelong glances and the sudden stillness surrounding them, he reached down and picked up her suitcase.

'I suggest we finish this in private.'

Turning, Ram walked purposefully across the departures lounge. Inside his head, though, he had no idea where he was going. Or what to do when he got there.

You're the father!

Three words he'd never expected or wanted to hear.

Then—*boom!*—there they were, blowing apart his carefully ordered world.

His chest grew tight. Only this wasn't just about his life anymore; there was a new life to consider now.

Through the haze of his confused thoughts he noticed two empty chairs in the corner, next to a vending machine, and gratefully sat down in one.

His head was spinning. Seeing Nola pregnant at the office, he'd guessed that he might be the father. But it had been just that. A guess. It hadn't felt real—not least because he'd spent all his life believing that this moment would never happen.

Only now it had, and he would have expected his response to be a mix of resentment and regret.

But, incredibly, what he was actually feeling was resolve. A determination to be part of his child's life.

Now all he needed to do was persuade Nola of that fact.

Glancing over to where Ram now sat, with that familiar shuttered look on his handsome face, Nola felt resentment surge through her. How could he do this? Just stroll back into her life and take over, expecting her to follow him across the room like some puppy he was training?

He had said he wanted to know the truth and so she'd told him, hoping that would be the end of their conversation. Why, then, did they need to speak in private? What else was there to say?

Her eyes narrowed. Maybe she should just leave him sitting there. Leave the airport, catch a train, or just go and hide in some nameless hotel. Show Ram that she wasn't going to be pushed around by him.

But clearly he was determined to have the last word, and trying to stop him doing so would be like trying to defy gravity: exhausting, exasperating, and ultimately futile.

The fact was that he was just so much more relentless than she could ever be, and whatever it was that drove his desire—no, his determination to win, she couldn't compete with it. Whether she liked it or not, this conversation was going to have to happen, so she might as well get on with it or she would never get on that plane.

Mutinously, she walked over to him and, ignoring the small satisfied smile on his face, sat down next to him.

Around her people were moving, picking up luggage and chatting, happy to be going home or going on holiday, and for a split second she wished with an intensity that almost doubled her over that it was her and Ram going away together. That she could rewind time, meet him in some other way, under different circumstances, and—

Her lip curled.

And what?

She and Ram might share a dizzying sexual chemistry, but there was no trust, no honesty and no harmony. Most of their conversations ended up in an argument, and the only time they'd managed to stay on speaking terms was when they hadn't needed to speak.

Remembering the silence between them in the lift, the words left unspoken on her lips as he'd covered her mouth with his, she felt heat break out on her skin.

That night had been different. That night all the tension and antagonism between them had melted into the darkness and they had melted into one another, their quickening bodies hot and liquid...

She swallowed.

But sex wasn't enough to sustain a relationship. And one night of passion, however incredible, wasn't going to make her change her mind. It had been a hard decision to make, but it was the right one. A two-parent set-up might be traditional—desirable, even—but not if one of those parents was always halfway out through the door, literally and emotionally.

Breathing out slowly, she turned her head and stared into his eyes. 'Look, what happened three months ago has got nothing to do with now...' She paused. 'It wasn't planned—we just made a mistake.'

For a moment, his gaze held hers, and then slowly he shook his head.

'We didn't make a mistake, Nola.'

'I wasn't talking about the baby,' she said quickly.

His eyes rested intently on her face.

'Neither was I.'

And just like that she felt her stomach flip over, images from the night they'd spent together exploding inside her head like popping corn. Suddenly her whole body was quivering, and it was all she could do not to lean over and kiss him, to give in to that impulse to taste and touch that beautiful mouth once again—

Taking a quick breath, she dragged her eyes away from him, ignoring the sparks scattering over her skin.

'You said you wanted to finish this, Ram, but we can't,' she said hoarsely. 'Because it never started. It was just a one-night stand, remember?'

'Oh, I remember every single moment of that night. As I'm sure you do, Nola.'

His eyes gleamed, and instantly her pulse began to accelerate.

'But this isn't about just one night anymore. Our one-night stand has got long-term consequences.' He gestured towards her stomach.

'But not for you.' She looked up at him stubbornly, her blue eyes wide with frustration. 'Whatever connection we had, it ended a long time ago.'

'Given that you're pregnant with my child, that would seem to be a little premature and counter-intuitive,' he said softly. 'But I don't think there's anything to be gained by continuing this discussion now.' He grimaced. 'Or here. I suggest we leave it for a day or two. I can take you back to the city—I have an apartment there you can use as a base—and I'll talk to my lawyers, get some kind of intermediate financial settlement set up.'

Nola gazed at him blankly.

Apartment? Financial settlement?

What was he talking about?

This wasn't about money. This was about what was best for their child, and Ram was *not* father material. A father should be consistent, compassionate, and capable of making personal sacrifices for the sake of his child. But Ram was just not suited to making the kinds of commitment and sacrifices expected and required by parenthood.

She had no doubt that financially he would be generous, but children needed more than money. They needed to be loved. To be wanted.

Memories of her own father and his lack of interest filled her head, and suddenly she couldn't meet Ram's eyes. Her father had been a workaholic. For him, business had come first, and if he'd had any time and energy left after a working day he'd chosen to spend it either out entertaining clients or with one of his many mistresses. Home-life, his wife and his daughter, had been right at the bottom of his agenda—more like a footnote, in fact.

Being made to feel so unimportant had blighted her childhood. As an adult, too, she had struggled to believe in herself. It had taken a long time, her friendship with Anna, and a successful career to overcome that struggle. And it was a struggle she was determined her child would never have to face.

But what was the point of telling Ram any of that? He wouldn't understand. How could he? It was not as if he'd ever doubted himself or felt that he wasn't good enough.

'No,' she said huskily. 'That's not going to happen.' She was shaking her head but her eyes were fixed on his face. 'I don't want your money, Ram, or your apartment. And I'm sorry if this offends your *romantic sensibilities*, but I don't want you in my baby's life just because we spent eight hours on a sofa in your office.'

Recognising his own words, Ram felt a swirling, incoherent fury surge up inside him. Wrong, he thought savagely. She had *belonged* to him that night, and now she was carrying his baby part of her would belong to him for ever.

Leaning back, he let his eyes roam over her face, his body responding with almost primeval force to her flushed cheeks and resentful pout even as his mind plotted his next move.

What mattered most was keeping her in Australia, and losing his temper would only make her more determined to leave. So, reining in his anger, he stretched out his legs and gazed at her calmly.

'Sadly for you, that decision is not yours to make. I'm not a lawyer, but I'm pretty sure that it's paternity, not romantic sensibilities, that matters to a judge. But why don't you call your lawyer just to make sure?'

It wasn't true but judging by the flare of fear in her eyes, Nola's knowledge of parental rights was clearly based on law procedural dramas not legal expertise. Nola could hardly breathe. Panic was strangling her. Why was he suddenly talking about lawyers and judges?

'Wh-Why are you doing this?' she stammered. 'I know you're angry with me for not telling you about the baby, and I understand that. But you have to understand that you're the reason I didn't say anything.'

'Oh, I see. So it's *my* fault you didn't tell me?'

He was speaking softly, but there was no mistaking the dangerous undertone curling through his words.

'*My* fault that you deliberately chose to avoid me at the office today? And I suppose it'll be my fault, too, when my child grows up without a father and spends the rest of his life feeling responsible—'

He broke off, his face hardening swiftly.

She bit her lip. 'No, of course not. I just meant that from everything you said before I didn't think you'd want to know. So I made a choice.'

Ram could hear the slight catch in her voice but he ignored it. Whatever he'd said before was irrelevant now. This baby was real. And it was his. Besides, nothing he'd said in the past could excuse her lies and deceit.

'And that's what this is about, is it? *Your* choices? *Your* pregnancy? *Your* baby?' He shook his head. 'This is not *your* baby, Nola, it's *our* baby—mine as much as yours—and you know it. And I am going be a part of his or her life.'

Nola stared at him numbly, her head pounding in time with her heart. She didn't know what to say to him—hadn't got the words to defend herself or argue her case. Not that it mattered. He wasn't listening to her anyway.

Shoulders back, neck tensing, she looked away, her eyes searching frantically for some way to escape—and then her heart gave a jolt as she suddenly saw the time on the departures board.

The next second she had snatched her suitcase and was on her feet, pulse racing.

'What do you think you're doing?'

Ram was standing in front of her, blocking her way.

'I have to go!'

Her voice was rising, and a couple of people turned to look at her. But she didn't care. If she missed this flight she would be stuck in Sydney for hours, possibly days, and she had to get away—as far away from Ram as quickly as she could.

'They've called my flight so I need to check in my luggage.'

For a moment he stared at her in silence, and then his face shifted and, leaning forward, he plucked the suitcase handle from her fingers.

'Let me take that!'

He strode away from her and, cursing under her breath, she hurried after him.

'I really don't need your help,' she said through gritted teeth.

Tucking the suitcase under his arm, he smiled blandly. 'Of course not. But you have to understand I don't fly commercial, so all this rushing around is very exciting for me. It's actually better than watching a film.'

He sounded upbeat—buoyant, almost—and she glowered at him, part baffled, part exasperated by this sudden change in mood.

'That's wonderful, Ram,' she said sarcastically. 'But I'm not here to be your entertainment for the evening.'

'If you were my entertainment for the evening you wouldn't be getting breathless from running around an airport,' he said softly. And, reaching over, he took her arm and pulled her towards him.

Her breath stuttered in her throat, and suddenly all her senses were concentrated on his hand and on the firmness of his grip and the heat of his skin through the fabric of her shirt.

'You need to slow down. You're pregnant. And besides...' he gestured towards the seemingly endless queue of people looping back and forth across the width of the room '... I don't think a couple of minutes is going to make that much difference.'

Gazing at the queue, Nola groaned. 'I'm never going to make it.'

'You don't know that.' Ram frowned. 'Why don't we ask at the desk?'

He pointed helpfully to where two women in uniform were chatting with a group of passengers surrounded by trolleys and toddlers. But Nola was already hurrying across the room.

'Excuse me. Could you help me, please? I'm supposed to be on this flight to Edinburgh but I need to check in my baggage.'

Handing over her boarding pass, she held her breath as the woman glanced down at it, and then back at her screen, before finally shaking her head.

'I'm sorry, the bag drop desk is closed—and even if we rush you through it's a good ten minutes to get to the boarding gate.' She grimaced. 'And, looking ahead, all Edinburgh flights are full for the next twenty-four hours. You might be able to pick up a cancellation, but that would mean hanging around at the airport. I'm sorry I can't be more helpful...'

'That's okay,' Nola said stiffly. 'It's really not your fault.'

And it wasn't.

Turning away, she stalked over to where Ram stood, watching her unrepentantly.

'This is your fault,' she snapped. 'If you hadn't been talking to me I'd have heard it when they called my flight and then I would have checked in my luggage on time.'

He gazed at her blandly. 'Oh, was that your flight to Edinburgh? I didn't realise it was that important. Like I said, I don't fly commercial, so—'

Nola stared at him, wordless with disbelief, her nails cutting into her hands. 'Don't give me that "I don't fly commercial" rubbish. You knew exactly what you were doing.'

He smiled down at her serenely. 'Really? You think I'd deliberately and selfishly withhold a vital piece of information?' He shook his head, his eyes glittering. 'I'm shocked. I mean, who would *do* something like that?'

She was shaking with anger. 'This is not the same at all.'

'No, it's not,' he said softly. 'I stopped you catching a flight, and you tried to stop me finding out I was a father.'

'But I didn't do it to hurt you,' she said shakily. 'Or to punish you.

And she hadn't—only how could she prove that to Ram? How could she explain to him that she had only been trying to prevent her child's future from inheriting her past? How could she tell him that life had taught her that no father was better than a bad father.

She shivered. It was all such a mess. And she didn't know what to do to fix it. All she knew was that she wanted to go home. To be anywhere but at this noisy, crowded airport, standing in front of a man who clearly hated her.

Her eyes were stinging and she turned away blindly.

'Nola. Don't go.'

Something in his voice stopped her, and slowly, reluctantly, she met his gaze.

He was staring at her impassively, his eyes cool and detached.

'Look, I don't think either of us was expecting to have this conversation, and even though I think we both know that we have a lot to talk about we need time and privacy to do it properly. I also know that I need to get home, and you need a plane. So why don't you borrow mine?'

She looked at him dazedly. 'Borrow your plane?'

He nodded. 'I have a private jet. Just sitting there, all ready to go, thirty minutes from here. It's got a proper bedroom and a bathroom. Two, in fact, so you can get a proper night's sleep. I guess I *am* responsible in part for making you miss your flight, so it's really the least I can do.'

He looked so handsome, so contrite, and clearly he wanted to make amends. Besides, all her other options involved an effort she just couldn't summon up the energy to make right now.

Biting her lip, she nodded.

Exactly thirty-three minutes later, Ram's limo turned into a private airfield.

As the car slid to a halt, Nola glanced over to where Ram sat gazing out of the window in silence. 'Thank you for letting me use your plane,' she said carefully.

Turning, he looked over at her, his eyes unreadable in the gloom of the car.

'My pleasure. I called ahead and told the pilot where to take you, so you can just sit back and enjoy the ride.'

She nodded, her heart contracting guiltily as his words replayed inside her head. He was being so reasonable— kind, even—and like a storm that had blown itself out the tension between them had vanished.

Her pulse was racing. A few hours earlier she'd been desperate to leave the country, to get away from Ram. Only now that it was finally time to go something was holding her back, making her hesitate, just as she had three months ago when she'd crept out of his office in the early hours of the morning. It was the same feeling—a feeling that somehow she was making a mistake.

She held her breath. But staying was not an option. She needed to go home, even if that meant feeling guilty. Only she hadn't expected to mind so much.

Her heart was bumping inside her chest like a bird trapped in a room and, clearing her throat, she said quickly, 'I was wrong not to tell you about the baby. I should have done, and I'm sorry. I know we've got an awful lot to discuss. But you're right—we do need time and privacy to talk about it properly, so thank you for being so understanding about me leaving.'

His eyes were light and relaxed, and she felt another pang beneath her heart.

'I'm glad you agree, and I feel sure we'll see each other very soon.'

The walk from the car to the plane seemed to last for ever, but finally she was smiling at the young, male flight attendant who had stepped forward to greet her.

'Good evening, Ms Mason, welcome on board. My name is Tom, and I'll be looking after you on this flight with my colleagues, James and Megan. If you need anything, please just ask.'

Collapsing into a comfortable armchair that bore no resemblance to the cramped seats on every other flight she'd ever been on, she tried not to let herself look out of the window. But finally she could bear it no more and, turning her head, she glanced down at the tarmac.

It was deserted. The limo was gone.

Swallowing down the sudden small, hard lump of misery in her throat, she sat back and watched numbly as Tom brought her some iced water and a selection of magazines.

'If you could just put on your seatbelt, Ms Mason, we'll be taking off in a couple of minutes.'

'Yes, of course.'

Leaning back, she closed her eyes and listened to the hum of the air conditioning, and then finally she heard the engines start to whine.

'Is this seat taken?'

A male voice. Deep and very familiar.

But it couldn't be him—

Her eyes snapped open and her heart began to thump, for there, staring down at her, with something very like a smile tugging at his mouth, was Ram.

She stared up at him in confusion. 'What are you doing here?'

'I thought you might like some company.'

Company! She frowned. Glancing past him at the window, she could see that they were starting to move forward, and across the cabin Tom and his colleagues were buckling themselves into their seats.

'I don't think there's time,' she said hurriedly. 'We're just about to take off.'

He shrugged. 'Well, like you said, we do have an awful lot to talk about.'

A trickle of cool air ran down her spine, and she felt a pang of uneasiness.

'Yes, but not now—'

She broke off as he dropped into the seat beside her.

'Why not now?' Sliding his belt across his lap, he stretched out his long legs. 'Just the two of us on a private jet...'

Pausing, he met her gaze, and the steady intensity of his grey eyes made the blood stop moving in her veins.

'Surely this is the perfect opportunity!'

CHAPTER SIX

NOLA STARED AT him uncertainly. Beneath the sound of her heartbeat she heard the plane's wheels starting to rumble across the tarmac. But she barely registered it. Instead, her brain was frantically trying to make sense of his words.

He couldn't possibly be intending to fly to Scotland with her, so it must be his idea of a joke.

Glancing up into his face, she felt her breath catch.

Except that he didn't look as if he was joking.

Taking a deep breath, trying to appear calmer than she felt, she forced herself to smile. 'I couldn't ask you to do that,' she said lightly. 'It's not as if it's on your way home.'

His grey gaze rested on her face. 'But you're not asking me, are you? Nor am I asking *you*, as it happens.'

Her face felt stiff with shock and confusion. Slowly she shook her head. 'But this isn't what we agreed. You said I could borrow your plane—you didn't say anything about coming with me.'

He gazed at her blandly. 'I thought you said we had a lot to talk about.'

'You know I didn't mean *now*.' Her voice rose.

This was madness. Total and utter madness.

Except madness implied that Ram was acting irrationally, and there was nothing random or illogical about his decision to join her on the plane. He was simply proving a point, and getting his own way just like he always did.

She felt as though she was going to throw up.

'You tricked me. You made me miss my flight and then

you offered to let me use your plane just so you could trap me here.'

And, fool that she was, she had actually believed he was trying to make amends.

Her heart began to pound fiercely. Not only that, she'd apologised to him. *Apologised* for not telling him about the baby and *thanked* him for being so understanding.

But everything he'd said had been a lie.

How could she have been so stupid—so gullible?

Her cheeks felt as if they were on fire. 'Why are you doing this to me?' she whispered.

He shrugged. 'It was your choice. I didn't make you do anything. You could have waited for a regular flight.' His mouth hardened. 'Except that would have meant talking to me. So I made a calculated guess that you'd do pretty much anything to avoid that—including accepting the offer of a no-strings flight back to Scotland.'

'Except there *are* strings, aren't there?' she snapped. 'Like the fact that you never said you were coming with me.'

He looked at her calmly. 'Well, I thought it might be a little counterproductive.'

Her pulse was crashing in her ears. 'I can't believe you're doing this,' she said hoarsely.

Leaning forward, he picked up one of the magazines and began flicking casually through the pages. 'Then you clearly don't know me as well as you thought you did.' He smiled at her serenely. 'But don't worry. Now that we have the chance to spend some time alone, I'm sure we'll get to know each other a whole lot better.'

Her hands clenched in her lap. She was breathless with anger and frustration. 'But you can't just hijack this plane—'

'Given that it's my plane, I'd say that would be almost impossible,' he agreed.

'I don't care that it's your plane. People don't behave like this. It's insane!'

'Oh, I don't think so.' He gazed at her steadily. 'You're pregnant with my child, Nola. Insane would be letting you fly off into the sunset with just your word that you'll get in touch.'

'So you just decided to come with me to the other side of the world?' she snapped. 'Yeah, I can see that's *really* rational.'

For a moment she glared at him in silence, and then her pulse began to jerk erratically over her skin, like a needle skipping across a record, as he leaned over and rested his hand lightly on the smooth mound of her stomach.

'Whether you like it or not, Nola, this baby is mine too. And until we get this sorted out I'm not letting you out of my sight. Where you go, I go.'

Blood was roaring in her ears. On one level his words made no sense, for she hardly knew him. He was a stranger, and what they'd shared amounted to so little. The briefest of flings. A night on a sofa.

And yet so much had happened in that one night. Not just the baby, but the fire between them—a storm of passion that had left her breathless and dazed, and eclipsed every sexual experience she'd had or would ever have.

She'd known that night that a part of her would always belong to Ram. She just hadn't realised then that it would turn out to be a baby. But now that he knew the truth was anything he'd done really that big a surprise? She was carrying his child, and she knew enough about Ram to know that he would never willingly give up control of anything that belonged to him.

Still, that didn't give him the right to trap her and manipulate her like this, bending her to his will as though being pregnant made her an extension of his life.

'You didn't have to do this,' she said hoarsely. 'I told you I was going to get in touch and I would have done.'

'I've saved you the trouble, then.' He gave her a small, taunting smile. 'It's okay—you don't need to thank me.'

She glowered at him in silence, her brain seething as she tried to think up some slick comeback that would puncture his overdeveloped ego.

But, really, why bother? Whatever she said wasn't going to change the fact that they were stuck with each other for the foreseeable future.

Only just because he'd managed to trick her into getting on his plane, it didn't mean that he was going to have everything his own way. Remembering his remark back at the airport, she felt her breathing jerk, and she curled her fingers into the palms of her hands. She sure as hell wasn't going to spend the rest of this flight entertaining him.

'I'd love to keep on chatting,' she said coldly. 'But it's been a long, and exhausting day, and as you can imagine I'm very tired.'

Their eyes met—his calm and appraising, hers combative—and there was a short, taut silence.

Finally he shrugged. 'Of course. I'll show you to your room.'

Her room!

'No—' She lurched back in her seat.

She would have liked to brush her teeth, and maybe put on something more comfortable, but the thought of undressing within a five-mile radius of Ram made her heart start to beat painfully fast.

'Actually, I think I'd rather stay here,' she said quickly. 'These seats recline, don't they? And I'm not really sleeping properly at the moment anyway.'

He stared at her speculatively, and she wondered if he was going to demand that she use the bedroom.

But after a moment, he simply nodded. 'I'll get you a blanket.'

Five minutes later, tucked cosily beneath a soft cashmere blanket, Nola tilted back her seat and turned her head pointedly away from where Ram sat beside her, working on his laptop.

How was he able to do any work anyway? she thought irritably. After everything that had happened in the last few hours anybody else—her included—would have been too distracted, too agitated, too exhausted.

But then wasn't that one of the reasons she'd been so reluctant to tell him about the baby? Just like her father, he always put business first, pleasure second, and then the boring nitty-gritty of domestic life last. And, having offered to fly her home in his private jet, he probably thought he'd been generous enough—caring, even.

Stifling a yawn, she closed her eyes. Ram's deluded world view didn't matter to her any more than he did. He might have been her boss, and he might be calling the shots now. But that would change as soon as they landed in Scotland. Edinburgh was her home, and she wasn't about to let anyone—especially not Ram Walker—trample over the life she had built there. Feeling calmer, she burrowed further down beneath the blanket...

She woke with a start.

For a moment she lay there, utterly disorientated, trying to make sense of the soft wool brushing against her face and the clean coolness of the air, and then suddenly she was wide awake as the previous night's events slid into place inside her head.

Opening her eyes, she struggled to sit up, her senses on high alert.

Why did it feel as though they were slowing down? Surely she couldn't have slept for that long? Picking up her phone, she glanced at the screen and frowned. It didn't make sense. They'd only been flying a couple of hours, and yet the plane seemed to be descending.

'Good, you're awake.'

Her heart gave a jolt, and she turned.

It was Ram. He was standing beside her, his face calm, his grey eyes watching her with an expression she didn't quite recognise.

'I thought I was going to have to wake you,' he said coolly.

He was holding his laptop loosely in one hand, so he must have spent the last few hours working, and yet he looked just as though he'd had a full eight hours' sleep. She could practically feel the energy humming off him like a force field.

But that wasn't the only reason her pulse was racing.

With his dark hair falling over his forehead, and his crisp white shirt hugging the muscles of his chest and arms, he looked like a movie star playing a CEO. Even the unflattering overhead lights did nothing to diminish his beauty.

Was it really necessary or fair for him to be that perfect? she thought desperately. Particularly when her own body seemed incapable of co-ordinating with her brain, so that despite his appalling behaviour at the airport her senses were responding shamelessly to his blatant masculinity.

Gritting her teeth, hoping that none of her thoughts were showing on her face, she met his gaze.

'Why are we slowing down? Are we stopping for fuel?'

'Something like that.'

He studied her face for a moment, and then glanced back along the cabin. 'I just need to go and speak to the crew. I won't be long.'

Biting her lip, she stared after him, a prickle spreading over her skin. She sat in uneasy silence, her senses tracking the plane's descent, until she felt the jolt as it landed.

Something felt a bit off. But probably it was just because she'd never flown on a private jet before. Usually at this point everyone would be standing up and pulling down their luggage, chatting and grabbing their coats. This was so quiet, so smooth, so civilised. So A-list.

Glancing out of the window, Nola smiled. They might not be in Scotland yet, but the weather was doing its best to make her feel as if they were. She could hear the wind already, and fat drops of rain were slapping against the glass.

'Come on—let's go!'

Turning, she saw that Ram was standing beside her, his hand held out towards her.

She frowned. 'Go where? Don't we just wait?'

'They need to clean the plane and do safety checks. And then the crew are going off-shift.'

She gazed up at him warily.

'So where are we going?'

'Somewhere more comfortable. It's not far.'

Her heart began to thump. Maybe it would have been better after all if she'd just waited for another flight. But it was too late to worry about that now.

It was warm outside—tropical, even—but she still ducked her head against the wind and the rain.

'Be careful.'

Ram took hold of her arm and, ignoring her protests, guided her down the stairs.

'I can manage,' she said curtly.

But still he ignored her, tightening his grip as he walked her across the runway to an SUV that was idling in the darkness.

Inside the car, he leaned forward and tapped against the glass. 'Thanks, Carl. Just take it slow, okay?'

'I thought you said it wasn't far,' she said accusingly.

Turning back to face her, he shrugged. But there was a

small, satisfied smile on his handsome face that made her heart start to bang against her ribs.

'It isn't. But this way we stay nice and dry.' His eyes mocked her. 'Despite what you may have heard, I can't actually control the weather.'

She nodded, but she was barely listening to what he said; she was too busy squinting through the window into the darkness outside.

Stopover destinations to and from Australia usually depended on the airline. It could be Hong Kong, Dubai, Singapore or Los Angeles. Of course flying on a private jet probably meant that some of those options weren't available. But, even so, something didn't feel right.

For a start there were no lights, nor even anything that really passed as a building. In fact she couldn't really see much at all, except a tangled, dark mass of trees and vegetation stretching away into the distance. Her heart began to beat faster, and she felt a rush of cold air on her skin that had nothing to do with the car's air conditioning.

She forced herself to speak. 'Where exactly are we?'

'Queensland—just west of Cairns.'

Turning, she stared at him in confusion, her mouth suddenly dry.

'What? We haven't even left Australia? So why have we stopped? We're never going to get to Scotland at this rate!'

'We're not going to Scotland,' he said quietly.

That prickling feeling had returned, and with it a sensation that she was floating—that if she hadn't been gripping the door handle so tightly she might have just drifted away.

'What do you mean? Of course, we're going to Scotland—' She broke off as he started to shake his head.

'Actually, we're not.'

His eyes glittered in the darkness, and she felt her breath catch in her throat.

'We never were. It was always my intention to bring you here.'

She stared at him in silence. Fury, shock, disbelief and frustration were washing over her like waves breaking against a sea wall.

Here? Here!

What was he talking about?

'There is no *"here"*,' she said shakily. 'We're in the middle of nowhere.'

He was mad. Completely mad. There was no other explanation for his behaviour. How could she not have noticed before?

'You and I need to talk, Nola.'

'And you want to do that in the middle of a jungle?' She was practically shouting now. Not that he seemed to care.

She watched in disbelief as calmly he shook his head.

'It's actually a rainforest. Only parts of it are classified as a jungle. And clearly I'm not expecting us to talk there. I have a house about three miles from here. It's very beautiful and completely private—what you might call secluded, in fact, so we won't be disturbed.'

Her head was spinning.

'I don't care if you have a palace with its own zoological gardens. I am not going there now or at any other time—and I'm definitely not going there with *you*.'

He lounged back against the seat, completely unperturbed by her outburst, his dark eyes locking onto hers. 'And yet here you are.'

She stared at him in shock, too stunned, too dazed to speak. Then, slowly, she started to shake her head. 'No. You can't do this. I want you to turn this car around now—'

Her whole body was shaking. This was far, far worse than missing her flight or Ram joining her on the plane.

Leaning forward, she began banging desperately on the glass behind the driver's head.

'Please—you have to help me!'

Behind her, she heard Ram sigh. 'You're going to hurt your hand, and it won't make any difference. So why don't you just calm down and try and relax?'

Her head jerked round. 'Relax! How am I supposed to relax? You're *kidnapping* me!'

Ram stretched out his legs. He could hear the exasperation and fury in her voice—could almost see it crackling from the ends of her gleaming dark hair.

Good, he thought silently. Now she knew how he felt. How it felt to have your life turned upside down. Suddenly no longer to be in charge of your own destiny.

'Am I? I'm not asking anyone for a ransom. Nor am I planning to blindfold you and tie you to the bed,' he said softly, his gaze holding hers. 'Unless, of course, you want me to.'

He watched two flags of colour rise on her cheekbones as she slid back into her seat, as far from him as was physically possible.

'All I want is for you to stop acting like some caveman.' She breathed out shakily. 'People don't behave like this. It's barbaric…primitive.'

'Primitive?' He repeated the word slowly, letting the seconds crawl by, feeling his groin hardening as she refused to make eye contact with him. 'I thought you liked primitive,' he said softly.

'That was different.' Turning her head sharply, she glowered at him. 'And it has nothing to do with any of this.'

'On the contrary. You and I tearing each other's clothes off has everything to do with this.'

'I don't want to talk about it,' she snapped, her blue eyes wide with fury. 'I don't want to talk to you about anything. In fact the only conversation I'm going to be having is with the police.'

She sounded breathless, as though she'd been running. He watched her pull out her phone and punch at the buttons.

'Oh, perhaps I should have mentioned it earlier...there's pretty much zero coverage out here.'

He smiled in a way that made her want to throw the phone at his head.

'It's one of the reasons I like it so much—no interruptions, no distractions.'

Fingers trembling with anger, she switched off her phone and pressed herself against the door. 'I hate you.'

'I don't care.'

The rest of the journey passed in uncomfortable silence. Nola felt as though she'd swallowed a bucket of ice; her whole body was rigid with cold, bitter fury. When finally the car came to a stop at his house she slid across the seat and out of the door without so much as acknowledging his presence.

Staring stonily at his broad shoulders in his dark suit jacket, she followed him through a series of rooms and corridors, barely registering anything other than the resentment hardening inside her chest.

'This is your room. The bathroom is through there.'

She glared at him. 'My room? How long are you planning on keeping me here?'

He ignored her. 'You'll find everything you need.'

'Really? You mean there's a shotgun and a shovel?'

His eyes hardened. 'The sooner you stop fighting me, Nola, the sooner this will all be over. If you need me, I'm just next door. I'll see you in the morning.'

'Unless you're going to lock me in, I won't be here in the morning.'

He stared at her impatiently. 'I don't need to lock you in. It would take you the best part of a day to walk back to the airfield. And there would be no point. There's nothing there. And if you want to get to civilisation that's a three-day walk through the rainforest—a rainforest with about twenty different kinds of venomous snakes living in it.'

'Does that include you?' she snarled.

But he had already closed the door.

Left alone, Nola pulled off her clothes and angrily yanked on her pyjamas. She still couldn't believe what was happening. How could he treat her like this?

Worse—how could he treat her like this and then expect her to sit down and have a civilised conversation with him?

She clenched her jaw. He could expect what he liked. But he couldn't make her talk or listen if she didn't want to.

Her eyes narrowed. In fact she might just stay in her room.

She would think about it properly in the morning. Right now she needed to close her eyes and, climbing into bed, she pulled the duvet up to her chin, rolled onto her side, and fell swiftly and deeply into sleep.

Ram strode into the huge open-plan living space, his frustration with Nola vying with his fury at himself.

What the hell was he doing?

He'd only just found out he was going to be a father. Surely that was enough to be dealing with right now? But apparently not, for he had decided to add to the chaos and drama of the evening by kidnapping Nola.

Because, regardless of what he had said to her in the car, this *was* kidnapping.

Groaning, he ran a hand wearily over his face.

But what choice had she given him?

Ever since she'd forced him to meet her at that internet café she had challenged him at every turn. But she was pregnant with his child now, and her leaving the country was more than defiance. Even though she'd said she would be in touch, he hadn't believed her.

His face hardened. And why should he? She had kept the pregnancy secret for months, and even when she'd had the perfect opportunity to tell him about the baby she had chosen instead to avoid him. And then tried to run away.

But Nola was going nowhere now. She certainly wasn't going to Scotland any time soon.

He breathed out slowly. In fact, make that *never.*

If she moved back to Edinburgh, then he would be cut out of his baby's life. Not only that, his child would grow up with another man as his father—with another man's name instead of his. Worse, he or she would grow up believing themselves to be a burden not worth bearing, a mistake to be regretted.

He would do whatever it took to stop that from happening.

Crossing the room, he poured himself a whisky and downed it in one mouthful.

Even kidnapping.

His chest tightened.

What had he been thinking?

But that was just it. He hadn't been thinking at all—he'd just reacted on impulse, his emotions blindly driving his actions, so that now he had a woman he barely knew, who was carrying a child he hadn't planned, sleeping in the spare room in what was supposed to be his private sanctuary from the world.

Gritting his teeth, he poured himself another whisky and drank that too.

So why had he brought Nola here?

But he knew why. He hadn't been exaggerating when he'd said that the house was secluded. It was luxurious, of course, but it was completely inaccessible to anyone without a small plane or helicopter, and on most days communicating with the outside world was almost impossible.

Here, he and Nola would be completely alone and they would be able to talk.

His fingers twitched against the empty glass.

Except that talking was the last thing he wanted to do with her. Particularly now that they were alone, miles from civilisation.

A pulse began to beat in his groin.

For a moment he stared longingly at the bottle of whisky. But where Nola was concerned it would take a lot more than alcohol to lock down his libido. A cold shower might be better—and if that didn't work he might have to go and swim a few lengths in the pool. And then maybe a few more.

He'd do whatever was necessary to re-engage his brain so that tomorrow he could tell Nola exactly how this was all going to play out.

As soon as she woke Nola reached over to pick up her phone, holding her breath as she quickly punched in Anna's number. When that failed to connect she called the office, then Anna again, and then, just to be certain, her favourite takeaway pizzeria by the harbour. But each time she got the same recorded message, telling her that there was no network coverage, and finally she gave up.

Rolling onto her side, she gazed in silence around the bedroom. It was still dark, but unless she'd slept the entire day it must be morning. She wasn't planning on going anywhere, but there was no point in lying there in the dark. Sighing, she sat up. Immediately she heard a small click, and then daylight began filling the room as two huge blinds slid smoothly up into the ceiling.

She gasped. But it wasn't the daylight or the blinds or even the room itself that made her hold her breath. It was the pure, brilliant blue sky outside the window.

Heart pounding, she scrambled across the bed and

gazed down at a huge canopy of trees, her eyes widening as a group of brightly coloured birds burst out of the dark green leaves. She watched open-mouthed as they circled one another, looping and curling in front of her window like miniature acrobatic planes, before suddenly plunging back into the trees.

She had been planning on staying in her room to protest against Ram's behaviour. But ten minutes later she had showered, dug some clean clothes out of her suitcase and was standing by her bedroom door.

Her pulse began to beat very fast. If she opened that door she would have to face Ram. But sooner or later she was going to have to face him anyway, she told herself firmly.

And, not giving herself the chance to change her mind, she stalked determinedly out of her room.

In daylight, the house was astonishingly, dazzlingly bright. Every wall was made of glass, and there were walkways at different levels, leading to platforms actually within the rainforest itself.

No doubt it had been designed that way, she thought slowly. So that the wildlife could be watched up close but safely in its natural environment.

Her heart began to thump.

Only some of the wildlife clearly didn't understand the rules, for there on the deck, standing at the edge of an infinity pool, was one of the most dangerous animals in Australia—probably in the world.

Unfortunately there was no safety glass between her and Ram.

She was on the verge of making a quick, unobtrusive retreat when suddenly he turned, and her breath seemed to slide sideways in her chest as he began slowly walking towards her.

It was the heat, she thought helplessly. Although she

wasn't sure if it was the sun or the sight of Ram in swimming shorts that was making her skin feel warm and slick.

She tried not to stare, but he was so unbelievably gorgeous—all smooth skin and golden muscles. Now he was stopping in front of her and smiling, as though yesterday had never happened, and the stupid thing was that she didn't feel as though it had happened either. Or at least her body didn't.

'Good morning.' He squinted up at the sky. 'I think it still qualifies as morning.' Tilting his head, he let his eyes drift casually over her face. 'I was going to come and wake you up. But I didn't fancy getting punched on the nose.'

She met his gaze unwillingly. 'So you admit that I've got a reason to punch you, then?'

He grinned, and instantly she felt a tug low in her pelvis, heat splaying out inside her so quickly and fiercely that she thought she might pass out.

'I'm not sure if you need a reason,' he said softly. 'Most of the time I seem to annoy you just by existing.'

She gazed at him in silence, trying to remember why that was.

'Not always,' she said carefully. 'Only some of the time. Like when you kidnap me, for instance.'

There was a short, pulsing silence, and then finally he sighed.

'We need to talk about this now, Nola. Not in a week or a month. And, yes, maybe I overreacted, bringing you here like this. But you've been building a life, a future, that doesn't include me.'

Her heart gave a thump. 'I thought you *wanted* that.'

'What if I said I didn't?'

His eyes were fixed on her face.

She breathed out slowly, the world shifting out of focus around her.

'Then I guess we need to talk.'

'And we will.' His gaze locked onto hers. 'But first I'll give you the tour, and then you'd better eat something.'

The tour was brief, but mind-blowing. The house was minimalist in design—a stunning mix of metal and glass that perfectly offset the untamed beauty of the rainforest surrounding it.

Breakfast—or was it brunch?—took longer. A variety of cold meats, cheese, fruit and pastries were laid out buffet-style in the huge sunlit kitchen and, suddenly feeling famished, Nola helped herself to a plate of food and a cup of green tea while Ram watched with amusement.

'I have a live-in chef—Antoine. He's French, but he speaks very good English. If you have any particular likes or dislikes tell him. His wife, Sophie, is my housekeeper. She takes care of everything else. So if you need anything...'

Fingers tightening around her teacup, Nola met his gaze. 'Like what?'

He gave a casual shrug. 'I don't know. What about a bikini? You might fancy a swim.'

His eyes gleamed, and she felt something stir inside her as his gaze dropped over the plain white T-shirt that was just a fraction too small for her now.

'Unless, of course, you're planning on skinny-dipping.'

Ignoring the heat throbbing over her skin, she gave him an icy stare. 'I'm not planning on anything,' she said stiffly. 'Except leaving as soon as possible. I know we have a lot to talk about, but I hardly think it will take more than a day.'

He stared at her calmly. 'That will depend.'

'On what?'

He was watching her carefully, as though gauging her probable reaction to what he was about to say. But, really, given everything that he'd already said and done, how bad could it be?

'On what happens next. You see, I've given it a lot of thought,' he said slowly, 'and I can only think of one possible solution to this situation.'

Her nerves were starting to hum. She looked over at him impatiently. 'And? What is it?'

He stared at her for a long moment, and then finally he smiled.

'We need to marry. Preferably as soon as possible.'

CHAPTER SEVEN

NOLA STARED AT him in stunned silence.

Marry?

As her brain dazedly replayed his words inside her head she felt her skin grow hot, and then her heart began to bang against her ribs. Surely he couldn't be serious.

She laughed nervously. 'This is a joke, right?'

For a moment he looked at her in silence, then slowly he shook his head.

She stared at him incredulously. 'But you don't want to get married.' Her eyes widened with shock and confusion. 'Everyone knows that. You told me so yourself.' She frowned. 'You said marriage was a Mobius strip of emotional scenes.'

Watching the pulse beating frantically at the base of her throat, Ram felt a flicker of frustration.

To be fair, her reaction wasn't really surprising. He'd spent most of the night thinking along much the same lines himself. But, as he'd just told her, marriage was the only solution—the only way he could give his child the *right* kind of life. A life that was not just financially secure but filled with the kind of certainty that came from *belonging*.

He shrugged. 'I agree that it's not a choice I've ever imagined making. But situations change, and I'm nothing if not adaptable.'

Adaptable! Nola felt her breathing jerk. What was he talking about? As soon as she'd shown the first signs of not wanting to do things his way he'd kidnapped her!

'Oh, I see—so that's what this is all about.' She loaded her voice with sarcasm. 'Dragging me out here, trying to coerce me into marrying you, is just your way of showing me how *adaptable* you are.' She gave a humourless laugh. 'You're about as adaptable as a tornado, Ram. If there's anything in your path it just gets swept away.'

'If that was true we wouldn't be having this conversation,' he said calmly.

'How is this a conversation?' Nola shook her head. 'You just told me we *need* to marry. That sounds more like an order than a proposal.'

His eyes narrowed. 'I'm sorry if you were hoping for something a little more romantic, but you didn't exactly give me much time to look for a ring.'

She glowered at him, anger buzzing beneath her skin. 'I don't want a ring. And I wasn't hoping for anything from you. In case you hadn't noticed, I've managed just fine without you for the last three months.'

His gaze didn't flicker.

'I wouldn't know,' he said softly. 'As you didn't bother telling me you were having my baby until last night.'

Pushing away a twinge of guilt that she hadn't told him sooner, she gritted her teeth. It had been wrong of her not to tell him that she was pregnant. But marrying him wasn't going to put it right.

Only, glancing at the set expression on his face, she saw that Ram clearly thought it was.

Forcing herself to stay calm, she said quickly, 'And I've apologised. But why does that mean we need to get married?'

Ram felt his chest grow tight. Did he *really* need to answer that? His face hardened and he stared at her irritably. 'I would have thought that was obvious.'

For a fraction of a second his eyes held hers, and then he glanced pointedly down at her stomach.

'Because I'm *pregnant*?' She stared at him in exasperation, the air thumping out of her lungs. How could he do this? It was bad enough that he'd tricked her into coming here in the first place. But to sit there, so handsome and smug, making these absurd, arrogant statements... And then assume that she was just going to go along with them.

'Maybe a hundred years ago that might have been a reason. But it is possible to have a baby out of wedlock. People do it all the time now.'

'Not *my* baby,' Ram said flatly, his stomach clenching swiftly at her words.

How could she be so casual about this? So dismissive? Did she really think that having a father was discretionary? A matter of preference? Like having a dog or a cat?

He studied her face, seeing the fear and understanding it. *Good.* It was time she realised that he was being serious. Marriage wasn't an optional extra, like the adaptive suspension he'd had fitted on his latest Lamborghini. It was the endgame. The obvious denouement of that night on his sofa.

Shaking his head, trying to ignore the anger pooling there, he said coolly, 'By any definition this situation is a mess, and the simplest, most logical way to clear it up is for us to marry. Or are you planning on buying a crib and just hoping for the best?'

Nola felt her heartbeat trip over itself. How *dare* he?

She didn't know what was scaring her more. The fact that Ram was even considering this as an option, or his obvious belief that she was actually going to agree to it.

Looking up into his handsome face, she felt her skin begin to prickle. She couldn't agree. She might not have planned this pregnancy, but she knew she could make it work. Marrying Ram, though...

How could that be anything *but* a disaster?

They barely knew each other, had nothing in common,

and managed to turn every single conversation into an argument. She swallowed. And, of course, they weren't in love—not even close to being in love.

Her head was spinning.

All they shared was this baby growing inside her, and one passionate night of sex. But marriages weren't built on one-night stands. And, no matter how incredible that night had been, she wasn't so naive as to believe that a man like Ram Walker would view his wedding vows as anything but guidelines.

Her fingers curved into the palms of her hands. For her—for most people—marriage meant commitment. Monogamy.

But Ram could barely manage five days with the same woman. So how exactly was he planning on forsaking all others?

Or was he expecting to be able to carry on just as he pleased?

Either way, how long would it be before he felt trapped... resentful?

Or, worse, bored?

Remembering the distracted look in her father's eyes, the sense that he was always itching to be somewhere else and her own panicky need to try and make him stay, she felt sick.

She knew instinctively that Ram would be the same.

Wanting Nola to be his wife was just the knee-jerk response of a CEO faced with an unexpected problem. But she didn't want her marriage to be an exercise in damage limitation. Surely he could understand that.

But, looking over at him, she felt a rush of panic.

He looked so calm, almost too calm, as though her opposition to his ludicrous suggestion was just a mere formality—some twisted version of bridal nerves.

And with any other woman he would probably be right

in thinking that. After all, he'd almost certainly never met anyone who had turned him down.

Her heart began to pound.

Until now.

Slowly, she shook her head.

'I can't marry you, Ram. Right now, I'm not sure I ever want to be married. But if at some point I do, it will be because the man asking me *loves* me and wants me to be his wife.'

His face was expressionless, but his eyes were cool and resolute.

'And what happens if you don't marry? I doubt you'll stay single for ever, so how will that work? Are you going to live with a man? Is he just going to spend the occasional night in your bed?'

She felt her face drain of colour.

'I don't know. And you can't expect me to be able to answer all those questions now. That's not fair—'

His eyes were locked on hers.

'*I don't know* is not a good enough answer,' he said coldly. 'And the life you're planning for our child sounds anything but fair.'

'I'm not planning anything.' She stared at him helplessly.

'Well, at least we can agree on that,' he snarled. 'Believe me, Nola, when I tell you that no child of mine is going to be brought up by whichever random man happens to be in your life at that particular moment.'

'That's not—' She started to protest but he cut her off.

'Nor is my child going to end up with another man's name because its mother was too stubborn and selfish to marry its father.'

She stood up so quickly the chair she was sitting on flew backwards. But neither of them noticed.

'Oh, I see. So you marrying me is a *selfless* act,' she

snapped. Her blue eyes flashed angrily up at him. 'A real sacrifice—'

'You're putting words in my mouth.'

'And you're putting a gun to my head,' she retorted. 'I'm not going to marry you just to satisfy your archaic need to pass on a name.'

'Names matter.'

She shivered. 'You mean *your* name matters.'

Ram felt his chest tighten. Yes, he did mean that. A name was more than just a title. It was an identity, a destiny, a piece of code from the past that mapped out the future.

His eyes locked onto hers. 'Children need to know where they come from. They need to belong.'

'Then what's wrong with *my* name?' she said stubbornly. 'I'm the mother. This baby is inside *me*. How could it belong to anyone more than to me?'

'Now you're just being contrary.'

'Why? Because I don't want to marry you?'

He shook his head, his dark gaze locked onto hers. 'Because you know I'm right but you're mad at me for bringing you here so you're just going to reject the only logical solution without a moment's consideration.'

Nola felt despair edge past her panic. His cavalier attitude to her objections combined with his obvious belief that she would crumble was overwhelming her.

'I have considered it and it won't work,' she said quickly. 'And it doesn't have to. Look, this is *my* responsibility. I should have been more careful. That's why this is on *me*.'

'This is *on you*?' He repeated her words slowly, his voice utterly expressionless.

But as she looked over at him she felt the hairs on the back of her neck stand up. His eyes were narrowed, fixed on her face like a sniper.

'We're not talking about a round of drinks, Nola. This is a baby. A life.'

She flinched. 'Biology is not a determining factor in parenthood.'

He looked at her in disbelief. 'Seriously? Did you read that in the in-flight magazine?'

She looked at him helplessly. 'No, I just meant—'

He cut her off again. 'Tell me, Nola. Did you have a father?'

The floor seemed to tilt beneath her feet. 'Yes. But I don't—'

'But you don't what?' He gave a short, bitter laugh. 'You don't want that for your own child?'

She blinked. Tears were pricking at her eyes. But she wasn't going to lose control—at least not here and now, in front of Ram.

'You're right,' she said shakily. 'I don't want that. And I never will.'

And before he had a chance to reply she turned and walked swiftly out of the kitchen.

She walked blindly, her legs moving automatically in time to the thumping of her heart, wanting nothing more than to find somewhere to hide, somewhere dark and private, away from Ram's cold, critical gaze. Somewhere she could curl up and cradle the cold ache of misery inside her.

Her feet stopped. Somehow she had managed to find the perfect place—a window looking out into the canopy of the rainforest. There was even a sofa and, her legs trembling, she sat down, her throat burning, hands clenched in her lap.

For a moment she just gazed miserably into the trees, and then abruptly her whole body stilled as she noticed a pair of eyes gazing back at her. Slowly, she inched forward—and just like that they were gone.

'It was a goanna. If you sit here long enough it will probably come back.'

She turned as Ram sat down next to her on the sofa.

She stared at him warily, shocked not only by the fact that he had come to find her but by the fact that his anger, the hardness in his eyes, had faded.

'Did I scare it?'

Ram held her gaze. 'They're just cautious—they run away when something or someone gets too close.'

Watching her lip tremble, he felt his heart start to pound. She looked so stricken...so small.

His breath caught in his throat. In his experience women exploited emotion with the skill and precision of a samurai wielding a sword. But Nola was different. She hadn't wanted him to see that she was upset. On the contrary, she had been as desperate to get away as that lizard.

Desperate to get away from *him*.

An ache was spreading inside his chest and he gritted his teeth, not liking the way it made him feel, for he would never hurt her. In fact he had wanted more than anything to reach out and pull her against him. But of course he hadn't. Instead he'd watched her leave.

Only almost immediately, and for the first time in his life, he'd been compelled to follow. He'd had no choice—his legs had been beyond his conscious control.

He stared at her in silence, all at once seeing not only the tight set of her shoulders and the glint of tears but also what he'd chosen to ignore earlier: her vulnerability.

Shifting back slightly, to give her more space, he cleared his throat.

'There's always something to see,' he said carefully. 'We could stay and watch if you want?'

He phrased it as a question—something he would never normally do. But right now getting her to relax, to trust him, seemed more important than laying down the law.

She didn't reply, and he felt an unfamiliar twitch of panic that maybe she never would.

But finally she nodded. 'I'd like that. Apart from the odd squirrel, I've never seen anything wild up close.'

'Too busy studying?'

It was a guess, but she nodded again.

'I did work too hard,' she agreed. 'I think it was a survival technique.'

Staring past him, Nola bit her lip. She'd spoken without thinking, the words coming from deep inside. Memories came of hours spent hunched over her schoolbooks, trying to block out the raised voices downstairs, and then—worse—the horrible, bleak silence that had always followed.

Ram stared at her uncertainly, hating the bruised sound of her voice. This was the sort of conversation he'd spent a lifetime avoiding. Only this time he didn't want to avoid it. In fact he was actually scared of spooking her, and suddenly he was desperate to say something—anything to make her trust him enough to keep talking.

'Why do you think that?' he asked gently.

She swallowed. 'My dad was often home late, or away, and my parents would always argue when he got home. He'd storm off, and my mum would cry, and I'd stay in my room and do my homework.'

The ache in her voice cut him almost as much as her words, for he was beginning to understand now why she was so determined to stay single, so vehemently opposed even to letting him know about the baby.

'Are they still together?'

She shook her head.

'They divorced when I was seven. At first it was better. It was calmer at home, and my dad made a real effort. He even promised to take me to the zoo in Edinburgh for my birthday. Only he forgot. Not just about the zoo, but about my birthday too.'

Ram felt as though he'd been punched hard in the face.

He felt a vicious, almost violent urge to find her father and tell him exactly what he thought of him.

She breathed out unsteadily. 'About two months later I got a card and some money. The following year he forgot my birthday again. One year he even managed to forget me at Christmas. Of course when he remembered I got the biggest, glitziest present…'

Nola could feel Ram's gaze on her face, but she couldn't look at him. She couldn't let him see what her father had seen and rejected: her need to be loved. Couldn't bear for him to guess her most closely guarded secret. That she hadn't been enough of a reason for her father to make the effort.

'I thought he'd stopped loving my mum, and that was why he left. But he didn't love me either, and he left me too.'

'And that's what you think I'd do?'

Turning her head, she finally met his eyes. 'You have to put children first. Only sometimes people just can't do that, and I'm not blaming them…'

His grey eyes were searching her face, and she felt a rush of panic. How could she expect Ram to understand? He wouldn't know what it was like to feel so unimportant, so easy to forget, so disposable.

'Sometimes you have to give people a chance too,' he said quietly.

Nola bit her lip. His voice sounded softer, and she could sense that he was if not backing down then backing off, trying to calm her. But her heart was still beating too fast for her to relax. And anyway… Her pulse shivered violently… It wasn't as though he was going to change his mind. He was just trying a different tactic, biding his time while he waited for her to give in.

Suddenly she could no longer rein in the panic rising up inside her. 'I can't do this, Ram. I know you think I'm just being difficult. But I'm not. I know what marrying the wrong person can do people. It's just so damaging and destructive. And what's worse is that even when the marriage ends that damage doesn't stop. It just goes on and on—'

'Nola.'

Her body tensed as he lifted a hand and stroked a long dark curl away from her face.

'I'm not going to behave like your father did. I'm not walking away from you, or our baby. I'm fighting to make it work. Why do you think I want to marry you?'

She shook her head. 'You want it *now*. But soon you'll start to think differently, and then you'll *feel* differently. And we hardly know each other, Ram. Having a baby won't change that, and there is nothing else between us.'

His gaze seemed to burn into hers. 'We both know that's not true.'

She swallowed. 'That was one night…'

'Was it?' Ram studied her face. He could see the conflict in her eyes, and with shock he realised that it mirrored what he was feeling himself—the longing, the fear, the confusion. The pain.

He didn't want to feel her pain, or his own. He didn't want to feel anything. And for a fraction of a second he was on the verge of pulling her into his arms and doing what he always did to deflect emotion—his own and other people's.

But something held him back—a sudden understanding that if he didn't allow himself to feel, then he would never be able to comfort Nola, and right now that was all that mattered.

Not himself, nor his business, the launch, or even getting her to agree to this marriage, but Nola herself.

In shock, clenching his hands until they hurt, he gazed past her, struggling to explain this wholly uncharacteristic behaviour.

Surely, though, it was only natural for him to care. Nola was carrying his child.

Turning, he breathed out slowly, staring down into her eyes. 'I know you don't trust me. And if I were you I'd feel exactly the same. I haven't exactly given you much reason to have faith in me, bringing you here like I have.'

He grimaced.

'I just wanted to give us some time and some privacy. I didn't think we could sort things out with everything else going on, and I still think that. But I'm not going to force you to marry me, Nola. Or even to stay here if you don't want to.'

Reaching into his pocket, he pulled out a phone and held it out to her, watching her eyes widen with confusion.

'I didn't lie to you. There is no coverage here. That's why I have this. It's a satellite phone. If you want to leave you can call the pilot. If you stay, I want it to be your choice.'

Nola stared at him, her tears beaten back by Ram's words. This was a concession. More than that, it was a chance to get her life back.

She glanced down at the phone, her brain fast-forwarding. They could handle this through their lawyers. There was probably no need even to see one another again. But was that really what she wanted? What was best for their baby?

'I'll stay.' She held his gaze. 'But I might ring Anna later, or tomorrow. Just to let her know I'm okay.'

He pocketed the phone and nodded, and then after the briefest hesitation he reached over and took her hand in his.

'I know this is a big step for both of us, Nola. But I think we can make it work if we compromise a little.'

Nola gazed at him blankly. 'Compromise?'

He frowned. 'That *is* a word, isn't it?'

She smiled weakly. 'It is. I'm just not sure you understand what it means. Maybe you're thinking of another word.'

His grey eyes softened, and she felt her pulse dip as he lifted her hand to his mouth and kissed it gently. 'Let's see… I think it means I have to stop acting like a tornado and listen to what you're saying.'

She felt her stomach drop. Ram might have been difficult to defy when he was angry, but he was impossible to resist when he was smiling.

'That sounds like a compromise,' she said cautiously. 'But what does it mean in real terms?'

'It means that I think we need time to get used to the idea of getting married and to each other.'

She bit her lip. 'How much time?'

'As long as it takes.' He met her gaze. 'I'll wait, Nola. For as long as it takes.'

Her pulse was jumping again. For a moment they stared at one another, breathing unsteadily, and then finally she gave him a hesitant smile.

'That could work.'

And maybe it would, for suddenly she knew that for the first time she was actually willing to consider marrying him.

They spent the rest of the morning together, watching lizards and frogs and birds through the glass. Ram knew a surprising amount about the various animals and plants, and she found herself not only relaxing, but enjoying herself and his company.

So much so that as she dialled Anna's number the following morning she found it increasingly difficult to remember that he was the same person who had made her feel so horribly trapped and desperate.

'So let me get this right,' Anna said slowly down the phone. 'You're staying with Ram Walker in his rainforest treehouse. Just you and him. Even though we don't work for him anymore. And you think that's normal?'

'I didn't say that,' Nola protested, glancing over to where Ram lay lounging in the sun, a discarded paperback on the table beside him. 'Obviously nothing he does is normal. He's the richest man in Australia. I just said that me being here is not that big a deal.'

Her friend gave a short, disbelieving laugh. 'Is that why I wasn't invited?'

Nola grimaced. 'You weren't invited because you're in Edinburgh. With a broken foot and a husband.'

'I *knew* it!' Anna said triumphantly. 'So there *is* something going on!'

'No!' Nola froze as Ram turned and glanced over at her curiously. Lowering her voice, she said quickly. 'Well, it's complicated…'

She badly wanted to tell her best friend the truth. Sooner or later she would have to. Her fingers gripped the phone more tightly.

'I'm pregnant, and Ram's the father.'

Her words hung in silence down the phone and she closed her eyes, equal parts of hope and fear rising up inside her. What if Anna was disgusted? Or never wanted to speak to her again?

'That's why I'm here. We're talking things through.' Breathing out shakily, she pressed the phone against her face. 'I wanted to tell you before, but—'

'It was complicated?'

Nola opened her eyes with relief. Her friend's voice was gentle, and full of love. It was going to be okay.

'I'm sorry. I just couldn't get think straight.'

Anna laughed. 'That's okay. I forgive you as long as you tell me everything now.'

She didn't tell Anna everything, but she gave her friend an edited version of the last few days. But even while she was talking she was thinking about Ram. Having finally stopped fighting him, all she wanted was to concentrate on the two of them building a relationship that would work for their child.

That was, after all, the reason she'd decided to stay.

The only reason.

Her cheeks grew hotter.

Try telling that to her body.

Her mouth was suddenly dry. Staring across the deck at Ram, she felt her breath catch fire. It was true, she *did* want a relationship with him that would work for their child. But that didn't mean she could deny the way her body reacted to his. Even now, just looking at him was playing havoc with her senses. And up close he seemed to trigger some internal alarm system, so that she felt constantly restless, her body shivering and tightening and melting all at the same time.

But her relationship with Ram was already complicated enough. So it didn't matter that no man had ever made her feel the way he had. Giving in to the sexual pull between them would only add another layer of complication neither of them needed.

Her mouth twisted.

Maybe if she told herself that often enough, she might actually start to believe it.

'So,' Ram said softly, as she sat down beside him and handed him the phone, 'is everything okay?'

She nodded. 'Yes. I told her about the baby. She was a little...' she hesitated, searching for the right word '... stunned at first, but she was cool about it.'

Ram studied her face. Since agreeing to stay, Nola had seemed more relaxed, but he couldn't shift the image from his head of her looking so small and crushed, and impulsively he reached out and ran his fingers over her arm.

'You need to be careful. Are you wearing enough sun-block?'

She grimaced. 'Loads. I used to try and tan, but it never works. I just burn and then peel, so now I am fully committed to factor fifty.'

'Is that right?' His gaze roamed over her face. 'Then I'm jealous. I only want you to be fully committed to *me*.'

Nola blinked. He must be teasing her, she decided. Ram might want to marry her in order to legitimise this pregnancy, but he didn't do commitment. And jealousy would require an emotional response she knew he wasn't capable of or willing to give. But knowing that didn't stop her stomach flipping over in response to the possessiveness in his words.

Hoping her thought process wasn't showing on her face, she said lightly, 'You've got bigger competition than a bottle of sunblock.'

His eyes narrowed. 'I do?'

He let his fingers curl around her wrist, and then gently he pulled her towards him so that suddenly their eyes were level.

'I thought you said you didn't have anyone missing you,' he said softly.

She bit her lip. 'I don't think he does miss me. He's quite self-sufficient…' Glancing up at the stubble shadowing his jaw, she smiled. 'A little prickly. A bit like you, really. Except he's green, and he's got this cute little pot like a sombrero.'

Ram shook his head. 'I can't believe you're comparing me to a cactus.'

She laughed. 'There's no comparison. Colin is a low-maintenance dream. Whereas you—'

His eyes were light and dancing with amusement. 'I'm what?'

She felt her pulse begin to flutter. 'You have a private jet and a house in the rainforest.'

'And you care about that?'

She glanced up. Something in his tone had shifted, and he was watching her, his grey gaze oddly intent.

'No, I don't,' she said truthfully. It might sound rude, or ungrateful but she wasn't going to lie just to flatter him. 'It's lovely to have all this, but it doesn't matter to me. Other things are more important.'

Her father had taught her that. His gifts had always been over the top—embarrassingly so in comparison to what her mother had chosen for her. But there had been no thought involved, nothing personal about his choice. Nothing personal about the money he'd sent either, except that it had grown exponentially in relation to his neglect.

'Like what?'

Ram was gazing at her curiously, but just as she opened her mouth to reply, his phone rang.

Glancing down at it, he frowned. 'Excuse me. I have to take this.'

Standing up, he walked away, his face tight with concentration.

She caught bits of the conversation, but nothing that gave her any clue as to who the caller might be. Not that she needed any. It would be work-related, because of course, despite what he'd said and what she'd chosen to believe, work would always come first. She just hadn't expected to have it pointed out to her quite so quickly.

Finally he hung up.

'Sorry about that.' His face was impassive, but there was a tension in his voice that hadn't been there before.

Looking up, she forced herself to smile casually, even though she felt flattened inside. 'When do they want you back?'

'Who?' He stared at her blankly.

'Work. Do you need to leave now?'

Ram didn't answer. He was too busy processing the realisation that since getting off the plane he hadn't thought about work once. Even the launch seemed to belong to another life he had once lived. And forgotten.

He shook his head.

'It wasn't work. It was Pandora. My mother. I was supposed to have lunch with my parents today, only with everything that's happened I forgot.'

Catching sight of Nola's face, he shrugged.

'It's fine—honestly. My mother's portions are so tiny it's hardly worth the effort of going, and besides it gives Guy, my father, a chance to complain about me, so—'

'You could still go,' she said hastily. 'I can just stay here and—'

She stopped mid-sentence as his eyes locked onto hers.

'Why would you stay here?

'I don't know.' She hesitated. 'I just thought… I mean, obviously I'd like to meet them.'

Was that true? Her pulse jumped.

She was still wary of escalating their relationship too fast. But was that because her perception of marriage was so skewed by the past? Maybe lunch with Ram's family would help balance out her point of view. And, more importantly, it might give her some insight into the father of her child, for while she had talked a lot—about herself, her parents, even her cactus—Ram was still a mystery to her.

Take his parents. She didn't know anything about them. If she'd been shaped by her mother and father, then surely it was logical to assume that Ram had been shaped by his parents too. So why not take this opportunity to see what they were like? For the sake of their child, of course.

She glanced up at him hesitantly. 'Would you like me to meet them?'

Ram stared at her in silence, wondering how best to

answer that question. Nola meeting his parents had not been part of the equation when he'd brought her here. Yet clearly she was trying to meet him halfway, and as it had been he who had suggested they get to know one another better it seemed churlish to refuse.

But going to lunch with them would mean leaving the rainforest, and he didn't want to do that.

He wanted to stay here with Nola. For it to be just the two of them. There was no need to involve Pandora and Guy. Only how could he explain that without having to explain who he was and *what* he was…?

His chest tightened.

Lifting his face, he smiled coolly. 'Of course. It will give me a chance to drop in at the office. There are a couple of papers I need. I'll ring her back and see if she can do tomorrow.'

CHAPTER EIGHT

THEY FLEW BACK to Sydney the next day.

Gazing out of the window, Nola wished her thoughts were as calm as the clear blue sky beyond the glass. It was hard to believe that only a few days ago she'd fled from the RWI building. So much had happened since then. So much had changed. Not least her perception of Ram.

She had believed him to be domineering, insensitive and unemotional, but as she glanced across the aircraft to where he stood, joking with the cabin crew, she knew that he was a different man than she'd thought.

Yes, he had as good as abducted her from the airport but, seeing her upset, he had backed down, given her the option of leaving. And he'd been unexpectedly gentle and understanding when she'd told him about her father.

Shifting in her seat, she bit her lip. She still didn't really understand why she had confided in Ram. The words had just spilled out before she'd been able to stop them. But she didn't regret it, for they had both learnt something about one another as a result.

Yet now she was about to meet *his* parents, and she could feel all her old nervousness creeping over her skin. Glancing down at her skirt, she pressed her hands against the fabric, smoothing out an imaginary crease.

If only they could just stay here on the plane, circling the earth for ever...

She jumped slightly as Ram sat down beside her, and

plucked her hand from her lap. Threading his fingers through hers, he rested his grey eyes on her face.

'So, what's bothering you, then?'

'Nothing,' she protested.

'You haven't said more than two words since we got on the plane. And you're fidgeting. So let's start with the obvious first. What have I done?'

She shook her head again. 'You haven't done anything.'

'Okay. What have I said? Or not said?'

Despite her nerves, she couldn't help smiling.

'It's not you…it's nothing—' She stopped, suddenly at a loss for words. 'It's just been such a long time since I've done a family lunch, and spending time with my mum and dad was always so stressful.'

'Then you don't need to worry,' he said dryly. 'My parents are the perfect hosts. They would never do anything to make a guest feel uncomfortable.'

She frowned. There was an edge to his voice that hadn't been there before.

'Are you sure they don't mind me coming along too? I don't want to put them to any trouble.'

He smiled—an odd, twisted smile that made her heart lurch forward.

'Pandora is the queen of the charity dinner and the benefit dance. She loves entertaining, and Guy does as he's told, so you coming to lunch will absolutely no trouble at all.'

Her heart felt as if it were high up in her chest.

'And who do they think I am? I mean, in relation to you?' She hesitated. 'Have you told them about the baby?'

His face was expressionless. 'No. They don't need to know. As to who you are—I told them you used to work for me, and that now we're seeing one another.'

As she opened her mouth to protest, he shrugged.

'You're the first woman I've ever taken to meet them.' His grey eyes watched her steadily, his mouth tugging up at the corners. 'It was either that or pretend you were coming to fix the hard drive.'

They landed in Sydney an hour later. Ram's limo was waiting for them at the edge of the private airfield, and soon they were cruising along the motorway.

But instead of turning towards the city centre, as she'd expected, the car carried on.

'Didn't you want to go to the office first?' Frowning, Nola glanced over to where Ram was gazing down at his phone.

'I changed my mind.' He looked up, his face impassive. 'I thought you might like to freshen up, and I need to pick up a car.'

'Where are we going?'

He smiled. 'We're going home.'

She frowned. 'I thought you had a penthouse in the city?'

He shrugged. 'I do. It's convenient for work. But it's not my home.'

Home.

The word made her think of her flat in Edinburgh, her shabby sofas and mismatched crockery. But home for Ram turned out to be something altogether grander—a beautiful white mansion at the end of a private drive.

Stepping dazedly out of the car, Nola felt her heart jump. She'd recognised the name of the road as soon as they'd started to drive down it. How could she not? It was regularly cited as being the most expensive place to live in the country, and Ram's house more than lived up to that reputation.

'Welcome to Stanmore.' He was standing beside her, smiling, watching her face casually, but she could sense a tension beneath his smile, and suddenly she knew that he cared what she thought—and that fact made her throat tighten so that she couldn't speak.

'It's incredible,' she managed finally.

A couple of hours ago she'd denied being intimidated by his wealth, but now she wasn't sure that was still true. For a moment she hesitated, caught between fear and curiosity, but then his hand caught hers and he tugged her forward.

'I'm glad you think so. Now, come on. I want to show you round.'

As they wandered through the beautiful interior Nola caught her breath, her body transformed into a churning mass of insecurity. How could Ram seriously expect them to marry? This was a different world from hers. And no doubt his parents would realise that the moment she walked through their door.

'My great-great-grandfather, Stanley Armitage, bought this land in 1864,' Ram said casually as he led her into a beautiful living room with uninterrupted views of the ocean. 'I'm the fifth generation of my family to live here.'

Nola nodded. 'So you grew up here?'

His face didn't change but his eyes narrowed slightly.

'My mother moved out when she got married. They live just along the road. But I spent most of my holidays here, aside from the odd duty dinner with my parents.' He paused. 'Which reminds me... We should probably think about getting ready.'

Nola gazed down at her skirt and blouse in dismay. They had looked fine when she'd put them on that morning, but after two hours of travelling she felt sticky and dishevelled.

'I can't meet your parents looking like this.'

'So don't,' he said easily.

'But I don't have anything else.'

'Yes, you do.'

Before she had a chance to reply, he was towing her upstairs, through one of the bedrooms and into a large dressing room.

'I know you acted cool about it, but I thought you might worry about being underdressed, so I spoke to my mother's stylist and she sent these over this morning.'

Hanging from a rail were at least twenty outfits in clear, protective wrappers.

Nola gazed at them speechlessly.

He grinned, obviously pleased by her reaction. 'Pick something you like. I think there are shoes as well. I'm just going to go change.'

She nodded. But picking something was not as easy as Ram's throwaway remark had implied. The clothes were all so beautiful… Finally she settled on a pale blue dress with a pretty ribbon-edged cardigan that cleverly concealed her bump. Her cheeks were already flushed, so she didn't bother with any blusher, but she brushed her hair until it lay smoothly over her shoulders, and then added a smudge of clear lip gloss.

'You look beautiful.'

Turning, she caught her breath. Ram was lounging in the doorway, his grey eyes glittering with approval.

'So do you,' she said huskily, her gaze drifting over his dark suit and cornflower-blue shirt.

Holding out his hand, he grinned. 'Who? Me? I'm just here to drive the car.'

The car turned out to be a Lamborghini, low to the ground and an eye-catching bright blue.

As they drove the short distance to his parents' house she couldn't resist teasing him about the colour. 'Did you choose the car to match your shirt?'

He gave her a heartbreaking smile. 'No, your eyes,' he said softly. 'Now, stop distracting me.'

She bit her lip, her expression innocent. 'I distract you?'

Shaking his head, he grimaced. 'More like bewitch me. Since I met you in that café I haven't been able to concentrate on anything. I've hardly done any work for months. If I wasn't me, I'd fire myself.'

Glancing out of the window, with his words humming inside her head, she felt suddenly ridiculously happy—even though, she reminded herself quickly, Ram was really only talking about the sexual chemistry between them.

Two minutes later he shifted down a gear and turned into a driveway. Nola could see tennis courts and a rectangle of flawless green grass.

'It's a putting green,' Ram said quietly. 'Guy is a big golf fan.'

She nodded. Of course it was a putting green.

But then the putting green was forgotten, for suddenly she realised why Ram had taken her to his house first.

As he switched off the engine she breathed out slowly. 'You thought all this would scare me, didn't you? That's why we went to Stanmore first.'

He shrugged, but the intensity of his gaze told her that she was right.

Reaching out, she touched his hand tentatively. 'Thank you.'

He caught her fingers in his, his eyes gently mocking her. 'I was a little concerned at how you might react. But, as you can see, I'm way richer than they are…'

She punched him lightly on the arm.

'I can't believe you said that.'

Leaning forward, he tipped her face up to his. 'Can't you?' he said softly. 'Then your opinion of me must be improving.'

For a moment time seemed to slow, and they gazed at one another in silence until finally she cleared her throat.

'Do you think we should go in?'

'Of course.' He let go of her chin. 'Let's go and eat.'

Walking swiftly through the house, Ram felt as though his chest might burst. He couldn't quite believe that he'd brought Nola here. One way or another it was asking for trouble—especially as his relationship with her was still at such a delicate stage. But avoiding his parents wasn't an option either—not if he was serious about getting Nola to trust him.

Aware suddenly that she was struggling to keep up with him, he slowed his pace and gave her an apologetic smile. 'Sorry. I think they must be in the garden room.'

The garden room! Was that some kind of conservatory? Nola wondered as she followed Ram's broad back.

Yes, it was, she concluded a moment later as she walked into a light, exquisitely furnished room. But only in the same way that Ram's rainforest hideaway was some kind of treehouse.

'Finally! I was just about to ring you, Ramsay.'

Pulse racing, Nola swung round. The voice was high and clear, and surprisingly English-sounding. But not as surprising as the woman who was sashaying towards them.

Ram smiled coolly. 'Hello, Mother.'

Nola gazed speechlessly at Pandora Walker. Tall, beautiful and blonde, wearing an expensive silk dress that showed off her slim arms and waist, she looked more like a model than a mother—certainly not one old enough to have a son Ram's age.

'You said one o'clock, and it's two minutes past,' Ram said without any hint of apology, leaning forward to kiss her on both cheeks.

'Five by my watch.' She gave him an indulgent smile. 'I'm not fussing on my account, darling, it's just that you know your father hates to be kept waiting.

Glancing past them, she pursed her lips.

'Not that he has any qualms about keeping everyone else hanging around. Or ruining the food.'

Nola stilled. Goosebumps were covering her arms. For

a fraction of second it could have been her own mother speaking.

But that thought was quickly forgotten as, shaking his head, Ram turned towards Nola and said quietly, 'The food will be perfect. It always is. Nola, this is my mother, Pandora. Mother, this is Nola Mason. She's one of the consultants I hired to work on the launch.'

Smiling politely, Nola felt a jolt of recognition as she met Pandora's eyes—for they were the exact same colour and shape as Ram's. But where had he got that beautiful black hair?

'Thank you so much for inviting me,' she said quickly. 'It's really very kind of you.'

Pandora leaned forward and brushed her cheek lightly against Nola's.

'No, thank *you* for coming. I can't tell you how delightful it is to meet you. Ram is usually so secretive. If I want to know anything at all about his private life I have to read about it in the papers. Ah, finally, here's Guy. Darling, we've all been waiting...'

Nola felt another shiver run over her skin. Pandora was still smiling, but there was an edge of coolness to her voice as a tall, handsome man with blond hair and light brown eyes strolled into the room.

'Ramsay, your mother and I were so sure you'd forget I booked to have lunch with Ted Shaw at the club. Just had to ring and cancel.' He turned towards Nola. 'Guy Walker— and you must be Nola.'

'It's lovely to meet you, Mr Walker.'

He smiled—a long, curling smile that reached his eyes.

'Call me Guy, please, and the pleasure is all mine.'

Ram might get his grey eyes from his mother, Nola thought as she followed Pandora out of the room to lunch, but he'd clearly inherited his charm from his father.

To her relief, she quickly discovered that Ram had been

telling the truth about his parents. They were the perfect hosts: beautiful, charming and entertaining. And the food was both delicious and exquisitely presented. And yet somehow she couldn't shift the feeling that there was an undercurrent of tension weaving unseen beneath the charm and the smooth flow of conversation.

'So what is it you did, then, Nola? For RWI, I mean?' Leaning forward, Guy poured himself another glass of wine.

'I'm a cyber architect. I designed and installed the new security system.'

He frowned. 'That's a thing now, is it?'

Nola opened her mouth, but before she could reply Ram said quietly, 'It's been a "thing" for a long time now. All businesses have cyber security teams. They have to. Big, global companies like RWI even more so. They're a prime target for hackers, and if we get hacked we lose money.'

Guy lifted his glass. 'By *we* you mean *you*.' He smiled conspiratorially at Nola. 'I might have given him my name but it's not a family business.'

She blinked. Taken at face value, Guy's comment was innocuous enough: a simple, statement of fact about who owned RWI. So why did his words feel like a shark's fin cutting through the surface of a swimming pool?

'Actually, I think what Ram is trying to say is that hacking is like any other kind of theft,' she said hurriedly. 'Like shoplifting or insurance fraud. In the end the costs get passed on to the consumers so everyone loses out.'

Feeling Ram's gaze on the side of her face, she turned and gave him a quick, tight smile. He nodded, not smiling exactly, but his eyes softened so that for a fraction of a second she almost felt as if they were alone.

Watching the faint flush of colour creep over Nola's cheeks, Ram felt his throat tighten.

He couldn't help but admire her. She was nervous—he could hear it in her voice. But she had defended him, and the fact that she cared enough to do that made his head spin, for nobody had *ever* taken his side. He'd learnt early in life to rely on no one but himself. Some days it felt as though his whole life had been one long, lonely battle.

Not that he'd cared.

Until now.

Until Nola.

But spending time with her over the last few days had been a revelation. Having never cohabited before, he'd expected to find it difficult—boring, even. But he'd enjoyed her company. She was beautiful, smart, funny, and she challenged him. And now she had gone into battle for him, so that the solitude and independence he had once valued so highly seemed suddenly less important. Unnecessary, unwelcome even.

'I'll have to take your word for it.' Guy laughed. 'Like I said, I might be a Walker but I'm not a hotshot businessman like my son.'

Draining his glass, he leaned forward towards Nola.

'A long time ago I used to be an actor—quite a good one, actually. Right now, though, I'm just a party planner!'

Nola stared at him confusedly. 'You plan parties?'

'Ignore him, Nola, he's just being silly.' Pandora frowned at her husband, her lips tightening. 'We're having a party for our thirtieth wedding anniversary, and Guy's been helping with some of the arrangements.'

'Thirty years!' Nola smiled. 'That's wonderful.'

And it was. Only as Ram reached out and adjusted his water glass she felt her smile stiffen, for how did that make him feel? Hearing her sound so enthusiastic about his parents' thirtieth wedding anniversary when she'd been so fiercely against marrying him.

But then Ram only wanted to marry her because he

felt he should, she thought defensively. His parents, on the other hand, had clearly loved each other from the start, and they were still in love now, thirty years later.

'Oh, you're so sweet.' Pandora gave her a pouting pink smile. "It's going to be a wonderful evening, but there's still so much to sort out. Only apparently *my* input is not required.'

So that was why she and Guy were so on edge.

Glancing over to see Guy was pouring himself another glass of wine, Nola felt a rush of relief at having finally found an explanation for the tensions around the table.

Guy scowled. 'You're right—it's not.' He picked up his glass. 'Doesn't stop you giving it, though. Which is one of the reasons why there's still so much to sort out.'

For perhaps a fraction of a second Pandora's beautiful face hardened, and then almost immediately she was smiling again.

'I know, darling. But at least we have one less thing to worry about now.' As Guy gazed at her blankly, she shook her head. 'Ram's guest. You *are* bringing Nola to the party, aren't you, Ramsay?'

There was a tiny suspended silence.

Nola froze. That aspect of the party hadn't even occurred to her. But obviously Ram would be going. Her heartbeat resonated in her throat as he turned towards her.

'Of course.'

Breath pummelled her lungs as he held her gaze, his cool, grey eyes silencing her confusion and shock.

'She's looking forward to it—aren't you, sweetheart?'

She gazed at him in silence, too stunned to reply. Over the last few days she had spent some of the most intense and demanding hours of her life with Ram. She had revealed more to him about herself than to any other person, and she had seen a side to him that few people knew existed.

But his parents' party was going to be big news, and although it was unlikely anyone would be interested in her on her own, as one half of a couple with Ram...

Her pulse fluttered.

She knew enough about his private life to know that it wasn't private at all, and that as soon she stepped out in public with him there would be a feeding frenzy—and that wasn't what she wanted at all.

Or was it?

Suddenly she was fighting her own heartbeat. Definitely she didn't want the feeding frenzy part, but she would be lying if she said that she didn't want the chance to walk into a room on his arm. And not just because he was so heart-stoppingly handsome and sexy.

She liked him.

A lot.

And the more she got to know him the more she liked him.

Looking up, she met his gaze, and nodded slowly. 'Yes, I'm really excited.'

Pandora clapped her hands together. 'Wonderful,' she purred. 'In that case I must give you the number of my stylist...'

After lunch, they returned to Stanmore.

Ram worked while Nola sat watching the boats in the harbour. After a light supper he excused himself, claiming work again, and she went upstairs to shower and get ready for bed.

Standing beneath the warm water, she closed her eyes and let her mind drift.

The drive home had been quiet—supper too. But then both of them had a lot to think about. Introducing her to his parents had probably been about as a big deal for Ram as meeting them had been for her.

Turning off the shower, she wrapped a towel around herself. And then, of course, there was the party. Her heart began to thump loudly inside her chest. Was that why he'd been so quiet? Was he regretting letting himself be chivvied into taking her as his guest?

But as she walked back into the bedroom that question went unanswered, for there, sitting on her bed, was Ram.

She stopped, eyes widening with surprise. 'I thought you were going to do some work?'

Glancing past her, he shrugged. 'I was worried about you. You seemed…' He hesitated, frowning. 'Distracted.'

There was an edge to his voice that she couldn't quite pinpoint.

'I'm just tired.'

His eyes on hers were dark and filled with intent. 'That's all? Just tired?'

For a moment she considered leaving it there. It had been a long day, but for the first time they seemed to be edging towards a calm she was reluctant to disturb. Although if she didn't tell him what she was really thinking, what would that achieve? Okay, it might just be one night in their lives, but if it was bothering her…bothering him…

She took a deep breath. 'I just want you to know that you don't have to take me to the party,' she said quickly.

His eyes narrowed. 'I know I don't. But I want to.' He studied her face. 'Is that really what this is about? What *I* want. Or is it about what *you* want?'

Nola looked at him uncertainly. 'What do you mean?'

He cleared his throat. 'Are you saying you don't want to go with me?'

She shook her head. 'No, but you only— I mean, your mother—'

He interrupted her, his voice suddenly blazing with an emotion she didn't recognise.

'Let me get one thing clear, Nola. *I want you to be there*

with me. And my mother has got nothing to do with that decision.'

She nodded—for what else could she do? She could hardly demand proof. And she wanted to believe him. Of course she did. Besides, if they were going to work even at the simplest level, wasn't it time to move on? To put all the doubt and suspicion and drama behind them and start to trust one another?

Drawing in a deep breath, she lifted her chin and looked into his eyes.

'Thank you for telling me that,' she said simply. 'And thank you for taking me to lunch. It was lovely.' Remembering the strange tension around the table, those odd pointed remarks, she hesitated. 'What about you? Did you enjoy yourself?'

Ram stared at her in silence. Her question was simple enough but it stunned him, for he couldn't remember anyone ever asking him that before.

'I suppose,' he said finally. 'Although they were a little tense. But there's a lot going on—I mean, with the party coming up—'

She nodded slowly. 'Thirty years together is an amazing achievement.'

'Yes, it is.'

He watched her bite her lip, glance up, try to speak, then look away. Finally she said quietly, 'I get that it's why you wanted me to meet them.'

His heart seemed to still in his chest. 'You do?'

She nodded. 'You wanted me to understand why you want us to marry. And I do understand. I know you want what they have.'

Her blue eyes were fixed on his face, and he stared back at her, his breath vibrating inside his chest.

You want what they have…

He tried to nod his head, tried to smile, to do what his mother had always required of him.

But he couldn't. Not anymore. Not with Nola.

Slowly he shook his head. 'Actually, what they have is why I've always been so *against* marriage.'

He watched her eyes widen with incomprehension, and it made him feel cruel—shattering her illusions, betraying his mother's confidences. But he was so tired of lying and feeling angry. His chest tightened. Nola deserved more than lies, more than his anger—she deserved the truth.

He cleared his throat. 'You see, Guy has a mistress.'

Confusion and shock spread out from her pupils like shock waves across a sea.

There was a thick, pulsing silence.

'But he can't have—' Nola bit her lip, stopped, tried again. 'Does your mother know?'

As she watched him nod slowly the room seemed to swim in front of her eyes.

There was another, shorter silence.

'I'm so sorry, Ram,' she whispered at last. 'That must have been such a shock.'

He stared past her, his eyes narrowing as though he was weighing something up.

'Yes, it was,' he said quietly. 'The first time it happened.'

The first time?

'I—I don't understand,' she said slowly. 'Isn't this the first time?'

His mouth twisted. 'Sadly not. That honour went to an actress called Francesca. Not that I knew or cared that she was an actress.' An ache of misery was spreading inside him. 'I was only six. To me, she was just some woman in my mother's bed.'

Nola flinched. *Six!* Still just a child.

Watching her reaction, Ram smiled stiffly. 'Guy told me it would upset my mother if I said anything. So I didn't.'

He was speaking precisely, owning each word in a way that made her feel sick.

'I thought if I kept quiet, then it would stop,' he continued. 'And it did with Francesca. Only then there was Tessa, and then Carrie. I stopped learning their names after that. It was the only way I could face my mother.'

'But you weren't responsible!' Nola stared up him, her eyes and her throat burning. 'You hadn't done anything.'

His skin was tight over his cheekbones.

'You're wrong. It *was* my fault. All of it.'

She shook her head. Her heart felt as if it was about to burst. 'You were a little boy. Your father should never have put you in that position.'

He was looking past her, his eyes dull with pain. 'You don't understand. *I'm* the reason they had to marry.'

She shivered. 'What do you mean?'

'My mother got pregnant with me when she was sixteen. In those days girls like her didn't do so well on their own.'

Nola blinked. She had imagined many reasons for what had made him the man he was, but nothing like this. No wonder he was so confused—and confusing—when it came to relationships.

'But that's not *your* fault,' she said quietly. 'I know it must have been hard for both of them. But just because Guy became a father too young, it doesn't mean you're responsible for his affairs.'

He shook his head, his mouth twisting into a smile that had nothing to do with laughter or happiness.

'Guy's not my father. My biological father, I mean.'

She stared at him in silence, too shocked to speak, the words in her mouth bunching into silent knots.

He looked away. 'My mother was staying with a friend and they heard about a party. A real party, on the wrong side of town, with drink and boys and no supervision. That's where she met my father. They were drunk and careless and they had sex.'

'Who is he?' she whispered. 'Your real father?'

Ram shrugged. 'Does it matter? When he found out she was pregnant he didn't want anything to do with her— or me.'

His eyes were suddenly dark and hostile, as though challenging her to contradict him.

She swallowed. 'So how did she meet Guy?'

He breathed out unsteadily.

'My grandparents knew his family socially. His father had made some bad investments. Money was tight, and Guy's never been that interested in working for a living, so when Grandfather offered him money to marry my mother he accepted.'

Nola didn't even try to hide her shock.

'That's awful. Your poor mother. But why did she agree to it?'

Ram's face was bleak. 'Because my grandfather told her he'd cut her off, disown her, cast her out if she didn't.'

A muscle pulsed in his cheek.

'She couldn't face that, didn't think she could survive without all this, so she gave in. Guy got a generous life-time monthly allowance, my mother preserved her reputation and her lifestyle and my grandparents were able to keep their dirty linen private.'

The misery in his voice almost overwhelmed her.

She took a breath, counted to ten. 'How did you find out?'

'My mother told me.' This time his smile seemed to slice through her skin like a mezzaluna. 'We were argu-ing, and I compared her unfavourably to my grandpar-ents. I hurt her, so I guess she thought it was time I knew the truth.'

Nola could feel her body shaking. How could his mother have done that? It had been needlessly cruel. She had to swallow hard against the tears building in her throat before she could speak.

'How old were you?'

He shrugged. 'Eleven…twelve, something like that.'

Her eyes held his as she struggled to think of something positive to say. 'But you get on with Guy?'

He shrugged. 'When I was a child he more or less ignored me. Now I'm older I just avoid him. After my grandfather died he made a big scene about needing more money, so I give him an allowance and in return he has to be devoted to my mother—in public, at least. And discreet about his affairs. Or he's supposed to be.'

Nola looked up into his face. There was nothing she could say to that.

'What about your real father?' she asked carefully. 'Do you have any contact with him?'

His eyes hardened. 'I know who he is, and since he knows who my mother is, he must know who *I* am, and how to find me. But he hasn't, so I guess he's even less interested in me than Guy.'

His face was expressionless but the desolation in his voice made her fists clench.

'It's his loss,' she said fiercely.

He gave a small, tight smile.

'Are you taking my side, Ms Mason?'

His words burned like a flame. Was she?

For months there had been an ocean between them. Then, for the last few days, she'd been fighting to keep him at a distance. Fighting to keep her independence. Fighting the simmering sexual tension between them. Her mouth twisted. In fact just fighting him.

Only now the fight had drained out of her, and instead she wanted nothing more than to wrap her arms around him, ease the desperate ache in his voice and that terrible tension in his body. Her breath seemed to swell in her throat as she reached out and tentatively touched his hand. For a moment he stared at her hand in silence, then finally he reached out and pulled her against him.

Burying her face against his body, she let out a shuddering breath. Being here in his arms felt so good, so right. If only she could stay this way for ever. But this wasn't about her, it was about Ram—*his* pain and his anger, his past. A past that still haunted him. A past she was determined to exorcise now.

Lifting her head, she looked up into his face. 'Your mother was so young. Too young. And she was scared and hurt and desperate. People don't always do the right thing when they're desperate. But they can do the wrong thing for the right reasons.'

Their eyes met, and they both knew she wasn't just talking about his mother.

Breathing out shakily, he shook his head. 'I've been struggling to figure that out for nearly twenty years. It's taken you less than half an hour.'

She smiled a little. 'It's all those in-flight magazines I read.'

Mouth twisting, he clasped her face, his thumbs gently stroking her cheeks.

'I'm sorry for what I did. Lying to you, dragging you off to the rainforest like that. It was completely out of order.'

Ram was apologising.

Her throat ached. She could hardly breathe.

'We both behaved badly,' she said shakily. 'And we both thought the worst of each other. But I'm glad you did what you did, otherwise we might never have got this far.'

Her gaze fastened on his face.

'But now we're here, and I think it's about time we

started figuring things out. If we're going to make it work, I mean.'

The words were out of her mouth before she even understood what it was she wanted to say. What it was she really wanted. Her heart began to beat fiercely as his grey eyes searched her face.

'Make what work?'

It wasn't too late. There was still time to backtrack. Ram couldn't read minds, and she'd said nothing damning or definitive. But she didn't want to backtrack—for wasn't that their problem in a nutshell? Both of them looking back to the past, and in so doing threatening to ruin the future—their child's future? 'Our marriage,' she said after a moment.

'Are you asking me to marry you?'

He looked tense, shaken, nothing like the cool, sophisticated Ramsay Walker who could stop meetings with a raised eyebrow. It scared her a little, seeing him so uncertain. But it made her feel stronger, more determined to tell him how she felt—and maybe, just maybe, get him to do the same.

She hesitated. 'Yes, I am.'

He had confided in her, and she knew what each and every word had cost him. Knew too why he was so conflicted, so determined to do his duty as a father even as he pushed away any hint of love or commitment.

'Is this what's changed your mind?' he asked slowly.

She bit her lip. 'Yes, but also it was that night we spent in your office—I've tried not to think about it, but I can't stop myself. It was so different...so incredible. I've never felt like that with anyone, and I wanted to tell you that. I wanted to stay, but I was too scared—scared of how you'd made me feel.'

'I felt the same,' he said hoarsely.

She felt a sudden twinge of panic. 'But it was a long time ago. Maybe we don't feel that way anymore.'

His grey eyes locked onto hers.

'We do feel it, Nola. We've felt it and fought it.'

The heat in his voice made blood surge through her body.

'But I don't want to fight you anymore. In fact fighting is the opposite of what I want to do with you.'

She held her breath as he stared down into her eyes. Chaos was building inside her.

'What is it you want to do?' she whispered.

His gaze moved from her face down to the slight V of her cleavage.

'This…'

Holding her gaze, he reached out and slowly unwrapped the towel from around her body. As it dropped to the floor she heard his sharp intake of breath.

She swallowed, her imagination stirring.

His mouth was so close to hers—those beautiful curving lips that had the power to unleash a blissful torment of heat and oblivion. For a moment she couldn't speak. All she could think about was how badly she wanted to kiss him, and how badly she wanted him to kiss her back.

And then her breath lurched in her throat as, lowering his hand, he began stroking her breast in a way that made her quiver inside.

'I want you, Nola,' he said softly.

'For ever?' She couldn't help asking.

His gaze held hers, then his hands dipped lower to caress her stomach and her thighs and the curve of her bottom.

'For the rest of my life.'

She pressed her hands against his chest, feeling his heart beneath her fingertips, and then she was pushing him backwards onto the bed, and he was pulling her onto his lap so that she was straddling him.

Fingers trembling, she undid the button of his jeans, tugging at the zipper, freeing him. His ragged breathing abruptly broke the silence as she ran her hand gently up the length of him and guided him inside her.

He groaned, his body trembling. Leaning forward, she found his mouth and kissed him desperately. And then his hands were tightening on her thighs, and she was lifting her hips, heat swamping her as he shuddered inside her, pulling her damp, shaking body against his.

But it wasn't just desire that was rocking her body—it was shock. For mere sex, no matter how incredible, could not make you want to hold a person for ever.

Only love could make you feel that way.

It was like a dam breaking inside her, but even as she acknowledged the truth she knew it was not a truth she was ready to share with Ram. Or one he was ready to hear. But wrapped in his arms, with his heart beating in time with hers, it didn't seem to matter. For right now this was enough.

CHAPTER NINE

THE NEXT MORNING Ram woke early, to a sky of the palest blue and yellow.

Next to him Nola lay curled on her side, her arm draped across his chest. For a moment he lay listening to her soft, even breathing, his body and his brain struggling to adjust to this entirely new sensation of intimacy.

Waking beside a woman was something he'd never done before. In the past, even the thought of it would have made his blood run cold.

But being here with Nola felt good.

Better than good, he thought, breathing in sharply as she shifted against him in her sleep.

After last night there could be no doubt that they still wanted one another. They had made love slowly, taking their time, holding back and letting the pleasure build. And, unlike that first time in his office, there had been tenderness as well as passion.

Forehead creasing, he stared out of the window. But last night had not just been about sex. Exploring the lush new curves of her body had eased an ache that was more than physical.

He froze as Nola stirred beside him, curling closer, and suddenly the touch of her naked body was too great a test for his self-control. Gritting his teeth against the instant rush of need clamouring inside him, he gently lifted her arm and slid across the bed, making his way to the shower.

Turning the temperature to cool, he winced as the water hit his body.

For years he'd never so much as hinted at his parents' unhappiness to anyone. Even imagining the pity in someone's eyes had been enough to ensure his silence. But last night—and he still wasn't quite sure why or how—he'd ended up telling Nola every sordid little detail about his life. Not just his mother's miserable marriage of necessity, but Guy's serial affairs too.

The words had just tumbled out.

Only Nola hadn't pitied him. Instead she had helped him to face his past. More than that, she'd finally agreed to build a future with him.

Tipping back his head, he closed his eyes, remembering how she'd asked him to marry her. His mouth curved. Of course she had—and wasn't that as much of an attraction as her glorious body? The way she kept him guessing, and her stubborn determination to do things her way and at her pace.

Switching off the water, he smoothed his dark hair back against the clean lines of his skull. It ought to drive him crazy, yet it only seemed to intensify his desire for her. And now that Nola had finally come round to his point of view he was determined that nothing would get in their way.

Whatever it took, they were going to get married—and as soon as possible.

'I need to drop by the office later, so I was wondering if you'd like to go into town?'

They had just finished breakfast and Ram was flicking through some paperwork.

Looking over at him, Nola frowned. 'Is there a problem?'

He shook his head. 'I just need to show my face—otherwise there might be a mutiny.'

'I doubt that. Your staff love you.'

He laughed. '*Love* might be pushing it a little. They respect me—'

'Yes, and respect is a kind of love,' she said slowly. 'Like duty and faith. Love isn't just all about passion and romance—it's about commitment and consideration, and sacrifice too.'

He leaned back in his chair. 'Then I take it back. I must be very loved. So must you.'

She felt her skin grow hot. Of course he wasn't talking about their relationship but his staff, and probably her friendship with Anna. Aware, though, of his sudden focus, she grasped helplessly towards his earlier remark.

'When are you thinking of going into the office, then?'

'Whenever suits you.'

'In that case, maybe I'll stay here. It's not as if I really need anything.'

He was silent a moment, and then he said quietly, 'Apart from a dress?'

A dress?

She stared at him. 'Oh, yes, of course—for the party.'

His gaze rested on her face. 'Are you having second thoughts?'

His tone was relaxed, but there was an intensity in his grey eyes that made her heart beat faster.

'About the party?'

'About agreeing to marry me?'

Looking up, she shook her head. 'No. Are you?'

Gently he reached over and, smoothing her hair back from her face, he gave her one of those sweet, extraordinary smiles that could light up a room.

'If I could walk outside and find a registrar and a couple of witnesses, you'd be making an honest man out of me right this second!'

She burst out laughing. 'I thought the bride was supposed to be the pushy one?'

His face grew serious. 'I don't want to push you into anything, Nola. Not anymore. I just want you to give me a chance—to give us a chance.'

Heart bumping into her ribs, she nodded. 'I want that too.' Taking a quick breath, she smiled at him. 'So what happens next?'

There was a fraction of a pause.

'I suppose we make it official,' he said casually. 'How do you feel about announcing our engagement at the party?'

Her pulse darted forward. *Engagement?*

But of course logically their getting engaged was the next step.

Only up until yesterday marrying Ram had been more of a hypothetical option than a solid, nuts and bolts reality. And now he wanted to announce their engagement in three days.

Three days!

Ram watched with narrowed eyes as Nola bit her lip. Taking her to the party was a statement of sorts, but announcing their engagement there would escalate and consolidate their relationship in the most public way possible. Clearly Nola thought so too, for he could see the conflict in her eyes. Only instead of making him question his actions, her doubt and confusion only made him more determined than ever to make it happen.

But he'd learnt his lesson, and he wasn't about to make demands or start backing her into a corner.

'It does make sense,' she said finally.

And it did—but that didn't stop the feeling of dread rising up inside her. For how was everyone going to react to the news? Her heart gave a shiver. She might have finally come to terms with the idea of marrying Ram, but this was a reminder that their marriage was going to be conducted in public, with not only friends and family having an opinion but the media too.

'What is it?'

The unexpected gentleness of his voice caught her off guard, and quickly she looked away—for how could she explain her fears to him? Ram didn't know what it felt like to be hurt and humiliated in public, to have his failures held up and examined.

A lump filled her throat as she remembered the first time her father had let her down in front of other people. She'd been on a school trip, and he'd promised to collect her in his new car. She had been so convinced that he would pick her up, adamant that he wouldn't forget her. In the end one of the mothers had taken pity on her and driven her home, but of course the next day at school everyone had known.

She clenched her fists. And then there was what had happened with Connor. It had been bad enough splitting up with him. To do so under the microscope of her colleagues' curiosity and judgement had been excruciating.

Even thinking about it made her feel sick to her stomach.

She took a breath. 'It's just…once we tell everyone it won't be just the two of us anymore.'

'Yes—but, like I said, if we go to the party together then they'll know about us anyway.' He frowned. 'I'm confused—I thought you *wanted* to get married.'

'I do. But what if our marriage doesn't work?' The words were spilling out of her—hot, panicky, unstoppable. 'What happens then? Have you thought about that? Have you any idea what that will feel like—?'

She broke off as Ram reached out and covered her hands with his.

'Slow down, sweetheart. At this point I'm still trying

to get you down the aisle. So right now I'm not thinking about the end of our marriage.'

Gently, he uncurled her fingers.

'Is this about your father?' he said quietly.

She shook her head, then nodded. 'Sort of. Him and Connor. He was my last boyfriend. We worked together. He told a couple of people in the office some stuff about us, and then it all got out of hand.'

'What stuff? And what do you mean by "out of hand"?'

She couldn't meet his eyes. 'Some of my colleagues went to the pub after work. Connor had been drinking, and he told them—well, he told them things about us. You know…what we'd done together, private things. The next day everyone was talking about me. It was so embarrassing. Even my boss knew. People I thought were my friends stopped talking to me, I was overlooked for a promotion, and then Connor dumped me.'

'Then, quite frankly, he was an idiot,' Ram said bluntly. Cupping her chin in his hand, he forced her face up to his. 'Correction. He's an idiot and a coward, and if ever I meet him I'll tell him so—shortly after I've punched him.'

She couldn't stop herself from smiling. 'You don't need to worry about me. I can fight my own battles.'

His gaze rested on her face, and he gripped her hand so tightly she could almost feel the energy and strength passing from his body into hers.

'Not anymore. You're with me now, Nola. Your battles are my battles. And, engaged or not, nothing anyone says or does is going to change that fact, so if you don't want to say anything, then we won't.'

Nola stared at him in silence. She knew how badly he wanted to get married, but he was offering to put his needs and feelings behind hers. Neither her father nor Connor had been willing to do that.

She couldn't speak—not just because his words had

taken her by surprise, but because she was terrified she would tell him that she loved him.

Finally, she shook her head. 'I do want to announce it. But I think I should ring my mum and Anna first. I want them to know before anyone else.'

He dropped a kiss on her mouth. 'Good idea. Why don't you call them now? And then you'd better come into town with me after all, so you can choose a dress.'

It was the afternoon of the party.

Slipping her feet into a pair of beautiful dark red court shoes, Nola breathed out softly. She could hardly believe that in the next few hours she would be standing beside Ram as his fiancée. Just days ago they had been like two boxers, circling one another in the ring. But all that had changed since they'd made peace with their pasts, and she had never felt happier.

Or more satisfied.

Her face grew hot. It was crazy, but they just couldn't seem to keep their hands off one another. Even when they weren't making love they couldn't stop touching—his hand on her hip, her fingers brushing against his face. And on the odd occasion when she forced Ram to do some work he'd stay close to her, using his laptop and making phone calls from the bed while she slept.

In fact this was probably the first time they'd been apart for days, and she was missing him so badly that it felt like an actual physical ache.

Her breath felt blunt and heavy in her throat. It was an ache that was compounded by the knowledge that, even though she loved him, Ram would never love her. She lifted her chin. But he did *need* her, and he felt responsible for her and the baby—and hadn't she told him that duty was a kind of love?

But she couldn't think about that now. There were other

more pressing matters to consider and, heart pounding, she turned to face the full-length mirror. She stared almost dazedly at her reflection. It was the first time she had seen herself since having her hair and make-up done, and the transformation was astonishing. With her dark hair swept to one side, her shimmering smoky eye make-up and bright red lips, she looked poised and glamorous—not at all like the anxious young woman she was feeling inside.

Which was lucky, she thought, picking up her clutch bag with a rush of nervous excitement, because soon she would be facing Sydney's A-listers as Ram's bride-to-be.

Downstairs, Ram was flicking resignedly through the pages of a magazine. If Nola was anything like Pandora he was going to be in for a long wait. Or maybe he wasn't! Already Nola had surprised him, by being sweetly excited by the party, whereas Pandora was just too much of a perfectionist to truly enjoy *any* public appearance. She saw only the flaws, however tiny or trifling. And of course that led inevitably to the reasons for those flaws.

His mouth tightened. Or rather *the* reason.

There was a movement behind him and, turning round, he felt his heartbeat stumble.

Nola was standing at the top of the stairs, wearing a beautiful pleated yellow silk dress that seemed to both cling and flow. It perfectly complemented her gleaming dark hair and crimson lips and, watching her walk towards him, he felt his breath catch fire as she stopped in front of him. She met his gaze, her blue eyes nervous, yet resolute.

'You look like sunlight in that dress,' he said softly and, reaching out he pulled her towards him. 'You're beautiful, Nola. Truly.'

'You look pretty damn spectacular too,' she said huskily.

The classic black dinner jacket fitted his muscular frame perfectly, and although all the male guests at the party would be similarly dressed, she knew that beside Ram they would look ordinary. His beauty and charisma would ensure that.

He glanced down at himself, then up to her face, his grey gaze dark and mocking. 'I doubt anyone's going to be looking at me.'

She shivered. 'Hopefully they won't be looking at me either.'

'They can look. But they can't touch.'

His arm tightened around her waist and she saw that his eyes were no longer mocking but intent and alert. Tipping her chin up, he cupped her face in his hand.

'You're mine. And I want everyone to know that. After tonight, they will.'

She felt her heart slip sideways, like a boat breaking free from its moorings. But of course he was just getting into the mood for the evening ahead, and it was her cue to do the same.

'I'll remind you of that later, when we're dancing and I'm trampling on your toes,' she said lightly. 'You'll be begging other men to take me off your hands.'

His face shifted, the corners of his mouth curving upwards, and his arms held her close against him.

'And what will you be begging *me* to do?'

Their eyes met, and she felt her face grow warm. She hadn't begged yet, but she hadn't been far off it. Remembering how frantic she had felt last night, how desperate she had been for his touch, the frenzy of release, she swallowed.

'We shouldn't—'

He nodded. 'I know. I just wish we could fast-forward tonight.'

She could hear the longing in his voice. 'So do I. I wish it was just the two of us.'

'It will be.' He frowned. 'I know you're nervous. But I'll

be there with you, and if for some reason I'm not—well, I thought this might help. I hope you like it.'

He lifted her hand and Nola stared mutely as he slid a beautiful sapphire ring onto her finger.

A sweet, shimmering lightness began to spread through her body. 'It—It's a ring,' she stammered.

His eyes glittered. 'You sound surprised. What were you expecting?'

'Nothing. I wasn't expecting anything.'

'We're getting engaged tonight, sweetheart. There has to be a ring.'

She nodded, some of her happiness fading. He was right: there did have to be a ring.

'Of course,' she said quickly. 'And it's lovely. Really…'

'Good.' Pulling out his phone, he glanced down at the screen and grimaced. 'In that case, I guess we should be going.'

Bypassing the queue of limousines and sports cars in the drive, Ram used the service entrance to reach the house. As they walked hand in hand towards the two huge marquees on the lawn Nola shivered. There were so many guests—several hundred at least.

'Do your parents really know this many people?' she asked, gazing nervously across the lawn.

He shrugged. 'Socially, yes. Personally, I doubt they could tell you much more than their names and which clubs they belong to.'

He turned as a waiter passed by with a tray of champagne and grabbed two glasses.

'I'm not drinking.'

'I know. But just hold it—otherwise somebody will wonder why.'

He smiled down at her and she nodded dumbly. He was

so aware, so in control of everything. In that respect this evening was no different for him than any other.

If only she could let him know how different it was for *her*.

But, much as she longed to tell him that she loved him, she knew it wasn't the right time. For there was a tension about him, a remoteness, as though he was holding himself apart. It was the same tension she'd felt at lunch that day with his parents. And of course it was understandable. This was a big moment for him too.

The party passed in a blur of lights and faces. She knew nobody, but it seemed that everybody knew Ram, and so wanted to know her too. Clutching her glass of champagne, she smiled and chatted with one glamorous couple after another as Ram stood by her side, looking cool and absurdly handsome in his tuxedo as he talked in French to a tall, elderly grey-haired man who turned out to be the Canadian Ambassador.

Later, ignoring her protests, he led her onto the dance floor and, holding her against his body, he circled her between the other couples.

'Are you having fun?' he said softly into her ear.

She nodded. 'Yes. I thought people might be a bit stiff and starchy. But everyone's been really friendly.'

His eyes glittered like molten silver beneath the soft lights. 'They like you.'

She shook her head. 'They're curious about me. It's *you* they like.'

'And what about you? Do *you* like me?'

Around them the music and the laughter seemed to fade, as though someone had turned down the volume, and the urge to tell him her true feelings welled up inside her again. But she bit it down.

She smiled. 'Yes, I like you.'

'And you still want to marry me?' He met her gaze, his

grey eyes oddly serious. 'It's not too late to change your mind...'

She shook her head. 'I want to marry you.'

'Then maybe now is a good time to tell everyone that.' Glancing round, he frowned. 'We need my parents here, though. Let's go and look for them.'

His hand was warm and firm around hers as he pulled her through the dancing couples and onto the lawn, but after ten minutes of looking they still hadn't found Guy and Pandora.

Nodding curtly at the security guards, he led her into the main house.

'My mother probably wanted to change her shoes or something. I'll go and find them.'

His eyes were fixed on her face and, seeing the hesitancy there, she felt her heart tumble inside her chest.

Taking his hands in hers, she gave them a squeeze. 'Why don't I come with you? We can tell them together.'

There was a brief silence as he stared away across the empty hallway. Then his mouth twisted, and he shook his head. 'It's probably better if I go on my own.'

She nodded. 'Okay. I'll wait here.'

He kissed her gently on the lips. 'I won't be long.'

Walking swiftly through the house, Ram felt his heart start to pound.

He could hardly believe he'd managed to get this far. Bringing Nola to the party had felt like a huge step but this—this was something almost beyond his comprehension, beyond any expectations he'd had up until now.

It hardly seemed possible, but by the end of the night he would be officially engaged to Nola. Finally, with her help, he had managed to bury his past, and now he had a future he'd never imagined, with a wife and a baby—

Abruptly, his feet stilled on the thick carpet and his

thoughts skidded forward, slamming into the side of his head with a sickening thud.

His heartbeat froze. Beneath the throb of music and laughter, he could hear raised voices. Somewhere in the house a man and woman were arguing loudly.

It was Guy and his mother.

His heart began beating again and, with the blood chilling in his veins, he walked towards the doorway to his mother's room. The voices grew louder and more unrestrained as he got closer.

And then he heard his mother laugh.

Only it wasn't a happy sound.

'You just can't help yourself, can you? Couldn't you have a little self-control? Just for one night?'

'Maybe you should have a little *less*, darling. It's a party—not a military tattoo.'

Ram winced. Guy sounded belligerent. And drunk.

For a moment he hesitated. There had been so many of these arguments during his life. Surely it wouldn't matter if he walked away from this one? But as his mother started to cry he braced his shoulders and walked into the bedroom.

'Oh, here's the cavalry.' Turning, Guy squinted across the room at him. 'Don't start, Ram. You don't pay me enough to take part in that gala performance downstairs.'

'But I pay you enough to treat my mother with respect,' he said coolly. 'However, if you don't think you can manage to do that, maybe I'll just have to cut back your allowance. No point in paying for something I'm not actually getting.'

For a moment Guy held his gaze defiantly, but then finally he shrugged and looked away. 'Fine. But if you think I'm going to deal with her in this state—'

'I'll deal with my mother.' Ram forced himself to stay calm. 'Why don't you go and enjoy the party? Eat some food…have a soft drink. Oh, and Guy? I meant what I said about treating my mother with respect.'

Grumbling, still avoiding Ram's eyes, Guy stumbled from the room.

Heart aching, Ram stared across the room to where his mother sat crying on the bed. Crossing the room, he crouched down in front of her and stroked her hair away from her face.

'Don't worry about him. He's been drinking, that's all. And he's had to get up before noon to make a couple of phone calls so he's probably exhausted.'

She tried to smile through her tears. 'That must be it.'

'It is. Now, here. Take this.' Reaching into his pocket, Ram pulled out a handkerchief and held it out to her. 'It's clean. I promise.'

Taking the handkerchief, Pandora wiped her eyes carefully. 'I just wanted it to be perfect, Ramsay. For one night.'

'And it is. Everyone's having a wonderful time.'

She shook her head, pressing her hand against his. '*You're* not. You'll say you are, but I know you're not.'

Ram swallowed. Whenever his mother and Guy argued there was a pattern. She would get angry, then cry, and then she would redo her make-up and carry on as if nothing had happened. But tonight was different, for he could never remember her talking about him or his feelings.

He looked at her uncertainly. 'You're right—normally. But it's different tonight. I really am enjoying myself.'

His mother smiled.

'That's because of Nola. *She's* the difference and you're different with her. Happier.' She squeezed his hand. 'I was happy like that when I found out I was pregnant with you. I know it sounds crazy, but when that line turned blue I just sat and looked at it, and those few hours when it was just you and me were the happiest of my life. I knew then that you'd be handsome and smart and strong.'

A tear rolled down her cheek.

'I just wish I'd been stronger.'

Ram dragged a hand through his hair. He felt her pain like a weight. 'You *were* strong, Mother.'

Shaking her head, she let the tears fall. 'I should never have married Guy. I should have had the courage to stand up to your grandfather. I should have waited for someone who wanted me and loved me for who I was.'

Looking up into Ram's eyes, she twisted her lips.

'But I was scared to give all this up. So I settled for a man who was paid to marry me and a marriage that's made me feel trapped and humiliated for thirty years.'

She bit her lip.

'I'm sorry, darling, for acting so selfishly, and for blaming you.'

Ram couldn't breathe.

His mother was apologising.

For so long he'd been so angry with her. Never to her face, because despite everything—the hysterics, the way she lashed out at him when she was upset—he loved her desperately. Instead he'd deliberately, repeatedly, and publicly scorned the very idea of becoming a husband and a father.

And he'd done that to punish her. For giving him a 'father' like Guy, for making choices that had taken away *his* choices, even though she'd been little more than a child herself.

'Don't,' he whispered. 'It wasn't your fault.'

'It was. It *is*.' Reaching out, Pandora gently stroked his face. 'And I can't change the past. But I don't want you to repeat my mistakes. Promise me, Ramsay, that you won't do what Guy and I did. Relationships can't be forced. There has to be love.'

'I know.'

He spoke mechanically, but inside he felt hollow, for

he knew his mother was right. Relationships couldn't be forced—and yet wasn't that exactly what he'd done to Nola? Right from the start he'd been intent on having his own way—overriding her at every turn, kidnapping her at the airport, pressuring her to get married.

He'd even 'persuaded' her into announcing their engagement tonight, despite knowing that she was nervous about taking that step.

His breath felt like lead in his throat. Whatever he might like to believe, the facts were undeniable. Nola wasn't marrying him through choice or love. Just like his mother, for her it would be a marriage of convenience. A marriage of duty.

Gazing into his mother's tear-stained face, he made up his mind.

He'd never wanted anything more than to give his child a secure home, a future, a name. But he couldn't marry Nola.

Now all he needed to do was find her and tell her that as soon as possible.

Glancing up, Nola saw Ram striding down the stairs towards her. Her heart gave a lurch. He didn't look as if news of his engagement had been joyfully received.

Standing up, she walked towards him—but before she had a chance to speak Ram was by her side, grabbing her hand, towing her after him, his grip on her hand mirroring the vice of confusion and fear squeezing her heart.

'What did they say?' she managed as he wrenched open the door, standing to one side to let her pass through it.

'Nothing,' he said curtly. 'I didn't tell them.'

She gazed at him in confusion.

'So what are we doing?'

'There's been a change of plan. We're leaving now!'

Five minutes later they were heading down the drive towards the main road. Cars were still arriving at the house, but even though Ram must have noticed them, he said nothing.

Several times she was on the verge of asking him to stop the car and tell her what had happened. But, glancing at his set, still profile, she knew that he was either incapable of telling her or unwilling. All she could do was watch and wait.

She was so busy watching him that she didn't even notice when they drove past Stanmore. In fact it wasn't until he stopped the car in front of a large Art Deco–style house that she finally became aware of anything other than the terrible rigidity of his body.

He had switched off the engine and was out of the car and striding round to her door, yanking it open before she even had a chance to take off her seatbelt.

'This way!'

Taking her hand, he led her to the front door, unlocking and opening it in one swift movement. Inside the house, Nola watched confusedly as he marched from room to room, flicking on lights.

'What is this place?' she said finally.

'It's a property I bought a couple of years ago as an investment. I lived here when Stanmore was being renovated.'

'Oh, right…' It was all she could manage.

Maybe this was some kind of bolthole? She flinched as he yanked the curtains across the windows. If so, he must have a good reason for coming here now. But as she stared over at him anxiously she had no idea what that reason might be. All she knew was that she wanted to put her arms around him and hold him tight. Only, he looked so brittle, so taut, she feared he might shatter into a thousand pieces if she so much as touched him.

But she couldn't just stand here and pretend that everything was all right when it so clearly wasn't.

'Are you okay?' she asked hesitantly.

'Yes. I'm fine.'

He smiled—the kind of smile she would use when sharing a lift with a stranger.

'I'm sure you're tired. Why don't I show you to your bedroom?'

'But don't you want to talk?'

Watching his expression shift, she shivered. It was like watching water turn to ice.

'No, not really.'

'But what happened? Why did we leave the party?' She bit her lip. 'Why didn't you tell them about the engagement?'

He stared at her impatiently, then fixed his eyes on a point somewhere past her head.

'I'm not having this conversation now. It's late. You're pregnant—'

'And you're upset!' She stared at him in exasperation. 'Not only that, you're shutting me out.'

His eyes narrowed. 'Shutting you out? You sound like you're in a soap opera.'

She blinked, shocked not so much by his words but by the sneer in his voice.

'Maybe that's because you've behaving like a character in a soap opera. Dragging me from the party. Refusing to talk to me.'

'And what exactly do you think talking about it will achieve?'

'I don't know.' Her breath felt tight inside her chest. 'But I don't think ignoring whatever it is can be the solution.'

He gave a short, bitter laugh. 'You've changed your tune. Not so long ago you managed to ignore me for three months without much problem.'

Nola felt her whole body tighten with shock and pain. Then, almost in the same moment, she knew he was lashing out at her because he was upset, and even though his words hurt her she cared more about *his* pain than her own.

'And I was wrong.'

'So maybe in three months I'll think I was wrong about this. But somehow I don't think so.'

She gritted her teeth. 'So that's it? You just want me to shut up and go to bed?'

His face hardened. 'No, what I want is for you to stop nagging me, like the wife you've clearly never wanted to be.'

'I *do* want to be your wife.' The injustice of his words felt like a slap. 'And I'm not nagging. I'm trying to have a conversation.'

He shook his head. 'This isn't a conversation. It's an interrogation.'

'Then *talk* to me.'

His jaw tightened. 'Fine. I was going to wait until the morning, but if you can't or won't wait, we'll do it now.'

'Do what?'

'Break up. Call it off.' His voice was colder and harder than his gaze. 'Whatever one does to end an engagement.'

Watching the colour drain from her face, he felt sick. But knowing that he could hurt her so easily only made him more determined to finish it there and then—for what was the alternative? That she spent the next thirty years trapped with him in a loveless marriage?

A marriage that would force their child to endure the same dark legacy as him.

No, that wasn't going to happen. His child deserved more than to be a witness to his parents' unhappy marriage. And Nola deserved more than him.

Across the room Nola took a breath, tried to focus, to make sense of what Ram had just said.

'I don't understand,' she said finally.

But then, staring at him, she did—for the man who had held her in his arms and made love to her so tenderly had been replaced by a stranger with blank, hostile eyes.

'You want to end our engagement? But you were going to announce it tonight...'

He shrugged. 'And now I'm not.'

But I love you, she thought, her heart banging against her ribcage as though it was trying to speak for itself. Only it was clear that Ram had no use for her love, for any kind of love.

'Why?' she whispered. 'Why are you doing this?'

'I've changed my mind. All this—us, marriage, becoming a father—it's not what I want.'

'But you said that children need to know where they come from. That they need to belong.' His words tasted like ash in her mouth.

His gaze locked onto hers. 'Don't look so surprised, Nola. You said yourself I'm not cut out to be a hands-on daddy. And you're right. I'm not. What was it you said? No father is better than a bad father. Well, you were right. You'll do a far better job on your own than with me messing up your life and our child's life. But you don't need to worry. I fully intend to take care of you and the baby financially.'

Nola stared at him in silence.

He was talking in the same voice he used for board meetings. In fact he might just as easily have been discussing an upcoming software project instead of his child.

Her heart was beating too fast. Misery and anger were tangling inside her chest.

'Is that what you think matters?' she asked, reining in her temper.

He sighed. 'Try not to let sentiment get in the way of

reason. Everything that baby needs is going to cost money so, yes, I think it *does* matter.'

'Not everything,' she said stubbornly. 'Children need love, consistency, patience and guidance, and all those are free.'

His mouth curled. 'Tell that to a divorce lawyer.'

Reaching into his pocket, he pulled out his car keys.

'There's no point in discussing this now. You can stay here, and I'll call my lawyers in the morning. I'll get them to draw up the paperwork and they can transfer this house into your name tomorrow.'

'What?' She stared at him, struggling to breathe.

'I'll work out a draft financial settlement at the same time. As soon as that's finalised we can put all this behind us and get back to our lives.'

Her skin felt cold, but she was burning up inside.

So was that it? Everything she had been through, that *they* had been through, had been for this? For him to pay her off. Just like her father had done with his ostentatious but impersonal presents.

Anger pounded through her. And, just like those presents, giving her this house and an allowance were for *his* benefit, not hers. He was offering them as a means to assuage his conscience and rectify the mistake he clearly believed he'd made by getting her pregnant.

'I don't want your house or your money,' she said stiffly.

He frowned. 'Please don't waste my time, or yours, making meaningless remarks like that. You're going to need—'

She shook her head. 'No, you don't get to offer me money. Aside from my salary, I've never asked for or expected any money from you, and nothing's changed.'

His eyes narrowed. 'Give it time.'

She felt sick—a sickness that was worse than anything she'd felt in those early months of pregnancy. For that nausea had been caused by the child growing inside her, a child she loved without question, even when she felt scared and alone.

Now, though, she felt sick at her own stupidity.

Ignoring all her instincts, she had let herself have hope, let herself trust him. Not just trust him—but love him too.

And here was the proof that she'd been wrong all along.

Ram was just like her father, for when it came to sacrificing himself for his family he couldn't do it.

He was weak and selfish and he was not fit to be a father to her child.

Wide-eyed, suddenly breathless with anger, Nola stepped forward, her fingers curling into fists.

'Get out! You can keep your stupid financial settlements and your paperwork. As of this moment I never want to see or speak to you again, Ramsay Walker. Now, get out!'

He stared at her in silence, then, tossing the house keys onto one of the tables, he turned and walked swiftly across the room.

The door slammed and moments later she heard his car start, the engine roaring in the silence of the night and then swiftly fading away until the only sound was her ragged breathing.

It was then that she realised she was still wearing his ring. Unclenching her fingers, she gazed down at the sapphire, thinking how beautiful it was, and yet how sad.

And then her legs seemed to give way beneath her and, sliding down against the wall, she began to sob.

CHAPTER TEN

FINALLY IT WAS time to stop crying.

Forcing herself to stand up, Nola walked into the kitchen and splashed her face with cold water. Her mascara had run, and she wiped it carefully away with her fingertips. But as she tried to steady her breathing she knew it would be a long time—and take a lot more than water—to wash away Ram's words or that look on his face.

Her chest tightened, and suddenly the floor seemed to be moving. She gripped the edge of the sink.

Ram giving up like that had been so shocking—brutal, and cruel.

Like a bomb exploding.

And she still didn't really understand what had happened to make him change his mind—not just about the engagement but about everything. For her, cocooned in her newly realised love, it had begun to feel as though finally there was a future for them.

She felt anger scrape over her skin.

But what use was love to a man like Ram?

A man who measured his feelings in monthly maintenance payments?

Steadying herself, she lifted her shoulders. She wasn't going to fall apart. For what had she really lost?

Even before she'd thrown him out she had felt as though the Ram she loved had already left. He'd been so remote, so cold, so ruthless. Changing his mind, her life, her future and their child's future without batting an eyelid, then offering her money as some kind of consolation prize.

Her throat tightened, and suddenly she was on the verge of tears again.

And now he was gone.

And she knew that she would never see him again.

Somewhere in the house a clock struck two, and she felt suddenly so tired and drained that standing was no longer an option. There were several sofas in the living room, but she knew that if she sat down she would never get up again, and lying on a sofa in a party dress seemed like the worst kind of defeat. If she was going to sleep, she was going to do it in a bed.

Slipping off her shoes, she walked wearily upstairs. There was no shortage of bedrooms—she counted at least seven—but as she opened one door after another she began to feel like Goldilocks. Each room was beautiful, but the beds were all too huge, too empty for just her on her own.

Except that she wasn't on her own, she thought defiantly, stroking the curve of her stomach with her hand. Nor was she going to lie there worrying about the future. Her mother had more or less brought her up on her own and, unlike her mother, *she* was financially independent. So, with or without Ram, she was going to survive this *and* flourish.

Getting undressed seemed like too much of an effort, though, and, stifling a yawn, she crawled onto the next bed and slid beneath the duvet.

She didn't remember falling asleep, but when she opened her eyes she felt sure that she must have dozed off only for a couple of minutes. But one glance at the clock on the bedside table told her that she had been asleep for two hours.

Her skin felt tight from all the crying, and her head was pounding—probably from all the crying too. Feeling a sudden terrible thirst, she sat up and wriggled out from under the duvet.

The house was silent and still, but she had left some of the lights on during her search for a bedroom. Squinting against the brightness, she made her way towards the stairs. It was dark in the living room, but her head was still so muddied with sleep that it was only as she began to grope for a light switch that she remembered she had also left the lights on downstairs.

So why were they off now?

In the time it took for her heart to start beating again she had already imagined several nightmare crazed intruder scenarios—and then something, or someone, moved in the darkness and her whole body seemed to turn to lead.

'It's okay…it's just me.'

A lamp flared in the corner of the room, but she didn't need it to know that it was Ram sitting in one of the armchairs. She would recognise that voice anywhere—even in darkness. And even had he lost his voice she would still have known him, for she had traced the pure, straight line of his jaw with her fingers. Touched those firm, curving lips with her mouth.

She felt a sudden sharp stab of desire, remembering the way his body had moved against hers. Remembering too how much she'd loved him. How much she still loved him. But with loving came feelings, and she wasn't going to let herself feel anything for this man anymore, or give him yet another chance to hurt her.

'How did you get in?' she asked stiffly.

'I have a spare key.'

Her heart began to race with anger, for his words had reminded her of the promise he'd made only a few hours ago. Not to love her and his child, but to take care of them financially, provide a fitting house and lifestyle.

Glancing round, she spotted the keys he'd left behind earlier, and with hands that shook slightly she picked them up.

'Here, you can have these too.' She tossed them to him. 'Since I'm not planning on staying here I won't be needing them. In fact...' She paused, tugging at the ring on her finger. 'I won't be needing this either.'

'Nola, please—don't do that.' He struggled to his feet, his mouth twisting.

'Don't do *what*, Ramsay?' She stared at him, a cloud of disbelief and anger swirling inside her. 'Why are you even here? I told you I never wanted to see you again.'

'I know. But you also said that ignoring this wasn't the solution.'

His voice was hoarse, not at all like his usual smooth drawl, but she was too strung out to notice the difference.

'Well, I was wrong. Like I was wrong to give you a chance. And wrong to think that you'd changed, that you could change.' Meeting his gaze, she said quickly, 'I know I've made a lot of mistakes, but I'm not about to repeat them by wasting any more of my time on you, so I'd like you to leave now.'

He sucked in a breath, but didn't move. 'I can't do that. I know you're angry, but I'm not leaving until you've listened to me.'

Her eyes widened, the pulse jerking in her throat. She didn't want to listen to anything he had to say, but she could tell by the set of his shoulders that he had meant what he said. He was just going to stand there and wait—stand there and wait for her to grow tired of fighting him and give in. Just as she always did, she thought angrily.

Blood was beating in her ears.

Taking a step backwards, she folded her arms protectively around her waist and looked at him coldly. 'Then say whatever it is and then I want you to leave.'

Ram stared at her in silence.

Her face was pale and shadowed. She was still wearing her dress from last night, and he knew that she must have slept in it, for it was impossibly crumpled now. But he didn't think she had ever looked more beautiful, or desirable, or determined.

Or that he had ever loved her more.

He stood frozen, his body still with shock. But inside the truth tugged him down and held him fast, like an anchor digging into the seabed.

He loved her.

He hadn't planned to. Or wanted to. But he knew unquestioningly that it was true.

And, crazy though it sounded, he knew it was the reason he'd broken up with her.

He'd told himself—told her—that he had never wanted to marry or have children. That he wasn't a good bet. That he would only ruin everything. And all of that had been true.

But it wasn't the whole truth.

He loved her, and in loving her he couldn't force her into a marriage of convenience. For, even though she had agreed to be his wife, he knew that she didn't love him. And he'd seen with his own eyes the damage and misery that kind of relationship could cause. He only had to look at his mother or look in the mirror for proof.

No, he didn't wanted to trap her—only he couldn't bear a life without Nola, a life without his child.

But how he could salvage this?

He took a deep breath. 'I know I've messed up. And I know you don't have any reason to listen to me, let alone forgive me, but I want a second chance. I want us to try again.'

For a moment she couldn't understand what he was saying, for it made no sense. Only a couple of hours ago he had said that he wanted to break up with her, to go back to his old life, and yet now he was here, asking her for a second chance.

But even as her brain raged against the inconsistency of his words her heart was responding to the desperation in his voice.

Only she couldn't do this again. Couldn't start to believe, to hope.

Ignoring the ache in her chest, she shook her head. '*You* gave up on *me*. And on our baby. Or have you forgotten that you were supposed to announce our engagement last night—?' She broke off, her voice catching in her throat as pain split her in two.

He took a step towards her, and for the first time it occurred to her that he looked as desperate as he sounded. There were shadows under his eyes and he was trembling all over.

'I haven't forgotten, and I'm sorry—'

'You're *sorry*!'

She shook her head. Did he really think that saying sorry was somehow going to make everything right again? If so, she had been right to throw him out.

'Well, don't be—I'm not. You know what? I'm *glad* you broke it off, because there's something wrong with you. Something that means that every time we get to a place of calm and understanding you have to smash it all to pieces. And I can't—I don't want to live like that.'

'I know, and I don't want to live like that either.'

He sounded so wretched. But why should she care? In fact she wasn't going to care, she told herself.

Only it was so hard, for despite her righteous anger she still loved him. But thankfully he would never know that.

'Then it's lucky for both of us that we don't have to,' she said quickly. 'As soon as I can get a flight back to Scotland I'm going home.'

She watched as he took a deep breath, and the pain in his eyes tugged at an ache inside her, so that suddenly she could hardly bear looking at his stricken face.

'But this is your home…'

She shook her head. 'It's *not* my home. It's a pay-off. A way for you to make yourself feel better. I don't want it.'

Ram stared at her in silence. The blood was roaring in his ears.

He was losing her. He was losing her.

The words echoed inside his head and he could hardly speak through the grief rising up in his throat. 'But I want you. And I want to marry you.'

Her heart began to beat faster. It was so tempting to give in, for she knew that right now he believed what he was saying. But now was just a moment in time: it wouldn't last for ever. And she was done with living in the moment.

Slowly she shook her head. 'Only because you can't have me. I don't know *what* you want, Ram. But I do know that you can't just break up with me and then two hours later come and tell me that you want me back and expect everything to be okay again. Maybe if this was a film we could kiss, and then the credits would roll, and everyone in the cinema would go home happy. But we're *not* in a film. This is real life, and it doesn't work like that.'

Tears filled her eyes.

'You hurt me, Ram…' she whispered.

'I know.'

The pain in his voice shocked her.

'I wish I could go back and change what I did and what I said. I panicked. When I went to find my mother she told me not to make the same mistake that she had. That relationships can't be forced. That they need love. That's why I couldn't go through with it.'

She nodded. 'Because you don't love me—I know,' she said dully.

'No!' He let out a ragged breath. 'I broke up with you because I *do* love you, Nola, and I didn't want to trap you in a marriage that you didn't want. That you never wanted.'

He took a step towards her, his hands gripping her arms, his eyes glittering not with tears but with passion.

'I *love* you, and that's why I want to marry you. Not out of duty, or because I want the baby to have my name. But I know you don't love me, and I've hurt you so much already. Only I couldn't just walk away. I tried, but I couldn't do it. That's why I came back—'

He stopped. There were tears in her eyes.

Only she was smiling.

'You love me? *You love me?*'

He stared at her uncertainly, his eyes burning, wishing there was another way to tell her that—to make her believe. But even before he'd started to nod she was pressing her hand against her mouth, as though that would somehow stop the tears spilling from her eyes.

'You're so smart, Ram. Easily the smartest person I've ever met. But you're also the stupidest. *Why* do think I agreed to marry you?'

'I don't know...' he whispered.

'Because I love you, of course.'

Gazing up into his face, Nola felt her heart almost stop beating as she saw that he too was crying.

'Why would you ever love me?'

His voice broke apart and she felt the crack inside her deepen as his mouth twisted in pain.

'How could you love me? After everything I've said and done? After how I've behaved?'

'I don't know.' She bit her lip. 'I didn't want to. And it scares me that I do. But I can't help it. I love you.' Her mouth trembled. 'I love you and I still want to marry you.'

His hands tightened around her arms, his eyes searching her face. 'Are you sure? I don't want to trap you. I don't want to be that kind of man—that kind of husband, that kind of father.'

Her heart began to beat faster. 'You're not. Not anymore. I don't think you ever were.'

Breathing out unsteadily, he pulled her close, smoothing the tears away from her face. 'Your parents married because it was the next step,' he said slowly. 'My mother married Guy out of desperation. They didn't think about what they were doing…it just happened. But we're different. We've fought to be together, and our marriage is going to work just fine.'

She breathed out shakily. 'How do you know?'

His eyes softened. 'Because you know me,' he said simply. 'You know everything about me—the good and the bad. And you still love me.'

Her lip trembled. 'Yes, I do.'

'It scares me, you knowing me like that.' He grimaced. 'But I trust you, and I love you, and I always will.'

Gently, he uncurled her arms from around her body, and as one they stepped towards each other.

Burying her face against his chest, Nola sighed with relief as Ram pulled her close.

'I love you, Nola.'

She lifted her head. 'I love you too.'

For several minutes they held each other in silence, neither wanting to let go of the other, to let go of what they had come so close to losing.

Finally Ram shifted backwards. 'Do you think it's too late to tell my mother?'

Tracing the curve of his mouth with her fingers, she laughed. 'I think it might be better for us to get some sleep first. Besides, what's a couple of hours when we have the rest of our lives together?'

'The rest of our lives together…' He repeated it softly, and then laying one hand across the swell of her stomach, he pulled her closer still, so that he and Nola and the baby were all connected. 'That's a hell of a future,' he whispered, kissing her gently on the forehead.

Looking up into his handsome face, Nola felt her heart swell with happiness. All the hardness and anger had gone and there was only hope and love in his grey eyes.

'Although, from where I'm standing, the present looks pretty damn good too.'

She bit her lip, her mouth curling up at the corners. 'I think it would look even better lying down.'

'My thoughts exactly,' he murmured, and with his heart beating with love and joy he scooped her up into his arms and carried her towards the stairs.

EPILOGUE

STEPPING UNDER THE shower head, Nola switched on the water and closed her eyes. If she was lucky, she might actually get to wash her hair today. Yesterday Evie, who was four months old today, had woken just as she'd stepped under the water. Not that she really minded. Her tiny daughter was the best thing in her life. The joint best thing, she amended silently.

Tipping her face up to meet the hot spray, she smiled as she thought back to the day of Evie's arrival. Ram had not only turned into a hands-on daddy, he'd practically taken over the entire labour ward.

It had been a small and rare reminder of the old work-hard, play-hard Ram, for nowadays she and Evie were the focus of his passion and devotion. He still loved his job, and the launch had been the most successful in the company's history—but he was happiest when he was at home.

And she was happy too. How could she not be?

She had a handsome, loving husband, a job working with her best friend, and a baby she adored.

Evie was beautiful, a perfect blend of both her parents. She'd inherited her pale skin and loose dark curls from Nola, but she had her father's grey eyes—a fact which, endearingly, Ram pointed out to everyone.

Her skin prickled as the fragrant warm air around her seemed to shift sideways, and then she gasped, her stomach tightening as two warm hands slid around her waist.

'Hi!'

Ram kissed her softly on the neck and, breathing out unsteadily, she leaned back against his warm naked body.

'Hey! That was quick.'

'I haven't done anything yet.'

The teasing note in his voice matched the light, almost tormenting touch of his fingers as they drifted casually over her flat stomach. Turning, she nipped him on the arm, softening it to a kiss as he pulled her closer.

'I meant the interview. I thought you were seeing that super-important woman from the news network?'

Tugging her round to face him, he looked down into her eyes, his mouth curving upwards into one of those sexy smiles she knew would always take her breath away.

'I talked really fast. Besides, I have two far more important women right here!'

'And in about half an hour you'll have three.' She pulled away slightly and smiled up at him. 'Pandora rang. She went shopping yesterday, and she wants to drop off a few things for Evie.'

Ram groaned. 'I presume she went shopping overseas? There can't be anything left in Australia for her to buy.'

Since the night of her anniversary party Pandora had been working hard to rebuild her relationship with her son, and Nola knew that, despite joking about her shopping habits, Ram was touched by his mother's efforts to make amends. She had separated from Guy, and now that they were no longer forced to live together the two of them had begun to enjoy each other's company as friends.

Nola laughed. 'You can talk. Every time you go out of the door you come back with something for me or Evie.'

'She deserves it for being so adorable,' Ram said softly as she glanced down at the beautiful diamond ring he'd given her when Evie was born. 'And you deserve it for giving me such a beautiful daughter.'

And for giving him a life, and a future filled with love.

Gently he ran his hand over her stomach. 'I miss your bump. I feel like I'd just got used to it, and then she was here. Not that I'm complaining.' His eyes softened. 'I can't imagine my life without her *or* you.'

Nola felt a pang of guilt. She knew how much he regretted not being there for the early stages of her pregnancy, for they had no secrets from one another now. That was one of the lessons they'd learnt from their past—to be open with one another.

'I miss it too. But there'll be other bumps.'

'Is that what you want?'

His face had gentled, and she loved him for it, because now everything was about what they *both* wanted.

'It is. It all happened so quickly last time.'

She hesitated, and then, leaning closer, ran her hand slowly over his stomach, her heart stumbling against her ribs as his skin twitched beneath her fingers.

His eyes narrowed, and a curl of heat rose up inside her as he pulled her against his smooth golden body.

'I'm happy to go slowly. On one condition.'

The roughness in his voice made her blood tingle.

'And what's that,' she asked softly.

'That we start right now.'

And, tipping her mouth up to his, he kissed her hungrily.

* * * * *

If you enjoyed
KIDNAPPED FOR THE TYCOON'S BABY
by Louise Fuller
why not explore these other
SECRET HEIRS OF BILLIONAIRES *stories?*

THE GREEK'S PLEASURABLE REVENGE
by Andie Brock
THE SECRET KEPT FROM THE GREEK
by Susan Stephens
CARRYING THE SPANIARD'S CHILD
by Jennie Lucas

Available now!

MILLS & BOON®

MODERN™

POWER, PASSION AND IRRESISTIBLE TEMPTATION

A sneak peek at next month's titles...

In stores from 16th November 2017:

- **His Queen by Desert Decree** – Lynne Graham *and*
  A Night of Royal Consequences – Susan Stephens
- **A Christmas Bride for the King** – Abby Green *and*
  Captive for the Sheikh's Pleasure – Carol Marinelli

In stores from 30th November 2017:

- **Legacy of His Revenge** – Cathy Williams *and*
  Carrying His Scandalous Heir – Julia James
- **Christmas at the Tycoon's Command** –
  Jennifer Hayward *and* **Innocent in the Billionaire's
  Bed** – Clare Connelly

Just can't wait?
Buy our books online before they hit the shops!
www.millsandboon.co.uk

Also available as eBooks.

MILLS & BOON®

EXCLUSIVE EXTRACT

Reluctant Sheikh Salim Al-Noury would rather abdicate
than taint the realm with his dark secrets.

But could one exquisitely beautiful diplomat convince
him otherwise?...

Christmas means heartbreak to Charlotte, and this overseas assignment offers the perfect getaway. But Salim
proves to be her most challenging client yet, and his
rugged masculinity awakens untouched Charlotte to
unimaginable pleasures!

Read on for a sneak preview of Abby Green's book
A CHRISTMAS BRIDE FOR THE KING
Rulers of the Desert

She looked Salim straight in the eye. 'Life is so easy for
you, isn't it? No wonder you don't want to rule—it would
put a serious cramp in your lifestyle and a dent in your
empire. Have you *ever* had to think of anyone but yourself,
Salim? Have you *ever* had to consider the consequences of
your actions? People like you make me—'

'*Enough.*' Salim punctuated the harshly spoken word by
taking her arms in his hands. He said it again. 'Enough,
Charlotte. You've made your point.'

She couldn't breathe after the way he'd just said her
name. *Roughly.* His hands were huge on her arms, and firm
but not painful. She knew she should say *Let me go* but
somehow the words wouldn't form in her mouth.

Salim's eyes were blazing down into hers and for a
second she had the impression that she'd somehow...*hurt*
him. But in the next instant any coherent thought fled,

because he slammed his mouth down onto hers and all she was aware of was shocking heat, strength, and a surge of need such as she'd never experienced before.

Salim couldn't recall when he'd felt angrier—people had thrown all sorts of insults at him for years. Women who'd expected more than he'd been prepared to give. Business adversaries he'd bested. His brother. His parents. But for some reason this buttoned-up slender woman with her cool judgmental attitude was getting to him like no one else ever had.

The urge to kiss her had been born out of that anger and a need to stop her words, but also because he'd felt a hot throb of desire that had eluded him for so long he'd almost forgotten what it felt like.

Her mouth was soft and pliant under his, but on some dim level not clouded red with lust and anger he knew it was shock—and, sure enough, after a couple of seconds he felt her tense and her mouth tighten against his.

He knew he should draw back.

If he was another man he might try to convince himself he'd only intended the kiss to be a display of power, but Salim had never drawn back from admitting his full failings. And he couldn't pull back—not if a thousand horses were tied to his body. Because he wanted her.

Don't miss
A CHRISTMAS BRIDE FOR THE KING
By Abby Green

Available December 2017

www.millsandboon.co.uk